AND YOU THOUGHT BEING

DEAD

WAS ALL THERE WAS!

EVELYN C. WOODWARD

Ordering Information:

Prime Seven Media
518 Landmann St.
Tomah City, WI 54660

Printed in the United States of America

TABLE OF CONTENTS

CHAPTER 1

"Hey lady! Are you all right? Are you hurt?"

I opened my eyes and shut them quickly. Light seared pain into the back of my eyeballs. My head was spinning, and I was pretty sure I was going to vomit. I didn't know what was happening.

"Lady! Can you hear me?"

That voice was very annoying.

I took in a painful breath to try to speak. "What?" I didn't recognize my own voice. An unintelligible croak came out. I was beginning to feel more in my body and it was bad. I have never felt so much pain in my whole body. Maybe when my appendix burst. I thought it was bad, but this was much worse. These thoughts wandered through my brain. I think I was trying to avoid the reality that I was going to die.

"Oh good! Stay with me here. You've been in an accident. You need to stay awake."

Accident? I didn't remember any accident. It hurt to breathe. My ribs felt like fire wrapping around my heart. Shallow breaths.

"Who?" I breathed out painfully.

"Who? Me? I'm Peter Tait. I was driving the car. You ran out in front of me! Why did you do that? I tried to miss you, but..."

Car? I ran in front of a car? That was stupid. I am not usually stupid. At least I didn't think I was stupid. "Hurt."

"Yes, you have been hurt. You did a pinwheel off the hood of my car, and... Well, you don't need the details right now. Stay with me and you will be all right."

He didn't sound like he believed what he was saying. He sounded like he was afraid.

"You hurt?" I managed to gasp. I tried to raise my arm over my eyes to block the burning light. Pain shot through my shoulder. My arm wouldn't move.

"Me? I... I'm all right." He sounded confused. "It's you I'm worried about. You need to stay awake."

His voice took on an unpleasant whine. I wished that he would shut up and let me go into the oblivion that would be painless.

"Can you hear that?" He interrupted my drifting thought.

I listened. I heard the familiar crackling of a fire. It made me think of the many camping trips I had gone on as a child. Was I on a camping trip? I couldn't remember. It didn't smell like a campfire. Beyond the sound of the fire, I heard sirens. They sounded so far away...

"Don't go to sleep!" He squawked.

How did he know?

"Over here!" He yelled. The sirens stopped abruptly.

"Here's one!" A strong male voice called.

I heard the clank and clatter of the stretcher.

"She looks pretty battered up. We need the backboard and neck brace." The deep voice said. "Ma'am, can you hear me?"

"Yes," I managed on an exhale.

"Good. Can you tell me where it hurts?"

I didn't think I had enough breath to answer. "All... over."

"Okay. This will be rough, but we will go as quickly as possible. Ready? One, two, three..."

Pain! Shocking, burning, throbbing, stabbing, like I had been run over by a steamroller pain. I didn't realize I was holding my breath until I let it go after they stopped moving me. Still shallow breaths. My lungs hurt.

"Let's go," the deep voice said to people around him.

"What about the other one?" Someone asked.

"We can't do anything for him. Team Two can deal with it.".

I was lifted. Blood rushed to my head as my feet were tilted up. Then it went the other way when they bumped the stretcher into the vehicle. I guess that meant my circulation was working, but it really hurt. I gasped in pain, which made my lungs scream in waves of agony. I was bumped along into a noticeably cooler place. *Inside the ambulance*, I thought. *Better.* I started to drift again.

"No no no! Don't go to sleep! You know you can't do that! You'll die! Stay with me!"

Shit, he was annoying.

"Pete," I breathed. "Shut up."

"What was that?" The deep voice asked. "There's no Pete here. Now, I have to check your eyes."

He pulled my unwilling eyelids up and shone a light in them. The light was bright, but not as bright as the earlier light. All I could see was bright circles with big black dots in the center. I tried to see the man, but the blackness covered everything. I couldn't see. Not the deep voiced medic; not Pete, who must've been behind him and not the other guy who was poking painful needles into my arm.

"I can't see!" I squeaked. That used too much air. I had to make it clear. I didn't want more damage from their bungling around. I breathed painfully into my tender lungs, and let it out more clearly. "I can't see!"

"Really?" The deep voice responded. He took the painful light away. "We'd better be safe and cover your eyes, ma'am."

I felt the gauze being wrapped around my head and pads covering my eyes. The darkness was welcome. Why did it still feel like my eyes were burning? I sighed and let myself drift away from the pain.

"Lady! You can't sleep! I told you that! You have to stay here!"

"Why?" I whispered.

"Excuse me ma'am? I didn't quite hear you," the deep voice asked.

"Because you may have concussion or something! All the books I've read say that an injured person should be kept awake until a doctor sees them. And, no offense to you boys, but these guys are *not* doctors."

I tried to turn my head, but the neck brace prevented movement. I could move my eyes behind the bandages. Hovering over me were four bright lights, tinted red, probably from the blood in my eye lids. The one at my left shoulder seemed to coincide with the deep voice. The one over my head must be Pete. I had not heard enough to single out the other two. It felt strange to visualize a person like that...

The ambulance turned a corner. I felt my body shift painfully to one side. The agony sent me into an oblivion that even Pete could not penetrate.

"Wake up Suzette! You have to wake up. They are all waiting for you to wake up. If you don't wake up soon, they will think you had brain damage. You don't want brain damage, so wake up!"

That annoying voice! I vaguely remembered hearing the voice before, and it was annoying, then. Who was this guy, always talking in my ear, disturbing my sleep. I breathed in a lung full of air and remembered - I had been in an accident. My ribs hurt; my lungs felt burned; my skin felt like it had been peeled off of my body and whatever was left could not hold me together anymore.

"That's it! Wake up! You can do it Suzette!"

"Shut up," I mumbled. "Who are you?"

"I'm Pete!" He sounded surprised. "Peter Tait. I've been so worried about you!"

"Why?" I asked.

"Because I'm the one who hit you with my car. I tried to swerve around you, but the front bumper still clipped you and sent you flying. Why did you run out in front of me like that?".

"Hit by a *car*? I can't remember that." My voice was croaking so bad, I could hardly understand myself. How he could was beyond me.

"That's okay, Suzette. The doctor said you had head trauma. You may remember more later."

"Why are you calling me that?"

"What? Suzette? That's what they wrote on your chart. Isn't that right?"

"Not if I can avoid it. My friends call me Susie. My family calls me Sue." Talking took my breath away. I was *so* tired!

I drifted back toward the peace of sleep, but Pete squawked again.

"Susie! You can't sleep yet! After the doctor sees you, then you can sleep. Doctor! Nurse! She's awake! Why don't you come?"

"Pete, let me be," I mumbled, becoming all too aware of the pain in my body. "It hurts."

"I know that. Believe me, all I want to do is help you. Nurse!"

"Pull the cord," I groaned.

"Right! The cord! Where is the cord? Oh, you have it in your hand. There's a button under your right thumb. Push the button. *Susie*! Push the button!"

"Hmm?" I was drifting away again, but his shout made my hand spasm, and I pushed the button.

Seconds or minutes later, the room was full of people. The sound of them was overwhelming. The redness from their light in my eyes hurt like staring into the sun.

"Hello Miss LaMarre. I am Dr. Menzies. You have been in an accident. There is some damage, but we are confident that we can fix it." His voice was cool and soothing. With a voice like that, he must know what he is doing. "You have some internal injuries, Miss LaMarre. We are going to have to operate to patch you up. Do you understand?"

"Internal injuries," I repeated, barely croaking it out. From the feel of my guts, I could readily believe my internals were injured. "Operate. When?"

"In about twenty minutes. We also have an ophthalmologist coming to inspect your eyes.. Don't worry. We will have you better in no time."

A cool voice is nice and all, but I suspected that it would take much longer than no time to make me better.

"Pete?" I asked.

There was no response. They must've moved him out of the room. Good. Maybe I could sleep. I felt myself being lifted and moved. Then everything went black....

*

"S...s...s...Susie, Beautiful Susie, you're the only g...g...g...girl that I adore. When the m...moon shines over the cowshed, I'll be waiting at the k...k...k... kitchen door."

What an old song! I remember my grandmother singing that to me. Of course, she had a better voice. She emanated love when she sang to me. This voice... well, he couldn't really sing. His voice was scratchy and off key. He sounded kind of nice, though. Except that he woke me up. Why couldn't he let me sleep? I turned my head toward the voice and groaned.

"Hey Susie! Welcome back! You're going to be alright! Isn't that great?"

"Great? Hmmm! Who?" My throat felt raw and my voice was rasping painfully over the damaged tissue.

"You remember me! I'm Pete. Peter Tait. We met under some very trying circumstances, but it will be better now."

"Pete. Right. I can't see."

I said it, but it wasn't really true. I could see the form of him as a reddish light through my closed eyelids. I could see him move closer to the bed. Weird. I'd never noticed people giving off a light before.

"Your eyes are still covered with bandages. They are worried that your retinas were damaged by the fire."

"Fire? What fire?"

"Well, after my car hit you, I lost control and ran into a gas station. There was a fire, but we got you away. Oh! Here's the doctor back."

I heard the sound of the door opening and people coming in. Through my eyelids. I could see the bright shapes of three separate people.

"Hello, Miss LaMarre. I'm Dr. Menzies. We met before your operation. You may not remember, you were quite out of it. Everything went well. We stitched up several bleeders in there and put everything back in its rightful place. Now, all you have to do is rest and give your body time to heal."

"My eyes?" I asked, looking towards his light.

"Doctor Enns had a good look inside your eyes. He wants us to keep them covered for a few days so they can heal. He will be in on Friday to take the bandages off. It is best if you leave the bandages in place until then. All right?".

"All right," I agreed, watching one of the other people move away from the group. I heard water running, then the person came over to the other side of the bed and put something on the table in front of me.

"Here's some fresh water for you," a female voice came from the figure. I saw where she was, but, of course, I couldn't see the water. Oh well. Later.

"I am confident that we will have you up and around in no time," the Doctor said, patting my leg before he turned to leave.

"That is encouraging!" Pete said from beside the bed after the doctor left.

"I'm seeing the strangest things," I said.

"Your eyes are covered. How can you see?"

"I don't know. People are shining through my eyelids as if they were full of light."

"Light? Like who?"

"The doctor for one; his nurse who got me water and a third person who just stood behind the doctor. And you."

"Third person? There was only the doctor and a nurse, and no one got water. You already have water on your table."

"So, I'm seeing things and hearing things? Hallucinating? How hard did I bump my head anyway?"

"I don't know. By the time I found you, you were fading fast."

I watched Pete pace back and forth in front of my bed. He was upset. He seemed to have lost some memories himself. "Let's see if we can jar some of our memories loose, okay?" I asked.

"Like what?"

"Like what you had for breakfast."

"Boiled eggs and toast. You?"

"Oatmeal with flax, cooked in apple juice."

"Apple juice? Is that good?"

"Yes. Very. Add a little cinnamon and it is wonderful. After breakfast, what did you do?"

"I grabbed my briefcase with my laptop, and I went out to my car."

"Where were you going?"

"To work. I work at High Tech Industries, HiTi."

"HiTi? Aren't they the ones that invented that new computer game console?"

"Yep. I did that."

"Nice. I read about it in Popular Science. What did you do then?"

"I drove to work... at least, I tried. When I got to Ellis and Wall, you ran out into the street right in front of me! I swerved to miss you, but I couldn't quite make it. The car hit you! I was terrified that I had killed you!"

"It's okay. You didn't kill me. What happened then?"

"The car was out of control. It hit something... there was fire. I went to you as quickly as I could. *Why* did you run into the street?"

"I don't remember." I said, feeling confused. "After breakfast, I left to go to work. I'm an artist. I've been teaching glass bead making. I had to go to the Stained Glass place on Sargent. I didn't get there... I was waiting for a bus, and this man came up to me. He flashed a knife and started talking dirty..."

As I talked, I knew my respiration and heart rate were increasing. I didn't know I was being monitored. A nurse came in.

"What's wrong here?" She asked as she checked my blood pressure.

"We were just trying to figure out what happened," I said. It was fascinating, being able to see her moving through my closed eyelids and the bandages. "I got scared all over again." Listening to my words, I wondered how she could understand my hoarse voice. I could barely understand myself.

"You were scared?" The nurse asked. "Before the car hit you?"

"Yes. A disgusting man with a knife was threatening me. I tried to run away, but he followed me. That's why I ran into the street. I was watching him, not the cars."

"Oh, dear. I hope you can give a description of him to the police. We need men like him off the streets. But first, you need to calm down, and heal. Sleep and let nature make it better."

"Nature! How trite!" Pete said from the other side of the bed.

"Hush," I said, turning to him.

"That's right," the nurse agreed. "I will dim the lights to let people know not to make noise. Ring the bell if you need anything. The doctor will be back later today." She went out, totally ignoring Pete.

"I knew I was nondescript, but I'm feeling more and more like a fly on the wall than a person," Pete snorted. "But she's right. Sleep now. I'll be back later."

I saw Pete move to the door that the nurse had used. His light faded the same way hers had. Feeling exhausted, I drifted back into sleep.

CHAPTER 2

Every time I woke up, I had to go to the bathroom. The nurses were usually good when I pushed the button for help. After all, I couldn't see. What was I supposed to do? I found out on the second morning. I pushed the button, and someone rushed in, turned it off and left without saying a word. We did this at least five times before I gave up and got out of bed to go by myself. I was gratified that the pain in my stomach had eased and I could stand more or less upright. I was impressed by the pain medicines they were giving me. Any previous pain problems I have had, they did not work as well.

Looking through my eyelids and the bandages, everything was black, other than the red lighted forms of the people around me. My room was empty and I was in the dark. First, I stubbed my toe on a chair that was pushed close to my bed. Another step away, I felt a pull on my hand, reminding me of the intravenous tubes they had put in me. I carefully felt along the tubes back to the pole that the medicine bags were hanging from. The pole was on wheels, so I grabbed it and pushed it in front of me. Unfortunately, I was turned around. Which way was the bathroom? I turned and pushed the pole in every direction that I could, finally finding an open space that I could step into. I stabbed the same toe on one of the wheels. That hurt! Somehow, I managed to get into the hallway. I only knew where I was by the number of people's lights I could then see. The place seemed to be extremely crowded. Assuming that there was furniture or contraptions connected with most of the people, I carefully stepped around them, apologizing if they flinched. I didn't want to hurt their toes the way I hurt mine. There were so many people, it was hard to dodge them with any speed.

"Miss LaMarre! What are you doing?" I recognized one of the nurses voices.

"Mary?" I asked.

"That's right. What do you need?"

"The washroom! I can't find it!"

"Oh dear, come this way." She put my free hand on her arm and led me back to my room. "I don't understand. Why didn't you ring the buzzer?"

"I did. Five times. Someone kept turning it off." I know I sounded whiny, but I still really had to pee.

"Turned it off? No one's supposed to do that. Do you have any idea who it was?"

I looked straight at her. "No. No smell... no sound... just her light."

"Light? Here we are. Can you manage from here?"

"Yes," I said, moving as quickly as I could under the circumstances into the small cubicle. I sat there for a few minutes, catching my breath and my bearings. When I opened the door again, Mary was patiently waiting to help me back to bed.

"Thanks Mary," I sighed. "I can't believe how quickly I get tired!"

"Your body has been through a lot. Healing requires energy." Mary sounded like she wasn't paying attention to her words. When she had me comfortable, she became more attentive. "What did you mean about the 'light'," she asked.

"I don't know," I mumbled. Her interest was making me uncomfortable. "People seem to be glowing a reddish light in my eyes."

"Really?" She sounded sceptical.

"Maybe it's an aura or something," I suggested, hoping she would drop it.

"People don't usually see auras, let alone when they are blindfolded."

"I know. I've never seen auras before. I don't know what I'm seeing. Probably nothing. Or damaged nerve endings firing off randomly and my brain is interpreting them as an image?" That sounded good to me as I said it. I would have to remember it for future questions.

"I suppose. I've never heard of it before. I wonder what Dr. Enns will say."

"I don't know," I said, rolling over on my side and hoping she would go away.

*

"Susie! Sue... are you awake?"

"I am now," I mumbled, recognizing the voice. It was Kimmy, my best friend. I was sleeping with my eyes buried in a pillow and my free arm over them to block out the light of so many people coming and going in my room. I rolled toward her voice and saw her light bouncing at the foot of the bed. "Hey Kim."

"Susie, what happened!? Are you all right? Why are your eyes covered? Does it hurt? What can I do?"

"I'm all right," I said. I always knew she was bouncy. I hadn't realized exactly how much she really bounced until I saw her as a red silhouette. She moved so much I thought she was vibrating. "It's okay, Kim. Are you all right?"

"Me? What could be wrong with *me*? I get a call from the hospital, telling me that my best friend was in an accident and could I bring her toiletries to her... you.... My heart almost stopped! And after making that pronouncement, they wouldn't tell me your condition, because I wasn't immediate family! So I don't know what happened!"

She stopped for a breath, but before I could say anything she was off again.

"What kind of accident? You weren't driving, you took the bus. You look a mess, you know..."

Partway through her speech, a figure came into the room.

"Hi Sue. Who's this?"

"Hi Pete. This is my best friend, Kimberly Foton. She talks nonstop when she is excited or upset. I would say she is more upset today than excited."

Kim stopped talking mid-word. I saw her shape turn around, looking around the room. She even went over to the doorway and looked out into the hallway. She came back to the bed and stopped right beside me. "Who are you talking to?"

"Pete," I said. "Pete was unfortunately driving the car that I ran into. He has been worried about me ever since."

"Hello Kimberly," Pete said pleasantly.

"Pete? Car...? You ran into a car!? Are you nuts? You could get killed! Why would you do that?"

"That's what I keep asking," Pete agreed.

"I was being chased," I sighed. "I thought that guy was going to hurt me. Or kill me! I was more afraid of him than anything else."

"Oh my God! Did you report him? Have you identified him to the police? Are they looking for him or is he still out there? What are they going to do?"

"Does she always talk like that?" Pete asked. I could see him lean across the bed to look more closely at her.

"Yes," I giggled. "Kimmy, slow down. You talk too fast!"

"I know that," she said, looking around the room again. She walked over to the window to look out. Then she turned back to me. I was turned in her direction. She tiptoed silently across the room while watching me. I turned with her.

"How do you know where I am?" She demanded. "Can you see through those bandages?"

"Not exactly," I said. "Shhh, Kimmy. Come closer. I don't think I want the doctors to know about this."

"About what? What happened to you? And why?"

"I don't know. I don't know anything except that I almost died and when I woke up, even though my eyes are covered up, I can see people through everything."

"See how? What do they look like?"

"They are, like, silhouettes of red light."

"Red like fire?"

"No… more like red from the blood in my eye lids. I would think people's light would be more of a white, wouldn't it?"

"And you don't want the doctor to know because…"

"They already think I'm strange. I heard them talking about my necklace as if it was something spooky! They wanted it off for the surgery, but couldn't get it off."

"So, there's no clasp. So what?"

"I don't know! I would have been upset if they had broken it, but I got the impression that they *couldn't* break it. Gramma would have rolled over in her grave if that happened! She put it on me…" I was lost in thought for a second, remembering my Grandmother putting the fine gold chain over my head and telling me to never, ever lose it. It held a tiny, intricate key which she told me was the key to her heart. Just the thought of someone trying to take it off of me made me feel sick. "I just want to go home to sleep. There are way too many people coming and going in here."

Just then, a person entered the room moving quickly, I assumed a nurse. I watched her bustle to the bed opposite mine, grab something, take it to the sink, fill it with water and return it to the bedside table. Then she bustled out.

"That's strange," I said.

"What's strange?" Kim asked.

"That nurse. She got fresh water for that bed, but the bed is empty."

"What nurse? No one came into the room."

"What? Are you sure? Check the glass over there. Is there water in it? Cold water?"

Kim went to the spot and did find a glass of cold water. "To be this cold, it has to have been fresh. But *I* didn't see her."

"Neither did I," Pete added. "And I was watching."

"If neither of *you* saw her, then why did I? I'm getting a little freaked out."

"What do you mean, neither of you? Who else is here?"

I saw her turn around again, looking around the room.

"Pete is here! I introduced you! Kimmy, this is not funny."

"I'm not laughing, Sue."

"Neither am I!" Pete said, moving closer to Kim. He reached out to touch her, but before he connected, she jumped up, heading for the door.

"I'll be right back," she said.

"Now what," I sighed.

"That's what I want to know," Pete said. "People around here have been ignoring me, but I thought that was because they were so busy."

"There has to be a reasonable explanation," I said, watching Pete pace the room again.

*

Kim returned sometime later. To me, in the dark, it felt like hours. She was no longer bouncing. Her movement was more like a cat that had been in a fight. Jumpy and ready to run.

"Kim?" I asked, not sure it was her who had entered the room.

"Yes," she said quietly. Too quietly. "Is he still here?"

"Who? Pete? Yes he is here. Why? What's going on?"

"In your accident, you ran into the street, just as a guy, Peter Tait, was driving by. He was going too fast and you ran right in front of him. He swerved. Hard. He almost missed you. His back end clipped you. The car was out of control. There wasn't the usual traffic to slow it down. The car spun into the gas pumps at the Co-op gas station there. It exploded. The car and everything in it... gone."

"Pete...?"

"Died instantly."

"What!?" Pete kind of stumbled over to a chair and sat down heavily.

"Oh no! That can't be!" I felt my heart thumping in my chest. "Pete? Are you all right?"

"I'm..."

"If he's here now, that means he's a ghost... or something. Doesn't he know he died?"

"Kimmy! Hush... please!"

"I don't feel different. The world still feels solid to me.... I don't understand! I have to think." He got up and walked out of the room.

"Well, now you've done it," I sighed. "He's gone."

"Me? I'm not the one talking to dead people! How could he have not known that he was dead?"

"He was so worried about me, he never thought about himself. I am ready to have these damn bandages off. What day is it?"

"Friday. Why?"

"Doctor Enns is supposed to take them off Friday... Then maybe they will let me go home."

"Home! What happened to your clothes?" She bustled over to the cupboards near the door. I heard the doors open and close. "Oh dear! Just as I thought. Your clothes are ruined! They are burned! How injured are you?"

"I don't know. They operated for internal injuries. They are afraid my eyes were burned...." I couldn't remember. My skin did feel like I had a bad sunburn and my belly felt punched. That wasn't too bad.

"I'll go get you some clothes," Kim said as she hurried toward the door.

I was left, wondering what was going on. Why? Why wasn't I hurt worse? Why could I see people? Why could I see Pete? I lay back and dozed for a while.

CHAPTER 3

"Okay, Miss LaMarre. I'm Doctor Enns. We are going to check your eyes now."

I awoke with a start. I couldn't believe I had actually slept. I lifted my arm to rub my head, but I could only move a few inches. I flexed my arms and discovered that I was tied down with padded bracelets. "What's going on?" I cried. "Let me go!" Panic edged into my voice. I am normally a calm person, but don't tie me down. *Never* tie me down. That may be one of the few things in the world that would set me off in a blind rage or panic.

"It's all right, Miss LaMarre!" A man's voice soothed. "We have been concerned about you. We don't want you to hurt yourself."

"Hurt myself? Why would I do that?"

"When a person hallucinates, they may be led to do almost anything."

"Hallucinate? What are you talking about?"

"You have been seeing people, or something, right through your bandages. You talk to people when there is no one there."

Memories of the last few days flowed over me. Doctors reassuring me; nurses helping me eat and go to the bathroom; and Pete being there, talking for hours, helping the time, and the pain pass through me without the stress. I sensed that this doctor was not the type of person to believe what was happening to me. People can't see through eyelids period, let alone when covered by bandages. He would never understand.

"You're a doctor! You *know* that an injured brain interprets nerve signals as anything it can. Take these bandages off and give me something real to see. Please."

"All right. Stay calm. Nurse, please dim the lights."

He was gentle about removing the many layers of gauze. Too gentle. He even rolled it up as he went. Maybe that is why he had me tied up. I would have had no restraint at all. I would have reached up and yanked the damn things right off. Finally, he was down to the pads over my eyelids. He pulled them off and gently wiped my eyelids with a wet cloth.

"All right. Don't rush it. Try to open your eyes."

"They feel caked shut," I muttered, wishing I could rub the stuff away.

"They are. It is just your body pushing dirt out."

He wiped the stuff away more firmly so I could open my eyes. I could see! I didn't realize how afraid I had been until then.

"I can see," I said, looking him in the eyes. "Will you take these shackles off now?"

"Of course. Hold still for a minute." He shone a flashlight into my eyes, looking carefully deep inside my eyeballs. "Everything looks good on the inside. What can you see?"

"I can see you," I said. "Everything beyond you is fuzzy, because I don't have my glasses on, and the lights are off."

"Yes, of course," Dr. Enns said, motioning for the nurse to turn the lights on.

The room seemed to be full of people! Most of them were fuzzy.

"I need my glasses," I said, looking around at my bedside table.

"I have them!" Kimmy's voice came from the doorway. "I thought you would need them. I brought your spares from home." People moved aside for her to come to the bed. She handed the doctor my extra pair of glasses and he put them on me.

Kimmy looked worried, but hopeful. Her bounce was back, making her blonde curls move continuously. I looked past her and saw the nurse, Mary. Gathered around her were five people, dressed in hospital gowns. I was going to ask why she brought other patients into my room, when I realized that I could almost see through them. They where opaque, rather than transparent. I turned and looked at the doctor. Standing quietly behind him were two patients with bandages over their eyes, how could they follow him if they couldn't see? While I was looking, a nurse bustled into the room and refilled the water glass of the bed beside mine. She seemed a little less opaque than the others, but I had no doubt that she must be a ghost too. Ghosts. I glanced back to the doorway and saw a tall, slim man dressed in a neat shirt and pants. He looked like he was in shock. I nodded to him and looked back at the doctor.

"All right, doctor, I can see. Could you please remove these shackles? My nose is itchy."

"Oh. Of course," the doctor said.

I don't think he knew what to expect. He obviously had a fear of mental illness. Or me. Why would anyone be afraid of me? He fumbled with the buckles, but eventually released my arms.

"I want you to come to my office in six months, as long as there are no major changes in your vision. If things go dark like a curtain falling in front of them, or it looks like a swarm of black bugs in front, the retina may be detaching. In that case, come see me right away. All right?"

"All right. Thank you, Dr. Enns."

All of the people left the room, including Kimmy, who waved goodbye as she left. All except the man standing by the door.

"Pete?" I asked.

"Yes," he said, coming over to the bed.

"Are you all right?" I didn't mention that he looked like he had seen a ghost.

"Physically, I feel fine." He sounded surprised. "I have no pain, no hunger, no fatigue. My senses still work, I think. I can smell stuff. But, I can't seem to leave."

"Leave? The hospital?"

"I think it's you. I think I'm stuck to you."

"Me! Why?"

"I don't know yet. It seems there are rules, but I haven't seen anyone that can explain them."

"How can that be? This place is *full* of ghosts. I think that if I wasn't sedated, I would freak out at seeing so many ghosts."

"It is? How can you tell? I don't think I've seen any." He looked worried.

"When I look at them, I can see through them. They are not quite solid."

"Everyone I see is solid."

"Yes, but to *my* eyes, *you* are not solid. I wonder if you can pass your hand through something solid."

He reached out promptly and touched the tray table with his hand. He tried to lift the mirror lid, but it wouldn't budge. He slapped down on the surface with his hand. I saw his hand pass slowly through the table.

"It feels like syrup," he said. "I don't understand."

"Understand what?" I asked.

"I always thought that when you die, that's it, you're dead. Gone. Maybe, if you're lucky, there's a white light of peace to go into... or maybe even those Golden Gates of Heaven! But this? What *is* this?"

"I honestly don't know. And I have no idea who to ask! Who is the expert?"

I watched while Pete wandered around the room, pushing his hands and feet through the dense furniture. The more he tried, the smoother his action became, but he was still slowed down in his attempts to pass through solid objects. He was standing in the middle of the bed opposite when Dr. Menzies came into the room..

"Well, Miss LaMarre. I hear you are doing better today. Your eyes are all right!"

"That's right," I agreed. "I don't think I realized how scared I was."

"Well, that's a relief. Everything is healing remarkably well. You are a very lucky woman, you know."

"Why?"

"I saw pictures of the accident site. It is as though you were being protected from the flames. You should have been way more burned than you are."

I glanced over at Pete. He had pushed himself up through the bed and was sitting cross-legged on top. The doctor said. "It's a miracle." And Pete grinned and shrugged.

"But, because of me, the driver is dead," I said, sadly.

"The way he was driving, it was only a matter of time," the doctor snorted. "He was going way too fast. Driving like that, he had a death wish or something."

Pete made a face at the doctor, while shaking his head. I didn't believe Dr. Menzies either.

"Doctor, can I go home now?"

"Home? Do you have anyone to help you at home?"

"Oh yes. My best friend Kimmy will stay with me. She is better than a Jewish mother."

"In that case, I have no objections. As long as you promise to come back if you start feeling worse. Do you have any other questions?"

"No..., yes.... Do you believe in ghosts?" I was watching five of them standing close to him, hanging on every word he said..

"Ghosts! No, I have seen no evidence to say ghosts exist."

"But what if?" I asked.

"Are you asking because of the images you saw when your eyes were covered?"

"Yes, that..."

"Whenever we lose one of our senses, the brain compensates. I am sure that everything will return to normal as you heal. All right?"

"Yes...." He really was a kind man. At least he didn't tie me up to talk to me.

"Good. I'll sign the forms. You can go home this afternoon."

"Thank you...."

He was out the door quickly, followed closely by his entourage of ghosts.

"I wonder if they go home with him and everything," I muttered.

"Who?" Pete asked.

"His ghosts! Didn't you see them? There were five of them!"

"I didn't see anyone. What did they look like? Were they emotional?"

"They were dressed in hospital gowns. They were all different in how opaque they were. One old man was so transparent, I could hardly see him. The others were much more substantial. A woman, the one I saw clearest, looked at him with so much hate and anger, I could almost feel it."

"And the others?"

"They seemed more interested or curious. They were watching. The oldest man, though, seemed bored, like he didn't want to be there anymore."

"Maybe that's a clue!" Pete said. "But why can't *I* see them?"

"That fits with why I can."

Just then the nurse that kept refilling the water glasses bustled into the room.

"Nurse!" I said, looking straight at her. "Nurse, I can see you! Talk to me!".

"You can see me?" She asked, stopping in front of me. She looked to be in her twenties. "How can you see me? What do you want?"

"I don't know how or why, but I want answers."

"Answers to what?"

"There seem to be rules around ghosts. What are they? And why?"

"Ghosts?" She looked around apprehensively. "There are ghosts here?"

"As far as I can tell, *you* are a ghost."

"Me? Oh. Yeah. I guess I am. Well, that's because I was killed in the fire. I seem to be stuck here. So, I keep working."

"When was the fire?"

"Don't you know? It wasn't *that* long ago. It was in March of 1950."

"It is 2010 now. You have been doing this for sixty years!"

"Sixty! Oh my." She sat on the nearest chair looking stricken. "It doesn't feel like that much time has passed. I don't want to do this forever...."

"Can you see or talk to the other ghosts in here?"

"Other ghosts? What other ghosts?"

"Well, Pete, for one." I pointed straight at Pete, who had moved closer to me. He was obviously trying to see who I was talking to.

"I don't see him," she sounded confused. "Are there many more?"

"From what I can see, lots." I said. "If you guys are spirits on the same plane, why can't you see each other? Pete, you should see her!"

"I don't think *should* has any bearing in this place," he said. "We seem to have bypassed all the physical laws. What is her name?"

"What is your name?" I asked the nurse.

"Nancy Fieldman," she said automatically. She seemed to flicker a tiny bit brighter to me.

"Hey! What was that?" Pete asked, looking at the chair.

I had an idea.

"Nancy, get mad. Or excited. Feel your emotions. Bring them to the surface!"

Sure enough, as she thought about emotions, she became easier for me to see.

"I can see her!" Pete said, in excitement. "She's cute."

"Oh my!" She said at the same time. "I can see him! What happened to him?"

"A car crash and a fire," I said, watching the two of them trying to communicate. Pete held his hand out, and she reached out to shake it. Her hand passed through his. They both snatched their hands back as if they had been burned.

"What was that?" I asked.

"An electric shock type of sensation," Pete said.

"Right, but not really painful," she agreed.

"Really! How did *that* happen?" They were looking closely at each other assessing their reactions.

"It must have to do with the touch," he said. Nancy nodded agreement.

"If you are leaving, can I come too?" she asked quietly. "I really don't want to do this forever. I want to be able to talk with someone. I have been so lonely."

"Of course you can," Pete said before I could respond. "Hold my hand and we can do it."

"Do you think it will work?" she asked fearfully.

"Sure! I have learned to walk through furniture and doors. I think we can do other things!"

"Well well," I said, deep in thought. "I wonder what else you can and cannot do?"

"Do?" Kimmy asked from the doorway. "Sue, looks like you're talking to yourself again. Not a good sign around here."

"Kimmy! I can go home!" I cried, ignoring her statement.

"I know. Dr. Menzies cornered me in the hallway and made me promise to stay with you for a week or more. He seems to think you were less than honest when you said you felt better."

"Ah, Doctors. They don't know everything," I said, making a face. "I want to go home. It is *way* too busy around here.".

Kimmy brought my clothes to me. Before I stripped, I pointed to Pete and gestured with my finger that he had to turn around. Kimmy gave me a strange look, but helped me get dressed anyway.

CHAPTER 4

I still dodged around the people in the hallway on the way out of the hospital. My own entourage was big enough. Kimmy and I led the way, closely followed by Mary, the nurse who had been kind to me. Pete followed, not far away, and right behind him, holding his hand, was Nancy. She looked so scared, I wished I could hug her, to bolster her resolve. But, she had more strength than even she realized. I turned and watched her leave the building. She looked as if she was walking chest deep in the river against the current. It looked much harder than pushing through solids had been for Pete. By ten feet away, it looked as though the water was waist deep and by twenty feet, knee-deep. We kept going. By the time we got to Kimmy's car, Nancy was skipping happily.

"I'm free! Thank you so much!" She cheered.

"Okay. So now what?" Pete asked. "Where do you go from here?"

"Go?...." Panic showed on her face.. "I don't know! Can I go with you?" Her fear was written all over her.

"Only if you do not attach yourself to us the same way you were attached to the hospital here," I said. "You may be able to learn things and teach us."

"Sue, who are you talking to?" Kimmy asked nervously.

"Nancy," I said, while Kim helped me into the car.

Kimmy looked all around us. "You mean, you can still see ghosts?"

"Yes. Better than ever. Now I see the whole of them, not just their light."

"And one is coming with us?"

"Two, actually. Pete seems to be attached to me.".

"Pete. The guy in the car that hit you."

"Right." I watched Pete and Nancy jump out of the way as Kim walked around the car. They may have known that they were dead, but they still thought as if they were solid. When Pete realized that he couldn't open the car door for Nancy, he pushed his way through and perched himself on the back seat. Nancy, who probably had much more practice with closed doors, followed easily. "That wore me out. Let's go home," I said, sinking back into my seat.

Kimmy got me home without incident. She helped me up the stairs to my bedroom and arranged every pillow she could find so I could sit and relax comfortably. Then she went to the kitchen to make us a meal.

"Nice place you have here," Pete said, wandering around my tiny bedroom.

"It is small," I said, shrugging. "But it suits my needs. The price was right."

"But you have used colour to make it cozy rather than cramped. I like that.".

"What is it that you do... did again?" I asked, looking at him sideways.

"I design cool gaming equipment. Like consoles and things."

"Oh yes. I remember. The one that looks like it came straight out of a science fiction movie."

"Yes, but it really works! It is like a multi-surface touchpad with sliders and lights. It can be programmed to work with any system out there! And I have ideas for improvement."

"Now, *that* is going to become frustrating," I said.

"Why? Oh... yeah. Right." He sat on the foot of my bed looking dejected.

"What are you guys talking about?" Nancy asked..

"Computers," I said. "Pete is an expert. Probably one of the best."

"Computers? Please explain."

Pete quietly started in on the history and function of computers. He kept his voice low, so I could doze off.

When Kimmy came with a tray of food, they were still talking quietly together. They had managed to put themselves into a small space in a corner of the room. I don't think they realized that they were occupying space that was too small for even one person to be in comfortably. I guess Pete was right. Physics does not apply in whatever plane of existence they were in.

"Are they here?" Kimmy asked, looking around the room.

"Yes, but they are talking to each other. We aren't all that interesting right now."

"But why are they here? Why can you see them? What is going on?"

"I don't know!" I cried and burst into tears. I don't cry easily. I never have. I'm the type of person who keeps her head and deals with each situation as it comes. All of a sudden, every sorrow, every crisis, every crushing experience in my life overwhelmed me. My mother's early death and then my Grandmother; the bullies I had to deal with at school; feeling inadequate because we had no money; trying to live on an artist's income. I cried and cried until I was out of breath and

had the hiccups. Kimmy put her strong arms around me, which swept more emotion into my heart, but I felt better. I couldn't believe that crying could give me that kind of release.

"It's okay, Sue. Let it out. It's going to be all right." Kim kept saying these words softly in my ear. It was comforting.

I took a deep breath and sat up straighter. "I don't know about that," I said. "The world has turned upside down, and I don't understand it."

"Sue, what's wrong?" Pete asked. He and Nancy were standing closer to me, looking worried.

"Pete, none of this makes sense. There must be reason behind whatever is going on with you and the other ghosts and me. I just don't understand the reason."

"I agree," Pete said, his brow furrowed. "I hold science in great regard. I want to know more."

"How?"

"One experiment at a time. I am going to try to leave here with Nancy. Maybe we can find someone who knows. In the meantime, sleep. Get better. We will come back."

"I'd say be careful, but of what, I have no idea."

"What is he saying? What's going on?" Kimmy asked, squinting her eyes in an attempt to see Pete.

"Pete and Nancy are going to try to leave to find the answers. I am going to sleep."

*

For the next two weeks, my life slid into a routine of sleeping, eating, exercising and talking with Kimmy, Pete and Nancy. Pete could not go beyond fifty feet from me, no matter how hard he tried. Nancy, once away from the hospital, could go anywhere she liked. She had her own adventures, going back to her home and family. She did locate her brother living in her parent's old home. He was eighty five years old and fearful. She was pretty sure that if she *could* reveal herself to him, he would suffer a heart attack. She really didn't want to deal with him then.

After that, she started to enjoy herself. At first she walked or took a bus or even hopped on a car to go from one place to another. After a while, she discovered that she just had to think about a place or person and, poof, she was there. She returned every day to report on her findings. Sometimes she was excited, and sometimes she was obviously affected by what she had seen.

"Sue! You've got to help her!" Pete said one day, tears shining in his eyes. "She shouldn't have gone there!"

"Slow down Pete!" I urged. "Where did she go?"

"We were talking about where she could go and whether she had to have been there before she thought herself to the spot." He paused, looking quite sick.

"Okay," I nodded.

"Well, we were looking through your magazines for a clear image that she could use."

"Pete, where did she go?"

"The World Trade Center. Or at the least, the monument."

"Oh no. What did she see? She can't see other ghosts, can she?"

"Only when there is strong emotion in the ghost. Do you remember that day?"

"I remember. Emotion was strong in the whole world that day. Shock, horror, fear, anger, hate. The anger and hate are still pretty strong, I think."

"Exactly. She went just after you had lunch. It was dark there, in the middle of the day! All those people still filling the park and streets. They suck the life out of everyone they touch. They felt Nancy's presence and surrounded her, gluing her to the spot. She said it was harder to get away from them than it was the hospital. Now, she just sits and cries."

"It's as if hell is right here!" I blurted out. I avoid talking religion with most people. My beliefs usually differ from others just enough to stimulate strong emotions.

"Hell or limbo," Pete agreed.

"But why are people stuck here? I'm certain that there were many good people that died that day. Why can't they move on or whatever?"

"I'm pretty sure some of it is connected to their emotions," Pete said.

"Emotions!?"

"The stronger the emotions of the dead person, the more they can be seen here in this place and the tighter the hold that is keeping them here."

"Even if the emotions are good?"

"Like love?"

He smiled as I nodded.

"I suspect love is the strongest of all. But, I may be wrong. I can't go out and I can't see them. I just have Nancy to talk to and she is a little freaked out right now."

"Let's go talk with her," I suggested. We went downstairs to the dining room, where Nancy was sitting in a corner sobbing. "Nancy! Talk to me!"

"Leave me alone!" she cried.

"I can do that, but I would much rather help you. You suffered a trauma out there. The world is not as nice a place as you expected. You probably feel betrayed."

"Yes. How did you know?"

"I've had my share of betrayal in my life. I know what it feels like. Do you want to go back to the hospital?"

"I can't! I tried! It's not the same anymore!"

"You know too much?"

"Right! The more I wander around, the more I can see the ghosts! Why?"

"I think that is because of your own emotions. You are so much stronger in *your* emotions, you are seeing more around you."

"I don't like it!"

"I don't blame you. I'm sorry, Nancy. I think this is all my fault."

"Your fault? I guess it is, but I came away willingly. I wandered those hallways for sixty years! That is no way to die! I don't understand."

"Neither do I. I think we should go out into the neighbourhood. There is a professor at the University who teaches a course on death and dying. Maybe he knows something."

CHAPTER 5

Kimmy had to go shopping, so she dropped me off at the University so I could meet the professor while she got the groceries. I have to say that I was afraid that he would kick me out when he heard my story.

I'm not an aggressive person. I'm not the type to push my way into a place where I'm obviously not wanted. But, when I got as far as the University, I was feeling very jumpy. I needed to find out what was going on. Everywhere I looked, I could see ghosts following people. Some of the young people, who were students at the University, were closely followed by old, wrinkled ghosts, who looked like they were prodding the younger ones along. I assumed the ghosts were grandparents, but if they were trying to help... I couldn't see how what they were doing was any help at all.

I saw a young black man walking across campus. He was surrounded by ghosts. I would guess over twenty, but it was hard to tell. They kind of overlapped each other as they pushed to be close to him. He looked like he had a hard time breathing, as if they were taking his air. They all looked very angry and focussed on him, ignoring the rest of the world completely.

"That is a scary sight," Pete said from beside me.

"You can see them?" I asked, surprised.

"I've been practising," he said proudly. "I'm pretty sure seeing them is connected to emotions. Their emotions make them visible and my emotions let me see. Knowing that, I can push the envelope so to speak, and I can see a lot of them. I need you to tell me if I've missed some."

"If everything is connected by emotions, then we have a problem." I said, looking up into his eyes.

"Why? What do you mean?" he asked seriously.

"You are having too much fun! If you are happy, you will stay by me forever!" I never, in my whole life, imagined that I would hear a ghost laugh. It was like the echo of laughter, and it made my heart feel good.

"So, do you know this prof we're going to see?" Pete asked.

"I've met him at my church," I said. "He was a guest speaker one Sunday. It was very interesting. I called him this morning and he agreed to meet at two. We will see what he thinks."

The religion department was on the fourth floor of a very old building. I had the impression that they were put out of the way, so they could be ignored. When I thought about the age of the building, it occurred to me that I should see lots of ghosts, but as I walked through the ancient hallways, I saw no people and no ghosts.

"Is it my perception, or is this place really free from ghosts?" Pete asked.

"Seem to be none here," I agreed. "Maybe they went to the lectures and fell asleep."

We arrived at the right door and I knocked.

"Come in, come in. Hello Miss LaMarre. Come on in. Have a seat."

Doctor Hamilton was a small round man. His head was round; he had no visible neck. His body was round and his arms and legs stuck out at awkward angles. Cheerfulness was written all over his round face.

"Doctor Hamilton, thank you for seeing me."

"No problem, my dear. Sit. Relax. Now, how can I help you, Miss LaMarre?"

"Please, call me Sue."

"All right, how can I help you Sue?"

"Doctor Hamilton, you are the expert on death and dying. I recently had a near death experience, and my life has been changed forever because of it."

"Yes, yes. That often happens. We get a renewed look at our life. Sometimes a new sense of purpose. That is a good reaction. There are occasions when one person dies, and the other lives, that the living one feels guilt for having survived. That too is normal. Sometimes you just have to give it time."

"That's not exactly what I mean." I said, trying not to stare at the ghost on the other side of the room. She was his wife. I recognized her from the lecture he gave at church. "Ever since the accident happened, I have been able to see dead people. Ghosts. And it is not like everyone says! There is no light to go into. No heaven. Hell seems to be right here on earth and there is no escaping."

"Ghosts? Well really Miss LaMarre, there is not much evidence that spirits remain with us. There are theories of reincarnation..."

I could see that this was going to be difficult. "When did your wife pass away?" I asked.

"My wife? Last April. Why? How did you know?"

"She is sitting over there on that huge pile of magazines. She looks much better than she did when you both came to the church. She is no longer in pain. She is looking at you with love in her eyes."

"Martha?" He swung around to look, but of course he couldn't see her. "This is preposterous!"

"Don't frighten him, dear," she said to me. "His heart is not strong enough to take the shock."

"But why do you stay?" I asked her.

"There is no place else to go," she said. "I tried. Believe me, I have heard all the myths and beliefs. I waited for the light. It didn't show. So I stayed with the only man I ever loved."

"Who are you talking to?" Dr. Hamilton blustered.

"Your wife loves you," I said. "She says you are the only man she ever loved."

"It wouldn't take much research to figure that out," he snorted.

"You may be right," I agreed. "But why would I want to? I want to know what's going on! In every religion that I know of, the dead move on to some other plane of existence or they are just gone. Very few mention spirits staying, haunting the people they have the most emotion for... to... I don't know. But I will tell you that it is mighty crowded around this world!"

"But... she's not in pain?"

"She's not in pain."

"Tell him I've not felt this good since the kids were born. He doesn't need to worry about me, I'm here with him always."

"I'm not sure that's what he wants to hear," I said.

"What?" he asked.

I repeated what she said. At first, he looked pleased, then he thought about it some more and looked uncomfortable.

"Always?" He repeated. When I nodded, he looked upset. "You are right. This is not the way it is supposed to be, but what happened to change it? I've got to think."

"Just because we always believed that people 'move on' or something when they die, doesn't make it a fact," Pete said, trying to touch Martha's hand. When she got the idea that he wanted to shake her hand, she reached out. I could almost see the spark they both felt.

"That was the most physical sensation I have felt since I died!" she said, looking brighter. "What was it?"

"I don't know," I said.

Dr. Hamilton looked up at me, but I was looking at Martha. I knew he wanted to ask, but he sank back into thought. "You have been talking to these ghosts, right?" He asked me. I nodded. "What years did they die? Who is the oldest?"

"Oldest?" I asked, looking at his wife.

"Not age before they die, age from when they die."

"All right. Nancy died in nineteen fifty. I haven't talked to all that many. Some are pretty intimidating."

"They are ghosts!" he said. "What can they do to you?"

"Pete protected me from the fire, or I would be dead too. If one newly dead spirit can do that, I have no idea what experienced ones can do. They are full of emotions, most of them anger."

"But how did he do that?" Dr. Hamilton asked.

"He put himself between me and the fire," I shrugged. "I think he did it on instinct. That's the kind of person he is."

"Good job, young man!" Martha said, nodding to Pete. "Your mother would be proud."

Pete closed his eyes grimacing. The look was funny and I laughed. He had not mentioned his family to me. They could still be alive, but he showed no interest in contacting them. Curious.

"Martha is praising Pete for being a hero," I told Dr. Hamilton when he looked confused at my laughter.

"She would," he smiled. "That's what she was like. I miss her.".

"So now, if you wander around at home talking to her, you know she is listening," I said, going with a hunch. "Even if she can't talk back."

"Doing *that* has made the kids think I'm losing it," he grumbled. When he frowned and looked sad, his wrinkles showed more, and he looked a little less round. "A selfish part of me wants her with me," he said, "but most of me wants her to go to a place of peace."

"I disagree," I said, "and so does she. She is nodding in agreement."

"Something must have happened," he said decisively, ignoring my comment. "Something had to have altered our reality sufficiently to change how our spirits deal with death."

"But what?" I understood what he was getting at, but how on earth do you find answers to a question, no one knows has been asked.

"If we can find out when, we may be able to decide what or where."

"We will need Nancy," Pete said. "She is the only one who can go around the world at will."

I repeated what Pete said. Dr. Hamilton agreed. "I have two more classes today. How about I come to your house tonight? We can try to learn more then."

I agreed and left the office with Pete close behind. I felt tired, so I sat on a bench outside the library to watch the world go by.

"What can you see?" Pete asked. "I can only see a few ghosts, and they're very fuzzy to me."

"There are so many of them," I said quietly. "They crowd the people they are following. Some are just there, following, as if they are balloons tied to the person, just bobbing along. They are faded and hard to see. Others are marching so close to their person, they appear to be occupying the same space. You know, the more I look, the more I see. This is a little overwhelming."

CHAPTER 6

"Come in Dr. Hamilton, Martha. Can I get you anything?" My habit of being a good hostess came from my Grandmother. I will jump up to get something for my guests, no matter how I feel. By that evening, I felt lousy. I was tired and sore from the internal injuries that had not completely healed yet. I ushered them into the living room, where Kimmy and Nancy were waiting. "Dr. Hamilton, this is my best friend, Kimberly Foton."

They shook hands and we sat comfortably around the room.

"Martha, this is Nancy Fieldman. She was a nurse at the hospital when there was a fire. We managed to free her from the hold of the building."

Martha and Nancy tried to shake hands with the help of Pete. The spark of their connection even made Kimmy and Dr. Hamilton jump, even though they saw nothing.

"My mother used to talk about that fire," Martha said. "It happened while I was being born. They were evacuating the building at the same time that they were telling her to push. They were still on the second floor when I was born and the nurses took me away to be checked. My mother was so upset that we were separated.... Anyway, the fire blocked the way for them to bring me back and there was so much smoke.... A young nurse risked her life to bring me back to my mother. Mother found out later that the nurse was overcome from smoke and died. It was very sad."

"I remember that!" Nancy said, surprised. "I didn't know why they took the baby away at a time like that. It was procedure, not necessity. There was a crash that distracted the other nurses, so I grabbed the baby and took it back to its mother. I don't remember much after that."

"That was you?" Martha said gladly. "You saved my life! At the expense of your own! How do I thank you for something like that?"

I had been quietly repeating what they were saying to each other. Dr. Hamilton sat quietly, looking amazed. Kimberly, who was getting used to such conversations, listened attentively.

"Imagine that!" Kim said. "It's a small world."

"I think of it more as the Interconnected Web of Life, like we say at our church." I said, sitting back and observing Dr. Hamilton.

"This just changes everything!" he said, obviously upset. "It breaks all the rules!"

"Rules?" Kim asked. "There are rules to dying? I don't believe it!".

"No no, not rules to dying exactly, but, in almost all religions, when people die, they move on to another plane of existence. They don't interact with us.".

"Hmmm. I always question absolutes, when there is no proof either way," Kimmy said disapprovingly.

"All right, guys," I said, shaking my head. "Martha said that when she died, she looked for the white light, but it wasn't there."

"That's right, dear. I saw a hint of it, just before I died, but once I left my body, it was gone."

"I didn't look for a white light," Pete said, "but from everything I've heard, you can't miss seeing it. I might have known that I was dead a lot sooner if I had seen it."

"When I died... everything was bright from the fire. There were a few of us that died that night. I kept busy trying to help people, but after a while, the others were complaining about not 'crossing over'. I didn't know what they were talking about. As the days passed, they complained more, so I moved into the new building as soon as it was built. I can't stand whiners and I like to keep busy."

I repeated what they said, trying to be accurate. I was getting a headache, listening and speaking at the same time. I closed my eyes and sat back in my chair. I could still see their light through my eyelids. I turned my head, looking at them all. I could see six red energy shapes in the room.

Startled, I opened my eyes. Kimmy, Dr. Hamilton, Martha, Pete, Nancy. Five. I closed my eyes again and pointed at the sixth person..

"Who are you?" I asked.

"Me?" The voice was soft and gentle and not gender specific.

I opened my eyes, staring at the spot and saw the flicker of a person, very faint in the bright light of my living room. "Yes. You. Who are you? Why are you here? Why were you hiding from us?" I felt a bit like Kimmy, questioning like that. Everyone else in the room was looking at me and the spot I was pointing at.

"I am Naomi," the ghost admitted. "I've been listening to your talk about dying. I used to live here... until I was murdered."

"Murdered!" I squawked. "Here?!"

Her light flickered brighter, as she thought about her death. "Yes, here. I don't really mind, though. Death allowed me to be my real self, not the pretend one I had to be in life."

"I don't understand," I said.

As she spoke, she became easier for me to see.

"Human beings destroy the things... people... who are different. I was different."

Pete, Martha and Nancy moved nearer to her, holding out their hands to her. Timidly, she touched each one, surprise showing on her face at the physical reaction.

"How were you different, dear?" Martha asked kindly.

"I was born into a male body, but, as you can see, I am female."

Looking at her, sitting calmly near the table, I could see that she was a very beautiful woman. Her features were delicate, her eyes bright. But she emanated a feeling of sadness that touched my heart.

"What year did you die?" Kimmy asked, when I finished repeating Naomi's words.

"In nineteen forty five. I had just moved here to start a new life. I didn't realize how bad this area was until it was too late."

"How old were you?" I asked, thinking she looked under thirty.

"I was forty five," she smiled. "I went overseas in the war. That was horrible. I was injured by a land mine, and almost died then. But they patched me up and sent me home. Life was so much worse here.”

“When you almost died, did you see a light?” Dr. Hamilton asked.

“Yes, I did. I was going toward it when something happened to it. I felt kind of dragged back to my body. I always thought my living was why the light shut down for me, but when I really died, the light was still gone.”

“What date was that, when the light shut down?” Pete asked, an odd look on his face.

“August sixth, nineteen forty five,” Naomi said, thinking back.

Pete and Dr. Hamilton each looked horrified by that date.

“What?” Kimmy asked.

“Hiroshima.” Dr. Hamilton said, a catch in his voice. “Seventy thousand people dead instantly. Another seventy thousand dead from radiation sickness or cancer directly related to that bomb. One bomb.”

“That’s right!” Naomi said. “I remember everyone talking about that. In Europe, the war was over, but Japan refused to stop. The Americans convinced them.”

“If the war was over, how did you get hurt?” Nancy asked.

"I crossed a field to save a child from bullies. I didn't know it was a minefield. Blew my testicles right off. Life became much quieter for me after that."

I couldn't miss her smile of satisfaction over that. Sex change operations were a long ways away, for someone in her generation.

"Until you came here," Pete said, shaking his head.

"That is such a sad story," Martha said, tears running down her cheeks.

"Don't cry for me!" Naomi said, reaching out to Martha. "My life was hard and sad, but my death has been quietly happy. I look good, I feel good. No one bothers me. And now, I have new friends! It just keeps getting better!"

"It would be better yet, if we had the choice to go into the light," Pete said, looking at Nancy.

"Do you suppose it was the splitting of the atom or the killing of so many people at once that did it to the light?" Kimmy asked.

"Well," Dr. Hamilton started, going into lecture mode. "They had done many tests to determine how to build the bomb. But, Hiroshima, and Nagasaki are the only times that nuclear weapons have been used to kill people. I cannot imagine the repercussions on *other* planes of existence. *This* one was bad enough."

"Obviously, the repercussion was the closing of the Gate between us," Kimmy said, looking disgusted. "Men and their wars."

"So now we need to find out how to open it again," Pete said.

CHAPTER 7

That was a strange gathering in my living room that night. Three living people and four ghosts, discussing the afterlife as though all our lives were affected by it. Of course, they were. The thought of dying, and having nowhere to go, horrified me. But what could we do? We ended the evening with more information than we started with, but we felt at an impasse.

We decided that we had to meet again in a place where many people died and find out if any of them knew what was going on. But where to go? The cemetery? No. No one died there. That's just where the bodies were kept. The hospital? I had already been there. The ghosts seemed oblivious to the outside world. Maybe because of the illnesses that killed them. We needed an accident site or natural disaster, where healthy people were killed, and they stayed there with nowhere else to go. Kimmy suggested a car crash, where no one survived. Sadly, not far away, west of Winnipeg, there was a stretch of the highway that seemed to get the worst of the weather. There had been several bad pileups there over the last few years. Kimmy and I went there in her car with our pair of ghosts. Naomi did not want to leave the house yet. Dr. Hamilton agreed to meet us there after his first class of the day.

"What a beautiful day for an outing!" Kimmy exclaimed, pointing out the various colours of the trees. "I love this time of year. All my best love affairs have happened in the fall."

"How can you tell?" I asked, teasing. "There have been so many of them."

"Just because *you* can't get serious with anyone, don't bug me because *I* can. You know, it's better to have loved and lost than never to have loved."

"Ouch. You may be right. I have liked quite a few men, but, there is always something missing. Oh, there!" I pointed to the other side of the highway.

Kimmy drove on to the next crossroad so we could turn around to the other side of the highway. We drove back, and I told her to stop just where a crowd of about twenty ghosts were standing around. When we got out of the car, several of the ghosts came toward us, shouting.

"No! No! Don't stop here! It's too dangerous! You could be killed!" That was a woman who seemed to be genuinely concerned for our safety.

"Let them be, Marg. If they get killed, we will have someone new to talk to."

"Ben, that is the most selfish thing I've heard you say, and I've heard a lot from you."

Ben looked younger than Marg. She looked to be around thirty and wore clothes that were popular in the eighties. Ben looked closer to twenty wearing full motorcycle regalia. That stuff has been popular for fifty years, but he didn't look like he had grown into his clothes yet.

Kimmy popped the hood of the car, so she could look busy, while I stood back and watched the interactions. Pete and Nancy stayed back with me, not trusting what they saw or heard.

"It's worked before," Ben shrugged.

"Worked? What are you talking about?" Marg asked.

"I... encouraged... and accidents happened. I wasn't alone any more! I must say, though, I would have had more entertainment if I had let *you* go by."

"What!? *You* killed me? You... you... I am going to do something to you. I don't know what... yet. But you *will* regret your actions."

Ben came over to the car and pulled on the rod that held the hood up. He was putting a lot of effort into this action and I could see the rod start to move.

"Kimmy, step back from the car," I said quietly.

Kimmy did as I said, prepared for almost anything in these weird circumstances. Still, she screeched when the hood banged down in front of her.

"Darn, she moved," Ben said.

"Good," Margaret retorted. Then she looked at me. "You can see us!"

"You can?" Ben walked through the car to get in front of me. "Why? Who are you? Are you the Ferryman? Where have you been?"

"The Ferryman?" I asked. "No. I'm just someone who can see ghosts for some reason. Who are you?".

"I'm Marg Williamson. We have been here a long time. The only time people stop here is because of another accident, which his Majesty claims are his fault."

"Hello Marg, Ben," I said, looking each one in the eye. "Who are the others over there?"

"They were a big mistake," Ben grumbled. "They were travelling together in a private bus. I thought it was a rock group or something entertaining. Instead, I've got a busload of super religious eggheads that cross themselves and pray whenever they look at me.".

Ben's disgust was funny in spite of the fact that he deliberately caused the deaths of so many people.

"Serves you right," Marg snorted. "You deserve worse."

"Worse! It can't get worse than this!" He really looked like he believed that this was about as bad as the afterlife could be.

I laughed. "Really? What if that bunch could physically touch you and push you around?"

"Well... I'm already dead. What can hurt me now?"

"Pete, can you see Marg or Ben?" I asked.

Pete came up beside me, his eyes squinting in the morning light. "Is this one Marg?" he asked.

"That's right. Marg, this is Pete. Shake hands with him."

Pete held his right hand out and Marg hesitantly reached out to touch him. She jumped and squealed at the shock that passed between them.

"Oh my God, what was that?" She yelled, jumping back.

Ben hurriedly took several steps away and didn't see the grin on her face.

"Just getting to know you," Pete said from an angle where Ben couldn't see his face. "Come and meet Nancy." Pete and Marg stepped over to Nancy, Pete still holding her hand in a way that made him appear to be dragging her unwillingly.

"Wow," she whispered after Nancy grabbed her other hand. "Does this mean I can leave this place?"

"If you want to, we can help," Nancy said quietly. "But what about the others?"

"They are all waiting for something. Or someone. The religious group, say Saint Peter and Ben says The Ferryman. They are all convinced that someone has to escort them to heaven or the white light. Or something. Since it has been several years, I think they are deluded."

"Dr. Hamilton is here!" Kimmy said, moving around the car, away from the ghosts in relief.

"Hello, my dear," Dr. Hamilton greeted her as he got out of his car. "What have we got here?"

"A number of ghosts," Kimmy said. "Martha, stay away from the biker, he's dangerous."

Dr. Hamilton and Kimmy grinned, since neither of them knew for sure that Martha was nearby or heard the advice. "This is so weird," Kimmy added.

I saw Martha join Pete and Nancy, so I joined Kimmy and Dr. Hamilton. I told them everything I had heard so far.

"The Ferryman? That's a song!" Kimmy said.

"Yes, but the concept does thread through most religions in one way or another," Dr. Hamilton said thoughtfully.

I noticed Pete urging the others to slowly move towards us. Ben kept his distance, watching for other cars to pass by, and the group from the bus were kneeling and praying.

"Some aboriginal peoples believe a bird takes them. Most give it a name like Death. The term Death fills the role."

"Role?" I asked. "What role?"

"Gatekeeper!" he said brightly. "Everyone seems to glimpse the white light, but they can't go to it. No one has seen a Gatekeeper! That's the point where everything stops."

I was starting to feel somewhat uncomfortable with this talk. "Are you saying you *believe* there is a *person* that escorts people to their final destination?"

"Well... a spirit. Yes. Why not?"

"It is preposterous," I said. I don't know why I was so ill at ease about the idea. "What happened to the last one?"

"August sixth, nineteen forty five," Kimmy said dryly. "You know this. Seventy thousand died right away. Another seventy thousand over the next few days, months, years. And then another eighty thousand died three days later. We shattered the atom. What if we shattered the ghost of the Gatekeeper and the Gate, too?"

"It boggles the mind!" Dr. Hamilton said, not looking the least bit boggled. If anything, he looked cheerful.

"So, we may know why the world is filling up with ghosts," I said. "So what? What do *we* do about it?"

"We find the new Gatekeeper, of course," Dr. Hamilton said, cheerfully. "It would need to be someone who could talk to both the dead and the living. Someone who is not bound by any single religious belief, but understands them all. Someone who can stand up to all and not be bullied."

"You know, Sue." Kimmy was grinning at me! "That sounds just like you!"

"No!" I was shocked at the suggestion. "I *survived* that accident, and am very glad I did. This Gatekeeper Spirit sounds dead. I don't want to be dead! I like life!" My voice was rising toward panic. "This isn't funny!"

"No, of course it isn't," Martha said, coming over to me. "You two should be ashamed of yourselves!"

"Martha, that would be a more helpful comment if they could hear you," I said, trying to calm my racing pulse. "Look... think of someone else. In the meantime, you guys see if you can help Marg leave this place, but not Ben. He is not nice. He caused her death just so he wouldn't be alone. He deserves a busload of religious fanatics surrounding him. Then, let's go."

I saw Kimmy and Dr. Hamilton exchange knowing looks, but I wasn't sure why. I just wanted to leave and not think about it anymore. I watched Pete, Nancy and Martha walk down the road with Marg. They encouraged her when she had a difficult time moving. Having them cheer her on, was the key to letting her leave. The further down the road, she went, the easier it got.

They were quite a long distance away, when Ben realized they were leaving him. He screeched and ran after them. The barrier that held him to the place where he died, made him bounce back and fall on his rear end. For the first time since we arrived, the busload of people noticed Ben's predicament and they ran over to him. I couldn't believe my eyes when they surrounded him, praying to their God. His wail sounded painful and distant.

"Come on, let's go," I urged Kimmy and Dr. Hamilton. "We can pick up the others on top of that hill." I felt a great deal of relief, leaving Ben to the ministrations of the ghosts he had murdered.

CHAPTER 8

Every time I got home, there were more ghosts following me. They stayed back and were respectful, but I felt like a pied piper. Marg had joined our group, and Sam and Elliott two gay gentlemen in their fifties followed us home from the grocery store. Apparently, they had been victims of a prank in the parking lot. No one knew if the live wire was placed there deliberately or not, but the rain created the hazard. Sam and Elliott wore leather soled shoes. Stepping into the puddle, they died quickly. Their hair was still smoking, five years later!

Dr. Hamilton had to go back to teach another class, so Kimmy and I went back to my little house. We sat on the front porch, enjoying the weather and chatting. I watched the coming and going of many ghosts who did not stop to introduce themselves.

"There are so many of them!" I said quietly to Kimmy.

"Like the mosquitoes," Kimmy grumbled, slapping another bug.

"Just a minute," I said. "I can at least fix that!" I went inside and grabbed a citronella candle. I took it outside and lit the candle.

The strangest thing I've ever seen in my life happened then. Every ghost I could see, crowded around me and the candle, pushing to get closer.

"Is that the light? May I go into the light? Where have you been Gatekeeper? Let us go into the light."

"Oh no!" I shrieked, staggering back.

"What is it, Sue?" Kimmy jumped up and helped me sit. She took the candle and put it on the table between us. "What are they doing?"

"They think *that* is the Light, and *I* should let them cross over." I said, watching in horror as a younger boy ghost sat on the candle. I could still see it burning through him. "No! No, boy, that's *not* the light!"

"Well, where is it? Take me there. I want my family! I've been here too long! I want my Mommy!" He started to cry.

"Let's go inside," I said to Kimmy. "This is too much!"

"I can tell," she said, looking frustrated. "I don't understand why they are coming to *you*. What can *you* do?"

"Besides see them and hear them?" I snorted. "I don't know. Pete! What do they want?"

"You know, *I* can't see that many of them," Pete said defensively. "I'm feeling a little overwhelmed myself. But I don't think they're coming into the house. I think Naomi is stopping them."

"That's right. I am," Naomi said, popping into view. "You are going to have to do something about this, Sue! My yard is full. They are trampling the flowers and the noise they are making is horrible!"

"*Me* do something!? What can *I* do!?" I was feeling pushed in a direction I did not want to go, over a situation *not* of my making. "This is all crazy! Can you guys leave me alone and let me rest? I'm tired!"

"That's a good idea!" Kimmy said. "I'll cook something nice for supper. You go to sleep. Maybe an idea will come to you in your sleep." She herded me into my tiny bedroom and tucked me into bed. "If any of you ghosts are here, be nice to her and let her sleep! You won't get anything from her if she gets sicker."

I know she couldn't hear them, but I heard the grumbled assent as everyone left the room. I was alone at last.

Time drifted, I'm sure I was asleep for a while. I know I didn't wake up with a start or anything. I was just drifting with my eyes closed when a really bright light entered my room. I opened my eyes, but had to shade them with a hand, the light was so bright.

"Who are you?" I asked.

"A Messenger." The voice was soft and clear. I could not determine if it was male or female. It didn't seem to matter.

"What for?" I asked.

"You have been chosen for a very important job."

"Chosen? By who? For what job? What if I don't want to do it." My heart quickened it's beat, I think from fear or anticipation.

"The job is Gatekeeper."

"Oh no. That sounds bad." After what I had learned in the last two weeks, I did not want to deal with more ghosts. Why couldn't anyone understand that?

"The last Gatekeeper was destroyed. The overwhelming influx of souls in one instant was too much. He lost the battle. We have not had a suitable replacement since then. The bureaucratic backlog is horrendous."

"I'll bet," I grumbled. "I don't believe in you, or your Gate, and certainly not your God. Find someone else!"

The Being smiled at me. I sat up and placed the pillows behind my back so I could see better. The radiance from the Being kept me calm, even though I was terrified. "You do not have to believe in a thing for it to believe in you."

"That makes no sense," I grumbled. "Things don't believe. They are inanimate objects."

"The Gate is very animated," the Being laughed.

I felt as if rose petals had floated down from the ceiling, covering me and my bed. I couldn't see them, but I felt them on my hands and face and I smelled them everywhere. "I don't understand."

"It really isn't a difficult job. All you have to do is touch the spirit, ghost as you call it, and the Gate will allow them to pass into whatever realm they belong in."

"Whatever realm? You mean 'heaven' or 'hell'?"

"Those are two of the concepts. Nirvana; a big field of daffodils; floating on clouds. Different people have different beliefs. The Gate knows."

"Why me? Why not someone who believes in this stuff?"

"Because belief can get in the way of service. You were raised to be open to all beliefs. Your Grandmother knew the need. Now you can talk to spirits and hear and see them. They will come to you. All you do is reach out with your right hand and touch them. You will understand when you do it."

"But I don't want to! I want my quiet life back."

"You don't always get what you want." The Being was still smiling, as it faded away.

I kind of expected the room to feel dark when the bright light left, but there was a residue of light shining in the background. I stared at the empty space for a long time, thinking.

"Sue! Susie are you awake?" Kimmy called from the doorway.

"I'm awake. What smells so good?"

"Roast beef, Yorkshire pudding, all the fixings. You need a treat."

Kimmy went to a lot of trouble to make that. I felt overwhelmed. So, of course, I started to cry.

"Hey Susie, what's wrong? It's going to be okay. Really. Didn't you sleep? Are you in pain?"

"No, no, not that," I burbled. "This Being.... Spirit.... Angel.... Ghost.... Person came here. It told me..." I stopped on a sob.

"What? What did it say?"

"I have to be the Gatekeeper!"

"What!? Why?"

"I don't know! Because I can see them and talk to them! There has to be more people that can do that!" I recognized a definite whine in my voice, but I didn't care.

"I would expect there are lots that can do that. If they picked you, you must have something more."

"Right. I don't believe in religion!"

Kimmy stopped, stared at me for a minute and breathed out heavily. "That makes sense," she said. "The Gate has to be there for all religions. You have always said that your church believes there are many paths to the truth. Someone who believes that their religion is the only truth, won't be willing to let anyone else near the Gate."

"It makes sense!?" I squawked. "It's crazy! I can't do it!"

"All right," Kimmy said, nodding. "Come down and eat. You'll feel better then."

I had no argument. I cooperated with Kimmy, ate her delicious meal and relaxed, trying not to think about my future. Just before Kimmy brought out a desert, Dr. Hamilton arrived with Martha in his wake. He joined us for some of Kimmy's Apple pie and listened while Kimmy explained to him what I had told her.

"All you have to do is touch them?" he asked. "That doesn't sound too bad. It's not like you have to decide where they should go. *That* would be tough."

"I don't even *know* where they would go!" I said, feeling fragile and imposed upon.

"So are you going to do it?" Pete asked.

"No! This is so arbitrary! Who is this Being that says I have to do this? I have been chosen! Don't *I* have any choice? I don't want to do *any* of this."

"Sue," Nancy came and stood before me. "I have been around the world for you. There are places so full of spirits, there is only darkness left. Living people have trouble breathing there. The spirits are unhappy at staying. I have seen too much. Never mind the rest of them, could you please touch me? I need to find my family. I need to move on."

I knew Nancy had been crying a lot since she returned from the World Trade Center. I felt responsible for taking her away from the hospital and putting her into such an unhappy state. Slowly, reluctantly, I reached out to touch her hand.

It was as though time stopped. I looked around and saw Kimmy and Dr. Hamilton frozen still. Even Pete and Martha were moving very slowly. Martha was moving towards me, and Pete moved away. I looked back at Nancy and saw great relief on her face. Our fingers touched, and there was a quick flash of white light. Then, she was gone. I blinked and everything was back to the way it had been before.

"She's gone!" Pete cried.

"It's okay Pete," I said. "She went happily. The bad stuff is over."

"So, it was a good thing, what you did?" Dr. Hamilton asked.

"I guess…. Dr. Hamilton, Martha wants to go next."

"She does? Wait just a minute…. Martha, I have loved you all of my adult life. I tried to give you everything that you deserve, but I couldn't do it all. If you go away now, will you wait for me on the other side… whatever that is?"

"Roger, of course, I will. We have gone through life as a team. I'm sure we can do the same in the afterlife."

I repeated what she said as she moved closer to me. I reached out again and time stopped again. She smiled an angelic smile as if she could see what was coming. The crack of thunder and light made everyone flinch. Then, she was gone.

"Martha?" Dr. Hamilton called.

"She's gone," I responded. "There's something really good waiting for them. They saw it as I touched them."

"So, they are in a better place?" Kimmy asked.

"Yes," I agreed.

"So, this job is a good one! All you have to do is touch ghosts, and they move on, leaving you in peace? Cool."

"But, it is a monumental job!" Dr. Hamilton said. "Do you know how many ghosts there must be by now? Sixty five years of deaths! How is it possible?"

"If you touch one per second, nonstop, you could do over two million a day... fourteen and a half million a week... seven hundred and fifty five million a year...." Pete was computing in his head. "But, you seemed to move much faster than one second."

Repeating what ghosts were saying, had become such a habit, I barely noticed I was doing it. I had to stop and think before I could respond. "To me, it seemed like everything else stopped... or at least, slowed down. The ghosts can't run away from me!"

For some reason, I thought that was very funny. I was thinking about Ben, trying to run away down the highway. I wondered what *he* would see on the other side.

"Pete, don't you want to cross over?" I asked. "You moved away."

"I am enjoying myself here, with you," he said. "I want to help you."

"Well, I'm ready!" Marg said.

I had barely noticed her. She had stayed in the background listening and watching since we returned from our stop on the highway.

"I guess I am too," Naomi agreed. "Time for the next great adventure."

They both came towards me and stood patiently while I hesitated.

"They need you," Kimmy said, encouragingly.

I sighed and reached out to each of them. The flash of light still made me jump.

"Wait, did you...?" Kimmy asked, an odd look on her face.

"Yes, why?"

"You barely moved. It was like moving under a strobe light. You were here, and then you were there, and then, back. Weird."

"Who is left here now?" Dr. Hamilton asked, looking around the room apprehensively.

"Just Pete," I said, rubbing my arms. "He wants to stay and help. Pete, do you know how Naomi kept the ghosts out of the house?"

"No. I have to study it. It seems to be still working, even though she is gone."

"Good. I'm tired. I don't want to think about it tonight."

"You're right," Dr. Hamilton agreed. "I'll go home and see if the house feels different with Martha gone."

While Kimmy showed him out, I rubbed my arms, trying to put my nerves back into their normal unaroused state.

"All right, what happened?" Kimmy asked, coming into the room and sitting opposite me, so she could look me in the eyes.

"Happened?" My voice cracked. I had to clear my throat.

"Yes. What has you blushing so red I'm going to worry about your blood pressure?"

"Oh. That. Well...." Kimmy and Pete were both sitting, eagerly hanging on every word. "When I touched the ghosts, I saw this flash of light and what feels like a back surge of energy. The energy must be aimed at the pleasure center in my brain."

"Pleasure center? What do you mean?" Pete asked..

"I mean... the only way I can describe it... is that I had a body wide orgasm."

"Really?" Kimmy asked, a sparkle in her eyes. "A good one?"

"Mind blowing," I agreed.

"Each time?" Pete asked, sounding horrified.

"The first was big. The ones that followed were a bit toned down, but still mind blowing. What's on your mind?"

"I have... had... whatever. I have an addictive personality. I know how easy it is to become addicted to something. A person can become addicted to pain, in order to get the painkiller release. Do you have any idea how addictive *this* could be?!"

"Umm. Yes. I have a very good idea." I looked at Kimmy's face. She was patiently waiting for me to explain. "Pete thinks I'm going to be addicted right away. You know, like what happens with crack?!"

"Instantly!" Kimmy said, watching my reactions. "Well, there has to be something in it for you. Why else would you do it? Even Saints must get tired. I'm just wondering if it isn't more like cigarettes than cocaine."

"What do you mean?"

"Do you remember when we started smoking? We were seventeen."

"Vaguely."

"The first few puffs, made us feel lightheaded, as if we were floating above our bodies. Our fingers tingled and our lungs tried to shut down. It felt good. Pleasurable. Except for the coughing."

"Right," I agreed, trying to follow her line of reasoning.

"Then, after a while, those puffs didn't do anything much. We felt good for a while. It became the norm."

"Until we quit," I said, raising my right eyebrow.

"Until we quit," Kimmy agreed. "You quit so easily! *I* was the one who had such a hard time. *You* stopped cold turkey!"

"So.... Nothing to worry about!" I said, feeling relieved.

I thought about how I felt, and I know I had a silly smile on my face. I was relaxed, happy, ready to face the world, or ready to sleep.

"There are a bunch of ghosts in the front yard. Let's get rid of them," I said, getting up, ready for more. I knew there was hesitation and apprehension from both Kimmy and Pete, but, they followed me anyway.

Out in front of my porch, there was about a dozen ghosts, eagerly waiting for something. The boy, right up front, desperately wanted to go to the next level. He held out his hand saying: "I know you can do it. Please do me!". I reached out, touching his hand in a loose clasp. Light energy flashed and I caught a glimpse of a Gateway. I am a fan of Science Fiction and I have been a fan of Star Trek most of my life. That Gateway looked more like a Star Trek wormhole made from white light, rather than a true Gate with an old guy on a throne telling people where they belonged. I was truly relieved that *I* did not have to make *that* decision.

"How about me?" An old woman stepped forward. She had a beautiful smile.

I reached out again, amazed at how beautiful she was even at her apparent age.

"Thank you dear," she said, being pulled gently into the light. As I got used to the sensations, time slowed even more. I could see the Gate open and close after it accepted the ghost.

After that, the ghosts in the yard approached in an orderly fashion. Each time I deliberately touched them, I felt the pleasure in my body. It had lessened enough to allow me to control it, if I had to. I have read about some studies with rats. Too much stimulation of the pleasure center of their brain caused them to die. This wasn't like that. As Kimmy suggested, it was just enough to become a pleasure to walk through the crowd of ghosts and send them on their way. I moved faster than the ghosts. One last man had come to the yard, out of curiosity. He hung to the back. When he realized what was happening to the ghosts, he tried to leave. I walked in front of him, blocking the way. He was dressed in a suit and tie with a fedora hat. He looked like the pictures of gangsters from nineteen thirty or so.

"What's wrong?" I said, staying in front of him. "Don't you want to pass through the Gate?"

"Not really," he said defensively, trying to back up.

"Why? Are you afraid of where you will go?"

"I don't know *where* I will go. Do you? Do you choose where to send me? Don't make me go there...." He was starting to panic.

"I'm sorry," I said, reaching out. "I cannot leave you here." When I touched him, the light I was expecting didn't come. He was sucked into a darkness that left me with the impression of bone freezing cold.

I stopped and the rest of the world came into focus. Kimmy and Pete were sitting on the porch, trying to see everything that was happening.

"Sue! How did you get over there?" Kimmy asked. "What happened?"

"I have gone all the way around the house and yard, sending about thirty ghosts to the Gate. Time changes while I do that. To me, living people are stopped and ghosts are slowed *way* down and *I* am sped up amazingly!"

"But, how can you do that?" Kimmy asked.

"I don't know. I reach out with the intention of sending someone to the Gate and time changes! Like some quantum leap or something."

"Quantum!" Kimmy started to bounce eagerly.

"Or something... Why? ... What?"

"Don't you remember? Your Grandmother would say we were going into Quantum Time whenever we ran too fast for her!"

"Oh yeah! I do remember that! I asked her why she called it that and she touched the key and said I would understand some day." I reached up to my throat and fingered the tiny ornate key resting there. "Quantum Time. I guess it fits."

"How do you feel physically?" Pete asked, worried.

"I'm feeling *very* good. But not crazy good. I think Kimmy is right. It's just incentive."

"Incentive!" Kimmy squawked. "I could use some of that! I haven't had a guy in... well, a long time."

"Ha ha ha!" Pete laughed. "She's cute."

"Yeah, cute," I agreed. "I wish you two could see or hear each other. Parroting is tiring."

"I'm trying!" Pete said earnestly. "Tell her not to be afraid. I'm trying."

"All right," I said, watching his look of serious concentration. "Kimmy, Pete is trying very hard for you to see him. Don't be afraid if he succeeds. He can't hurt you."

"Oh! That would be nice."

"In the meantime, I'm going to bed. What a day. What a long long day." I left them in the living room, both concentrating hard to communicate. I knew Kimmy very well. One way or another, she would set up a line of communication, even if she had to use a Ouija board.

CHAPTER 9

The ghosts came to the house. I had been assuming that they would stay attached to the place or person that was involved in their death forever, but for most, it had been a long time. People died. The next generation died. Buildings collapsed. Time wore on and the bonds loosened. Who would have thought ghosts would gossip! I was learning more and more every day. I was very thankful for the protection that Naomi had done to the house. Otherwise.... I have never had a panic attack in my life, but just thinking about ghosts crowding around me, pushing to get near me, not letting me sleep.... I would seriously panic. I guess I am a control freak. I want to be in control of everything in my life. That is how I cope.

So, every morning, I went out into the yard and dispatched a hundred or so ghosts. I would stop for breakfast and go out to find another group of a hundred waiting patiently. If I stopped, I could see them coming down the street. I had to stop occasionally, just to reassure myself that I was still part of the land of the living.

"Sue!" Kimmy hollered from the house. "Come in, please? We have a problem!"

She had my attention. I went in, finding her with a pile of bills in front of her.

"What's wrong?" I asked.

"We are broke," she groaned. "I have tried to keep it going, I gave up my apartment to move in and take care of you. That helped, but I quit my job. Employment Insurance won't kick in for several weeks. Your income has dwindled down to nothing, even though I sold all of your best pieces of art. Now, you are way too busy to do more art and I'm way too busy to get another job. Taking care of you is a full time occupation!"

"So we need money," I said, sitting down next to her at the table.

"You could do 'Ghost Busting'," Pete suggested from the other side of the table. "You know, rid 'Haunted Houses' of their ghosts!"

"I do that anyway," I said, not following.

"Yes, but you could do it for a fee."

"Oh, really. I don't think I should. The costs of funerals are bad enough."

"For new ghosts, right. But what about the ones that are still haunting the family house? They should move on!"

"True, but to charge a fee?"

"I had lots of money," Pete interjected. "You could have it all!"

"And where would it be?" Kimmy asked. "In a bank? Dead people can't have bank accounts."

Pete and I stared at Kim, open mouthed.

"You heard him?" I gasped.

"Yes, but we can't use it," she said.

"You heard me!" Pete shouted.

"You don't need to shout!" Kimmy said. "I heard you without... I heard you... I can hear you! Oh my god, I can hear Pete!"

"That's great!" I cheered. "That will save me a lot of time and energy. So, Pete, how do we get to your money?"

"Well, Kimmy's right about the bank accounts. They would be frozen. But I don't really trust banks."

"You don't? Why not?" Kimmy asked.

"Banks crash. Investment companies crash. It hasn't been that long since the last recession. So I put my money into collectibles."

"Collectibles? Cool!" Kimmy said.

"Where? How could we touch them any better than your bank? They are your estate!"

"My parents are dead. I had no brothers or sisters, just business partners who didn't care about my personal life as long as I invented the next great thing. I was paranoid. There is *no* paper trail to a storage place with a combination lock. They warned me that they couldn't stop someone with a combination. Only if they had bolt cutters would they be considered thieves. Lousy security. That's why I chose them."

"That's crazy," I said. "You should take better care of your things!"

"Next time around," he laughed. "You know, I'm not the only paranoid person around. I bet there are lots of ghosts that would contribute to the cause of keeping you healthy."

"So, how do we do any of it," Kimmy asked.

"Kijiji," Pete said quickly. "It is like a local eBay online and is connected with local newspaper classified ads."

Kimmy and Pete quickly became engrossed in plans to acquire funds. I was glad they could do it together, so I could go back outside to deal with the influx of ghosts. I don't know how the word had spread throughout the world, but they kept coming. They were getting more polite about it too. I heard more: 'Bless you child!' Than: 'It's about time!'. I felt good, like I was helping the world in a way. I stopped when I was hungry or tired and left the rest of the daily details to Kimmy and Pete. Time passed without my being aware of it.

"Sue, we have got to go out today," Kimmy said at breakfast a number of days later.

I knew I was losing track of time, but it couldn't have been all that long, could it?

"We do? All right. Where are we going?" I was willing.

"The Fort Garry Hotel," Kimmy said, grinning. "They have ghosts and they want them gone."

"Is this your 'Ghost Busting' business?"

"Yes it is. If you get rid of these ghosts, our reputation will be made and we will be able to go out to the ghosts and the world.."

"Go out .... Right. Am I missing something?"

"Yes!" Pete and Kimmy chorused.

"You step out the door and kind of disappear into the yard. We know you are there, but we can't really see you. That's okay. We understand, but *nobody... not one person...* will enter the yard when you are out there. We have had to arrange for a box office for mail delivery because the mail person just walks past as if the lot was empty! And *we* can't leave either. If I'm not out before you in the morning, I can't go! There is a force that feels like rubber or something that keeps me inside! Pete can't go because his tie to you is still too strong! So *we* are going *stir crazy*! All we can hope is that you can escort us out of here!"

"Wow Kimmy, I'm sorry! I didn't realize it was an issue! How long has it been?"

"Two months!" They chorused again.

"Two months? Since the accident?"

"No!" Kimmy squawked. "Two months since you opened the Gate and sent Martha and Nancy and Naomi through."

I was stunned. No way it felt that long. That was seriously unfair to Kimmy and Pete. Being stuck like that might make *him* want to cross over and *then* what would Kimmy do? I had at least been observant enough to see the growing bond between them.

"All right," I said, decisively, "let's go."

I was surprised at the animosity that started building when I went to the car instead of into the front yard. "I will be back," I told the crowd of ghosts. "I have to do something else right now."

"But we have come so far. We have waited so long!" An old woman cried.

"I will be back," I said firmly.

"Yo, Bitch! You got no business going anywhere else! *This* is your obligation and you will do it, or else!"

I don't like it when people push me, physically or mentally. "Or else what?" I asked coldly.

"Or else your life could be short and painful!" The big ghost threatened.

"Do you not know who I am?" I asked, my teeth clenched.

"You are the one to touch, so I can finally get out of here. So do your job!"

"No," I said, turned my back and climbed into the car. I could feel the ghosts trying to grab me, as if touching me would do the same as my touching them. It tickled, nothing more. Kimmy put the car in gear and got us out of there. We actually drove the car through some of the ghosts. One passed through Kimmy and I saw her shiver. Another deliberately lined up to pass through me. Again, it tickled. The old woman looked angry when we left them behind. It felt good to get away.

The Fort Garry was a grand old hotel, built for the guests and passengers of the Canadian National Railway. All of the old hotels built along the route had an age and majesty that could not be reproduced in current building styles. I really loved all of them.

Kimmy led the way to the manager's office, looking businesslike and assured. We passed a large mirror and I realized that I looked anything but businesslike. I wore a white cotton sundress that flowed around my legs and my light brown hair flowed down my back. When I dressed in the morning, I thought I would be outside in the sun. Oh well, I thought I was looking pretty.

"Good morning Miss Foton, Miss LaMarre. Thank you for coming so quickly. I am Eric Handry. He gestured for us to sit in his spacious office.

"Good morning Mr. Handry," Kimmy said, shaking his hand. "Your request sounded urgent."

"Well, yes. We do a lot of conventions here. Many of them are annual. Our largest income comes from repeat customers." He fidgeted with papers on his desk before he could go on. "Last year we had a large group from one of the Government Departments for the first time. They have a three day conference every year and are considering coming here every year. This is a *very* lucrative contract. There were complaints, however, that someone encountered our ghosts. Most people are not sensitive enough to see the ghosts, but this person saw three. They have made it clear that we must make every effort to rid the hotel of ghosts or they will never return. They could spread the word and ruin our business!"

"How many ghosts do you have?" I asked, looking at two of them who were resting behind him on the windowsill. A man and a woman, dressed in fifties styles.

"I have no idea," he said. "I have been told of a little girl who wanders around in a nightgown on the fourth floor. There's a woman in the public washroom off the main lobby and I have heard of different men and women on the first and second floor. The trouble is, all the descriptions are different. The child and the woman are the only ones that have been described consistently."

"All right," I said, still watching the two behind him. "I need a quiet location where I won't be disturbed…"

"The Queen's bedroom," the woman ghost said, standing eagerly.

"The Queen's bedroom," I repeated.

"The… how do you know about that?" He looked shocked. "It hasn't been called that since nineteen ninety seven. She stayed there in nineteen seventy for the Centennial and the name stuck unofficially. We insisted on renaming it when an anti-monarchist trashed the room in ninety seven." He shook his head in wonder and maybe suspicion.

"It's all right," I said calmly. "Could we go there?"

"Of course," he agreed. He still looked a bit annoyed. He took us back out into the lobby and over to the elevators. I watched the woman from the washroom watch us as well as several others that had been hiding amongst the decorations. They followed. She stayed. As we travelled up to the third floor, more and more ghosts joined the procession. Mr. Handry looked like he was having difficulty breathing. He unlocked the door and was about to enter, but Kimmy put her hand on his arm to stop him.

"I think we will be more effective if we go in ourselves," she said firmly. "We will try not to take too much of your time."

"Oh. Well.... since you've come this far." He shrugged his shoulders and stepped back. "I will be in my office if you need me."

Kimmy closed the door and we sat on the end of the bed. For the first time, since we entered the building, Pete showed himself to me, looking troubled.

"There seems to be a lot of them," he said nervously. "What do you want us to do?"

"Take down names," I suggested. "I don't think Handry will believe that we did anything unless he can look them up."

"Good idea!" Kimmy said, taking a notebook out of her large bag.

"All right now," I said, looking around the circle of ghosts. "Is everyone here?"

The ghosts murmured to each other and then turned back to me, nodding.

"Why don't you tell me your name and why you are here and then I can help you move on to the next level."

"Can you really do that?" A young voice asked. The little girl walked through the crowd of ghosts and stopped in front of me. She looked too sad and tired to be hopeful.

"Yes, I can," I assured her. "Tell me what happened to you. Why are you here?"

"I was visiting my Grandma," she said. "Everybody was getting sick. The hotel people and my Grandma. My Auntie kept me here so I wouldn't get Grandma sicker, but it didn't work. We both got sicker and so did my auntie. When I died, I didn't *know* the people who came to take me away. I didn't know where to go. So, I've stayed here ever since."

"What year was that?" I asked, suspecting the flu pandemic of nineteen eighteen.

"Nineteen nineteen," she said sadly. "I miss my Mommy."

I reached out to her and took her hand. As usual, the light was bright and calming in a rainbow of light. All the ghosts in the room cheered her passing and lined up, ready for their own turn. I slowed the process myself by having Kimmy write down the names and dates of dying of each ghost before I touched them. This was a historical building and the ghosts that lived there were part of its history. In all, there were thirty two ghosts that came to me in that room. None of them looked like Handry's description of the woman in the washroom, so we went downstairs to look for her.

"How will I know they are gone?" he asked, coming out of his office when we reached the base of the Grand Staircase. "You don't have any equipment! How do you get them to leave?"

"I talked to them," I said, looking closely at him. "They are not here to bother anyone. They just didn't know where else to go. Now, where is this washroom?"

"Over here," he led us to a small door that had been painted over to disguise the presence of a washroom.

Opening the door, he revealed cleaning supplies and equipment taking up all the available space. He stood back and let Kimmy and me enter. I didn't notice him following us into the cramped space.

"Hello," I called. "Are you here? What is your name?"

"Name?" It was a whisper coming from the pipes.

"Yes. Your name. Who are you? Why are you stuck here? Let me help you."

"You can help, girl?"

"Yes, I can." I saw a flicker of light from the farthest stall. I moved slowly toward it.

"I am Bertha. I have always been here."

"Why?" I asked. Surely she died before nineteen forty five. She must have had an opportunity to cross over then.

"This is where they put me. I stayed."

"Put you? In a washroom?"

"No... in the cement. They killed me and put me here. I won't leave until my body is moved." She was flickering into a more stable image for me. Looking to be barely over twenty, she was dressed in a hundred year old dress style. Her finger steadily pointed to one spot on the floor.

Pete moved over next to her and slowly sank down through the floor. In a second, he popped back up, looking upset. "She's right!" He squawked. "There is a body there, between the floors!"

My knees felt weak. I grabbed at the nearest object, a sink piled with a box of paper towels on top, to steady myself. I heard Kimmy's gasp, because she had heard Pete.

"What is it?" Mr. Handry asked.

"Mr. Handry, there is a body of a woman lodged in the cement of this floor," I said, pointing to the spot. "Someone stuffed her in there when the floor was being laid. Since the tiles are still original, there has been no reason to dig her out... until now. She won't leave until she gets a proper burial."

The ghost smiled at me. She was so beautiful, and so young, her death was a tragedy that should never have happened.

"Oh no! I guess I'd better call the police, or someone."

I didn't understand his hesitation until a while later, a police officer arrived on the scene.

"You're telling me that there is a dead body in this floor that has been there for... what?... a hundred years? Talk about a cold case. How do you know that it's there?"

The officer was an older man, probably nearing retirement. He had at least twenty ghosts crowded around him. They looked angry at him. One young man kept poking him high on his chest, making him stop to cough every once in a while. I reached out to the ghosts, going into Quantum Time. "I understand that you may want to punish this man, but I assure you, there is a better place for you."

"Since when?" The young man asked. "I've been here since he was a stupid rookie! Moron shot me in the back!"

"And you are having fun?"

"Some," he laughed. "I will come to you later, when it's not fun anymore."

The other ghosts around the officer seemed to be in agreement. They were enjoying making his life more difficult.

"Officer, I know that there is a body there. I just don't know who should dig it up," I said. "It was a woman who was murdered, but what do you do when everyone involved must be dead? Does it become a history issue, or what?

"Murder? Look, lady. You can do what you want! *If* you find a body, *then* the police will get involved. Before *that*, it is all speculation."

"I understand officer," I said, turning to Mr. Handry. "Mr. Handry, do you think the maintenance staff would have a heavy hammer of some type?"

"You want to break the floor?!" he gasped.

"Mr. Handry," I said, looking him in the eyes. "You want this ghost to leave. For that to happen, you must smash the floor of this room, which you can't use anyway because of her. I think replacing the floor would be cheaper than not getting those contracts, don't you?"

"I'll be right back," he said, moving quickly out the door.

I watched Pete chat with the ghosts around the police officer. I knew he was giving them information for future reference about finding me in order to cross over.

We waited, crowded into the small washroom, unwilling to chat around the closed minded officer and totally unwilling to chat with him.

"I'm back," Mr. Handry said, coming through the door. "This is John, the maintenance man. John, please break through the floor in that spot there."

The maintenance guy had a sledgehammer and goggles. After a couple of blows, the rest of us backed out of the room and watched through the doorway. He was efficient at the job. Bits of tile, grout and cement were flying around the room. Before too long, his hammer went through to a hole that shouldn't have been there. Carefully, he smashed the edges back until he exposed a hand to show to the police officer.

"Now that we have a body, does it become a police investigation?" Mr. Handry said sarcastically.

"I guess it might. I'll call it in. Don't disturb the scene anymore," the officer said.

"Mr. Handry, when the body has been given a proper burial, this ghost will leave too." I watched her smiling agreement to that. "All the others have moved on, including the little girl. Poor thing died in the flu pandemic, but so did her family. When they didn't come to take her away, she didn't know what to do. She was lost."

"How do you know all that?" He asked.

"I talked with her," I said. "She has crossed over now. She will be much happier."

"How do I know you are telling the truth?" He asked, belligerently. "You hide in a room for a while and then *claim* the ghosts are gone?"

"The only proof is the absence of the ghosts," Kimmy said. "You may have to have another sensitive person come to check it out."

"You may take my word for it," I said, staring into his eyes. "Or, I can invite other ghosts to come visit this newly vacated hotel. I can't guarantee their cooperation at being quiet, of course..."

"Are you threatening me?" He said aghast.

"Stop now, before anyone says or does something they will regret!" Kimmy intervened, placing herself between us. "Mr. Handry, you hired us to do a job that there was no way to prove, right from the start. We did the job. You will pay the agreed on fee and enjoy the added interest that you will get when flocks of people come to see the spot where the murdered woman was buried, only to be revealed by her ghost! If you don't think that is a money draw, you are a fool."

Kimmy wasn't even winded! Mr. Handry reached into his pocket and brought out an envelope with a cheque in it. Kimmy checked the amount, put it in her bag and nodded to him. "It has been a pleasure doing business with you," she said, turning and taking my arm, leading me out of the building.

"Well done, Kimmy!" I said. "I was getting angry with him."

"To put it mildly," she grinned. "Threatening to bring down a horde of ghosts!"

"A little over-the-top," I nodded. "The ghosts would have had fun, though."

"Speaking of fun, let's go for lunch," she said, turning us down the street toward the old part of the city.

There used to be factories in the great old buildings. When the factories shut down, stores took over, but the area got seedier. Every city has such an area and they all seem to tackle them the same way. Clean, rebuild, bring in boutiques and restaurants to draw the wealth; revamp historical sites into colleges; up police details and make the area undesirable for the gangs and drug dealers. The process just moves the dealers and prostitutes a few blocks over. But, the well-to-do have quaint places to go to, to have lunch and buy new clothes. So, usually this area, just before lunch, is considered safe, until an older man, down on his luck, apparently living on the streets, stepped out in front of us with a large hunting knife in his hand.

"Give me all your stuff," he snarled.

"All right!" Kimmy squealed, she was going to give our paycheck and everything to this man!

"No!" I said. "You can't have it! We worked hard for what we have. What do *you* do?"

"I have partners," he snarled, stepping closer to me. His breath was so bad, it brought water to my eyes. I waved my hand in front of my face to avoid the noxious smell and to distract him. I didn't know what would happen, but I was determined to try. He waved his knife, following my hand. I reached out to him in the manner that I do to open the Gate for ghosts and I touched him.

The Gate opened! It was more dark than light. Slowly, it sucked the terrified soul out of the old man's body. He slowly collapsed onto the ground.

"Sue, what did you do?" Kimmy asked.

"Umm, I'm not sure." I scratched my eyebrow, looking at the body at my feet. I looked around me, studying the usual gathering of ghosts that seemed to follow wherever I went. "Does anyone want a body for a while?"

"Really?" they chorused.

"Well, *he's* gone. The heart is still beating. Why not?" I shrugged.

"He's probably full of drugs," one elderly woman sniffed and backed away.

"Hey, I beat *that* before! No problem!" A ghost who looked about the same age as the body stepped forward. It might be a good fit. He reached down to touch the man, trying to figure out how to take over. "I think I need help here."

I reached out with my left hand on instinct and thought about the soul merging with the body. To my amazement, it worked! The old man stood up, brushed himself off and grinned at me.

"This guy is drunk!" He said laughing. "That will end today!"

"I hope you have a long, healthy life," I said, shaking his hand.

"Thank you! Bless you!"

"Susie, did you just do what I think you did? How did you do that? How is it possible? Do you know what the ramifications are?"

"Umm... Yes; I'm not sure; I don't know and probably not." I answered her, taking her arm and directing her to the nearest restaurant. When we were sitting in a quiet corner, I turned to her. "Kimmy, I moved on instinct. I had no intention of removing someone's soul from their body!"

"Soul?" she asked, looking nervous.

"Yes soul. We beat around the bush talking about ghosts, but they are souls. Souls of the dead. Somehow, I sent a bad man's soul to the other side and I put another man's soul into the body."

"This makes the term 'feeling like a whole new man', take on a really creepy turn," she said, making a face.

"I know! Can you imagine it? I have a friend that says if you believe in reincarnation, you are recycling bodies! She only wants to go through this life once. After *this*, I don't know what to think.

"Well, I think you get what you believe in," Kimmy said, thoughtfully. In order to reincarnate, don't they have to go through the Gate first?"

"In order for it to be a whole new life, I would think so."

"Susie, you could be a very dangerous person now," Kimmy said quietly, sliding away from me on the bench.

"I think you are right. I'm close to freaking out right now. Where's Pete?"

"Isn't he here? The last time I heard him was just after the old man stood up. He swore and ... nothing. He can't be far, can he?"

"I don't think so, but he may not want to talk to me right now." I said sadly. Had I alienated my only friends? "This job sucks!"

CHAPTER 10

Kimmy organized our lives into a very strict schedule. She even posted the schedule on the front porch where the ghosts could see it. She let me do the job throughout the day, but after supper, it was rest and recuperation time. It seems that I was the only one to not notice how much weight I was losing. Pete did some calculations while I did the Gatekeeping job and he figured that for every hour I spent in the ghost plane of existence, in real time, I worked for four hours in my body's time. I was working thirty two hours in every twenty four hour day. No wonder I was tired!

All the time that I was working, out in the yard, I didn't know what Kimmy was doing. I knew she had to arrange in advance with me before she could go out, but her schedule included that. Pete became our timekeeper since he could communicate in both planes of existence.

Kimmy seemed happy. Almost driven, actually. I didn't find out what she was doing until she came home with the mail, so excited she was dancing.

"I did it! They want it! Pete, they sent me a contract!"

"Really? That's fantastic!"

"What?" I asked, feeling lost.

"I wrote a book!" She said. "And it's going to be published!"

"That's wonderful! What's it about?"

"You!"

"What?!" All kinds of wild ideas went through my mind. People can't know about me! I was having a hard enough time as it was! How could she do that to me?

"Before you blow up, read it," Kimmy said, pulling a big pile of papers out of her desk drawer. "Trust me!"

"All right. I have always trusted you Kimmy."

I sat down with the manuscript. The title "My Best Friend, The Gatekeeper" made me nervous, but I read on. The story is about two girls around eleven years old. One of them gets into a serious accident but, with the help of a ghost, survives. For some reason, not clear in this story, she sees and talks to any ghost near her after the accident, but she doesn't freak out, she tries, with the help of her best friend, to figure out what is going on. They travel around the town and countryside on their bicycles, looking for answers. Finally an angel approaches her to tell her that she has been chosen to be the Gatekeeper. The Gatekeeper is there to allow spirits into the afterlife. If they don't go with the help of the Gatekeeper, they become lonely ghosts, haunting the places that are familiar. The best friend can see the angel as well and is instructed to take care of her.

The girls have an adventure in a local factory where there had been a tragic disaster with many deaths, about ten years earlier. The Gatekeeper manages to cross over all the spirits that come to her from the area. The best friend talks to the police who arrive because they are trespassing. She manages to convince them that they are not in a dangerous area and they are staying out of danger. The story ends with the girls promising each other that they will help each other for as long as they live.

"Wow!" I said, amazed. "When you change our age, you change everything!"

"Right! As far as the world is concerned, this is pure fantasy! And to top that, the publisher has suggested that I make it a series of Continuing Adventures of the Gatekeeper!"

"Continuing Adventures! For kids! This job is hard enough at *my* age! I suppose you will get ideas from what I run into?"

"With a few changes, sure. But I have a pretty good imagination. I could dream up other adventures."

"I'm absolutely certain you could," I smiled. "There's just one thing missing."

"What?"

"Pete!"

"Oh, yeah. Well, I didn't want to complicate the story with a ghost like that. But Pete has helped me through it all. He read it and made suggestions. He doesn't *want* to be in the story."

I looked at Pete and recognized his melancholy look. It was the look of a man who is deeply in love with someone he believes is out of his reach. I wondered what the problem was, she really liked him too. I had been watching their love grow deeper every day.

Then, in a flash, I remembered that Pete was a ghost. Kimmy could hear him, but not see him. They could not touch each other. Talk about unrequited love!

"Pete, how far away from me can you get now?" I asked.

"I haven't tried," he said, surprised.

"Try," I pushed. "It may be beneficial for you to go with Kimmy when she is out and about. You need some independence." As I said it, my heart tightened. I realized, when the word came out, that I was very dependent on Pete myself. I did not want to lose him.

"All right," he said, going to the door and waiting. "I'm willing to try."

We all went out to the porch. It was late autumn already. The leaves on the trees had changed colour and most had fallen to the ground. A crowd of ghosts had gathered as usual in the yard. I signalled for them to give us space. They begrudgingly cooperated.

Pete easily went down the path to the gate. He stepped through it and met with resistance. Pushing against the limits, the way he had encouraged Nancy to do it, he put one foot in front of the other, slowly, one step at a time. I saw the effort. Kimmy heard the effort. The crowd of ghosts, when they realized what we were trying to do, cheered the effort. One young woman in particular, went over beside Pete urging him on.

Then, one step at a time, each step got easier. I could see him straighten up, square his shoulders and walk easily down the street. He stopped and looked back. The look was not exactly happy. He waved for me to join him, so I did.

"Why do you want me to do this?" He asked, obviously troubled.

"Because, if you stay, I want it to be because you want to, not because you have to. I want you to have the freedom of choice."

"And... what about Kim?"

"I want you to have the freedom of choice," I repeated. "Pete, we have been through *so much* in a really short time. I don't think I could have coped at all without you. Now, both you and Kimmy are keeping me going. I appreciate it more than you will ever know... I don't want either of you helping me because you feel you *have to*. Whether it is because you are bound to me or because the one you love is bound to me. You must always have the choice, or I will not be able to work. Do you understand?"

"Yes," Pete said, grinning happily.

"Yes," Kimmy said from behind me.

"Oh! You startled me!" I said, swinging around.

"Sue, you don't have to be so selfless," Kimmy said, shaking her head. Her blonde curls were bouncing around her shoulders again. I wondered if it was a barometer to her happiness. "I am here helping you because I love you. I'm writing the stories because it is amazingly fun and might get us travelling around the world on book tours. I talk with Pete because he is intelligent, funny, compassionate, exciting, stimulating and wonderful to be around. *I'm* happy. Are you?"

"I am now," I said, giving her a hug.

We walked back to the house thinking all was right with the world. It's funny, and probably the reason I needed Kimmy so much by that point, my view of the world around me was more focussed on the ghosts than on the living. Just as we reached the gate, an old man staggered up to us. He looked familiar, but I wasn't sure why.

"Sue!" Kimmy shook my arm. "Susie, it's the old guy who tried to rob us and then you put another in the body..."

"Oh! Right!" I looked carefully at the man. He looked terrible. "What's wrong?"

"I thought I could handle anything!" The old man said, moving with great difficulty. "I was wrong. This body is full of cancer! There is more pain than any human should have to bear! You have to get me out of this. Please, I'm begging you!"

"Oh dear! I'm so sorry! Did anything good come out of this?"

"No!.... Wait... yes. I went to see my family. I didn't talk to them... that would scare them too much, but

I've only been dead two months. They are getting on with their lives. *This* body has no family, so I arranged to give everything to my kids."

"He was robbing people!" Kimmy said, aghast. "It should be given back!"

"Right, I did. For anything that was traceable. Most of what he had was cash. A lot of cash. I think he was a thief all his life and never got caught! I put it in a box with a letter and mailed it to my family."

He was rocking back and forward on his feet, holding his arms across his stomach. Beads of sweat ran down his cheeks, mixing with the tears from the pain. "I did the best I could to make things better. I just can't take it anymore."

"All right," I said and reached out to him before Kimmy had a chance to intervene.

The Gate was a much brighter light than it had been for the body's original occupant. I saw the relief on his face as he was drawn out of the body. He blew me a kiss just as he reached the Gate. The body collapsed before us onto the street. At least it looked much cleaner this time.

Kimmy called nine-one-one to say a man collapsed on the sidewalk in front of her house. Could they send an ambulance?

They came quickly; efficiently; not effectively. I heard the boss of the crew say 'coma', so they loaded up the stretcher and drove away.

"I wonder how long a body will live without a soul?" I muttered, watching them go.

"I'll find out," Pete said, enjoying his new independence.

"Pete!" Kimmy cried. "Don't!"

"What? What's wrong?" He asked.

"Don't do anything heroic or stupid," she said. "Be careful."

"I'm just looking. I won't *do* anything," he assured her.

I had the impression that there was more to it than what either one of them said. Was Pete thinking about finding a body? Well, he couldn't do it without me, so I dropped the thought.

*

I went back to work. Looking at each of the faces of the ghosts, I tried to figure out when and where they lived. Their costumes gave me information, but sometimes I just had to stop and talk with one. I saw a young woman in a nondescript house dress that was so worn out, I could see her body through most of it. She was patiently standing back, obviously hoping I would see her behind the pushy ones. I didn't think much of it until I got close. There were lines, like scars, all over her body. One of the scars went right around her neck.

"What happened to you?" I asked. "Who did this to you?"

"Some came from my father, the rest from my brother." Her voice was hoarse and scratchy. I had to bend closer to catch all her words.

"What did they do?" I asked.

"They used me until I was all used up and then they threw me away."

"Did the police catch them?"

"The police didn't know I existed. How could they know I disappeared?"

"So, they got away with it?!"

"Until they died in New Orleans, during Hurricane Katrina. They thought protecting their secret was more important than their lives. Maybe it was. But now, they've followed me here too."

"Here! In the yard here?" At her nod, I scanned the faces near me. Nothing extraordinary, but far in the back, looking uncomfortable, two men stood together. "Come with me," I said to her. "Stay behind me."

I walked straight toward the two. The older one was arrogant the way he stood and stared at me. The younger looked uneasy, but without remorse.

"You are lucky that I am not the one to choose where you go from here," I told them. "The Gate does that."

"Why do we need you, then?" the younger one snarled.

"I am the Gatekeeper," I said. "In order to move on, you must see me. You have done great evil in your lives. You deserve the worst place available."

"Then, forget it! We'll stay here!" the older man barked, backing up.

I was getting a real appreciation for my ability to move fast. Before they could get away, I reached out and touched each of them. The opening of the Gate was the weirdest I had yet seen. It was a light, but more like a black light. Everything pale in colour around the two men shone in the ultra-violet spectrum. The two spirits resisted the pull, but they had no choice. They were being sucked into a very dark place. Each of them screamed as they passed through the Gate, whether it was from what they saw, or what they felt, I didn't know.

Once the Gate closed again, the yard became brighter. I turned around to see the poor abused woman.

"They can't hurt you ever again," I said, smiling compassionately. "They went to a different place."

"How do you know I won't go there?"

"I can tell from your aura," I said, reaching out to her. "May your future be *way* better than your past."

The Gate opened to a bright white light. I could feel the light itself lift my spirit. By the look on the young woman's face, she felt it too. The scars faded as she was gently pulled to the Gate.

"Why does the light look different every time the Gate opens?"

I turned and found myself staring into Pete's blue eyes.

"It has to have something to do with how they lived their lives," I said. "The young and innocent who have not hurt anyone, seem to go into a bright white light. Those who have done evil, get a black light. Most people are not all good or all bad. Sometimes, they go to a rainbow place. I guess even the afterlife is not all black and white."

"The Wisdom of The Gatekeeper!" Pete grinned. "We should keep track of that."

"Don't you dare!" I squawked. "I'm nothing special! I don't need to be quoted! That is a truly disturbing thought!"

"Relax," Pete grinned. "If Kim puts it in her stories, it will be changed enough to keep you safe."

"Yes, but..."

"What's wrong?"

"You guys are treating me like something is different. Something new! As if I had some special new-found wisdom! I don't! Really! I'm just me!" I didn't think that I was expressing myself very well. The look in Pete's eyes told me that he was going to say whatever I wanted to humour me. I couldn't win!

"Sue, have you noticed that the crowds are thinning?" Pete asked, changing the subject.

"Thinning? Are they?" I turned and really looked at the ghosts gathered in the yard. Pete was right. There were maybe half as many in the yard as there had been when I started the Gatekeeping. "What does it mean? Am I getting caught up with the backlog?"

"I don't think so," Pete said, watching more walking down the sidewalk towards us. "The ones here were not seriously tied to a person or place and somehow they heard about you. There must be a lot of them still stuck someplace, waiting to be released somehow. Someplace stronger than how I was stuck to you."

"What kind of place would have that kind of hold?"

"You remember, Nancy wanted to learn about the world's history since she died. She went to a lot of places, just to find out what was happening. She found some emotionally charged places, but she was all right. Then she went to New York, to the World Trade Center Monument. She came back changed."

"Right. She cried a lot, but she wouldn't tell me about it. What happened?"

"The people are still there and their emotions are still strong. They can't leave and when Nancy was there, she couldn't leave either. She was very frightened by the time she got back to us. She said it was much harder than leaving the hospital, and you remember how hard *that* was."

"So, I have to *go* to New York?"

"I would say so," Pete agreed. "Kimmy's publisher is in New York. We could launch her book from there."

"Right. In the mean time, I guess, we should drive around town here to see which ghosts are unable to come here."

I turned back to the ghosts in the yard, letting Pete carry on with whatever he was doing.

*

"I've thought of a place here in town," Kimmy announced at suppertime. "I've been doing my research and there is an area where gang wars went on for ten years straight. This city is the murder capital of the country and this city block is the murder capital of the city. We can see if any ghosts are stuck there!"

"All right. That makes sense," I agreed. "We can go in the morning. I have had a feeling that most of those that find me here are not bad or malevolent. The worst I have seen are mainly confused. Except for that old guy and the frightful pair today, of course."

"Yeah and you took him out of his pain," Kimmy said. "I'm just wondering how eager the really bad ones are to go to the Gate. Will you have to chase them? Will you be able to catch them unawares? Can they hide from you?"

"Right," I said. "I can move faster than any I have found so far. Since they come to me, I don't have to sneak up on them, but I suspect they could hide from me. I don't know."

*

Early the next morning, we drove downtown into what had been the poorest area of the city ten years earlier. It wasn't that poor any more. There had been a program to fix the houses and sell them to families in an effort to change the economic status of the area. The houses looked Victorian in style with enough cheerful colours to make me think of Easter eggs.

Kimmy parked the car in front of a pale blue house and pointed to the back.

"About ten years ago, there was a shoot-out between two gangs right here," she said. "All together, eleven men and two women were shot. Seven of the men and both the women died on the spot. The other two died in the hospital a few days later. This is the most violent event to have happened in the city in the past sixty years. If there are bad ghosts around, this would be the place."

"All right," I said, getting out of the car. "Stay here. Stay safe."

I stood on the sidewalk and looked into the yard. An apple tree had been planted a few years ago. It stood straight and tall with a few apples still hanging onto the top branches, out of reach. The rest of the yard was somewhat neglected, but green with growth. I thought that the evil couldn't be too strong if the plant life was so hardy. I was guessing. Walking to the corner of the lot, I kept looking for any flicker of a ghost, but I saw nothing. I closed my eyes, shading them from the sun and almost screamed. I was closely surrounded by the red glow of several ghosts.

"Show yourselves to me," I said quietly, opening one eye.

"No!" a female voice rang in my ear.

I turned toward her. "I won't hurt you."

"That's what *they* said! But look what they did to me!" Her voice was panicky.

"I can help you," I said, reaching out for her. I was faster than her. She didn't know what to expect. The Gate opened. I got a glimpse of a dark haired, dark skinned girl. She looked like a teenager.

"Oh! Thank you!" Her voice drifted back to me as she went through the Gate.

"What did you do?" a male voice snarled from behind me.

"I opened the Gate, so she can move on to the next step in her life," I said, turning to the voice. I kept my left eye closed so I could see their positions. "I can help you too." I turned to another, smaller figure. "Do you like it here?"

"No!" It was another girl. This one sounded even younger.

"Here," I moved quickly, touching her before she knew I was going to do it.

Again, the Gate opened. The light for both the girls had been bright and beautiful.

"You can put this behind you," I said, turning to the men. They were close, trying to be intimidating, even though I could only see them through my closed eye. I decided that I would have to get them all quickly in case some of them tried to run away.

"We don't want to go to the next step," the snarling voice came from close beside me.

"All right then," I said, moving quickly. I reached out and touched each and every one of the red glowing spirits in my closed eye vision. The Gate opened with some light showing for the first ghost. After that, it darkened until I felt like I was inside a very dark fog. Each of the men were sucked into the Gate, screaming as they went. Once the last passed through, the Gate closed with a snap and the horrible sound stopped. A fresh ray of sunshine streamed between the houses.

"Thank you," a voice said from behind me. I swung around, trying to locate the voice. "I'm here!"

I looked up and saw the ghost of an old woman sitting in the upper branches of the apple tree.

"You're welcome," I smiled. "I can help you too. I'm pretty sure you won't go where they did."

"Well, I guess I don't have to protect the place any more..." she hesitated for a minute before she floated down from the tree, landing in front of me. "I've been helping the tree."

"I can see that," I said, looking up into the branches again. "It is well established. It can grow on it's own now."

"Right," she said, standing in front of me. She braced herself, as if for something bad when I touched her. When she saw the clear bright light of the Gate, a look of great peace went over her face.

*

"*That* was one of the best and one of the worst experiences I have run into so far," I said to Kimmy, getting into the car. "I did not think that light could be so dark."

"Dark? How?" Kimmy asked.

"Kind of like ultra violet. I've seen the images in the movies where a bad person is chased and swallowed up by shadows, but it's not like that. They still need the Gate."

"And the Gate changes?"

"Right. Even when I move as fast as I can, each ghost has it's own interaction with the Gate. It can go from bright white light to black light and back to white in an instant. It is beautiful to see! But frightening."

"I wonder what happens after the Gate? Do the really bad ghosts have to do penance? Are they reincarnated into frogs?"

"I don't know. They should have to, but we would have many more frogs than we do. They *are* on the endangered lists, you know."

"Well, we'd better keep going," Kimmy said. "The woman in that house is watching us."

I looked up and saw a younger version of the woman in the tree standing in the window. I smiled and waved as we pulled away. I didn't see if she waved back.

We drove around the area for a while. The neighbourhood's reputation was a long list of poverty and violence. I expected to see more evidence of that, but even when I got out of the car and closed my eyes, the ghosts evaded me.

"This isn't going to work," I grumbled. "If they don't come out, how can I help them? I can't go into every house in the city!"

"You need a way to call them to you," Kimmy said thoughtfully. "You know, like the ice cream trucks call the children with their bells."

"Right! Like *that* would work!"

"It might work." Pete's voice came from behind us.

We both jumped, not realizing that he was there.

"Pete! When did you get here?" I gasped.

"I've been here all along. I was just afraid to come out with all those malignant spirits around."

"Did you see more than I did?" I asked.

"No, I didn't *see* them. I *sensed* them. *All over* that neighbourhood. They are in hiding."

"So how do we get them to come out?" I asked. "How can we call them without drawing attention to ourselves?"

"Call them on a wavelength that only they can hear," Pete suggested.

"How can we do that?" Kimmy asked.

"We could hack into the cable companies' computers and send high frequency messages to everyone."

"We could?" Kimmy asked. "How could we do that? *I* don't know how to do that!"

They got into a very technical discussion that I zoned out of. On our way home, I did see a few ghosts through the windows of some older homes. I had so much difficulty getting rid of the ghosts in this small city. How on earth would I be able to deal with all the ghosts on the planet? Especially if they don't want to be found!

"Ultra High frequency!" Pete asserted. "We broadcast to the whole city that the ghosts should go to Assiniboine Park at a specific time and then you do your thing. It will work. We can make a CD to send it through the car speakers, so they can find you. It's simple."

I had a feeling that it wasn't going to be all that simple, but we had to do something. When we got home, Pete and Kimmy went to the set of connected computers that he had directed her to build. He had tweaked the whole thing into some kind of super computer.

In the mean time, I went back to work in the yard.

"How did you know to come here?" I asked.

"We were called," a little old woman said impatiently. "There is a musical voice. Now do your job. Please!"

I reached out and sent her to the Gate. Then I turned to another; an old man. "What kind of musical voice? What did it say?"

"It's not very loud," the old man said, turning his right ear towards me as if he had been deaf in life. "It's like a hundred voices talking in unison. They say to follow them. That brings us here."

Maybe the process would be easier than I thought. Since the ghosts themselves could find me, maybe all I had to do was amplify the sound. That was a cheering thought.

"But who are they?" I asked, confused.

"Us. When we understand that you are the Gatekeeper, our own voices join the many. It is very crowded in the world right now. I have been here a long time. Can I go on now?"

"Yes," I said. "Thank you. Be well."

"I hope so," the old man said as he was drawn into the bright white light of the Gate.

I cleared the yard twice that day. I was finding that I had to stop and wait for the ghosts to come down the street. Still, the ghosts that hurried to me had been good in their lives. The Gate was bright white most of the time. Was I going to have to trick all the evil ghosts into crossing over. Or, worse yet, would the only ghosts left in the world be the ones full of hate and violence. Somehow, I believed that *that* much of a shift in the energy of our world would be very dangerous for all the people, living or dead.

CHAPTER 11

⌘

"Sue, I have the tickets! We leave tomorrow!" Kimmy was all excited.

"Tomorrow? So soon? I lose track of time around here."

"I know. You have to tell those ghosts outside that you will be away for a few months, but you will be back."

"Months? I don't understand."

"We are going on a book tour all over the States and Canada. That takes time, you know."

"Of course it does, but how will I sleep?" All of a sudden, I felt exposed. I was going to lose control and it scared me.

"Sleep? In a hotel, I would think... oh!... The ghosts in hotels can be pushy, right?"

"Right. I need to know what Naomi did to this house to keep other ghosts out."

"Pete! Do you have any idea?"

"No. She left before I got it out of her. I have found, though, that I can only come and go with one of you and *that* only through the front door."

"Well, that's a start," I said, jumping up.

I went to the door and examined it carefully. I had always been impressed with the weather stripping on the doors. It was well done. The drafts stayed out and I hadn't needed to replace any of it in all the years I lived there. Down on my hands and knees, I felt along the bottom of the door. What I found was a surprise.

"There's a long tube of something attached to the door," I said, knowing Pete and Kimmy were not far away. "It feels water proof, but flexible. I can feel something inside of it."

"Something like what?" Kimmy asked.

"I don't know. Large pebbles and small sand." I grabbed one end of the tube and pulled it away from the door. It had been glued in place. Some wood from the door came with it. "Okay. It's nylon. Well protected." I took out a pocket knife and undid some of the stitching and poured some of the contents into my hand. I sniffed it, and carefully tasted it. "Salt! It's rock salt! Why would she put salt across her doorway?"

Kimmy dashed into her room and came running back with a needle already threaded. "Stitch it back up," she urged. "I'll get some glue."

"What is it Kim?" I asked, wondering at her urgency.

"I have been reading up on myths about ghosts. Several of them say that a ghost cannot cross a circle of salt. This must literally be the doorway. I'll bet that there is something full of salt going all around the house."

Quickly, I repaired the tube of salt and glued it back in place. We went outside and discovered two inconspicuous holes on either side of the doorway that went through the floor of the porch. Brass fittings on the ends of a black rubber hose told us what Naomi had done. She filled the hose with rock salt and wrapped it around the house, ending at the doorway. She used the cloth tube on the door to overlap the ends of the hose, thus making a complete circle of salt.

"I would never have thought something as basic as salt would have any power over ghosts!" I said, straightening up. "But how does this help us in big hotels and such?"

"We make a cloth circle full of salt and wrap it around your bed?" Kimmy looked worried.

"I need more room than that. I need to be able to eat and relax in peace."

"Sounds like we need a bus or RV or something," Pete suggested. "Then you can go anywhere you want."

"A bus! Right! That could work!"Kimmy was very excited at the prospect. "In the mean time, I guess we need a supply of salt."

"I want to try something first," I said, heading for the kitchen. "Let's make sure we are right." I came back with a box of salt. We went into the front yard which, as usual, was crowded with ghosts. I leaned over and sprinkled a thin trail of salt in a large circle, enclosing the three of us. Just before I closed the circle, I made sure that Pete was the only ghost present. All of the others stood back as if they were around a bonfire that gave off too much heat.

"What are you doing?" The ghosts were yelling and calling to me. I could barely hear them.

"Pete, can you hear them?" I asked.

"Not really. They are muffled."

"Can you move out of this circle?"

"No. It is like a wall, straight up and down."

Pete looked like a mime in a box. His hands flattened against the invisible wall created by the salt.

"Strange," I muttered. "I wonder what would happen in places with salt flats?"

"Salt flats?" Kimmy asked, her brow furrowed.

"You know, Salt Lake City. Plus, there are mines all over the world. The coastlines along oceans! Evaporation makes a lot of salt all along the shore."

"Oceans," Kimmy said, shaking her head. "Can you imagine where they must go when they die at sea?"

"Ghost Ships!" I said.

Kimmy giggled.

"Umm, ladies, I hate to push or anything, but can I get out of here?" Pete looked very claustrophobic in our small circle.

I kicked the circle of salt apart in several places. Pete moved away in relief while Kimmy and I stayed, looking at the ground.

"A stiff breeze or rain will wash this away," Kimmy said, "But it makes you think about all the salty areas of the world. What *do* ghosts do?"

"That book tour includes all of the States and Canada, doesn't it? We will find out." I shrugged. "I like the bus idea. I wonder if the publisher will like it?"

"I'll find out," Kimmy said, leaving me to go back to work.

*

We flew to Toronto and then to New York. New York's reputation has always unnerved me just by the idea of so many people living in such a small area. When we got there, I was even more overwhelmed.

All the publishers in New York work out of a few buildings on the same street in the same zip code. That did make it easier to find the right one. The building went up forever. We saw the names of all our favourite publishers all in the same building!

"Aren't they competitors?" I asked Kimmy, who had done the research on them.

"They are, but at one time, most of them worked for one of the big companies. As the editors and executives learn more, they branch off. One big company had a small program for Science Fiction. They only put out a few books a year. An editor, who saw all the good manuscripts out there, decided to branch off and form a company that does only Sci Fi. He made a good choice and his fortune. That kind of thing happens all the time. Sometimes it works, sometimes it doesn't. They still know each other, though."

"And printers! Look! There's a printer in the building!"

"Why send things out when they can be done right here?"

We arrived on our floor then. Getting off the elevator put us right into a huge office space. Quiet, but fast paced music came to us over a speaker system. Most of the people were at desks working on computers. Some had their feet up and were reading pages of manuscripts. I wondered how many of them were from new writers trying to get into the field.

We were led to a small meeting room off to one side of the main space.

"Miss Foton, welcome!" a sharp eyed woman in a business suit hurried toward us. "I'm Samantha Blake."

"Hello," Kimmy said, nervously. "This is my partner, Susie LaMarre."

"Oh? Well, welcome Miss LaMarre," the woman said, barely breaking stride.

She shook our hands firmly, as if to prove she was stronger than any man.

"Partner!" Pete squawked behind us. "Do you know what that means? What they will think now? They will think you are lesbians! Do you want them to think you are lesbians?"

"Shhh," I whispered. "It gives us strength. They have to deal with both of us."

"Oh!... Well... all right then," Pete sighed. "I'll be quiet then."

We sat at a large table and watched as three other people joined us. A young woman entered pushing a cart with refreshments on it and parked it behind us, against the wall. It wasn't until I turned to look that

I realized that she was a ghost. She was still strongly in the present. So much so that she could manifest a trolley of goodies. Unfortunately, they faded when she did.

"Hmm," I said to the room at large. "I just got a whiff of tea, coffee and spice cake! Then it was gone! Isn't that odd."

"It's an old building," Samantha Blake said brusquely. "Strange drafts everywhere. Can we get you some tea or coffee or anything?"

"No, thank you," Kimmy said nervously.

"All right, then, down to business. This is the cover art for the book, right off the presses."

The picture showed two girls; one watching the other. The second girl was standing beside a large Gate that looked like it was made of pearls and gold. A line of ghosts that looked like children's costumes made from bed sheets were waiting for the Gatekeeper to let them through. It looked quite childish.

"Wow!" Kimmy said. "It looks... different."

"We have a group of children in the age range as consultants. They thought this cover would have them wanting the book much more than the others we considered."

"All right," Kimmy said. "That's what we're after then. Big sales."

"Right!" Samantha said. "Which is also why we do book tours. You sent an e-mail saying you want a bus? That's not the usual way we do it."

"What do you do?" Kimmy asked.

"We fly you from city to city, catching all the big centers. We put you up in good hotels. We arrange talk shows and book signings in each place. It takes two months to cover North America."

"Well, we propose that we drive to every large and middle sized city across the country. *You* arrange for the book signings and interviews. *We* go everywhere in North America in six months, selling as many books as you can print. If you keep making announcements the week ahead of us, we will do *much* better. We will have our own accommodations no matter where we are, so we will sleep better. I don't believe a bus and its gas costs more than air flights and hotel rooms when you consider the seriously increased amount of sales."

"Who will drive the bus?" one of the quiet executives asked.

"We will," Kimmy answered. "We both got our class one licenses six years ago. We can drive anything."

"After a while, you will get too tired and want to quit!" another executive, an older man, said sceptically.

"Put days of rest into the schedule," Kimmy said. "This is the chance of a lifetime. While we are touring the country, I can see it first hand! I can do research for the next book... or two!"

Samantha looked toward the man, who sat, thinking. He looked up at her and nodded once. That was it, the meeting was over. They kept going, pretending there was more to be worked out, but I knew, the decision was made. They set up an appointment for us to go the next day and inspect busses to find one that we would want. The whole meeting took less than an hour.

We had the afternoon to ourselves. Kimmy and Pete did not want to go to the memorial for the World Trade Center, so they went shopping while I took a taxi to the site.

Pete was right. To my eyes, it looked as bad as it had on the day it happened. The air was full of dust and ash and smoke. The ghosts... the souls of the people... were covered in soot, some - only their eyes revealed their presence amongst the wreckage. The remains of the buildings' girders stuck up into the air like the bare bones seen in an elephant's graveyard.

I knew the building had been big, but I come from a small city. Big is relative. My brain could not grasp the immensity of the place even as I stood in the rubble. I closed my eyes for a second and saw the thousands of souls standing there, hurt and angry, bright red in my vision.

Opening my eyes quickly, I was in the peaceful park that memorializes the catastrophic event. Then, I was back in the rubble; the image projected by each and every soul that died that day.

"Hello," I said, quietly. "I came to help you."

"Help? How?" a young woman asked.

"I can take you away from this," I said. "It is time to move on to the next stage in your life."

"So they can forget?" a man yelled angrily.

"No! No, they will *never* forget. But *you*, you have not finished! I am the Gatekeeper and I am here to help you cross over."

"Cross over to what?" The young woman sounded hopeful.

"To the light! Your families think you crossed over that day, but here you are, still in the rubble and dirt of it. The sun is shining right now! You have been here long enough! The world has been horrified enough for all of you. Your anger is warranted, but your death will have no peace unless you let it go."

"Ok, what do I do," the young woman said, stepping closer.

I reached out to her and touched her arm. She must have been special; the Gate was a beautiful bright white. It could be seen through the dust and dirt like a beacon. The young woman floated gently up to it, looking angelic above the crowd.

"This is *incredible!*" she said, loud enough to be heard. "You should *all* come here." She reached the light, merged with it and the Gate closed.

"I want that too!" another woman demanded from behind some large men. As an afterthought, she added, "Please?"

"All right," I agreed. "Just line up here. It won't take long."

"No!" one of the angry men said, blocking the way.

"Look," I said, feeling a little impatient. "I can only stay here for a little while. You do not have the right or the power to stop anyone from going to the light. If *you* choose to stay here until I return or you seek me out, fine, but stand aside and let the others past."

"I don't think so," the man said, trying to look tough.

I reached out quickly and touched his arm, the chest of the man beside him and the shoulder of the man on the other side. They yelled as the

Gate opened and pulled them towards it. I noticed that the colour was not dark, but kind of average. A rainbow, as if through a prism showed the way. They were not bad men. They were just so angry about their death.

A few men moved quickly away from me while more moved closer. I worked quickly. One by one, I sent over three thousand souls to the light until all that was left was a small group of angry men.

"There is a better place to be than here," I urged. "There is a war being fought because of this incident. It has not been forgotten."

"War! So more innocent people are going to die! That's not what we want!" The man had been a firefighter. His gear made him look even bigger than he really was.

"When people come here, to the memorial, they can feel your anger. They still see the images, burned in all our minds forever. *Your* emotions are so strong, *their* emotions become involved. And what *they* want is revenge. Is that what *you* want?"

Nobody spoke. Looking at their feet, or the rubble behind them, they did not want to commit.

"All right," I sighed, sadly. "I don't know when I'll be back. You can walk away from here if you try. It will be hard, but believe me, it can be done. Once away, the voices will tell you how to find me." I turned to walk away.

"Wait! The fireman said. "I don't want to propagate the hate. I didn't know we did that. I will go."

"Great!" I said, letting him approach me.

As I sent the fireman to the Gate, the other men lined up for their turn. Some looked unhappy and many looked nervous, but they stepped forward with determination. It did not take long for me to touch them all.

All, that was, except for six men hiding in the bushes. As I looked around, the rubble faded away, leaving the memorial in the sun and the air clean and crisp.

I turned back to the men. "Well, are *you* going to stay here?"

"This is *not* what Allah promised us," one of the men whined. "We were supposed to go straight to heaven with one hundred virgins and anything we could wish for."

I looked at them carefully. They must be the ones who hijacked the planes and flew them into the twin towers. They were the direct cause of all this death and destruction. I knew that I had no control over where they went after the Gate, but I was pretty sure that it would be unpleasant. Staying here would be better, if they understood that. I was determined not to let them avoid their consequences.

"Allah's promise comes *after* the Gate," I said. "*I* have to let you through the Gate first."

"How do we know you speak the truth?" one of them asked belligerently.

"You have been watching me for the past hour or two. You have seen me send all of these people through the Gate. If you don't believe your own eyes, what *do* you believe?"

"That Allah will reward us," a third man said with a heavy accent. "What do we care where the infidels go?"

"All right, then," I said, gesturing for them to come out from the bushes. I wanted them close together so I could touch them quickly.

Nervously, they crawled out from under the branches and stood before me.

"I am the Gatekeeper," I said. "I only have the power to send you through the Gate. Where the Gate sends you is up to Allah, not me." I moved quickly down the line, touching them all before the Gate opened for the first.

The Gate, in its wisdom, was barely visible. It wasn't black light as it had been with the blood thirsty gang members. I saw what looked like the absence of light. As the men were pulled into the darkness, they lost form and appeared to dissipate into the nothingness. Then they were gone.

I sat in the park for a long time, thinking about what the Gate had done. Who really controlled the Gate? Was there really a God? In my whole life, I had not seen sufficient evidence to tell me there was. I am Humanist, believing that we humans are accountable for our actions. If we make a mess of things, we have the responsibility to fix it. There is no absolution. The Gate was showing me that there are other forces involved, whether I believed in them or not.

I waited patiently until Kimmy and Pete showed up.

"Susie, are you all right?" Kimmy asked, rushing over. "Is it done?"

"It's done," I sighed. "They are all gone."

"All?" Pete repeated, looking around carefully. "What about the ones who did it?"

"Them too," I said. "I am very glad that I am not the judge. Even if I knew where they went after the Gate, I would not want to decide that."

"Where did they go?" Kimmy asked.

"Well, in spite of being stuck here with their victims for all these years, they still believed that they were going to heaven to have their hundreds of virgins."

"What do the virgins have to say about that?" Kimmy asked, horrified.

"We will never know," I smiled. "I don't think it will be an issue. They went somewhere dark. Very dark."

"Are you all right?" Pete asked. "It must be hard sending anyone there."

"I'm okay, but yes it is. That's why I'm glad it's not me making the decision. I just moved quickly so they couldn't avoid the consequence."

"Well done!" Pete cheered.

"Where do we go now then?" Kimmy asked.

"To eat and rest and then Central Park," I said, looking around, seeing the gathering of ghosts from other areas of the city.

"Central Park? At night? Are you nuts?" Pete squawked.

"Night?" I looked around me. Sure enough, it was getting darker. "Oh, all right. In the morning." I looked over at a gathering of ghosts a distance away. They got the message. They were nodding among themselves, understanding where to go.

"They got the message?" Kimmy asked, watching me.

"They got the message! I like this. Now, let's go have some fun."

We went back to our hotel to drop off Kimmy's parcels and to freshen up. I know that the ash and dust wasn't really there, at ground zero any more, but it felt real. I felt covered in it still and had difficulty breathing. After a shower, I was happily ready to have an enjoyable time, but when we went outside to get a taxi, a young man grabbed Kimmy's purse, trying to snatch and run.

Kimmy, however, had been nervously holding her purse tightly and did not break her hold. There was a few seconds of a tug of war between them. I was instinctively ready to reach out to the man and send him away, but Pete intervened first.

Creating an image of himself as a huge angry lion, Pete stood in the man's immediate personal space and roared. This image flashed in the man's vision several times, making him drop his hold on the purse and scramble backwards, falling on his backside. He kept moving as Pete kept flashing the lion at him. The man struggled to his feet and ran away screaming.

"Pete! Where did you learn to do that?" I exclaimed.

"I've been practising," Pete said proudly. "I can only hold an image for a fraction of a second, but I can flash it many times. Kimmy thought a lion would be scary enough."

"It worked," Kimmy whispered, shaking and looking around us.

For some reason, no one interfered or acknowledged that something had happened. They moved around us like tide water around a rock. Unsettled, we found a cab and went for a meal.

"Is it just New York, or is it everywhere?" Kimmy asked, still shaken.

"It is everywhere," I responded. "Do you remember in Winnipeg, when that guy saw his ex-wife walking along Portage Avenue one afternoon? He was really pissed at her, so he jumped out of his vehicle, caught her and stabbed her to death. None of the bystanders, and there were many, would intervene. Some guy said 'STOP', but that was it. She died."

"I remember. You know, something like that can't happen in a book, though. Editors would call it contrived."

"You have notes from your editor?" I asked, smiling at the look on Kimmy's face.

"You were there! They signed the contract, *then* they came up with about a million changes I have to make! They want final printing done right away, so I have to do it fast!"

"So, you will be busy while I'm in the Park tomorrow."

"Right." She didn't look happy.

"Kimmy, do the changes alter the story?" I asked. She shook her head. "Do they make what you are saying a bit clearer?" She nodded her head. "Then, don't fuss. This will be a best seller if we let it. It will give us the book tour. Life is good!"

"You're right. And it will take several days for them to fix up a bus to our needs. I will still be able to do some more shopping."

Even Pete laughed at her priorities. I saw the love in his eyes when he looked at her. I wished I knew what I could do to help them.

CHAPTER 12

We had a bus! It had a bedroom and extra bunks and a kitchen with a dining space as well as a satellite TV and a desk for Kimmy to write. I knew we would be comfortable in it. It was our new home.

We were in New York for a week. Kimmy worked on the book and I worked on sixty five years of ghosts. Even with Quantum Time, I worked dawn to dusk every day we were there. It felt good to leave.

Creating a salt circle wasn't as difficult as I feared. The bus had compartments under the living space. We used Naomi's hose idea and looped a hose filled with rock salt all around the storage compartments. The only break was in the door. Pete could still come and go with Kimmy when the door was open. It worked! Our first night was quiet and comfortable.

Our route across the Country was convoluted. We were to stop at every community with a book store. Kimmy would do a book signing and I would go to a local park.

Because we were on the move, I couldn't rely on the ghosts to tell the others quickly enough, so we revisited Pete's idea of High Frequency radio waves. We put some small outdoor speakers on the roof of the Bus. Pete and Kimmy made the hardware work. Then Pete and I chose the message: 'The Gatekeeper is here. It is time to cross over into the light. Come to the Gatekeeper in the largest park in town today.'

We thought it sounded good.

Pete eagerly stayed with me the first day we broadcast the message. We stopped in the park's parking lot, letting the message run.

"Look!" Pete said, "There's a bunch! They heard us!"

"Oh good. We can let it play until we have a good crowd. They can probably take over after that."

I got out of the Bus and joined the growing crowd of ghosts. They did not have many questions for me. Many of them looked too tired to care why they had been left for so long. All of them cheered up when I sent the first to the Gate.

"Why are you whistling that awful noise?" one old man asked as he approached.

"I needed to let you know to come to me," I said. "It worked, didn't it?"

"We hear it," the man said, looking disgruntled. "But so do they!"

I turned where he pointed and saw at least a hundred dogs of all sizes and breeds howling as they ran towards the bus. Many of them trailed leashes or tie up cords behind them. Some of them were baring their teeth at each other and me!

"Oh no!" I cried. I dashed back to the bus to turn the noise off. Fortunately, Pete and Kimmy had put the switch just inside the driver's window. It was an easy reach.

Once the broadcast was turned off, the dogs stopped howling. They became more like regular dogs in a park, some fighting; some finding the females in heat; some playing chase. Things should have calmed down so I could carry on. What I didn't foresee, was the effect that ghosts have on animals, specifically dogs.

The first dog to walk through one of the ghosts yelped as if it had been burned. It tried to run away, but by then, the park had too many ghosts in it. The dog owners were away in the distance, running to find their dogs, but it would take time to sort out the chaos. The dogs were spread in front of me yelping and screaming as if they were being shocked by electricity.

The ghosts were getting impatient, not caring about the dogs or anything else, other than the Gatekeeper. I just hoped no one had a camera. Before the dog owners arrived and demanded an explanation, I walked quickly toward the other side of the park.

The ghosts followed me. I stopped in the middle of a group of trees. There was a path, but it was not wide. The area was quiet and secluded. As the ghosts joined me, I quickly sent them to the Gate. I was relaxed, enjoying the work. The fiasco around the bus moved to the back of my mind. Only a dozen ghosts were left waiting when a man on a bicycle came down the path at top speed.

"Look out!" he yelled at the last second.

I whirled, startled to see anyone there, let alone someone moving so fast.

He swerved to avoid me, his wheel hit a root clump and he went flying over the handlebars. If he hadn't been wearing a helmet, I'm not sure he could have walked away. His head bashed into the solid trunk of a very old elm tree. Branches from the smaller bushes scratched and scraped his whole body as he passed through. He landed, crumpled into a heap further down the path.

"Pete!" I called. "Is there anyone with him?"

"He was riding alone," Pete said, appearing beside me. "But there are more coming down the path right now! They are not moving as fast, but be careful!"

I went over to the man and felt for a pulse on his neck. It was strong and steady.

"Hello! Can you hear me?" I called to him. "You should wake up now!" I heard the other bicyclists coming down the trail. I decided that I did not want to deal with explanations, so I stepped through the trees and left the path completely. I could still hear the sounds from the path, so I heard the next bunch of bicyclists stop and exclaim over the man. They seemed to know him. I heard one of them call emergency on a cell phone, so I knew I was not needed. I walked slowly back to the bus, talking to the last of the ghosts on the way.

"Well, this was not as well done as I hoped," I said, looking around.

"Why did you call the dogs?" an elderly woman asked.

"I wasn't trying to call *them*!" I said, stricken. "I was trying to call *you*!"

"But, that's not necessary, dear," the woman said. "As soon as one of us realizes you are here, *we* put out the call. *We can* find *you*!"

"You can? How?"

"You give off your own music," she said. "I can't describe it, but we are drawn to it. All you need to do is go to a park for a while, we will all go to you. At least, until you let us through the Gate..."

"Oh! Of course!" I happily sent the last of the group through the Gate, thinking about what she had said.

"Pete? You're awfully quiet," I said, going back to the bus.

"I'm sorry, Susie. I should have known about the dogs. We hit the exact frequency they find most annoying."

"Pete, we are all learning here. We all know about dogs and high frequency sound. We should all have known better. But I did not know *I* give off a sound! Do you hear it?"

Pete stopped, staring at me and listening carefully. "Yes! Now that you mention it! It is beautiful."

"What does it sound like?"

"The voices of a thousand angels singing about Peace? I don't know... It started just after our accident, I guess. At first it was quiet, but it has built over time. I have been around you so much, I didn't even realize it was there!"

"Hmm. I wonder if salt mutes that too..." I stepped into the bus and closed the door, letting the salt protect me. Pete stayed outside, listening. After a few minutes, he waved at me through the windows. I opened the door and let him in.

"When the salt is around you, your music is muffled, but still there. I suspect that when the ghosts hear it, they can pass it on for others to hear. Susie, our biggest worry is taken care of! Now you can really enjoy this trip! Let's go get Kimmy and tell her!"

I laughed at his obvious need to be close to Kimmy. We drove to the mall where the bookstore was located. They had her sitting in a conspicuous place where she could talk to people and sign their books. Pete and I stood back watching. She looked like she was in her element. Parents and kids alike complimented her on her writing.

"Are you done already?" she asked when we came closer. "Did the call system work?"

Pete told her all about our adventure in the park. No one else could hear what he said, so she did get some strange looks when she burst out laughing over the dogs. She sobered up at the bicyclist, but murmured that he should have been going slower when he did not have good visibility. Then she looked overjoyed that I was making my own music to call the ghosts to me.

"The Gatekeeper has her own angelic choir," she said, ostensibly to herself and me.

"That's a good idea!" one of the mothers said, coming up for an autograph. "But soon, isn't it going to get difficult for a living person to get to some of the places where ghosts may hide?"

"Like where?" I asked, curious.

"Oh, you know, where there has been a nuclear reactor melt down. Or under the ashes of a volcano. Those places are too dangerous for people to enter."

"So it is good if the Gatekeeper can call them out," I said.

"That will help," the woman agreed. "And then, there is the issue of ships sinking. What happens to *them*?"

Kimmy had not mentioned salt and its effect on ghosts in the book. This woman was keeping up with us even though she did not have all the information.

"We will have to go out to sea and see if we can figure it out," Kimmy said. "The Gatekeeper's job must have some special talents with it, or she couldn't do the job. I don't see a point in setting her up for failure."

"I like that!" the woman cheered. "I like your imagination and how you express it. I'm looking forward to reading more."

"Thank you!" Kimmy said, lifting her eyebrow up at me.

Eventually, the afternoon was over. I had a small gathering of ghosts, waiting patiently for me to go to them. I felt conspicuous sending them to the Gate in the parking lot, but I had no choice.

"Do you know what that looks like from the outside?" Kimmy asked, while she drove us on to the highway toward the next town.

"Looks like? What?"

"It looks kind of like Tai Chi." She spoke in a whisper, trying not to disturb her concentration.

"What do you mean?" I asked, feeling tired.

"You! When you are out in the yard or a park. The way you move is like a dance in slow motion. I know you are moving so fast, we can't see it, but *my* brain at least, interprets it as a slow motion exercise. You reach out and back. You swing around. You bend your knees to go down, possibly for short ghosts and you pivot on your heels and toes. It actually is soothing to watch."

"Really?! Wow! Maybe I should wear exercise clothes. People wouldn't be inclined to stop and ask so many questions." It was early yet, but I had run into several instances where people stopped me to ask what I was doing. I had not come up with an acceptable explanation yet. "I can't call it Tai Chi, though. As soon as I do, someone will correct my steps and try to improve my stance."

"I can see that," Kimmy laughed. "All right, you need a costume and a name for it. Maybe we can even put some quiet music through the speakers to complete the picture."

We slept in the outskirts of the next town. We had a small television in the bus that could pick up local stations. Just before we went to sleep we saw a news item about 'dogs gone wild' in the park where we had just been. There were pictures of the dogs and of our bus, but luckily, they missed me. That was attention I did not want.

So, when we woke up the next morning, we were motivated to go to the mall and find some appropriate clothes and music to mask my mission. I am quite self conscious about my body. I am not over weight exactly, but I am not a skinny model either. My belly sticks out a bit and my joints, hips, knees, and elbows are knobbly. When I put tights on, every flaw is accentuated in my eyes. Kimmy suggested black tights, but I had an instinct to avoid that much darkness when I sent people to the light. I chose instead, a white leotard and tights with a multicoloured skirt and vest made from sheer scarves and a sheer sash of bright colours to drape across my bulges.

When I twirled in front of the mirror, I felt like a ballerina.

"Wow, Sue!" Pete said, after I put it on, "you are looking like the Gate! You have the same balance of colours as it has!"

"That's the nicest thing anyone has ever said to me!" I said happily. "Let's see if it looks better today."

The ghosts were right. As soon as I stopped in the park, they came toward me, slowly first, then in greater numbers. I turned the music on and joined them on the green, lush grass in the park. The music was a blend of nature sounds and choir voices to enhance the experience of meditation and relaxation. To try to stave off interruptions. I put the CD case on the picnic table along with an information sheet on: *Freedom Chi Dance'*, a title Kimmy came up with during the night.

It was wonderful! I did not have any interruptions. The ghosts were pleasant and cooperative. I managed to clear the area in two hours real time. The only problem arose when Pete told us afterward that someone had filmed me the whole time.

"Film? What will he see?" I asked. I did *not* want to panic...

"I don't know, but I know one thing. That guy has been around us before, I'm not sure when, I just remember seeing him."

"Well, there's not much we can do about it right now," Kimmy shrugged. "We just have to keep going. Maybe he has a crush on you Sue."

CHAPTER 13

So, that's what we did. We drove through every town and village in the North Eastern part of the United States. We found that we didn't have to stop. Passing through was enough to get the ghosts to follow us. Sometimes I worked while Kimmy was signing books and sometimes it was when she was cooking supper. I was energized by the Gatekeeping process and Kimmy was energized by the admiration for her work. We were having a good time.

About two months after we started the tour, Pete sat down with us over breakfast in the bus.

"We may have a problem," he said. "That guy who photographed you before is following us."

"Following us?" Kimmy asked. "Like stalking?"

"Maybe. It is Sue he is interested in. That first time I saw him, he used his cell phone to capture her image. He looked conspicuous standing there holding his phone out in front of himself. I saw him again in a car with a somewhat better camera. It looked like a digital snapshot camera that can do movies if you set it up right, but isn't designed for it. Then he had a handi-cam. They are pretty good. I saw him again with a much bigger camera several days later. He stood behind his car, trying not to be noticed.

"Yesterday, though, he had the kind of camera you see on television sets."

"Television sets? What do you mean?" Kimmy asked.

"You know! When they switch cameras on talk shows, sometimes you see the other camera men. News shows too! They have shoulder harnesses and waistline harnesses. They look to be worth a fortune!"

"So do you think he is a news reporter?" I asked.

"I don't know! But, those cameras can see a lot. They can be slowed down and sped up and they can show one frame at a time. There's no telling what they would pick up. He is following us and I don't know his motivation!"

"Maybe I should ask him," I said, calmly. "Pete, please stay with me, so you can try to verify his story."

"All right," he said, looking worried.

For Pete to stay with me is a sacrifice. He seemed to only be happy when he was around Kimmy. I had noticed that she felt the same. Of course, neither one of them were ready to admit the bond out loud.

Kimmy had a talk and book signing to do at a book store which was situated across the street from a large park. This was the first time that had happened and we were delighted. I left her introducing the book and starting her talk, while I crossed the street.

I sat at a picnic table, waiting to see what would happen.

"There he is!" Pete said, excitement putting a tremor in his voice.

I positioned myself so I could see without appearing to look at the man. I waited until he had his camera out, ready to roll, before I went after him.

He tried to run when he realized I saw him, but I can move much faster than normal people when I try. I cornered him against a building with a fence blocking the way.

"Why are you filming me?" I asked.

"Filming? I'm not! There's no film."

"Why are you taking my picture?" I growled. "Don't you try to argue intellectually with me. You don't have the ammunition."

He tried to make his face look innocent. A flash in his eyes meant he understood me, but he was trying to pretend to be stupid. "You are a beautiful lady," he stuttered. "I just like the way you move."

"So you get a huge expensive camera because you like the way I move. I'm not believing that. What do you want?"

"Nothing!" he said, belligerently. "I like to watch from a distance! It is like a dance."

"Your smaller cameras are good enough for that. You are looking for something. What?"

"I don't know what you're talking about!" he said, getting belligerent.

I reached out with my right hand, just to smack his cheek. I was not feeling threatened or surprised. I was in complete control of my actions. But, before my hand reached him, he screamed and sank down to the ground, fear coming off of him in waves.

"What?" I said, stepping back in surprise.

"He thinks he knows what you can do," Pete said from beside me. "We need to know what he saw."

I took the heavy camera from the man's limp grip and balanced it on my hip. "I am going to look at this," I said. "If you want the camera returned, you will have to join me. If you run away, it is mine. Got that?"

I heard a blubbery squeak from him, so I turned my back and crossed the street, going back to the picnic table. I was careful to sit so it would be difficult for anyone to sneak up on me. Of course, I *did* rely on Pete.

"Okay, how do I operate this?" I said, turning it over.

"The lens is there," Pete pointed. "There is a view screen back here. All these shading things around them are just to prevent too much sunlight from damaging the picture or your viewing of it. These buttons are the same as any viewer: Play, Fast Forward, Reverse, Pause and Slow. I would guess slow is what we are looking for."

The camera was digital. I pushed the play button and saw myself doing my thing for the first time. I recognized the background as the place we were at two days before.

Kimmy was right. It did look like Tai Chi or some other Martial Arts Katah. And the outfit looked quite good in an elfin, fantasy type of way. I was impressed.

Looking at the buttons again, I pushed the one for slow motion. Doing that, I sped up in the picture, which, of course, went against all logic. But, not only was I moving faster, I seemed to be surrounded by a light. I pushed the button again and the light haze started to look like individual images of people, many of them old, all of them tired. I appeared to spin in a circle and each person was replaced with another person. It was happening very fast. I pushed the button again, which would normally have the camera click one frame after another, stopping for a hundredth of a second on each frame. This, however, clearly showed me reaching out with my right hand to each of the people and they would almost dissolve and move toward a light just out of range in the viewfinder. That would be the Gate. I doubted that the Gate could ever show up on a photograph.

"Here he comes," Pete said calmly.

"Good. I wonder what he thinks is going on here?"

The man came over to the table and sat on the bench on the other side. He straddled the bench, obviously ready to run away if he had to.

"What is your name?" I asked.

"Christopher Remington," he said unhappily.

"Who do you work for?" I asked. I could see it would be difficult to get answers from him.

"I work freelance," he said. "I sell photographs to magazines. Who are you?"

"You are invading *my* privacy," I said. "*I* get to ask the questions. Who would you sell *this* to?"

"That depends on who or what you are," he said, watching my hold on the camera.

"*What* I am? Oh, *that's* rude!"

"No one can move the way you do... At the speed you do... It's impossible!"

"All right. So what? Your camera is broken. You have me move faster at a slow speed than at regular speed. That's backwards. And what's all this interference? You've superimposed faces around me! That's just weird."

"I didn't alter the picture and you know it."

"Do I? I don't think so. Pete, where is the storage card or whatever for this thing?"

Pete pointed to the spot where a tape cartridge fit. I pushed the button and out popped the tape.

"Double check that there isn't a hard drive as well," Pete suggested.

I looked back at the view screen, trying to play anything left on a hard drive of the camera. What I got was a tutorial on how to use the camera. It was a rental!

"Who's Pete?" Christopher asked, looking around nervously.

"A friend," I replied, irritated. "You mean, you can see those faces, but not Pete? You are looking in all the wrong places, my friend." My fingers clenched on the camera. I was finding it difficult to control my anger.

"Please don't break the camera. It is a rental! I can't afford to pay for it!"

"You should not have poked your nose in where it doesn't belong," I said, still gripping the camera angrily.

"Why? What are you doing?" he wailed. "What's so all fired important that you go through this charade."

"Charade? I exercise in the park and you call it a charade?"

"Exercise? You flicker! That's why I got the fancy camera. You must be moving at stupendous speeds! Normal cameras and even the human eye can't register movement that fast, so it makes you flicker! What are you? You can't be human!"

"There, now you're getting silly. I am as human as you."

"Then why..."

"He's not listening to me Pete!" I said, interrupting him.

"Maybe Kimmy can help. I will get her. Don't let him run away."

"No problem," I said, glancing up at Pete. When I looked back at Christopher, he was looking at the spot I had been looking at. He could not see Pete, of course.

"Who is Pete? I found no mention of a Pete in your past."

"You looked into my life? How? Why?"

"You know how... the internet! The why is obvious. You are strange! Strange people get investigated. You seem to be tagging on to your friend's book tour, pretending to be gay, but you don't sleep together. You seldom touch each other! She is afraid of your touch too!"

"No, I'm not," Kimmy said, making him jump. "You don't know anything."

"I know you never wrote anything before this. Your writing skills are pedestrian, at best. How it can be a best seller is beyond me!"

"Good marketing," Kimmy said dryly. "My people are good! So good, in fact, they sold a collection of books with nothing written in them. All the pages were blank, marketed as a future history of your life! *They* were on the best seller list!"

"But that's a journal," Christopher said.

"Of course it is," Kimmy nodded, her curls bouncing. "No one was journaling at the time. Now, journals are a big market. Probably because of my publisher and Oprah. *She's* big on journaling."

"What does that have to do with you?"

"He's not too bright, is he?" I said.

"*They* are marketing *my* book. *They* like it. You can call my writing whatever you want, but it is aimed at a young audience who read a different style than adults. So what has *my* book got to do with *you*?"

"Nothing!" He looked aghast.

"Then, why are you following us?"

"I'm following *her*," he said, pointing a finger at me.

"So you admit you are stalking her," Kimmy said with a wicked smile.

"I'm not *stalking* her. I'm following at a distance. She is... I will find out..."

"What? Find out what?" Kimmy asked.

"He thinks I'm not human," I said.

"Of course you're human. What else could you be?" She turned back to Christopher questioning. "Well?"

"An alien from outer space," he whispered. "No human can move the way she does."

"So, Kimmy, what do I do with him?" I asked.

"Did you get it recorded?"

"Of course," I said, taking my finger off the record button of the camera.

"Then let's call the police! They don't like men who follow women wherever they go."

"The camera! Did you record over the tutorial? The rental guys will charge me extra for that!"

"I deemed it necessary for my future safety." I said.

Kimmy called the police and we showed them what Christopher had done and said. They took him away to jail while one young officer stayed to take our statement.

"So, it's just the two of you driving across the country?" he asked.

"That's right," Kimmy said. "We have a schedule. Quite a number of people, like the publisher, know where and when we are at any given time. We check in regularly. And we are being cautious and observant."

"But you still got a stalker."

"*We* observed the stalker, caught him, and called in the police," I said. "If we thought he presented more danger, we would have called you guys first, but he may have run away before you got here."

"He could have been more dangerous. He still could be. I don't buy his story for following you. That's stupid. There is more to it. We can only hold him for a while. You are crossing State lines and he may follow you. Even restraining orders are impossible to enforce across the whole country! Next time he gets close, he may do something worse than take pictures."

"I appreciate your concern, officer," I said. "But he is more afraid of me than I am of him. That man thinks that I am an alien from outer space and that I can kill people with one touch."

"And are you?" the officer asked with a straight face.

Kimmy and I burst out laughing.

"I am Suzette LaMarre, born in Churchill, Manitoba, Canada. You can look up the date yourself. It is not that hard to follow my boring little life. This trip is the farthest away from my home in Winnipeg I have ever been. I may be a little strange, but coming from Northern Manitoba could account for that. Otherwise, I am as normally human as you!"

"Of course," he said, closing his notebook. "If you do find this guy following you across the state lines, call in the FBI. It becomes their jurisdiction."

"Thank you, officer," Kimmy said, holding out her hand to shake. She walked with him to his car while I turned toward the large number of ghosts gathered around me.

"How can I do this without being observed?" I asked in general.

"Night time," one woman suggested.

"Behind closed doors," a rather prissy looking man said.

"Shed your body," a younger man said, as if it was obvious.

"What?!" I reacted. "How could I do that?"

"You are the Gatekeeper! You can take any soul you want, including your own."

"Any soul *I* take goes straight to the Gate. Wouldn't that happen to me?"

"I don't think so," the man said. "*You* don't *know* all you can do. They plunked you into the job without telling you what you can do *now*, let alone when you are no longer burdened by flesh."

"I think I'll keep the burden for a while longer," I said dryly, wondering if the being had indeed only told me the bare bones of the job.

I went to work on all the ghosts in the area. The one that had suggested that I shed my body, hung back until the end, just watching what I did.

"So, don't you want to cross over?" I asked.

"Yes, indeed I do. I'm just wondering why they didn't tell you more."

"And I'm wondering how you know anything about it."

"I've been around since nineteen eighteen. I watched the old Gatekeeper work. For a while… years, I guess, I followed him. Then I got curious about the world and drifted, literally, on the winds. Then, when I was ready to cross over, a really terrible thing happened. You know about it on *your* level of reality as the atom bombs killing so many people at once. On *this* level… there was a huge wind blowing out from Japan. It collided on the other side of the globe taking millions of souls with it…"

His voice was hoarse. I could see tears in his eyes.

"Those who did not have a strong grip on a place, were swept out into space. At that time, the human version of reality included earth, the moon, which was uninhabitable, the planets, also uninhabitable and space, seriously uninhabitable. Space was *not* the current image of Heaven. Most of the souls believed that if they were in space, they would disintegrate into a million tiny pieces and become nothing. So they did. A few of us waited and caught the recoil wind that pulled us back to the earth. That was a seriously amazing ride. These kids and their computer games have no idea!...." His smile at the memory was striking. "Anyway, thousands of souls did not cross over then, they just fell apart! And the Gatekeeper. He fell apart too! He was attacked! I didn't see who it was... Who would have the strength to hurt the Gatekeeper? It is beyond me! The battle ended with both of them gone somehow. I don't know how he passed the job along to you... But, finally, you are here and you don't know everything involved in your job!"

"So, they are telling me on a 'need to know' basis," I grumbled. "Well, I guess if I need to know more, they will tell me, or provide the answers with someone like you."

"That may be true," he said, "but it seems inefficient. What if I hadn't said anything? What if I just went to the Gate."

"I believe they will send me a nudge. If I don't get it, they will send a smack. If I miss that too, they will run me into a brick wall that is impossible to miss. I am pretty sure that they are watching over me. I think they didn't want me overwhelmed in the beginning or I would have refused the job. Now, I'm committed to doing my best."

"That makes sense. Just remember: Whatever happens on one plane of existence, the repercussions happen in the other. I did not go to the Gatekeeper when I died, because it was so crowded with victims of the flu. I was shy. I have almost been destroyed many times over the years..."

"Then it is time. I don't know what awaits you, but I'm sure it is good."

He moved to a place right in front of me, waiting for me to touch him, but before I could, he backed away again.

"Not yet," he said. "I think I'd prefer to stick around for a while."

"To do what?"

"To help you. To answer questions. To give you a nudge."

"What is your name?"

"Derek Adams, from Vancouver, British Columbia, Canada, at your service." He smiled at me and my heart warmed. He was a very attractive man.

"All right Derek. Please don't interfere with Pete or Kimmy. They are collaborating on a new book while we tour around the country. They might get upset with another person joining the group. *I* don't need any more stress."

"Not a problem. Pete won't even know I'm here."

I thought Pete was smarter than Derek believed, but I would not argue. If this guy wanted to tag along, I had very little power to stop him. But if he became dangerous, I could send him to the Gate faster than he could blink. I didn't think he understood the speed I was working at. Somehow, I was bending time with the Quantum Key. Maybe he was right, though. Maybe, if I shed my body, I could also bend space.

CHAPTER 14

The police officer was right. Christopher Remington followed us. He kept his distance. When he took pictures, he stayed inside his locked car. He slept in his car and as far as we could tell, he did everything else there too. I didn't know what he had learned about me, but I couldn't see that it was much more than he had in the beginning. He was back to using his snapshot camera to film me.

"Pete, is there anything we can learn about him?" I asked one evening after the ghosts were gone.

"Like what?" Pete asked.

"I don't know. You're the expert on these things. Google him or something. Or sit beside him in his car and find out what he's doing or saying to whoever. Be a detective!"

"All right. I get the picture. I'll see you later."

Pete stayed with Christopher for the most part of the next week. Kimmy was getting miserable without him. Several times at night, I saw him looking through the window at her sleeping form. I got up to let him past the salt barrier, but he shook his head and left each time. I was getting worried.

Finally, he came back to us, looking disturbed. "I did not understand that people like him really existed," he started. "I've seen that type in movies and TV, but I always thought they were the exaggeration of creative writers."

"What are you saying?" Kimmy urged.

"Christopher has a ghost attached to him," Pete said. "Karen Biggs. She hasn't shown herself to you because she won't leave him. She hasn't figured out how to hurt him yet."

"Hurt him?" Kimmy asked. "Why would she want to hurt him?"

"Because he killed her," Pete said, obviously seriously disturbed. "He stalked her. A lot like he is talking Sue. She never even knew who he was. They did not meet. They did not talk. She has no idea why he chose her. When she found out that he was watching her, she called the police who did what they could, but it wasn't enough. She made friends with one special police officer. That triggered something in Christopher because he killed both her and the officer. The strange thing is that he was not caught. Not even questioned. No one looked at him!"

"So why did he start following Sue?" Kimmy asked.

"Because Karen and Sue could be sisters, they look so alike. I don't know what else would start him looking at you, Sue. But when he saw that you are different, he really became obsessed. He is bad news, no matter how you look at it."

"What does he have to incriminate me?" I asked.

"His pictures. He has put them on a website. They are mostly of you surrounded by translucent ghosts."

"Pictures like that can be faked," I said. "What else?"

"Well, he knows you are involved with the light somehow, but whenever the Gate opens, his camera goes blank. Overexposed or something. He hasn't figured out how to get around that." Pete chuckled and added. "I learned a whole new vocabulary from him."

"So what do we do?" Kimmy asked.

"If you don't mind a suggestion from outside, I have an idea."

Pete and I both jumped and turned toward the sound. Kimmy watched apprehensively.

"Who is this?" Pete asked me.

"Pete, this is Derek Adams. He has been dead much longer than he was alive. He has actually been helping me do my job."

"Don't sneak up on us like that!" Pete said. "We are a little jumpy right now."

"You're right. I'm sorry," Derek said pleasantly. "I'm sorry that I can't make Kimberly hear me yet, but that takes time and motivation. However, you have a number of problems and they all focus around that bad guy."

"Right," I said. "So what do we do? Wait until he kills me?"

"No! You must not die! That would close the Gate again!"

"Would it? Okay. What then?"

"He needs to be gone. Pete needs a body. Switch them."

"Switch...!" Pete was repelled by the idea, but I could see hope enter his eyes.

"That would be murder!" I said. "I can't arbitrarily just send a soul to the Gate! That would be wrong!"

"Even if it is self-defense?" Derek said. "You know he will try to kill you. I think he is working his way up to it now. He is afraid to get close to you, so you can't be the perfect woman he is looking for. Therefore, you need to be eliminated. You have to get him before he gets you."

Pete had been quietly telling Kimmy everything Derek was saying. She is the most nonviolent person

I know. It just isn't in her nature to want to hurt anyone, so I was very surprised when she said, "You have to protect yourself! Whether or not you put Pete in the body, the one in there now is obviously sick."

"Yes, but I don't think it is up to me to decide who deserves a body and who doesn't. That makes me no better than him! I have to think."

I went for a walk down to the river. It is one of those things in North America that most cities are built along a river or two and the riverbanks have parks with walkways down by the water. It made me feel at home to find a riverbank walk, as if *this* river was connected to the one at home.

I was hoping for inspiration, or maybe an angel to guide me. An angel started this quest of mine, wouldn't they come when I was at a crossroad? Did they *want* me to turn into a killer? Somehow I didn't think so. The water, moving swiftly pass me, had a calming effect on my psyche.

"Sue, step one foot to the left," Derek said urgently in my right ear.

I moved, partly to do what he said and partly to move away from something that close to my ear. An extremely loud noise rang in my ears. It was a gunshot! Aimed at *me*! I dropped to the ground, whirling around to try to see where the gunman was hiding.

He wasn't hiding! He expected to hit me on the first shot. He hadn't realized yet that he had missed. He was coming down the path to get me.

My first instinct was to go into Quantum Time. I was safe there. Time slowed, or I sped up, enough to dodge bullets that came my way. Not that I was going to take chances. Moving around the straight path of the bullets, I went to his side and pried the gun out of his fingers. I took the ammo from his shoulder bag and several knives from arm and leg holsters. Stopping in front of him, I let my time merge with his.

"You!" He cried out, trying to pull the trigger of the gun until he realized his hands were empty. I pointed to his knives, all lined up on the trunk of a tree, when he grabbed for the large one that had been on his belt. "How?" He gasped.

"Why do you want to hurt me?" I asked. "You tried to kill me!"

"Oh, you *will* die," he snarled, reaching into a back pocket that I had missed. He was fast. Amazingly fast. He had a garrotte out and almost around my neck before I realized what he was trying to do. The thing was just a wire between two wooden handles, but it was razor wire and would have cut my head right off.

I reached out to him and removed his soul as quickly as I could. His body slowly collapsed to the ground, leaving his ghost still standing, trying to wrap the wire around my neck. I stepped back, letting him realize what had happened to him.

"What did you do?" he screamed.

"I have sent you to the Gate," I said, watching him react. "You couldn't seem to understand. *I* am the *Gatekeeper.*"

"Gate? What Gate?"

"The one that lets you go into the light when *you* die."

"Die? I'm dead?" He seemed shocked.

"You, yes. Your body, not so much," I said. "But you are going to the Gate anyway." He was slowly being drawn away from me.

"Wait! You can't do that! I haven't done anything to you. Put me back!"

I chose not to respond to that. He was too busy flailing his arms, trying to stay put, to hear me.

"You are going to Hell!" A shrill voice came from the other side of him. It was a woman who did indeed look like me. She eagerly watched his struggle.

The Gate opened into an absence of light. The darkness seemed to draw the air as well as the light, maybe so he could scream longer. It did seem to take longer for him to get there than those who went to the White Light. Perhaps it was additional punishment. Finally, he was sucked screaming into the darkness and the Gate closed. Light returned to the world along with the birds singing.

"Thank you for doing that!" The woman said enthusiastically. "He actually deserved worse, but it is hard to plan when you can't move objects."

"You must be Karen," I said. "You can now go into the Light peacefully."

"Me?" She sounded nervous. "I don't want to go where *he* went!"

"Nobody does," I said, "but it is unlikely. The Gate decides what happens to you. You can leave hate and revenge behind now."

"Really? I can?" It surprised me that she had to think about it. "All right."

I reached out to touch her and was relieved to see the bright white of the light as she passed through the Gate.

"Sue! Susie! Where are you?" I could hear Kimmy breaking through the underbrush to get to me quickly. She sounded ready to panic. "Sue! Answer me!"

"I'm here!" I called. "I'm all right!"

She rushed up to me, throwing her arms around me, sobbing. "I heard a gunshot! We hadn't thought of that! What happened? Are you really all right? How did you manage to avoid the bullet?"

"I'm not hurt!" I laughed. "He forced the issue, though, and now we have *this*." I pointed to the body on the ground.

"Pete!" Kimmy called. "Did you want to do this?" She sounded hopeful.

"I thought I did," Pete said quietly beside us. "But I don't know. Right now, it feels like I would be putting on someone else's dirty underwear."

"Eeew, yuck," Kimmy responded.

"He could be cleaned up," I said, looking more carefully at the body. "According to the last time, the memories, the mind, does not stay with the body, remember? The pain from the cancer was the only problem. Does this body have cancer?"

"No," Pete said, looking at Kimmy. "All right, I will try it."

"Just remember one thing!" Derek said from the background. "You can only do this once. If she takes you out of the body, you will go to the Gate."

"I understand," Pete said, stepping up. "Derek, will you keep a watch out for Sue? Help her as no one living can?"

"I will, I promise," Derek said, as if they were handing me over, like a responsibility someone had to take.

"Humph," I snorted. "Men." I reached out with my left hand to Pete and the body, still unsure of my actions, but Pete went into the body as smoothly as Christopher had left it.

Pete drew in a deep breath and opened his eyes. They were green now. Kimmy and I helped him to stand and walk back to the Bus. He went into the shower and stayed there a long time.

Kimmy and I went to Christopher's car to find clean clothes and whatever incriminating evidence might be there. He didn't have much. His camera and his computer were full of pictures of me. Otherwise, he just had the tools to keep them running and clothes and blankets to let him live in his car. His weapons, we had thrown into the river.

By the time the hot water ran out and he had clean clothes on, Pete was ready to rejoin the land of the living. He came out of the tiny bathroom looking like a totally different person. He combed his hair differently, he had a different posture and attitude.

The change was way more than I expected. *Way* more than Kimmy expected too.

"Pete?" she whispered tentatively.

"Kim," he opened his arms and she ran into them.

Their kiss was passionate. I went out for another walk along the river, talking with Derek.

CHAPTER 15

"**I**f you knew, without a doubt, that a person was a serial killer, and had killed many people, getting away with it, would you put a stop to it?"

"Another morality question! Derek, it is hard to relax around you."

"Yes, but it is a good question," Pete said, from his spot beside Kimmy, who was sleeping quietly.

"How do I know he is a serial killer?"

"All the ghosts are angry and attached to him. They want him stopped."

"You are talking like it is not a hypothetical question," I said. "Who is he?"

"He is a twisted mind in an average body. I don't know what happened to him in his early life, but he has methodically found and killed fifteen women that look just like his mother did when she was twenty. He moves around the country, so even the FBI have had trouble finding him. You don't really see the trend until you see all fifteen lined up. They could be sisters. So, do you stop him?"

"I think I need an angel or being or someone to help me on this one," I said, looking up toward the sky.

"Don't hold your breath," Derek snorted. "Your angel doesn't seem too ready to get involved. Are you sure it was an angel?"

"It was a being within a very bright white light. When it laughed, I felt rose petals fall around me. I was overwhelmed by its presence."

"What did it tell you?"

"That I was chosen," I said, wrinkling my brow. "That the backlog was horrendous and that belief can get in the way of service. It said it was a messenger. I was to do the job."

"And you have done it admirably," Derek said. "If there was a problem, don't you think they would have stopped you?"

"All right, all right! My first instinct would be to stop killers before they could kill again. I did stop Christopher, didn't I?"

"Yes, but he was shooting at you at the time. It was self defence. You got to side-step the issue. That is different."

"What did the old Gatekeeper do?"

"If he was confronted by victim ghosts, he would try to find the killer, but he was too busy to seriously stop them. There were wars going on. Can you imagine what history would have been like if he had taken Hitler and his gang before all those people were slaughtered?"

"I can, sort of. Then it is too much for me and it boggles my mind. There are too many factors involved. I'm not ready for that. The concept is too big."

"Derek, what are you trying to do to her?" Pete asked. "Sway her beliefs to do your bidding?"

"Pete! I just realized that you can hear him! Can you see him too?" I cheered.

"Umm. Yes. I can see and hear the same things as I could before. Still not everything, but lots."

"I'm glad," I said. "I don't feel quite so alone."

Pete was staring at Derek with a hostile expression on his face.

"It's okay, Pete," Derek said cheerfully. "No. I'm asking a sort of hypothetical question. I have come across killers in my travels and I just wondered if there was a policy or morality laid down to the Gatekeeper."

"I think they chose Sue because she already has a deep personal code of morality. Rules take away from it, don't you think?"

Derek stopped, looked carefully at Pete and me and smiled a softer, truer smile. "Yes, I do, Pete. I have been watching the world for so long, I have become cynical. To answer my own question, I suppose the Gatekeeper will deal with each situation as it arises, to the best of her ability in the most fair way possible."

"Sounds good to me!" I smiled at both of them. "I would like it if I had both of you on my side, watching my back."

"You've got it!" they both said and laughed.

*

We continued the tour. Kimmy was happier than I have ever seen her. Now it wasn't just her blond curls that bounced, her whole self did. Pete was a good, kind man, who's entire focus was on making her life better. We both had to tell him to take care of himself. He would have forgotten to get rid of the incriminating evidence that Christopher had left on his computer and in his camera. Once that was done, he found people who could help change his identity back to Peter Tait. It was not possible to do it legally, but almost. His hand writing was the same as Peter Tait, not Christopher Remington. He made sure that all evidence of Christopher was gone.

We were a happy family travelling across the country. I think we could have continued indefinitely.

Unfortunately, Derek's question came back to us in a horrible way.

*

We stopped in a small city where Kimmy had a TV interview as well as a talk and book signing at the local bookstore. Her picture was on posters all over town. The park I stopped in was even close to the bookstore. We thought it was ideal.

Pete went with her to all her events. She should have been safe. But after an hour in the bookstore, she had to use the washroom... She was taken right out from under Pete's nose. He waited fifteen minutes and when she didn't return, he barged into the washroom. There were signs of a struggle. The small window had been broken. It was big enough to climb through.

Pete called the police and me.

"There is blood on the window," one of the police officers said. "As if she was dragged through. This guy seems to have thought of everything. There are no fingerprints, no evidence. Nothing to say where or why he took her. If it is money, can you raise a ransom?"

"I don't know," I said, watching the ghosts mingle amongst the police officers. "I'll have to call her publisher."

I called Samantha Blake, her publisher, explaining the problem.

"Well, I don't know," Samantha said. "The sales have been good. You were right that a tour would sell more books, but the tour is costing a lot too. We may be able to scrape ten thousand together in a hurry, but that's it. I don't understand why anyone took her. She's not on the Times Best Seller list yet. I think in a couple of months we may get her there, but for now..."

"Ten thousand?" I squawked. "What if he wants fifty? Or a hundred thousand?"

"We can contribute ten towards it. You may have to fool the bad guy or something. Let me know what you need."

"Is Derek around?" Pete asked me quietly.

"I haven't seen him since early this morning. He looked upset."

"Will he come if you call?"

"Call? How?"

"Go into the ghost level and yell!"

"The only way I go into that level is when I'm opening the Gate."

"Really? I thought you could, just by thinking about it."

"I'll try," I shrugged.

Pete was right! I love learning new things! I thought about the Gate and time seemed to stop for all the living people around me. The ghosts, realizing who I was, came toward me eagerly.

"Wait a little while, please," I said to them. "I need Derek Adams to come to me." A whisper of his name spread out from there like a ripple from a stone dropped in water. "Someone has taken my friend Kimberley and I need help finding her."

"I know where she is," a soft voice came to me.

I turned to look and my heart missed a beat. This woman looked exactly like Kimmy with blond curls and blue eyes. But, she had scars all over her face and body. Something bad had happened to her before she died.

"Oh dear! What happened to you?" I asked.

"The same thing that is happening to her," the woman said. "You have to hurry."

"We have to take the police with us," I said. "Wait a minute! Show us the way."

"We have information," I told Pete. He looked over at the ghosts that he could see and saw the battered woman. He staggered into the counter and almost collapsed on the floor.

"No Pete! That's not Kimmy! Her name is...."

"Mary."

"… Mary. She will show us the way!"

"Whoever did that, has Kim?"

"Yes! Let's go!"

Pete convinced an officer to follow us. We drove in Christopher's car, Mary sitting between us in the front seat. She led us to a huge old house in the oldest part of town. It was run down and overgrown with weeds.

The police officer tried to slow us down, saying we needed a search warrant and or protection.

"*You* need a warrant," I said. "*I* need my friend." I used a brick from the garden edging to smash a window in the door so we could unlock it. Then I let Pete kick the inner door in. We were at the top of the basement stairs. I hurried down, slipping into the Quantum Time unconsciously. The basement was full of ghosts of young women with blond, curly hair. They all had been tortured to death. They pointed to a door inserted into a cement wall. The killer must have been careless or overconfident. The door was closed, but the key was in the lock. I guessed he was inside.

I had to slow down to normal time in order to open the door, which gave him some warning, but I sped up again immediately.

The man was bent over a figure on the bed, a large hunting knife in his hands. He turned toward me, raising the knife as he spun. I saw Kimmy tied to the bed, half naked, blood oozing from many shallow cuts all over her body and face. Above her, Derek stood, shaking with the effort of holding the knife away from her.

"I couldn't stop him!" Derek cried. "I kept the cuts shallow, but I couldn't stop him!"

"Who are you?" the man yelled, moving toward me much faster than he should have been able to.

"I am the one who will stop you," I said, contemptuously. "You deserve to rot on death row for the rest of your life, but I won't take the chance that you might get away."

He lunged toward me, knife held in front. I side stepped and touched him, releasing his soul from his body and trapping it in the power of the Gate.

"What did you do?" he screamed.

The knife hit the floor, followed by his body.

That darkness is not something I will get used to. I suspect that if we could see a black hole, this is what it would look like.

"You have done enough violence in your lifetime. You could have had a good life. Instead, you chose to do this! *She* is my friend! Now, *you* have to go."

"Go where?" he gasped, trying to grab on to something to hold himself back. Of course, his fingers went straight through. He started to beg and plead, but the Gate didn't waste any time over him. The silence after he passed through the Gate was a relief.

"Kimmy!" I cried, stumbling over his body to get to her. "What did he do?" I looked up at Derek who still hovered protectively over her.

"You don't want to know," he said sadly.

"I don't want to know. You're right about that, but I must know. In order to help her, I have to know what happened."

"He saw her on the news," one tiny ghost woman with blond curls said. "He is rather fond of the look. When she went to the washroom, he knocked her on the head, made her breathe ether and tied her up. Then he dragged her to his van and brought her here.

"His methods are nasty. After he ties you up, he rapes you and cuts you. He likes to watch you bleed. He did rape her, not well, but before he started to cut her, *this* guy showed up."

"Derek," I said, seeing who she pointed to.

"Right. He put himself between her and the blade. I didn't know we had the power to move things like that! Derek is strong! But *he* is... was... stronger. He still cut her, just not as deep."

Kimmy groaned from the bed. I started to untie her wrists and ankles. As soon as she was released, she curled up into a ball, groaning.

"Kim!" Pete cried from the doorway. He grabbed a blanket from the floor and wrapped it around her, picking her up into his arms.

"Ambulance!" I called. "Has someone called an ambulance?"

"They are on their way," the officer said from the doorway. "What did you do to him?"

"Him?" I looked at the body crumpled at my feet. "I don't know. He just collapsed. Fainted or stroke maybe."

I shifted speed to talk with the ghosts. "He is gone, hopefully to his just reward. The body appears healthy. Does anyone want it?"

"He would go to jail, wouldn't he?" one of the women asked.

"Yes, you are right. You have been punished enough by him. The time has come, you can go into the light now."

"What will happen to the body?" another asked.

"I think it will be in a coma until it deteriorates and dies. It will probably be called brain dead."

"Brain dead? He was that long ago," the first woman snorted. "No. I would much rather go into the light now."

I reached out to them, one at a time, letting the Gate determine their future paths.

All except one. She looked like she had been there a long long time. Crouching at the back of the room, she only appeared to me when all the others were gone.

"This is the first," Derek said.

"The first?" I turned to her. "Then you know why! What made him become like this?"

"I don't know! He hated me! He was a perfect baby! A good boy! Why did he have to change... grow up?"

"She is his mother," Derek snarled contemptuously. "She kept him a baby until he was supposed to go to school! The other children were unmerciful.... Lady, you are as nuts as he was!"

"I'm sorry!" she sobbed. "I didn't know!"

"I should put you in his body to face the consequences of what you created," I said angrily.

"No! I want the light! Like the other girls got... I want the light!"

"You need to earn it," I said, reaching out with my left hand and placing her in the body.

The man on the floor gasped, opened his eyes and started to sob.

"No no no no! Don't make me stay!"

"The ambulance is here! The police officer said from the room behind me. "What's going on? What did you do?"

"I rescued my friend with your invaluable help," I said, turning to him. "You need to arrest this man for doing this to her."

He stepped past me and dragged the criminal to his feet. He was moving out as the stretcher came in.

Pete was still cradling Kimmy in his arms, whispering something soothing in her ear. The paramedics insisted that he put her on the stretcher and they wrapped her in warm blankets. She was hurt. Badly hurt.

Pete rode with her to the hospital while Derek and I followed in the car.

"Thank you, Derek," I said, tears in my eyes. "You saved her life."

"I don't think you should thank me yet. Trauma like that is hard to deal with. She will be scared both inside and out. Some of those women, the more recently killed, had a tendency to crawl into closets or under the bed and scream. The screams may be silent to the world, but they can be felt. Pete may be the only reason for Kimmy to hang on to her sanity."

"How did you manage to protect her? I didn't think ghosts had the strength to do any more than knock over ornaments and such."

"I guess you don't know your own strength until you need it. I put every bit of my being, whatever that is, into protecting her. I had never tried to do that much before. It makes me wonder."

"Wonder what?"

"What else I can do? I have new things to learn!"

We arrived at the hospital and met Pete in the waiting room of emergency.

"They won't let me in," he fretted. "I said she was my wife, but still... and you are her sister when they ask."

"Good. That will help. Derek is going to check on her."

"How did he *do* that? He was trying to protect her. I saw that, but how?"

"Necessity, I think. He is upset that he couldn't do more."

Derek appeared in front of us looking worried. "She needs you both," he said. "They have to come and get you..." he faded away again, leaving us feeling more upset than ever.

Fortunately, the doctor come out to talk to us. He looked grim. "Your wife was badly beaten," he said, leading us to her room. "Most of the cuts were superficial; painful, but not debilitating, but he hit her with something. A baseball bat maybe. She has internal bleeding everywhere. There are lumps on her head; her brain is swelling. Several ribs are broken. One arm and both legs are fractured. She fought him off with every bit of strength she had. But her pulse is thready, her blood pressure keeps dropping. We need to operate, but honestly, I don't think she will survive such an operation until she is stabilized, and we can't stabilize her. She is semiconscious right now, drifting in and out. Perhaps if she hears your voices, she will calm down and stabilize. Otherwise..."

We arrived by Kimmy's bed. Butterfly bandages were holding the cuts closed on her face, but the bruising and swelling was growing worse. She was almost unrecognizable.

"Kim!" Pete gasped, running to her side. "Dearest, you have to be strong! We have a life to live!"

He couldn't see Kimmy sitting half out of her body, but I could.

"I can't do it!" she whispered to me. "What that man did... I have to leave..."

"What do you mean, leave?" I asked.

"This, sort of. I don't know, but I separated myself from the pain and brutality of it. What happened to him?"

"He is gone," I assured her, telling her what we found and did when we arrived.

"Derek is a hero," she smiled sadly.

"Kim!" Pete said, squinting his eyes in an attempt to see her. "Don't leave your body! Don't quit on me now! Please!"

"Oh Pete, I just can't do it!" she cried. It felt really awful to have to repeat what she said to him. Definitely backwards. "I can't stop thinking about what he did. And the pain... I'm not strong like that. Please don't make me! I'll stay with you, I promise... just like you stayed with us... me."

"I can't force you to do anything you don't want to," I said.

"Neither can I," Pete said sadly. "At least we had a little while where I could touch you, feel your kiss."

"Oh Pete... I'm trying so hard not to just scream and scream and scream... Derek helped me... Why... What did I do...? Why me??"

"You did nothing!" I said, earnestly. "That man was sick in his head! Now his mother, who made him the way he was, will pay the price."

"You do know that this state has the death penalty, don't you?" Derek said. "I don't think she will be there that long. If she can find a way out, she will take it."

"When I see her again, I will let the Gate deal with her." I shrugged. "She should have been stopped before he became a monster."

The machine monitoring Kimmy's heart started to beep loudly.

"Oh sweet Kim," Pete whispered, holding her hand. "I'm going to miss kissing you."

The hospital crew with their crash cart came rushing into the small room to try to restart Kim's heart. We were ushered out of the way and Kimmy's spirit went with us. We watched through the doorway as they zapped her chest repeatedly. Finally, the doctor came out to us, shaking his head.

"I'm going to need all of the relevant information from you so we can make out a death certificate."

"Tell them it's you!" Derek said quickly to me.

"What?" Pete and I chorused.

"She didn't have her ID on her," the doctor said. I need you to fill in the forms.

"I'll do it," I said, going where the doctor pointed. "I know all her data."

I was left in a small booth with papers on a clipboard wondering what I was supposed to do.

"You will have to shed your body sooner or later," Derek said. "If you are already pronounced dead, there will be less paper work and mysteries later."

"My body... You are saying... You want me to..." I couldn't say it. Yet, he put it in my head. Did he *want* me to give my body to Kimmy?

"Not now! You are not ready for such a thing and neither is she. But some day in the future, it *is* possible. Think!"

I thought. I'll admit that I was finding the restrictions of a body a little frustrating at times. And if I had to shed my body, I preferred the idea of giving it to Kimmy rather than dying. It was just happening so fast.

So, I started to fill in the forms, writing Suzette LaMarre with all my medical numbers. By the time I had filled them in, I was crying. Pete joined me, reading the papers over my shoulder.

"I don't understand," he said, putting an arm around my shoulders.

"I know, but you will. Now, we have to arrange a funeral, or at least a cremation.

"But, who's idea...?"

"Derek. He's probably right, I guess. Just don't tell her yet."

"I can't see her," he said. "I don't understand it. I can almost hear her, but..."

"She's new as a spirit. You can only see and hear what you did before you got a body. Let's find her."

We went back to the room. A nurse had pulled a sheet over the body's face. Kimmy was standing beside the bed trying to pull the sheet back. Her hands couldn't grab the sheet.

"I can't see me!" she cried. "I want to see me one last time."

I went to the other side of the bed and pulled the sheet away from the face. In death, the muscles relaxed and the terror of the last hours left her face. She looked at peace. Kimmy, on the other hand, was frantic. She touched the cuts on her body's face; the bruising around her nose and the massive lump on her head.

I wasn't sure what she was doing until I looked closer. Each wound she touched on the body, disappeared from her ghostly appearance. I helped her to reach all of the wounds in order to remove them from her psyche. I hoped it would work. When we were done, she had tears running down her cheeks.

"What do you need now?" I asked.

"I need someone to hold me!" she cried. "It was so bad! I was so alone... I don't want to be alone again! Ever!"

"Oh sweetie, I don't know how!"

"I do," Derek said, appearing at the foot of the bed. "You wear a locket. We can use it."

I reached up to my neck. I had two gold chains: the locket and the key. I opened it showing a picture of Kimmy on one side and me on the other. We were quite a few years younger at the time. I unsnapped the chain of it and held it out.

"Kimberly, you can put yourself into that locket. Whenever you do, you will feel the love of whoever is holding it or wearing it. It will almost be as good as a hug. Maybe better."

Kimmy looked at Derek for a second and then the locket. "Will I be bound to it the way Nancy was to the hospital?"

"No. You can come and go as you please. This is a place you can go to when you need a hug and love. It rests over Sue's or Pete's heart. Because you know this, you will be safe and loved. Try it."

Kimmy disappeared for a minute, leaving us standing around the bed, me beside the body and Pete on the other side. She reappeared, smiling for the first time.

"Thank you Derek. You are right. I do feel safe there. We can go now."

She disappeared again. I handed the locket to Pete to put around his neck and we left the hospital.

"Now what do we do?" Pete asked.

"I would say a hairdresser is called for," Derek suggested.

"A hairdresser? What for?" Pete asked.

"Because I don't look like Kimberly Foton, the up and coming children's writer," I sighed. "I'm not so sure that this will work. It seems crazy to me. What will we tell Samantha?"

"We rescued Kimmy. She was hurt, but not as badly as we feared, but the guy laid a trap and Sue got caught in it. In our effort to rescue Kimmy, Sue was murdered. I don't think we need say more; talking about it makes us too emotional." Pete was very emotional, proving his point.

"Your collaboration with Kimmy is good!" Derek smiled. "You should write on your own too. You think on your feet."

"All I want is to be with Kim," Pete said sadly. "This idea seems crazy."

CHAPTER 16

We saw very little of Kimmy for the next few weeks. We continued with the book tour, but we were slowed down since I had to do the talks as well as the Gatekeeping. Pete sold the car so that he could drive the Bus while I slept.

I could not copy Kimmy's signature. I got close, but not exact. We covered it up by getting a hand splint and claiming carpal tunnel syndrome. I could sign the books, but it was not the same. Even Kimmy was impressed when she showed up to see what we were doing. Noises frightened her. The least little unusual event sent her back into the locket in a blink. She should have helped me at the talks, but she was terrified to be in an open area. Her fear was frustrating, but, over time, I believed she would do better.

The transformation that I went through to become Kimmy was not as hard as it seemed at first. We were the same size and age. We had been friends since we were children. I knew her mannerisms better than anyone. When we made my light brown hair into blond and curly, I started feeling more like her. I bounced more and talked a mile a minute asking a whole series of questions whenever I saw someone for the first time. Pete claimed it was spooky, I was so good at it. I kept practising as we drove.

Our route took us South through Florida and then New Orleans. I was surprised at how little difficulty we had throughout the States of Florida and Louisiana. They seemed to be full of contradictions between the wealth and the poverty. Many seniors retire there, so I expected the many older ghosts I saw. The younger gang members, who wanted to dominate the area in life, kept meeting with resistance even after death.

We stopped in a small park along the seaside one morning and waited, enjoying the view. By then, I knew all the ghosts would come to me.

"All right now, youse guys have ta line up dere. No one gets to her without Reggie's say so."

This boy - I call him that because he could not have been more than twenty when he died - sounded ferocious and had many of the seniors crouching away from him as if he could hurt them.

"Get out of my way!" an elderly woman snarled. She was almost spitting! "Who do you think you are, young man? Do you think *you* can do something scary to *me*?"

"Yes I can, you old fool. Do what I tell you and you might come out where you want to be."

The old woman walked with a walking stick. She must have needed it for years and years in order to have it still with her in death. I knew the stick was as insubstantial as she was, but the power of belief is a wonderful thing. I was prepared to intervene so the seniors would not be delayed by the gang of thugs, but the delightful old lady held her cane up high and smashed it down on the top of the young man's foot.

"Ouch! How did you do that!" he asked, stepping backwards.

"My stick is made of the same thing you are," the woman snorted. "Therefore, it will hurt you. You need to learn to be nicer to those who lived longer than you did. We can still hold our own!"

"I think that is always a good lesson to remember," I said, coming over to her.

"Who are you and what makes you think you can do anything different around here? Nothing changes in this place!" The old woman turned on me as if I was allied with the gangs.

"I am the Gatekeeper," I said, cheerfully. "I can help you go to the light. Are you ready?"

"Ready? I have been ready for sixty four years! Where have you been? What took you so long?"

She was really aggressive! Her emotion was stirring up the other ghosts gathered around. I started to wonder what a mob of ghosts could do when they were really impassioned. I needed to cool this off quickly."

"I wasn't born yet," I said. "The other Gatekeeper died... or something... They had a hard time finding a replacement. I've only been doing this for six months!"

"And of course, we are the last to go," the old woman grumbled.

"The last!" I laughed. "Hardly! I haven't been anywhere West yet. I've only worked the Eastern Seaboard in North America! I haven't even left the continent yet!" It was starting to sink into my brain. I had been working hard every day and I had really only handled a drop in the bucket! How on earth was I going to do such an insurmountable job?

The old woman seemed to read the expression on my face. Her aggression turned to compassion in a flash. "Don't worry dearie, you stay here and work and we will gather everyone together. You shouldn't ever have to chase anyone down."

"But some people are stuck," I said.

"Yes, I know. I have heard that, particularly in New Orleans at the Superdome after Katrina. That was unfortunate. But I haven't been here for sixty four years without learning a thing or two. We *can* help you."

Her about face made the day wonderful. I went through the crowds of ghosts, touching each one and sending them to the Gate. Time went on and on, but I was not tired. I knew I was in Quantum Time, but I didn't realize how much it changed time until I got to the end of a day's work and returned to normal time.

"Ready for a lunch break?" Pete asked.

"Lunch? How much time has passed?"

"Three hours, give or take…"

"Three hours? It felt like days!"

"Now you are getting it!" Derek said from beside me. "You can bend time any way you want to! You have as much time as you need to do the job at hand."

"But why aren't I tired or hungry?"

"You aren't tired because that zap of pleasure the Gate gives you, feeds your energy requirements. You aren't hungry because you ate three hours ago. Now it is lunch time."

"How many ghosts did you cross over?" Pete asked.

"Thousands," I said. "It seemed like thousands of thousands. It was non-stop for what felt like twenty six hours minimum."

"Why would it feel like hours?" Pete really couldn't understand the difference in Quantum Time, even though he had been there.

"I looked into every soul's eyes. I spoke to most of them. Some were too shy or too young. Babies and young children were brought by family ancestors. I had to reassure all of them! Especially those ones that travelled from the Superdome. What a horror that was. Not *that* many deaths, but the fear... Those who survived will probably have nightmares for the rest of their days. To do that with each and every one of them, took time." I shrugged.

"Unnecessary kindness," Derek snorted.

"I don't think so," I said seriously. "They chose *me*. I have to think it is for more reason than I could see the ghosts and am Unitarian!"

"You are right," Derek said. "That's why I'm staying with you. I like you."

"Okay," I said, looking for deeper meaning in Derek's brown eyes. He had mentioned before that he wanted to help me. He had not declared how he felt about me. "Thanks. I like you too."

What do you say to someone that you cannot hold hands with, or kiss, or touch in any way? I was starting to feel like I depended on him. Doing the Gatekeeping had become so much more pleasant since he arrived. I knew I was falling in love, but what could I do about it?

"So, how about lunch?" Pete asked, changing the subject.

We were content to sit in the park eating sandwiches and watching the gulls.

"What is that!?" I gasped, pointing out to sea.

There was a ship, floating in a fog that slowly appeared before me. It was an ancient square rigger with torn sails and one broken mast. I could see people climbing down from the rigging and overboard. Squinting my eyes from the sun, I saw them walk on top of the water.

"I think we are seeing what happens when people die at sea," Derek said. "They are walking above the salt!"

"You never tried to go out to sea?" I asked him.

"I hitched a ride on an aeroplane. Salt water burned my feet."

"I can't see what you guys are talking about!" Pete said. "It was more fun when I could see."

"Count your blessings," Derek grinned, but he described the whole scene to Pete, including the fact that the ghosts seemed unable to actually come ashore.

I walked down to the water's edge and saw the problem. There was a barrier of evaporated salt all down the coast line. Kicking an opening through the barrier, I let all the ghosts come ashore.

"Who are you?" a young man asked. "Why are you calling us?"

"Calling you?"

"With your music. We heard it for miles! Why do you call us?"

"I am the Gatekeeper. I can send you to the light."

"All right! It's about time!" I heard the cheers from many behind him.

"We've been here a long time. There is no light!" he snarled in disbelief.

I looked invitingly to the rest of the crowd and they swarmed past him.

"Are you telling the truth?" a young girl asked, looking deeply into my eyes.

"Yes I am," I smiled and touched her arm.

The Gate was a particularly beautiful rainbow for that young girl. There were 'oohs' and 'ahs' throughout the crowd, even from the young man.

I don't really notice how or when I go into Quantum Time when I work. It just happens. I suspect that when I think I must hurry to do them all, I am given enough time to do exactly that. I understand also that ghosts don't take up any space, so I shouldn't be surprised at how many came off of that old ship. It was sixty five years worth of deaths at sea across a huge area, maybe all of the Gulf of Mexico, maybe even the Atlantic Ocean. There were certainly enough nationalities represented. But, I did, eventually, get them all.

"*Now*, I'm getting tired," I said as I joined Pete at the picnic table. "How long did that take?"

"Two and a half hours," Pete said. "You look more tired this time.

"That's because she worked for comparatively another ten hours this time. That makes a work day of thirty six hours crammed into six."

"So, you need to eat! We are on the outskirts of New Orleans! It is famous for its cuisine. Let's go out!"

We enjoyed ourselves. It didn't matter where we went, we enjoyed ourselves. When we went to a restaurant, we sat in a booth so Derek and Kimmy could join us comfortably and we would talk for hours. Kimmy was getting stronger within herself.

Her fear was receding. She left the locket to join us for supper every day, but the way she looked at Pete, with so much love and longing, my heart was ready to break for her. Pete couldn't see her, but they had tried for a long enough time and finally, he connected with her sufficiently to hear what she was saying. What a relief *that* was!

"So where do we go next?" she asked.

"Texas," Pete said. "There are a lot of people in Texas."

"There are a lot of people everywhere," Kimmy said. "I did some checking. I compared the death rate to the world population each year from 1950 on. They don't say much before that. According to my calculations there have been approximately twenty nine million, nine hundred seventy nine thousand, six hundred and fourteen deaths since nineteen fifty. It went down for a while and then it went up again, but we can estimate five hundred fifty five thousand a year."

"Five hundred fifty five thousand! Approximately? That would be... one thousand five hundred twenty a day! Oh boy. You know, that is less than I expected, but more than I want."

"That is why you have to shed your body, sooner or later," Derek said. "The old Gatekeeper went from place to place with a thought. He had been everywhere by then, so it was easy."

"You keep saying it, but I can't figure out how to do it." I shook my head. "I'm not there yet."

Pete's phone rang. He didn't talk much, just listened to the other end. It was hard to read the expression on his face. When he hung up, he had the look of a deer caught in the headlights of a car at night.

"What is it? What's wrong? Why do you look so scared?" I said, feeling as nervous as Kimmy.

"Samantha is coming here! She left this afternoon and will be at her hotel in an hour. She wants to meet with us."

"Us?" I asked.

"Well, Kimmy, really, but she knows we are two steps from being married, so she included me. She has exciting news. Her assistant wouldn't say what. I guess she needs a signature."

"Oh no... I'm not good at that. Even with a splint, it looks forged."

"But what can we do?" Pete sounded panicky.

"Kimmy can share your body," Derek suggested. "Then she can do the talking and sign the papers."

"Two people in one body? Isn't that a mental illness?"

"Only when they don't know it. They get confused."

"We have to get going," Pete said, looking worried. He went to the front to pay the bill while I followed, listening to Derek and Kimmy debate the pro's and con's of sharing my body.

My body. That was a really big issue to me. It's not the same as changing your clothes. All of your emotions and sensations are all tied into the structure of your body. Sometimes, during sex, you may feel like you are sharing an experience, but not really. Your pleasure is your own and your pain is your own. But then, what do we really know about it. If more than one inhabit a body, the body is locked away in a mental institution and treated as insane. It was a lot to think about in our short drive to the hotel.

"So what do we do?" Pete asked.

"I'll just stay close and coach Sue on what to say and do." Kimmy said. "I didn't spend *that* much time with Samantha. She has to realize I've changed after losing my best friend.

"No," I said, sighing. "It is time we tried this. It has been part of the plan since Kimmy died. Derek, what do I do?"

"My guess is that you do the same thing you did for Pete so he could have his body. Use your left hand and think about it."

It sounds simple! But, it's not that simple. Not to me. I reached out to Kimmy, grabbing her hand and bringing it to my chest. I saw her being sucked into my body, but then, the scariest thing I have ever experienced happened to me. I felt like I had been punched in the stomach by a battering ram. As I doubled up from the agony, it kept pushing me backwards until I was several feet away, disoriented and in pain.

I looked over at Kimmy and realized what had happened. When I let her into my body, I was pushed out! She was swaying on her... my... feet, trying to keep her balance.

"Sue? Sue, where are you? Why can't I hear you?" she whispered.

"Because I'm not there," I groaned. "Man, that hurt!"

"Sue!" the three turned and looked at me, horrified.

"That wasn't supposed to happen!"

"Well, it did," I grumbled.

"Take it back!" Kimmy shrieked. "I'm not going to steal your body from you! Put yourself back in here!"

I had been pretending to be Kimmy for a few weeks by then. The look was good. I fooled lots of people. But watching Kimmy be present in the body, it *became* her. There was nothing to suggest that it was me. It was not my body any more, just like that!

I looked down at myself, rubbing my sore tummy. I was wearing the exercise costume we had designed, with the white tights and colorful sheer draperies. In the light of the streetlights, it was beautiful.

"Susie! Why are you looking like that? Take your body back, *now*!"

"No. It was time. Derek is right. I can't do my job properly if I am encumbered by a body. This is so different! I can float! You guys never told me what it feels like!"

"The necklace!" Kimmy said, moving closer. "You still have your Grandmother's key! How can that happen?" She was looking for it on her own neck.

I reached up to my own neck and sure enough, the tiny key was still hanging on its fine gold chain. "I don't know!"

"I should be able to touch it, or see it if it is really there," Kimmy muttered. She reached out to me to touch the key, but her fingers went right through it. "Weird. But Sue, it's not right for you to give me your body. The sacrifice..."

"Kimmy, you are more you in that body than I was me! You fill it with your energy. I have always been half there and half gone somewhere else. You know that!"

"Preoccupied..." Kimmy nodded. "But..."

"Sweetie, I am feeling one hundred percent present right now! *This is great!* Let's go to the meeting and see what happens, okay?"

She agreed, of course. By the time we were in the hotel lobby, she was steadier on her feet. I could see a light of joy in her eyes as she turned and kissed Pete passionately. Their joy would keep me going for a long time.

Samantha Blake is a passionate, energetic woman, a lot like Kimmy. She was looking for something changed in Kim. She never found out exactly what had happened to Kim and me and was suspicious. If we hadn't switched, she would have figured out that something was wrong.

"I was so sorry to hear about Suzette," she said to Kimmy, right off the bat.

"I was murdered!" I reminded Kimmy before she asked why.

"Oh, thank you. It has been hard," Kim said. "She was my very best friend."

"I would imagine, then, that she is watching over you now," Samantha said sincerely.

"I am sure of it," Kimmy grinned. "So what is the big deal that flies you half way across the country?"

"Warner Brothers wants to make a movie of the book."

"A movie! Really?"

"Really. They want to make it a teen type story. They are popular right now. And they are willing to pay a lot for it. We will both do very nicely."

"All right! So what happens now?"

"Well, the book tour has to be cut short. You can stop at a few main cities along the way, but you are going to Hollywood!"

I was feeling as excited as the others. I felt prickles all over me, like pins and needles without the pain. I started to float.

Kimmy and Pete could both see and hear me. I don't know why, since they both had intermittant abilities to see that plane of existence, but as I rose toward the ceiling, they both looked up at me, which started me laughing, which caused me to float more. The sensation was wonderful. For the first time in my life, I was free from aches and pains. I could do acrobatics as if I was swimming. I was just having a little difficulty staying down to earth.

"What are you looking at?" Samantha asked, looking right at me, but seeing nothing.

"Nothing!" Kimmy said, looking back down. "So, do we have paper work to do?"

"Yes. Absolutely. I have the contract right here."

Pete was still staring at me so Kimmy poked him in the ribs to get his attention. He anxiously waved a finger at Derek who was lounging on the bed, laughing. Finally, Derek got up and grabbed my ankle and pulled me back down beside him. I was not in any danger. I did not know how to go through walls and ceilings yet. I had a lot to learn. I love learning.

Kimmy cut the meeting short. Her nervousness showed. I'm sure Samantha thought she was just excited, but Kim didn't want to risk Pete saying anything. She walked to the door and paused for another handshake to give me time to get out of the room.

As soon as we were outdoors, we all laughed hysterically. Pete and Kimmy went straight back to the bus to explore her new body while Derek and I flew up into the air.

Derek did not loosen his hold on me. He held my hand! I gathered that in my new state, I had to have the intention of moving a soul to the Gate for it to happen. Otherwise, we were just holding hands. I hadn't done any hand holding since the accident with Pete. It was wonderful!

Derek stood with me, floating over the brightly lit city. He reached out to touch the key around my neck. To my surprise, his finger passed right through the tiny gold key and its chain. He leaned closer to admire it's intricate detailing.

"There is something about this key," he muttered.

"I know. I just don't know what. My Grandmother never explained."

Derek taught me how to move through space; how to go through solid objects; how to keep the wind from blowing me away; how to shrink to any size I wanted and how to dance on the head of a pin. By the time other ghosts started gathering around me, I felt like I had mastered my own actions. I felt powerful! Invincible!

"How did you find me?" I asked the first in line, always wanting to know.

"You give off music," a wizened old man said. "I don't know what you did, but yesterday I heard it faintly and started to come to you. Then tonight, it became loud and clear, like a beacon. As if *you* are the light! We *have* to go to you. So, if you're the light, what happens next?"

"I *am not* the light!" I was shocked. "I am the *Gatekeeper*. I *cross* you *over* to the light! *That is much* better than *me*!"

I sent the old man to the Gate and was cheered to hear him say how wonderful it was as he passed through the Gate. I was also surprised to feel the same pleasure in my body when I sent him over even though I did not have a body any more.

Time no longer meant anything to me. My only connection with the plane of the living was with Kimmy and Pete. I was going to have to remember to stop and talk with them every once in a while.

CHAPTER 17

"Kimmy, are you awake?" I called from the tiny bedroom door. "Pete, wake up!"

"I'm awake, I'm awake. What's wrong?" Kimmy asked, pushing the blanket off of her nude body.

"Kim!" Pete exclaimed, tossing her robe to her.

"If anyone has a right to see this body, it's her," Kimmy said, winking at me. "It used to be hers, remember?"

"Somehow, I never looked so sensuous and sexy in it," I said, considering the difference carefully. "You bring a whole new attitude with you. You are positively glowing!"

"Glowing?" Pete exclaimed, sitting up and staring at Kim. "You're not..."

"How could that happen? I'm not able..." Kimmy said.

Suspiciously, I looked carefully at and in Kimmy. Sure enough, I saw a tiny glowing lump in her uterus.

"No, my dear Kimberley, but, I *was* able. You are in a different situation now. You are pregnant."

"Pregnant! Really?"

They both seemed to be stunned by the idea. When she was young, Kimberley had to give up hope of having children because her reproductive organs were underdeveloped. I assumed Pete had come to terms with his life also. Now, both had new bodies and new beginnings.

"So, what's up?" Kimmy said, trying to change the subject.

"We will be in Dallas in the morning," I said. "I guess I'm a little nervous. So far, I haven't run into any really famous or important people."

"That you know of," Derek added from behind me.

"That I know of," I agreed. "I'll admit that my knowledge of history is limited, but I should have met some of them. Anyway, John Kennedy must be somewhere! If he is still where he was shot, he will be there. So, I'm nervous."

"Kennedy! You're right! We were near his family home months ago! And there have been a lot of assassinations as well as natural deaths of rich and famous people! You haven't seen *any* of them?"

"None. I'm starting to feel like I'm missing something."

"Like what?"

"Like, that Being didn't tell me anything! I go out there and do the job, thinking everything is fine, but something is being hidden from me. Those important people should be going to the Gate the same as everyone else, shouldn't they?" I looked at each of them, challenging them to contradict my thoughts.

"Well, they used to go to the Gate," Derek said, popping in behind me. "I saw Generals and Politicians rushing to the Gatekeeper even faster than the regular folks. *They* had the same attitude of entitlement in death as they had in life!"

"So where are they?" I asked.

"Something or someone must be preventing them from coming to you," Pete suggested.

"Someone? Who? Why? I don't understand!"

"I would say that this is the place to go looking," Kimmy said, putting her bath robe on. "Maybe you can ask the folks waiting for you if they have seen what happened to Kennedy?"

"Good idea! I'll see you later."

*

I went to a nearby park. I had found that it wasn't necessary to be in an open area to do the job, but I enjoyed it more. I could feel the sun or rain on my skin, even though, technically, I didn't have any skin.

Perhaps it was my mind creating the sensations, but I didn't care, I enjoyed it. I watched the city's ghosts make their way to me. Their determination was amazing. I could tell by the way they were moving, that they were attached to buildings or people, but they wanted to leave. A young woman was swearing softly as she pushed through the resistance.

"I did everything for you. I fed you and clothed you and made sure you were safe! What did I get back? Complaints and demands. You dragged me down when I was alive, I'll be damned to let you drag me down in death. Yours *or* mine. You have to learn how to survive on your own and I have to learn to stand up for myself. Well, this is it! You're on your own now!"

Amazingly, a younger man was following her, trying to get her attention. He looked so much like her, he had to have been her son. She was breaking the bond and he was very upset.

"Hello!" I said cheerfully. "I am the Gatekeeper. I'm here to help you cross over to the other side."

"It's about time!" a cantankerous old man grumbled. "What took so long?"

"The last Gatekeeper met with an accident. It took time to find a replacement. Now, I'm here."

"All right then, *where* are *you* sending us?"

"I send you to the Gate so you can cross over to the Light. It is so much better than anyone ever expects. But why are you saying it like that?"

"Like what?"

"As if someone else is sending people somewhere else?"

"Yep, that's about it. He is holding a whole big bunch of em over at the football stadium. His music isn't as nice as yours."

"Thank you," I said, looking over the heads of the throng of people to Derek. He looked as perplexed as I felt. He waved to me to carry on while he went to investigate. That made sense to me, so I went to work, starting with the old man.

I worked for a long time. The Gate was bright and beautiful for almost everyone. The level of goodness and love in that park was wonderful. Even the mother and her irritating son went to a bright warm place. When I was finished, I had an uneasy feeling. Something was wrong. I was relieved when Derek returned.

"I don't believe it," he said, worry written all over his face.

"What? What's going on?"

"There is a man who can call spirits to him the same way you do, but when they get there, he traps them. I don't know what holds them, but something does. Some can resist his hold, but not many. They may be some of the ones that made it to you, I can't tell. But, I do think that is where the rich and famous are. They are trapped."

"Oh dear, we had better go see," I said determinedly.

"Sue…"

"Yes?"

"This is a *really* bad guy. He is strong enough to bind thousands of ghosts to him. They are probably adding to his strength. You must be careful."

"All right," I smiled at his worry. "Don't worry." After all, what could happen to me? I was the Gatekeeper! I could dance on the head of a pin!

When we approached the stadium, I could see a cloud of darkness over everything. I couldn't separate it into individual spirits. Perhaps it was just their energy. Whatever it was, it would not touch me. Obviously, there was no way for me and my music to hide and sneak up on whatever was going on, so I walked right in with the darkness pulling back ahead of me and then closing in behind me. Derek stayed close, inside my bubble of light.

We went out to the field without incident until I saw who was apparently in charge of everything.

"Oh no! Andrew Rat! What is *he* doing here? How can this be possible?"

"Well, well, well, Suzette LaMarre! Fancy meeting *you* here. I thought you were too much of a loser to succeed at anything. Now, I'll prove it."

He was just as offensive and slimy as I remembered him in school.

"What is going on here?" I demanded. "What are you doing?"

"Me? I'm just gathering some energy."

"Energy? From Dead people's souls? For what?"

"You always were stupid," he sneered. "When I have the energy, I can take over all the *power* in the world. Then, living people will do what I say just as easily as these dead ones."

"Power? These souls need to cross over to the light! They have more to do in their existence!"

"The light? There is no light anymore! It is all darkness now, no matter how loud *you* are. You cannot beat me on this one, little girl. There is no one to tattle to. You are a weak woman who will shatter even more easily than your grandfather did. *My* grandfather did that and *I* will finish the battle. *You* will leave!"

He made a pushing gesture at me and I was lifted into the air and shoved away from him. I felt punched in the stomach much worse than when I left my body. I couldn't breathe. Closing my eyes as I doubled up, I felt my self bounce and bang around as if I was the ball in a raquette ball tournament. I felt pain. Lots of pain. It didn't matter that I didn't have a body and didn't need air. The pain was overwhelming. Eventually, I seemed to be far enough away from him to not be hurt further. I opened my eyes and gasped in surprise.

I was floating in outer space! In my upper left vision, the moon hung, absolutely enormous. I turned a bit and saw the earth. The beauty of the planet brought tears to my eyes.

Which reminded me that I had eyes. I brought my hand up to feel the wetness. If I had not met Derek, I may have stayed there, blown into bits by the solar wind. But Derek had been even farther out into space and returned because he knew he could. If he could, I could. I started to move back to the enormous planet that was my home.

It took longer to return than it did to get out there. I had to learn to move faster in the empty space. I hadn't realized that my movement at home was enabled by my interaction with the molecules in the air. There were way fewer molecules in space. When I did reach the atmosphere, I took the scenic route home, enjoying myself and thinking seriously about what had happened. What Andrew Rat had done to me.

CHAPTER 18

I did not know how much time had passed when I arrived in front of Kimmy and Pete. Their reaction said it was quite a while.

"Sue! Susie! Are you all right? What happened? Where did you go? What did he do to you? I missed you!" Kimmy burst into tears.

"He? What he?" I asked. "Have you seen Derek?"

"Yes! He is broken up! He thinks you were destroyed! He blames himself! Who *was* that man?"

"Hang on," I said, going outside to call Derek. We had a way to cut through the noise and talk. Distance slowed us, but if he was near, he would come.

Sure enough, he popped into view right in front of me.

"Sue! You're back! I was so scared! I thought you were gone! I couldn't hear you! Where were you? Where did he throw you?"

He swept me into a hug and kissed me in a way I hadn't been kissed in years. I felt every bit of it and it felt wonderful! I could feel his fear and worry as well.

"Throw is a good term," I said, taking his hand and pulling him back to Kimmy and Pete in the bus. "I was thrown into space. I got a good look at the moon. Earth is so beautiful from up there. It was Derek's story that made me understand that I could return safely and did not have to be shattered into millions of pieces. But it took a while to get back. How long?"

"A month," Kimmy said soberly.

"A month! Why are you still here? You should be in Hollywood by now!"

"She wouldn't let us go until we heard from you," Pete said. "She did not believe that you were gone, in spite of what has gone on."

"Gone on? What?"

"First things first!" Kimmy interrupted. "Was that really Andy Rat? The one from school?"

"Yes. I don't understand what he was talking about yet, but it was him in all his horrifying glory."

"Who was he?" Derek demanded.

"He has always been Sue's enemy," Kimmy said. "From the first time we saw him in grade one, he has bullied her. He would talk his friends into doing things to her. He started rumours about her. He called her all the names there are and made her life miserable."

"A bully," Pete said, nodding.

"There were four of them, but he was the ring leader. She couldn't get away from them."

"But how does he tie in with all of this?" Derek wondered. "He talked about your Grandfather and his Grandfather. I don't get it."

"My Grandmother had my mother out of wedlock," I said quietly. "She never told anyone who the father was. She just got a job and raised my mother. My Mom died when I was young. I don't remember her much. I was raised by my Grandmother. She put the key around my neck a short while after my Mom died. I always thought it was her way of creating a stronger bond between us. I never really knew my Mom. Gramma would not say who *my* father was. If Andrew was telling the truth, could it possibly be, that my Grandfather was the Gatekeeper?"

"That is a possibility," Derek said. "He had a body for quite a while. He shed it when the war broke out. He couldn't keep up with the volume of ghosts."

"Okay, but what about Andrew Rat?" Kimmy said it as if she had something bitter in her mouth.

"He was raised by his grandparents," I said, thinking back. "His Grandfather came to a career day thing at school in... grade three... maybe, remember? He was a horrible old man! I remember his eyes. They were black! I have never at any other time seen black irises around the black pupil. His hair was black too, even though he was really old, but his skin was white and pasty. He looked sick and weak. Across the room, he pointed at me and told Andrew something about me. Before that, I was one of many who that kid bullied. After that, I was the number one target. I couldn't get away from it. I think the old man died that year. Not a day went by that Andrew didn't say or do something horrible. People think surviving bullies makes you stronger, but it doesn't. It chips away at your self-esteem and weakens you. Surviving bullies is not enough. They must be stopped!"

"You are *stronger* than him!" Derek said. "You are a wonderful person! He couldn't take that away from you!"

"Derek's right, Sue," Kimmy said, quietly. "I know bullies are a pet peeve to you. I was there. I never understood why he did that. But, whatever he did in his life, it could not match you."

"Maybe we had better find out what he did," Pete said. "You guys rest. I have some research to do."

Derek and I agreed and went out into the park to talk, letting Kim get some sleep.

"What happened to you?" I asked Derek.

"I was blown away with you for a ways. I tried to stay close, but he was bouncing you around so fast, I lost you. Your light and music got farther and farther away and then it faded out. I thought he destroyed you!"

I put my arms around him and kissed him. We were two souls, without bodies, able to touch each other, kiss each other and love each other. I had never in my life experienced lovemaking so sensual. My heart was filled with the joy of it. For the first time since I left my body, I drifted into a deep, contented sleep, feeling safe in Derek's arms.

*

"Hey lady! Shiny lady! Help us!"

"Hmm? Oh!"

I sat up on a bed of flowers in the park and looked around me. There was a gathering of ghosts standing back respectfully. Derek stood up beside me and helped me to my feet.

"Of course I will help you," I said. "What's wrong?"

"I don't want to go to that dark one, but he says I have to. That there is no place else...," a young boy said.

"He underestimates me," I said. "I am the Gatekeeper. You *can* go into the light where you are *meant* to go."

"Oh thank you! He said you were dead and gone! He is a very bad man."

I went to work on the crowd around us. They were all grateful to see me. Afterward, Derek and I joined Pete and Kimmy in the bus.

"So what did the Rat make of his life?" I asked.

"Not much," he said. "After high school, he went to college, but dropped out. He did various jobs, waiter, gas jockey, labourer, each worse than the last until he got caught stealing cars. He was in jail off and on for twenty years. The last time, he seemed to clean up his act and behave himself. He behaved until he finished his parole and then disappeared. I can find no records of him over the last fifteen years. Somehow, I don't think he saw the light."

"Did he die?" Kimmy asked.

"Not in the usual way," Pete said, looking troubled. "There is no death notice."

"How about illness... like a coma?"

"I didn't think of that." Pete turned back to his computer and searched, but turned back more disgruntled. "I need a better system to hack into medical files. He could be anywhere under an assumed name. I'll keep looking, but it could take time."

"You did your job with a body, could he be doing that? Did he look solid?" Kimmy asked.

"We didn't get very close," I said, thinking back. Andrew's image flashed into my memory as he stood arrogantly laughing in my face. The lights of the stadium were on. I saw the dots of light through him, but his cloud of dark spirits blocked most of the other lights. "He was a spirit. Either his body is dead, or it is uninhabited."

"What was his Grandfather like?" Derek asked. "I know horrible, but did he have strength?"

"No," Kimmy and I said together.

"He could barely walk!" Kimmy added. "He shook all the time and he stunk! I remember that smell! My mother kept putting herself between him and me. She said she did not trust him. That he was as close to pure evil as she had ever seen."

"Astute woman," Derek said. "So, he wasn't destroyed when he killed the Gatekeeper, but he was weakened."

"*He* killed the Gatekeeper?" Kimmy gasped.

"That's what Andrew claimed," I said.

"To what end?" Pete asked. "He killed the Gatekeeper and the world filled up with ghosts. What else happened?"

"Quite a few power shifts," I said. "Technology has sky rocketed. I suspect that he was too weak to do what he wanted. He must have taught Andrew how to do whatever he is doing. I wish *my* Grandfather had done the same."

"Can you teach 'good or evil'?" Derek asked. "Is it not a fundamental part of your being?"

"I don't know," I said. "I never believed that the world was so black and white. It is not logical."

"Which is why you are a Humanist!" Kimmy smiled. "But this year has shown us that things are not always what we grew up to believe. Now, you are going to have to defeat evil."

"Defeat evil," I sighed. "Defeat evil. But how?"

"What do you have that he does not?" Pete wondered.

"The Power of the Gate." Derek said.

"The key," Kimmy added, "though we don't know what it does."

"Does it do something?" I asked, automatically reaching up to my neck. As usual, the key was cool to the touch. I needed to know if it could do something other than stay with me.

CHAPTER 19

"Is there something I can do that no one else can do besides send people to the Gate?"

"You can slow time," Pete said.

"Well, yes, but..."

"That's right. *I* can't do that," Derek said. "I've been around a long time. I would have enjoyed that sometimes."

"But isn't that part of the Gatekeeping?"

"Not really. Before the old Gatekeeper shed his body, he could for a while. I remember watching it. Then, he stopped doing it a short time before he lost his body. He could travel with a thought, but he did not slow time. He did his Gatekeeping in Real Time!"

"During a war? That's crazy!"

"The deaths would be close together, like in a battle or...," Kimmy said from behind Pete.

"Or a prisoner camp..." Pete finished, looking disturbed. "The ability to travel would let him keep up, but why give up the power over time?

"I don't know." I shook my head in frustration. Funny, I just noticed that my hair was back to my normal colour, but it was bouncy and curly almost as much as Kimmy's. Silly, the things you think about when you can't think of a solution to your problem. "I wish I could talk to Gramma. *She* would know."

"When did she die?" Derek asked.

"When I was nineteen. She suffered from Alzheimer's for a year or so, but she had a heart attack before she got to the point where she didn't know me. It was a blessing, but I miss her."

"Have you crossed her over?" Derek asked.

"No. I haven't seen her since she died...!"

"I wonder why not?" Derek muttered. "This may be really bad."

"Why? What are you thinking?"

"You are the only Gatekeeper, but you are not the only person collecting souls. If that Andrew Rat has been collecting them since he was young, he could *have* your grandmother too! And so many others..."

"I don't understand what he is doing to them," Kimmy said.

"He is draining their energy and leaving them in a cloud of darkness. I could not see any individual souls in the darkness, if that is what is happening. Could you Derek?"

"No. It just seemed to be a shadow. That shadow pulled away from *you* and would not touch you, but it did try to touch *me*. It has some kind of magnetism that draws more souls into it. It is very hard to resist."

"So what do I do now?" I was feeling very vulnerable by then.

"Use what *you* have that *he* does not," Kimmy insisted. She looked ready to do battle herself! "You once said that you could move faster than *any* ghost. That they cannot run from the Gate. So... send that cloud to the Gate!"

"But, I didn't see any individuals to send!"

"Then send them en masse!"

"She's right, sort of," Derek said. "We saw the outskirts of a darkness. If you went into the middle of it, you might see something different."

"All right. If nothing else, I could learn more. Information is power."

"I think you should practice an escape route first," Pete suggested.

"An escape route? What do you mean?"

"When Kim was too afraid to move, she spent time in the locket. She could run there in an instant. No matter what happened, she went there on instinct. You need a safe place to go to and you need to go there on instinct, without a thought."

"Pete's right! Derek said. "I never thought about it, but he's right. Who's wearing the locket now?"

"I am," Kimmy said, pulling it out from under her shirt. "It still gives me feelings of love, protection and safety. You should both go there. Then Pete and I just have to protect the locket."

I agreed. I thought about making myself small, so small that I could fit into the tiny space. As I shrank, Derek took my hand and shrank with me. Together, we popped ourselves into the locket.

Maybe, because I was still so new to the spirit world, I could not think of myself without thinking solid. I kept my form, still in my pretty flowing costume. The inside of the locket was strange. The inset heart that held the pictures in place formed a ledge in front of each picture. There was more space between the ledge and the picture on each side of the locket than on the ledges. Kimmy had an area on one side that looked comfortable. She had put fibers from the paper into the tip to cushion the spot into a bed. I looked up and saw that she had made her safe place at the base of my photo. I was touched that she felt safest there.

"I didn't realize how much light you gave off," Derek said from the other side. "You really light this place up!"

"Doesn't everybody?"

"No. Not so much. Everyone gives off a bit of light. Kimmy wasn't in total darkness here. She couldn't have handled that. But her light was a candle. You, my dearest, are a spotlight!"

"A spotlight?" I was so startled with his description that I almost overlooked his term of endearment.

"Well, it looks like she was comfortable," I said, reclining on her soft spot.

"Now, we need to make this *your* place."

"*Our* place," I interrupted. "I would not have made it this far without you Derek. I want you as safe as I am. We *are* in this together, aren't we?"

"We are." His voice got husky as he leaned over to kiss me.

Making love in a small, comfortable spot is a good way to make the spot your favourite place to be. In spite of my great sense of urgency in facing my enemy, Derek and I took a few days to practice going to the locket. We chose several signals which would make the return automatic. Darkness was a strong one of them, but it was hard to put me in darkness. I gave off light. Derek found places in the midst of black fabric to take me to. When things were *that* dark, I went to the locket... bang. Just like that. Derek was good at finding scary situations. I don't know if he developed that reflex to retreat to the locket by himself, but he was always close when I was there. I just had to hope. Once we felt protected, we needed to find Andrew and his cloud of darkness.

When you think about where evil would reside and not be noticed, all kinds of places can come to mind. I'm sure some would think Las Vegas or one of the gambling cities. Others might think Hollywood. I suspected that those spots were too obvious. Andrew Rat was a nasty piece of work, but he was not stupid. If he was going to hide anywhere, it would be in an unusual spot.

As usual, when I felt confused and at a loss in the spirit world, I turned to the ghosts who were gathering around me no matter where I was.

"Have you seen the dark cloud?" I asked the crowd.

"Yes, from a distance," a well dressed woman said as she came closer. "I got a really bad feeling from it, so I went the other way."

"Good for you! There is a bad man doing really bad things in charge of that cloud. I think I am going to have to do battle with him."

"He is too strong!" the woman said, shocked at the idea of a battle. "What if you lose? What happens to us then?"

"I would think it would be the same as it was before I started doing this. He is malevolent, but he can't have everyone."

"Have you not seen the decline of human society? The wars over religion? *That* is coming from him!"

She was sincere, albeit, in my mind, misguided.

"There have been wars over religion for as long as there has been religion. He has not been here that long!"

"Someone has!" a man behind her said. "I like to talk with people. I've talked with many who explored the world. There has always been that dark, festering cloud. Sometimes it is larger, sometimes smaller. It is growing right now. Those who go too close, never come back. Ever."

"Which means I need to stop him," I said. "Everyone has the right to cross over through the Gate to whatever it is that happens next! He does not have the right to interfere with that!"

"Maybe not the right, but he has the power!" the woman said. "I was a long ways away, but I felt the pull. He has a stone. It is what traps you. He has the power over the stone."

"But how can I find him?" I asked.

"Will you let us through the Gate before you leave?" the woman asked, letting her fatigue show.

"Of course! That is my job! I will always do my job first!"

"He goes to the places where people are dying, like hospitals, hospices, care homes. Sometimes he doesn't wait for them to die... he just takes them."

"How do you know this?"

"Some people are stronger than others. I met a young man who described it to me. He told me that he barely got away! The dark man was angry and chased him for a while. That was years ago. He didn't have so much power then. Now... our only hope is to run and, if we are lucky, find you."

This group of souls believed what this woman was saying. They were nodding their heads and moving a bit closer, as if they could be protected by my presence. I wasn't sure what kind of power they held. It wasn't electric or magnetic. How could he use it? I wasn't going to get more information from them, so I went to work, sending them to the Gate.

*

"Susie, where are you?"

I heard the call from Kimmy even though I was miles away. I don't know why I could hear her except that we had been best friends since childhood. We knew each other's thoughts. We could finish each other's sentences. A bond like that is special. I went to her immediately, letting a small crowd of ghosts follow me.

"What's wrong, Kimmy?" I asked, popping into view right in front of her.

"I may never get used to that!" Kimmy squeaked. "Never mind. I've thought about it and I know where the Rat must be *right now*! There was another earthquake in Haiti last night. The death toll is horrendous. You have to go there for those people, but I'd bet anything that he is already there capturing people."

"Oh dear! All right. All my dreams of visiting the Carribean did not involve buildings flattened into rubble. The survivors will be having a worse time than those who died."

"Unless the Rat gets them first."

"You're right. Derek! Are you around?" I was gratified at how quickly Derek responded to my call. It was reassuring to know how much he cared.

"I'm here," he said, popping into view beside me. "What's up?"

"There has been an earthquake in Haiti. I need to go there. The Rat is probably already there. What is my best route to get there?"

"We will go together. Bye Kimberley. Take care of the locket. I will take care of her." He took my hand and we soared above the world.

As we approached the island, we could see the clouds of dust still rising from the rubble in the capitol city. Any building over one story had been flattened. We could also see a black cloud sitting amid the debris of the slums.

We sank to the ground, standing off to the side on a pile of rubble.

"Derek! I'm having a hard time telling which ones are ghosts and which are alive! They all look so devastated!"

"We need to go somewhere that living people can't. Then the ghosts will come."

That sounded logical, but when we stood on top of the smashed Palace Dome, very few ghosts came to us. They stood back out of my reach.

"What's wrong?" I called. "I am the Gatekeeper! I can help you cross over to the other side! Why won't you come?"

"My baby is alone!" one woman cried. "There is no one to take care of her!"

"And my sister!" Another cried.

I heard the messages from so many. They could not leave until they knew their families were safe.

"But what about that dark cloud?" I asked, pointing to the murky area hovering over the worst of the slums in the city.

"Oh, we don't want that either!" A gray-haired old man said, shaking his head violently. "You must know, Miss, *that* man wants to take us away without giving us a thing! We lived the life of the righteous and we *will* go to our reward. *You*, you look like an Angel. I believe God sent you to help. I do not believe God had anything to do with *him*. He can talk all he wants, God *is* with us. He will protect us."

"Okay. So, at least, you're not going to *his* trap. What can I do to help you?"

"Wait for us! Help them find our bodies and make sure our families will be all right! *Then*, we will come to you."

"All right. I don't know if I can influence the living, but I *do* have to

deal with *him*. He will steal the children if he can."

"Our faith is stronger than him!" An elderly woman insisted.

I hoped she was right. I turned to look at the dark cloud. It hovered over the Cathedral. I could tell from where I was on the Palace that the roof had collapsed into the Cathedral, leaving the walls in place. Did he think the ghosts would go there to pray? He didn't understand the extreme poverty of the country if he thought that. These people held their religion in their hearts far more than in a church. They formed a church just by going to a spot together and praying. From my point of view as the Gatekeeper, I was impressed by the strength of faith in them, before *and* after death.

I took Derek's hand and we flew toward the darkness. We went over the heads of the people in the street and were gratified to see so many aid workers, there to help the survivors.

At the edge of the darkness, I peered into it and watched the behaviour of the people, living or dead, who were near it. Somehow, no one touched it. I knew the dead were convinced that the cloud was evil, but the living gave it a wide berth too. I don't think they were consciously staying back. There was enough trouble to make them stay away from the tall walls of the Cathedral, but there were similar walls down the street where people were climbing over the rubble to find the bodies.

I stepped into the shadow. It pulled back, away from me, but not before I sensed another presence, different from Andrew Rat.

"What is it?" Derek asked.

"Someone else. Over there." I pointed to the other side of the strongest wall left standing. Cautiously, I approached the building and entered through a window opening that had once held a beautiful stained glass window. Shards of red and green glass still glittered in the beams of sunlight where the black cloud could not stop them. On the other side of the wall, even though the roof had completely caved in, the darkness took over. I could not see beyond the edge of my bubble of light. I had to use my other senses to find my way to my enemy. Sadly, it wasn't that hard. There was a stench coming from the front. I went towards it, staying in real time, but ready to move in an instant.

I actually got within 10 feet of Andrew Rat before he noticed me. He had been talking to or arguing with a huge black man.

Andrew Rat, Derek and I were in the ghost plane of existence. From what I could see, this man was still alive. He had symbols painted all over his body with some kind of white paint. His skin was shiny with oil or sweat, but the symbols did not run. Maybe they were tattoos. Seeing him, I realized that there were aspects in this society that I had overlooked. He was clearly a practitioner of voodoo. I know of the good, healing arts of voodoo, but this man connected to the evil side of voodoo. Some people choose evil.

As long as I exist, I will never understand that.

"Who are you?" He bellowed at me. "What do you want?"

"She is a nosy do-gooder. *She* can't stop us," Andrew Rat sneered.

"I am the Gatekeeper," I said calmly, ignoring Andrew Rat's words. I still watched him carefully. "Many people have died. They need my help to cross over into the Light."

"There is no light!" the big man sneered. "Can you not see? It is only dark."

"Maybe for you," I responded. "But people have a right to go to the next level. You have no right to interfere."

"That is what you think!" He lifted his hand and pointed at me. Tiny pieces of rubble rose into the air and flew at me, as if they were swarms of insects.

I expected this stuff to go through me like all solids would, but they didn't! They hit and stung me like thousands of bees. I could feel the stings in my skin and the poison in my blood. I heard Derek slapping the stuff away, so I knew he was feeling them also. I had to stop it. I grabbed Derek's hand and stepped up my time response. Everything around us slowed down so we could step out of the path of the stones. I pulled Derek behind me as I went up to the two men. I stopped right in front of the big man, put my hand on his wrist and let time return to normal as I pushed his pointing finger towards Andrew Rat. The stones flew at Andrew Rat, putting him in a situation where he was too busy avoiding the bombardment to notice what else I was doing.

"What do you think you are doing?" I said in the man's face. "What is your purpose? What do you want?"

"Revenge!" the man roared. "They come in and take over our lives and tell us what to do and how to do it! Every time we blink, they are here!"

"Who?" I asked.

"Outsiders! The Bosses!"

"What Bosses?" I was confused.

"There are always Bosses! How did you do that?"

"I'm fast. Outsiders have come here to help the people after the earthquake. They are not Bosses! They bring food and water and medicine! What is wrong with that?"

"We can do it ourselves! I will stop them!"

"You *cannot* do it yourselves! There are too many injured and dead. It is *your* people dying. They need help!"

"Death is not the end. They will go on." He sounded adamant.

"Not without *me*, they won't!" I yelled. "They need to go through the Gate!"

He wrenched his wrist out of my grasp, ready to hit me. "That does not matter! They will do as *I* say!"

"Do what?" I quickly sidestepped the massive fist that could possibly hurt me. "What can they do?"

"They can go into the earth and make it move, so the sacred buildings of the outsiders are broken into bits." He looked in confusion at his fist and at me standing out of his reach.

"You *caused* the earthquake?" I gasped. "To demolish buildings? That makes no sense! You have *killed* these people! Your people!"

"I am here on the altar of their God saying I can destroy you! They forced their God on us! I proved him impotent. He could not stop me!"

"*Missionaries* forced their *religion* on your people, not God! But your people all around this ruined city are singing hymns in prayer to God. *Their* God! *Their* spirit is strong and their belief will see them through. All *you* have done is kill a lot of people! Your own people! You are not strong. You are pathetic."

Both of his fists came at me from the sides. I stepped away from them easily. This man was dangerous. I don't know how he controlled all those spirits, but I knew I couldn't let him go on. I reached out to his passing arm and sent his spirit to the Gate.

"What have you done to me?" he screamed. "You can't touch me! No God can touch me!" His body collapsed at my feet.

"Well, I'm not a God and I did," I said, dryly, watching his spirit being pulled toward a very dark place. It swallowed him up, but the dark cloud continued around me. I looked at Andrew Rat.

"What did you do?" he screamed. "He was to be *mine!* They *all* were! As soon as I had *him*, I would have them all!"

"How would you *get* them?"

"I have a signal. They come to the sound. They have no choice!"

"You won't get them here," I said looking around. "You create a cloud of poison that they *won't* enter. Their religion will keep them stronger than *you*. You may as well give up now."

"Give up? I don't know how you dodged his fists, but you can't dodge mine!" He pointed at me and I saw a ripple of energy pushing through the air towards me.

Derek, who still held my hand, yanked me away and in an instant we were in the locket.

"Whoa! That was quick!" I gasped. "Your reflexes are faster than mine!"

"I was waiting for it," Derek grinned. "Either he has no better arsenal, or he relies on the one talent above others. If all he can do is push you around, we can use it against him."

"We need to know how he traps the souls," I muttered. "And we need to get all those poor people out of his reach. Let's go find a park."

We went back. The city was big. There had been over three million people living in the city itself. Badly built buildings had collapsed everywhere, leaving rubble and bodies behind. The stench of rotting bodies was becoming the biggest horror to those left alive. I found a small grassy area that had once been a small park. I stayed still and waited. Derek stayed beside me, watching for any sign of danger.

Before long, the ghosts started to come to me. They looked like they had been in a war. Some had broken bones, unfixed of course. Some had gaping wounds. They looked tired, as if trying to find and protect the living was no longer important to them. Some appeared to feel the pain of their wounds. They no longer resisted coming to me. My guess was that the Voodoo man had influenced them before he died. Now they were free to follow their own hearts.

I started to send them to the Gate. After I touched them, the wounds and dirt went away. They went into the Gate as the people they were when alive. I think that was the biggest encouragement for the rest of them. They wanted the damage erased from their self image when they moved on.

I slowed time and worked hard. I encouraged people. I grieved for families smashed apart as violently as their buildings. I do not like having to send babies to the Gate, but when I did, the sight was beautiful enough to almost make me believe in God. Fortunately, that particular belief was not necessary for me to do my job to the best of my ability.

After a long space of time, I don't know how long, the crowd of earthquake victims dwindled to nothing. I was ready to leave, but Derek pointed out something strange coming our way. It was the other ghosts. The ones who had been caught and forced into service by the Voodoo Priest. They walked as if they were zombies with their their heads held down, stumbling their way towards me. They stopped a distance away from me, looking fearful.

"Come closer," I said. "It is time. You can go to the Gate now."

"What we have done," an old man broke. "We don't deserve going on."

"You were *forced* to do something. Did you *want* to do what he said?"

They all shook their heads in horror.

"Well then, he was strong, but he is not here now. You do not need to fear him or obey him anymore."

"Where is he?"

"He went to the Gate. It sent him to a dark place. Now you can go and rejoin your families. They are waiting for you."

I think that was the key. Family is very important to these people. They moved towards me and I worked hard again. There were not as many in this group. They were the ghosts from the time period after the last gatekeeper was destroyed. So far, their afterlife had been awful. I was relieved to see the Gate as a bright white light for most of them. By the time the last one had crossed over, I was tired, but content.

"What have you done?!"

Derek grabbed my hand as we both looked around for Andrew Rat.

"How could you *do* that?"

I saw Andrew Rat standing on top of a stone staircase that was left behind after the building collapsed. It looked appropriate that he would be on stairs that lead to nowhere.

"It's my job," I said coldly.

"But they were *mine*!" he screamed. "They had enough anger and hate to keep me powerful for a long time! There were so many! How did you do that so fast?"

"You're asking *me*? Consider it a job secret. Come closer Andrew Rat. It is time for *you* to cross over. I can't guarantee that you will go into the light, but you *will* go somewhere."

He was thrown off-guard trying to figure out how I worked so fast. He didn't notice that Derek and I had moved to the base of the staircase and were quietly moving up. I was being careful not to slow time too much in case he did something that I couldn't protect myself from. I was almost within reach when he noticed that I was there.

"*No!* Not happening!" he shrieked and disappeared.

"Well, well, well," Derek said softly. "*We* sent *him* running! I didn't expect that!"

"Neither did I! Let's go back to see Kimmy and Pete. Maybe they have learned something to help."

CHAPTER 20

"Sue! What happened? Are you all right? You looked terrible!"

"You're looking a bit off-colour yourself, my dear," I grinned. "What's wrong? Morning sickness?"

"Yes," she sighed heavily. "How could you tell?"

"I think it is the shade of green, wouldn't you say Derek?"

"Umm... you know, ladies, back in my time, nobody talked about such things. They were considered..."

"Private?" Kimmy guessed.

"Unclean?" I added. "Aha! The look on your-face tells the truth! I'm glad I didn't live in your time. Women died from having babies! Babies are what our bodies were built for! It *should* be as easy as breathing!"

"Well, sometimes *that* kills too," Derek said defensively. "I can't help when I was born and since I died, I have watched the dead far more than I watched the living. So, I don't know that much about life."

"It's all right, Derek," Kimmy smiled at his embarrassment. "We are teasing. What happened in Haiti? Why do you both look like you swam in an ash pit?"

I looked over at Derek and down at myself. Kimmy was right! We were covered in dust and grime. "Why is it sticking to us?" I asked him.

"Because when we walked through it, our minds could not separate the image from our reality. There was too much grime everywhere. We just have to think it gone."

We both thought about how we looked the night I gave my body to Kimmy. The dust and dirt went away, but, unexpectedly, it fell to the floor in the tiny kitchen area of the Bus.

"Wait! What did you do?" Kimmy shrieked, grabbing a broom. "Isn't this dirt supposed to be on a different plane? How did you drop it here?"

"I don't know!" Derek said. "This has never happened to me before! Could Andrew Rat have caused this?"

"How?" I was upset to think that Andrew Rat had any influence whatsoever in my existence.

"I think we should have this dirt tested," Kimmy said. "If he can push energy, maybe this is the residue of that push. Or maybe he can push solid objects." She took an empty jar from the cupboard and gathered the sweepings into it.

Funny, I felt less solid than ever, looking at the tiny stones and dirt gathered in the jar.

"Where's Pete?" I asked. "Where are we?"

"Don't you know?" Kimmy asked. "You came here from somewhere else, didn't you?"

"I came to you. I pictured you in my mind and here I am, looking at you. So, where is here?"

"We are in California!" Kimmy grinned. "They are auditioning to find a cast for the movie. I have met some really amazing people! Pete is staying in the background, though. He says it is my show."

"So where *is* Pete?"

"He went out to explore this morning. He should be back soon."

As if on cue, a taxi pulled up to the bus and Pete got out. He looked very upset.

"Pete! What's wrong?" I asked.

"Wrong?" Kimmy reacted. She rushed to the door to help him in.

"We didn't do our research," Pete said, rubbing his jaw.

"Research about what?" Kimmy asked, peering at the bruises forming on his face.

"Chris Remington," Pete said, wincing when Kim touched his eye. "We knew he was an unsavory character, but...."

"But what? Who did this, Pete?" Kimmy was getting frantic. "We need to call the police!"

"No... not that. That would be worse. I don't know what he did! He might be wanted by the police! *I* might end up in jail!"

"Jail!?"

"We *know* he committed murder at least once. I think those guys were loan sharks. They said something about fifty thousand dollars by tomorrow or I will swim with the fishies."

"Fishies? They said fishies?" I butted in.

"They said fishies. They weren't too bright. I don't know how they recognized me!"

"Maybe when we changed your look, it was back to what he had when he was here," Derek suggested. He looked worried.

"We have to change it again!" Kimmy shrieked. You aren't that man! We have no way to get that much money that fast!"

"How did he get in debt?" I asked. "Did he gamble?"

"Apparently," Pete nodded. "He liked to bet on horse races. I guess he lost a lot of the time."

"Most gamblers do," Derek said dryly. "Otherwise it wouldn't be gambling. So why don't we gamble with the boss and win?"

"Win! How can you do that?" Kimmy sounded frantic. She kept one hand protectively over her abdomen as she spoke.

"I can move things!" Derek said, lifting a spoon off the table and spinning it in the air. "Most bets are made around a physical event happening, whether it is the roll of the dice or the speed of a horse, I can make you a winner."

"But...." Pete shook his head and then grabbed it in pain. "I've never gambled in my life! I don't know the rules!"

"It's simple," Derek said. "You put some money on a longshot and Sue and I make sure *that* horse wins. Okay?"

"It sounds dangerous," Kimmy said. "Can't we just run away?"

"No!" Pete said. "These bruises are because he ran! Right to the opposite side of the country! The only way out of this is to settle with them!"

"All right, when and where?" I asked.

"Tomorrow morning at the racetrack," Pete said. "They told me to be there with the money or else."

*

Pete insisted that Kimmy stay home, but she would not listen. Her fear was genuine. The only person at risk was him and if something happened to him, she wanted to be there. Ultimately, we convinced Kimmy that putting the baby at risk was not her decision. She agreed to stay home and wait for our return.

At the racetrack, Pete went to the betting area where Derek and I met him.

"Are they here?" I asked.

"Who?" Pete asked. One of his eyes was swollen almost shut and the other was red and bloodshot.

"The guys that beat you up! Have you looked in the mirror today?"

"I've tried to avoid that," he said, looking around. "They said they would be here at noon. I need the money by then."

"Okay. We need a horse that is a longshot. Derek, do you know what all those numbers mean?"

"More or less. There is a horse in the first race that no one thinks can win. The odds are sixty to one. Go to that booth and put all your money on Longshot to win. Stupid name for a racehorse! How much do you have?"

"We could only get one thousand dollars at such short notice. Will it be enough?"

"If we do it right. Go quickly. Sue and I will check out the horses."

We watched Pete make the bet. The man behind the counter openly laughed at him. He shrugged, putting his ticket in his breast pocket and went to the stands to watch the race.

"Derek, I don't know anything about horses."

"That's all right, they don't know about you either. Here's Longshot. Good lord, is this really a horse?"

"What?" I looked in the stall at the animal. I could see why he said that. It just seemed out of proportion. The back legs looked longer than the front legs and the head looked too large for the neck. The horse looked straight at me, its nostrils flaring and eyes widening. "It's all right horse, I won't hurt you."

"Hey lady! What are you doing?"

I turned and saw a gathering of ghosts coming my way. "Hello," I said cheerfully. "I am the Gatekeeper. I can send you to the Gate, so you can cross over into the light."

"That's nice, but what are you doing to that horse?" One short man asked rather belligerently.

"I guess I am scaring him," I sighed. "The thing is, I need him to win this race or a friend of mine will be murdered."

"Win? Him? It ain't gonna happen lady," another man, dressed like a jockey said. "Not unless all the other horses run backwards. He was entered on a joke."

"What if I helped him win?" I asked.

"How could you help?"

"Umm... I could ride him and that would scare him into running fast."

"I could slow the other horses down," Derek offered from beyond the growing crowd of jockeys. "They seem to be able to sense us."

"No!" Several of the ghostly jockeys gasped. "Someone will get hurt! The rider or the horse! You can't do that!"

"Oh dear, you are right," I said, thinking out loud. "But the only way I can stop Luigi Petroni from having my friend murdered is if he wins big on a race to pay off his debt."

"Petroni? He is trouble! He does bad things just for fun. He has forced several of us into throwing a race for him. Those who didn't cooperate with him are over there."

The small man pointed at a small group of jockeys who looked miserable. They kept their distance from all the other jockey ghosts, looking afraid to come closer.

"He killed you?" I questioned.

"Well, he had his goons do it," one older man with a slight accent agreed. "You don't want to mess with him, Miss." They all nodded in agreement.

"That's no problem!" I laughed. "I am the Gatekeeper! He can't kill me! He can't even see me. He won't know what happened until it is too late."

"You really want to do this?" The first jockey asked. When I nodded, he went on, "if you can get Longshot to move down the track, we can make the others slow down. Horses can see us. They know *us* better than they know their owners *or* riders. Some of the riders have sensed us. They know there are ghosts here."

"How do they know that?" Derek asked.

"When we are right beside them or touch them, they get icy cold. We have fun with that. There's the bell."

The horses were led out to the starting gate, jockeys already perched on their backs. I knew I would have to wait until the last second to get on or the horse would freak too soon. I climbed the railing and stood right beside the jockey, ready to swing my leg over.

"Oh no. We don't want no ghost here!" He muttered, looking a bit wild. "Why are you here ghost? I don't want no ghost."

The light went on and the gates opened. I jumped onto the horse behind the jockey and held on tight. The horse freaked out. He turned his head and looked back at me as if to say: 'get off of me', so I kicked my heels into his ribs. He bucked, trying to get me off, but he wouldn't win if he didn't have a rider. I smacked his rear and shouted at him. "Run you stupid animal! Go!"

He did go, with a lopsided gait that made hanging on a challenge for me and the jockey. *He* was still babbling about ghosts. I looked over at the other horses to see how far ahead they had gotten. They were trotting down the track in a dance that looked exactly like the Canadian RCMP Musical Ride. They crossed the track back and forth, in a well choreographed sequence. It was beautiful.

Longshot finally got the momentum to pass through the line of horses to take the lead. We were halfway around the track. He was sweating profusely, his eyes bugged out and his nostrils flared. I could feel his heart beating through my legs. I was beginning to fear that he would have a heart attack before he reached the end.

I looked at the jockey to see if he could help the horse along, but he just sat there, eyes closed, hands loosely holding the reins, shaking and denying the presence of ghosts.

Looking forward, I saw the guy with the black and white checked flag. We were on the home stretch. Longshot was slowing down! The other horses were catching up, even though they were still dancing around the track. His gait was lopsided and choppy. Every step connected my butt with his.

"Go Longshot!" I yelled. "You can do it!" But it really didn't look like he could. Longshot kept bouncing toward the finish line. "Darn it horse! Have you ever heard of a glue factory?" I said in frustration.

I have no idea if he understood or not. All I know is that he sped up again and gave it his all. The last sprint to the finish held all the excitement you could ask for.

The next horse crossed within a second. It had been the favourite to win. Behind it, one at a time, the other horses crossed the line, nose to tail.

The crowd was going wild. People were screaming in the stands. I floated up off the horse, hoping he would calm down enough to prevent a heart attack. He was walking with his head held high. Somehow, he understood that he had done well in the race.

I joined Pete in the betting area.

"They say it's not possible!" Pete said. "The officials are trying to decide whether to allow the results, considering how strangely the horses behaved! This may have been a really bad idea."

A group of men came in the door, the one in front obviously the boss. I thought he looked more like a caricature of a mob boss than a person. He wore a dark suit with a white silk scarf around his neck. The Fedora hat on his head exactly matched the suit as did his shoes. I expected to see spats over his shoes, but he left them off. His entourage consisted of four beefy men dressed in cheaper looking dark suits that gaped where their guns would be holstered.

The room was filling with people, most of them upset about the race, a few cheering because they had made a bet on the longshot. Petroni walked straight to Pete and his men surrounded them, keeping the crowd at bay. The crowd, sensing something was happening, became quiet, almost holding their breaths.

"Christopher! You owe me money! Where's my money?" Petroni said loudly.

"Here is the betting slip from the race." Pete said quickly. "It is worth sixty thousand. Take it and let me go."

"The race? You call that a race? Somebody interfered with those horses! We put that horse Longshot in on a joke! He can't run! I must say though, it did look funny! How did you do it?"

"Do what?" Peter allowed himself to looked confused, but he was being wary. Two of the goons were in easy arms reach of him. Things could go bad really quickly.

"How did you make the horses dance around the track instead of run?"

Pete stepped forward and sideways and turning, took Petroni's arm and started walking them out toward the track and the next race.

"I have a special gift," Pete said confidentially to Petroni, as if he was divulging a deep secret. "I can see and hear dead people."

"Dead people? Waddya mean?"

"Their spirits, or ghosts. There are places that they like to go to. You know, to hang out. I guess it can be pretty boring, being dead."

"Yeah. So what good is it to talk to the ghosts? What can *they* do?"

"They can sit on a horse and scare it enough to run faster than it ever had. They can take the bridle of the other horses and walk them wherever."

Pete had walked them out into the open air, away from the crowd of innocent bystanders.

"So ghosts threw the race for you? Then they can throw a race for me! I want Sea Breeze to win!" He looked around glaring, as if he could see the gathering crowd of ghosts.

"Why would we do that?" A short aggressive man hissed.

"They ask why they should do that?" Pete said.

"Because, if you don't, I'll kill your buddy here!"

"Oh dear," Pete said, pretending to be more upset than he felt. "They are laughing! Most of them are saying *you* caused *their* deaths. I'm assured that it would be better to be dead than under your thumb. Personally, I would prefer a third option."

"That is?" Petroni asked, glaring ominously.

"You convince the officials that the race was won. It wasn't Longshot's fault that the other horses wasted their chance. Then, you cash in the ticket here and collect all that I owe you. After that, you let me go and our paths need never cross again!"

"Why would I want to do that?"

"Because you are being haunted. The ghosts have decided that you and your goons have bullied your way through life enough. That time is over. That sensation you have that you can't breathe? They are doing that."

Petroni was clawing his face, trying to pull the invisible hands away from his mouth and nose. I was standing right next to Pete in case the goons moved too fast. One of the goons pulled out his gun, pointing it straight ahead, as if he could kill a ghost. I pulled Pete sideways, out of the path of the bullet.

"Ma ha mph" Petroni yelled as his goon pulled the trigger.

There was chaos as the bullet slammed into Petroni's shoulder. One of the other bodyguards shot the first, even though both their faces were turning blue. Pete looked at the ghosts and asked them to stop for now.

"Why should we? He deserves it," they were all saying.

I stepped in, "because I am the Gatekeeper and I will send you to the Gate. You don't want to go to the light right after killing someone do you?"

A few of them crossed themselves and backed away. A few seconds later, the five men were breathing easier, but they were shaking and looking around wildly.

"Boss, I didn't mean to!" The man that shot him whined. "And Charlie shot me!" He was cradling his right arm as blood oozed between his fingertips.

Petroni was still clearheaded enough to assess the situation. He looked into Pete's eyes with only a flicker of fear in his own.

"*These* ghosts will cross over to the light soon," Pete said. "They don't want to stay here to interfere with you. But me? I am always surrounded by ghosts. They want to talk to me so they can send messages to loved ones and all that crap. Things have changed. Christopher Remington is gone, never to return. I, on the other hand, don't gamble. Wouldn't it be better to leave it at that?"

"All right, Christopher or whatever your name is. We have never met. None of us were here today. I'm sure I will never see you again. Boys, let's go."

They left the same way they came, as if they owned the place. Who knows, maybe Petroni did own the racetrack. He did seem to think that winning that race was personal.

I had the usual crowd of ghosts around me. I sent Pete to go home in a taxi while Derek and I sent everyone to the Gate. It's odd. I don't think I had run into a crowd of ghosts so predominantly male before. The few females appeared to be cashiers or prostitutes. A few of the jockeys looked female, but they kept their disguise. I wondered what the Gate would do with them, but it just opened to reveal the light and their faces showed the joy. When we were done, we went back to Kimmy.

"Where's Pete?" We both asked.

"He's supposed to be back here by now!" Derek said, looking worried. "Wait." Derek left and returned in a flash. "Sue, come with me," he said, grabbing my hand. "We'll be right back, Kim."

He took me straight to Pete who was laid out on a stretcher barely breathing.

"What happened?!" I gasped.

Derek looked bleak when he told the story. "They waited for him to be away from the ghosts... us... and they just machine-gunned the taxi and sped away. The taxi driver was killed instantly. Pete... he wants to be alive so badly...."

Everything around us lurched to the side, making me realize that we were in an ambulance, sirens blaring and a medic monitoring Pete's vitals.

"Pete?" I called quietly. "Pete, can you hear me?"

"Sue?" He mumbled without opening his eyes.

"That's right Pete. How bad is it?"

"It's bad. Worse than before. I can *feel* this."

"Sir, try not to talk," the medic said. "Save your strength for healing."

"Tell me what is damaged," Pete gasped.

"From what we can see, your internal organs are in a bad way from bullets. They will have to operate." The ambulance lurched the other way and Pete groaned from the pain. "There appears to be damage to your spine. We have you on a backboard to protect you. Don't try to move. Don't worry sir, we can fix you up."

"Susie, tell Kim...."

"Pete, *you* will tell Kim. I will not leave you alone. I will help you just like you helped me!"

Pete coughed and specs of blood sprayed over him and the medic. He breathed in once and his whole body relaxed, the air whistling as it passed out from his blood-filled lungs.

The ambulance came to a screeching halt and the rear doors opened. People grabbed the stretcher, pulling it through me, to take it into the emergency room. I followed them. Pete stood beside the bed watching their frantic efforts to bring him back to life.

"Pete! Aren't you going to try?" I asked.

"I did try! There is serious damage in that body! I would never walk again! There are two bullets in the spine! One grazed the heart. It won't last longer. I tried. Now I have to go back to Kim like *this*!"

"All right, let's go see her," I promised. "Derek! Are you all right?"

"I'm all right," Derek appeared in the hallway. "There was no way a person could have survived that barrage of bullets. They wanted to make a lesson of you Pete."

"Or at least a lesson of Christopher Remington. I wonder if it will work?"

"I'm sure something about it will work," I said dryly. "But Petroni is the one who needs a lesson! He can't run around killing people like that!"

"According to the jockeys, that is *exactly* what he does every time his will is crossed. The world around him is too frightened to tell the police. He just kills everyone who crosses him." Derek looked stormy.

"What do you want to do about him?" I asked, seeing the anger in both.

"He must be stopped!" They both said.

"All right, he can't hurt any of us now. Let's go see how he lives."

He lived in a mansion that he upgraded to a fortress. The house was made from huge stones, protecting the interior from assault. The windows were small and could not let much light or bullets in. The yard had two massive walls surrounding the property. The outside wall was decorative as well as functional. Between the walls, there was a deep moat and then the interior wall was topped with glass shards and spirals of razor wire. It would be impossible for anyone to enter the grounds without being seen or eaten by the pirana fish in the moat. The wall and grounds were kept under constant surveillance with a series of video cameras pointed every which way. I don't think we were observed as we floated over everything to go to the house. We found all of the men together in the large living room.

This scene was one that looked eighty years out of time. Petroni, the boss, was lying on the table while a doctor bent over him with various surgical instruments. He was trying to remove the bullet, but Petroni was still awake.

"Ow Doc! That hurts! Can't you just freeze it or something? Hurry up!"

"Relax Mr. Petroni! I've almost got it! You know this would be better done in a hospital. I don't have all the drugs you need. We are lucky I have antibiotics!" He pulled the bullet out of Petroni's shoulder with long bloody tongs and dropped it into a nearby vase. "All right, now we just stitch it up!" As he happily stitched Petroni's shoulder, I went over to the goon who had also been shot. His arm had been hit in such a way that the bones shattered. It would take a skilled surgeon with a passion for jigsaw puzzles to put the bones together. He was sitting on the sofa, cradling his arm and rocking. His pain must have been excruciating, but he did not speak. The doctor finished Petroni and went to check the man's injury. "This man must go to the hospital. I cannot fix it."

The man looked relieved.

"The police will be called and they will come back to me! No way!" Petroni said.

"We can say it was an accident, Boss," the man said plaintively.

"Bernie, an accident like that could break us! The cops would flood the place."

"But, I'll tell them I was home alone, at *my* place! It didn't happen here! I'll just go..."

Petroni wasn't going to let him leave, so I poked the crime boss in the shoulder just as he was going to say something. "Ow! What was that?"

"What?" The doctor asked, coming back to him.

"Something poked my wound!"

"Nerves were damaged," the doctor said, reassuringly. "It will take them time to reconnect the way they were."

"Who's he trying to bullshit?" Derek said.

"Petroni," I answered. "Derek, go over there and make loud noises. I want to know if they can hear us." I pointed to the wall beside a huge fireplace.

Derek stood there and started to shout. "Hey, morons! Wake up! You! Shit-for-brains, I'm talking to you! You flap your gums, but can you really talk? It sounds like a mouth full of excrement to me!"

I watched each of the people in the room to see if any of them could hear Derek. Pete was the one who saw that the goon that had shot Ernie flinched at Derek's words.

"Ah hah!" Pete said, "what's your name, asshole? You can't hide from us!"

"My name is Mac," the man said it clearly but quietly. "They already think I'm strange, I don't want it to get worse!"

"I need to talk to them," I said. "You are going to say it to them."

"No!" He squawked.

"What's wrong Mac? Were you hit too?"

"No Boss. It's just...."

"Out with it, man! It's just what?"

"The ghosts are back! Including Christopher Remington! It was a mistake to shoot him, Boss!"

"What do you mean they're back? Can you see them?"

"Not exactly, Boss. I can hear them!"

"Hear them? What are they saying?"

There was a loud booming sound that reverberated in the room. It became silent as if everyone was holding their breath. A column of smoke appeared in the center of the large room, drawing everyone's attention. Inside the smoke, a figure appeared. It was Andrew Rat!

"What are *you* doing here, bitch?" he spat.

"I could ask you the same," I snorted. "But this *is* the company you would keep."

"Mr. Petroni has provided me with many of my strongest allies," he said, sneering at me. "We have a cooperative thing going on here. *You* will not interfere!"

He raised his hand to push me away the way he had the first time, but I was ready for that. I moved sideways, letting the force of his push hit Mac in the chest and whamming him into the wall.

From the corner of my eye, I saw Derek take Pete's hand, ready to leave quickly.

"Where are you going, boys?" Andrew Rat asked, turning towards them. "I have something here that will interest you." He pulled a jewel that was set on a chain like a pocket watch, out of his vest pocket. It looked like a huge black diamond, but the darkness in the jewel moved and swirled as if it contained a life of its own.

I could see that both Pete and Derek were drawn to the stone. They reluctantly moved closer, Pete's hand reaching to touch the thing.

"Pete! Don't!" I yelled. It was a distraction, but did not stop them. Before they reached Andrew Rat and his stone, I moved in Quantum Time to put myself between them and him.

"Why are you doing this?"

"I will do anything I want!" he cried out, angry that I interfered. "I am a *God*! Don't you know *that* yet?"

"If you are a God, then what am I?" I asked, pushing the two behind me back a few steps.

"You are a lesser God," he snorted contemptuously. "Much lesser. You will learn not to interfere with *me*!"

Again he tried to push me, but I reacted faster than him. I spun around, grabbed Pete and Derek's joined hands and retreated to the locket. Leaving them, I returned to Petroni's living room in a different spot, behind where Andrew Rat stood. He did not notice me and the others could not see me, so I stood quietly, watching.

"Who was that?" Petroni gasped. "What did you do to them?"

"I threw them away," Andrew Rat snarled. "I have the power to do whatever I want. Remember that!"

I think he believed that he had done something to us. He wasn't looking for me. I could use that to my advantage.

"What do you want from me?" Petroni asked nervously.

"I want you to do another job for me."

"A job? I dunno," Petroni said, shaking his head fearfully. "We got a lot of pressure from the Heat the last time. They work harder when we knock off important people. The only reason we got off, is they couldn't figure out why I would want those guys gone! After today, they're gonna watch us again!"

"It's because of today you must do this!" The Rat screamed. "I want her! I want her and her abilities to stop interfering in my plans!"

"Her who? I didn't see no her!"

"No, but she was there, and she was here! She lives in the spirit world now. She has the power to move superfast! I want to know how she does that too!"

"Who is she?" Petroni asked in awe.

"She calls herself the Gatekeeper." the Rat snarled. "She sends spirits to the Gate, out of my reach."

"What's the Gate?" Petroni asked suspiciously.

"The Gate! You know: The Pearly Gate. The place you go in order to cross over to the other side. She's the only one who can do that!"

Petroni crossed himself revealing his Catholic upbringing. "Do you think it is a good idea to hurt her? People *need* to cross over. My mother, bless her soul, passed away last year. She should be in heaven, growing a nice rose garden. She loves roses."

"I'm sure your mother is fine," the Rat said quickly. "But, think about *your* life! It is the Gate that decides where you go. Do you really think you would be in the same place as your mother?"

"The priest always said...."

"Priests don't know everything! Bad deeds follow you after death! It would be better to use your power to help take over *this* world! Then we can do anything we want!"

"So what do I do?" Petroni asked.

"I have another stone," the Rat said. "If I can get close enough, I want to trap her in it!"

"But how can I help you? I can't even see her!"

"I want you to use all your contacts to find out where her friends are and what they are up to. She never left that other girl all through school, they still have to be together now."

"That won't work," I said from behind the Rat.

He whirled around looking panicky. "You're back!"

"I can move faster than you," I said, sidestepping another energy push from him. "You don't have the right to steal people's souls for your own purposes. What happens to them in your stones?"

"What, your Grandmother didn't tell you? Oh right, she died, didn't she. They stay there forever, lost in a darkness where they have no power left and no way to leave." He was smirking as he drew a fist sized gem from his pocket. The facets reflected the light except for the face directly aimed at me. It was a dark matte black that swirled and moved within the stone. I could feel the pull from the stone. It took all my effort to wrench my eyes away before he struck again. Again, I sidestepped his push.

"Is that all you can do?" I asked, wondering if I could provoke another ability in him, to see what I was up against.

"No!" he shouted, frustration and maybe a little fear starting to show. He pointed his left forefinger at me and a bolt of lightening burst forth.

"Oh dear, you broke Petroni's nice piano!" I said from beside Petroni who was shaking beside the smashed instrument. I couldn't tell if he was shaking in fear or anger. Personally, I would have been angry. The piano had been nice. "I told you I could move faster than you." Petroni was sweating into his blood stained, expensive suit.

"I will get you!" the Rat cried out, rushing towards me.

"Not today. Stay away from me and my friends!"I left for the locket long before he reached the spot.

CHAPTER 21

"Where did you go?" Derek asked immediately.

"Back. We have to talk with Kimmy. Come on."

I pulled Derek and Pete, who was reluctant to come out of the locket and face Kimberley.

"Kim, we're back," I said heavily.

"Did it go all right? Did the horse win?Could you pay off the debt? Where's Pete?"

"I'm here Kim," Pete said quietly. Looking at him, I saw his original look and heard his original voice. I only just realized that I had missed his voice after he changed his body.

"Oh no! Pete, what happened?"

"The mob does not like being made to look silly. We should have thought of that. They left the racetrack, but when I left, they shot up the taxi really badly. The driver and Chris Remington were both killed before they could make a statement. I must say, this time hurt a lot more than the first time. I did have time to decide the results."

"You chose this?" Kim croaked, her voice choked with tears.

"Sweetheart, I love you more now than ever. If that body could recover, which I doubt, I would have been a quadriplegic. I will not accept that. Not when I could be with you like this forever! That way would kill me sooner."

"Oh Pete. What am I going to do now?" She held her hands protectively over her barely swelling belly.

"You are going to move," I said firmly. "That Rat thinks that he can get to me through you. He has told those mob guys to look for you. We have to hide you. *You*, in the meantime, have to do what it takes to protect yourself and the locket while you are in hiding."

"You mean with guns? You want *me* to handle a *gun*?"

"They killed an innocent taxi driver to get to Pete, just because they were mad about the race. They are vicious killers. I won't have that happen to you again! We have to protect our body!"

"I won't leave her," Pete assured me. "I will practice lifting and throwing solid objects. We will do this!"

Kimmy drove the bus to the movie lot where there was more security. With Pete's help, she described the mob guys to the Security Chief and went to talk with the producer of the movie. Pete stayed with her, but I went with Derek, looking for a hiding place where Andrew Rat would feel safe.

We went straight up, looking for the cloud of darkness. With so much smog and pollution hovering over the city, it was difficult to separate. Some really dark clouds enveloped chemical storage lots. What we saw were the parts per million of the chemicals leaking out over the ground in the area. Living people could not see them. Probably they could smell them, but money and politics make the rules far more than consideration for the safety of the people. After going to the fourth of these places, I felt frustrated.

"We are looking in the wrong places!" I cried out. "Where could he go and feel at home?"

"I would say a Mental Hospital or a Jail," Derek suggested. "People there are really dark themselves. They have no expectation of going into the light."

"True. Or a place for the Criminally Insane! I remember one of those in Saskatoon. I wonder where they are around here?"

"Kimmy can find out. Locket."

That was our quick signal to go to the locket instantly. After leaving the locket, we found ourselves in a comfortable apartment with its own washroom, kitchen, entertainment systems, computers and anything else a person might need.

"Wow, this would be considered a really nice bachelor apartment back home," I said, peeking in the well-stocked fridge.

"It is cozy," Kimmy agreed. "Samantha wants me to stay here until we know I'm safe. When I told the producers that Luigi Petroni was after me, they got worried. He must be powerful in these parts. Anyway, what can I do for you?"

"We need to know where the criminally insane people are kept around here."

Kimmy tried to find something in the phone book but just ended up with a list of many hospitals. She went to the computer and found a list of Mental Hospitals for all of North America. Shortening the list, we headed first for Patton State Hospital in Bernardine County, California.

It did not take long for us to believe that Andrew Rat was indeed hiding there. The dark cloud around the buildings had to come from more than just the insane people living there. The internet search revealed that the turnover rate associated with that hospital was unmatched by any other place. After two or three years of treatment or therapy, murderers are let out on the streets again. At that point, I would guess that some of them might believe they could go to the light when they die.

I was eternally glad that I didn't have to make *that* choice.

"All right, what are we looking for?" Derek asked, landing in front of the massive old doors.

"We want to find any object associated with his abilities."

"You mean like your key?"

I put my hand to my throat, fingering the key. "Yes, like that. I think his diamonds or gems or whatever they are, are like it. The one he traps people in. But I wonder if there is something he cannot carry easily hiding here."

"Like a trunk?"

"Yes! A trunk or briefcase or even just more stones. There has to be a reason for his darkness to be here when he is not."

"He's not here? Are you sure?"

"Yes. If he spent more time here, I would have goosebumps all over my arms.... It's been like that since grade four. Let's see what we can find."

The first thing we found were a few very timid ghosts.

"Hello," I greeted them. "I am the Gatekeeper. I am here to help you cross over into the light."

One of the ghosts backed away from me looking seriously frightened.

"What is it?" I asked. "Are you afraid of where you will go?"

He nodded agreement, keeping distance between us.

"If you help me, things may go better for you," I suggested. "I need help."

He nodded and smiled. I began to realize that for some reason, he could not speak.

"Do you know Andrew Rat?"

His eyes widened in horror and he backed further away.

"I am *not* his friend!" I said quickly. "I must *stop* him! He is doing terrible things to people after they die!"

The little man stopped retreating, but he looked worried.

"Does he leave things here?" I asked. "Like a trunk or suitcase?"

The man nodded. His eyes were not still while he looked at me. He appeared to be trying to see everywhere at once. I could tell that he was trying to make a decision. Before I could guess more, he beckoned to me to follow him. He took us up ever narrowing staircases to the top of the old building.

Looking back, I saw all the ghosts in the place following, single file. We could have floated up through the floors, but trudging up all the stairs seemed to be some kind of rite of passage to these people. The higher we went, the brighter they looked. By the time we were all in the dusty attic, the place's ghosts looked young and happy, ready to go to the Gate.

All except the old guy who led us there. He seemed to be shrinking in on himself. He was very jumpy but still could not say a word. He pointed to a medium sized wooden chest that glowed in the darkness of the attic. Then he squared his shoulders and stepped toward me, ready to move on.

I reached out to him and sent him to the Gate. I think everyone there held their breath, waiting to see what the Gate would do to him. Fortunately, the light was pretty average in brightness. All the other ghosts lined up, silently demanding that I send them to the Gate as well.

It did not take long before Derek and I were alone in the dusty attic with the strange chest. It was carved from one piece of light coloured wood. The finish had turned the wood into a golden colour that reminded me of Kimmy's natural hair colour.

But this wood glowed in the darkness of the attic. I examined it closely to see if there was a lock or latch to open it. All I found was an indentation along the back for the hinges. The wood was carved into figures of people. I stared at it for a while before I realized that the people were carved as though they were trying to escape from the box, climbing on top of each other, all of them with a look of agony on their faces.

"This is not a pretty box," I mumbled, reaching out to it.

"Be careful!" Derek warned. "He may have traps in there!"

"I am quite sure he has," I said, lifting the lid. It was strange. Many of the figures were cut through, but the separating line was a jagged edge and all of the figures came apart at the neck, leaving them headless and gruesome. Inside, the chest had many of the large gem stones like the one I had seen him holding. Some of them were dark with a swirling smoky black cloud inside. A few had only wisps floating inside of them and one was flat black. It looked dead. I felt tight bands around my heart just looking at it.

"Can we take these?" I muttered checking the chest.

Derek reached out, trying to take one of the stones out of the pile. His hand passed right through the outside of the stone, but when his fingers touched the dark core, he stopped.

"I'm stuck!" He cried out. "Sue, it's pulling me in! I can't get away!"

He did not panic, but he was obviously afraid. I'd never heard that in his voice before. I moved quickly.

I grabbed his hand and reached instinctively for the stone to push it away from us. For some reason, I could hold the stone in my hand. I lifted it and pulled hard. With a strange thwock sound, Derek was released.

I held the stone, watching the black swirling cloud. It looked agitated. Angry maybe.

"We have to get out of here," I said. "I've got a feeling that he is looking our way.... I know! I still had Derek's hand. I lifted the carved chest under my other arm and got us away from there.

"Where are we?" Derek asked, looking around at a desolate landscape.

"Hawaii," I said smugly. What better place to deal with diamonds and stones than a volcano?"

"It looks as desolate and damaged as Haiti," Derek shook his head. "Without the devastated people. What are you going to do with those things?"

"There are people trapped in there. I have to try to get them out!"

"How?"

"I don't know." Still holding the stone, I put the chest down on the ground beside us and concentrated on the swirling black clouds. "I can feel the pull and the attraction, but I can resist it. It feels like sticky clay that clings to everything that touches it."

"Can you sense the people there?"

"Not as individuals. They are stuck together and I can't reach them through the stone. *You* can reach into the stone, but it was too hard to pull *you* back, let alone others that might stick to you. I think we need to smash the stone."

"Smash a diamond? Can you do that?"

"Yes. They are not as strong as everyone thinks," I said, looking up at his worried voice. "I had a girlfriend a few years ago who found her fiancé cheating on her. She took the diamond and smashed it into powder. He had to finish paying for it for seven more years! We were so scared that he would smash her face in, that I helped her to move away."

"What did she use?"

"A hammer." I looked around at the rocks strewn near our feet. Most of them looked like compressed volcanic ash or glassy lava. I saw a lump of something that looked different so I went to pick it up. My hand passed through the rock. "I can't do it!"

"Of course not," Derek grinned. "It takes a lot of practice to pick things up when you have no body. Let me try."

Derek picked the fist sized rock up easily and brought it back to the chest at our feet. "Now what?"

"Normally, we would wrap the diamond in a handkerchief or something to protect ourselves from the shards of the hardest substance known to man. Can you imagine the damage *they* could do?"

"It would be bad. I'm glad we don't have *that* problem anyway. Which one do we start with?"

I held up the darkest stone with the swirling black cloud inside and placed it on a flat area of the cooled lava. Derek hefted the heavy rock above it and smashed it into the diamond.

I don't know what we expected, but we were not prepared for what happened. A great burst of light flashed out of the stone and a wind whipped around us like a tornado. Dirt was swept up and sent whirling away. The wind moved back from the center, making an enlarging circle that in a few breaths slowed down. I could see the swirling darkness separate into individual people. They looked confused. I could tell from their clothes that Andrew Rat or, more likely his grandfather, had trapped them just after the Second World War. They milled around, bumping into each other as if they couldn't see what they were doing.

"Hello people!" I called, trying to get their attention. It didn't work. Waving a hand in front of a face didn't work. Feeling under pressure to deal with them quickly, I reached out to the nearest, a woman, and sent her to the Gate. That got their attention. They stopped moving and stared at me. One woman opened her mouth. I expected a scream. The look on her face read like a book of terror, but not a sound came out. Others, who may have comforted her in another time, looked like they would scream with her. The lack of sound was unsettling.

"I am The Gatekeeper," I said clearly, filling the silent hole. "I can help you. You can go into the light. It is time."

I saw relief on some of the faces, confusion on others. A few, like the screaming woman, did not seem to comprehend what happened to them at all.

I decided that she was probably the best person to start with. I stepped closer and touched her. The Gate was almost too bright to look at, but everyone there looked anyway. The woman floated gently toward the Gate. By the time she got there, she had stopped screaming. I think her look was eager anticipation or relief. I don't know. But the rest of them wanted to go there too. They crowded around me, pushing me in their eagerness. I slowed time. I didn't know I could feel claustrophobic from ghosts before that.

"Wait a minute!" I cried out after I moved from the center of the group to the outside. "You will all get your turn. Just give me some space! I guess your voices were taken away with your energy. If any of you can tell us what happened to you, please do. In the meantime, each of you *will* be able to cross over into the light."

I would guess that there were a hundred people trapped in that diamond. I don't think any were famous. They looked like ordinary people. The light from the Gate was quite bright for all of them. One man waited to be last, but when we gave him the opportunity to speak to us, he still had no voice. He shook his head, shrugged his shoulders and stepped up to be sent to the Gate.

"Wow!" Derek said quietly. "That was strange."

"Right," I sighed, feeling drained, "but we must go on.... I am concerned about what we will find in *that* one." I pointed to the flat black stone that looked so dead.

"We have to be careful. If you feel in any danger at all, don't wait for me. Go to the locket. I will get there too, all right?"

"All right. Let's do it."

I positioned the strange jewel and Derek hit it with the stone. The first one was amazing, but this... this was scary. When the stone hit the jewel, there was a bright red flash like a spark. Then there were many more flashes as if it was one of those huge starburst fireworks balls to go up in the air and burst into several layers of bright stars. Except this happened on the ground all around us. Some of the bright flashes flew through us. It didn't hurt, but I felt it.

Each bright red spark coalesced into a person. They gathered into groups as if assessing the situation. Then, before I could move, they converged on me. They pushed me to the ground, getting me on my back. I tried to slow time, to get away from them, but I was pinned down by their weight. I felt a sharp rock in my kidney. It was as if their touch made me more solid.

"Wait!" I cried out. "What are you doing? I am the Gatekeeper!"

They started to drag me over toward the lava flow.

"Derek!" I screamed. "Go! Get Pete! Get help!"

I looked into the crazed eyes of the person hovering over my head. The rage was so powerful, it made me feel sick to my stomach. I had never been so frightened in my life. I felt the heat from the lava as they pulled me closer. I didn't know if it would hurt me or not, but I didn't want to find out like that. How could they do this to me? I was *rescuing* them!

There was a huge sonic boom and a wind that blew the heat over us. By then, I was terrified. Was that Andrew Rat, come to trap me too? Whatever it was, it got their attention.

"What are you doing?" A familiar voice boomed loudly. It was Pete! He was a quick thinker.

"We will destroy anyone who traps us like that." I couldn't tell if it was male or female, it was so full of hate.

"She didn't trap you! She *released* you! Let her go!"

"She has the key! We ken what that means! She stole it from its rightful owner!"

"*She is* its rightful owner! She is the *Gatekeeper*! Let her go!"

A murmur went through the crowd around me. All I understood was the repetition of the word Gatekeeper. The rage still flashed in the eyes of those that I could see.

"I can help you," I said, trying to stay calm. "I can send you to the Gate to cross over into the light."

"No!" The one above me roared and backed away from me.

As if responding to an unspoken message, they all backed away from me, out of my reach. Except one. This man grabbed my right arm, hauled me to my feet and held me with my right arm painfully twisted up by back.

He knew what he was doing. I used my right hand to send people to the Gate. With him holding me like that, I couldn't send anyone anywhere.

"I do not believe thee!" He snarled. "This is what that witch, the one named Rat, told us before. Rather than the doorway, we were imprisoned with these heathens! Dost thou have any idea how many seasons have passed?!" His eyes looked black to match his clothes.

"When did he trap you?" I gasped, trying to pull away.

"The year of our Lord sixteen hundred and ninety-two. How did that Son of Satan enter our Holy Place? It was Consecrated ground! How did that *THING* trap our souls?"

"I don't know! Let me go! You are hurting me!"

"Thy pain is justified!"

"*No it is not!*" Pete bellowed loudly, a clap of thunder following his words. "You are hurting the person who *freed* you! *Let her go!*"

The man reluctantly let me go and stepped quickly out of my reach.

"Why don't you want to go into the light?" I asked. I knew, now that I was free, that I could use Quantum Time and send all of them to the Gate before they could flee, but I needed to know why they didn't want to go. "Were you bad in your lives? Did you do things that would send you to darker places?"

"What a thing to say to us!" a shrill voiced woman said from behind the Puritan man. "We were good God-fearing people! We should have gone to the arms of our Lord on the day we died!"

"So it is way past time!" I urged. "You can go now and find the peace you have missed out on." I guess I'm not as persuasive as I thought. They all stepped farther back, looking stubborn. "What are you going to do, then?" I asked, confused.

"We will hunt that son of a jackal down and destroy him."

"Then we are on the same side," I said. "I must stop him! You can help! We can work together."

"What can thee do to a devil like him? Thee are a small and weak female. *We* will go. For an eternity we have planned this. Do not try to stop us!"

They popped out of my vision quickly. I could do no more for them. I looked around and saw Derek and

Pete looking worried. I climbed away from the lava flow, rubbing my arm. "Thanks guys. That thunder got their attention. How did you do that?"

"Pete has been playing with clouds and weather while Kimberly is busy with the movie," Derek said, taking my hand to look at my arm.

I expected to be bruised all over. I did not expect blisters popping up as if something had burned me. "But his touch wasn't hot! It was cold! So cold, I can still feel the ache of it up my arm and across my back. I don't understand."

"I think we need to find out more before we break another stone," Derek said.

I picked the chest up and went back to Kimmy, to do more research.

CHAPTER 22

We arrived back at the bus to find Kimmy sitting at the small table writing. I slid into the bench opposite her to relax. It is silly really, when you don't have any muscles, how can they be tired? Perhaps the whole tired muscle thing has always been in my mind. I don't know. I set the chest on the table so I could brush the hair from my eyes. I opened it so we could all look at what we had to deal with.

"What are they?" Kimmy asked.

"You can see them?" Pete asked eagerly.

"Yes. Why not? Aren't they real?"

"Oh they're real all right," I said. We told her about our adventure. She looked proud that Pete rescued me. She seemed to know where he was, perched on the opposite countertop. "Kimmy, can you see him?" I asked.

"Sort of," Kimmy said, looking guilty. "I guess it comes from the whole being dead for a while, and your body could see them and all. I don't see everything, but Pete is kind of long and skinny now..."

"Can you see Derek?" I asked.

"Pretty much. It's like looking at them without your glasses on. They are a little fuzzy and it is hard to catch the details, like eye colour and such. I'm just glad I can see them now."

"We all are!" I laughed at the look of relief on Pete's face.

"I'm getting confused on who can do what in our group," Pete said, rubbing his nose. "Derek can move heavy objects and can see almost anything, but he can't pick up these gems, right?"

We all nodded.

"Can he touch the key?"

"No!" Derek answered. "My fingers go right through it the same as the gems."

"And the picking up of anything else is...?"

"Practice," Derek grinned. "I spent some winters in the Yukon. The caribou were having problems in one area crossing a river. I moved enough rock and stones for them to cross more easily. It worked. It's still there. People say it's a natural formation."

"So I can learn that?" Pete asked.

"Definitely," Derek agreed. "Can you teach me that thunder trick?"

"Right! What did you do?" I butted in.

"Well, I can't lift much, but I can blow hot and cold air around. If you know how weather works, it's not that hard. Timing is hard though. I was lucky today. I wouldn't want to rely only on that."

"It is a good distraction," I said. "It got them off of me."

"That's good, but I can't lift anything else. Not rocks, not these gems and not the key. How about you Kim?"

"Me? Well...." She reached across the table and lifted the key from the spot around my neck. "Maybe it's because it used to live here on this neck." She put her hand to her own throat.

I was getting to the point where I had forgotten that her body used to be mine! I was totally comfortable the way I was now.

Kimmy put her hand over the gems and touched one with the tip of her finger. She jumped back as if she got a jolt of electricity.

"What is it? Are you hurt?" Pete asked.

"No, no, not that. I felt the strangest thing there! Halfway between seeing and hearing. You don't want to break *that* one without protection!"

"What did you see and hear?" I ask earnestly.

"I saw an image of people crammed into a space like sardines in a can. They were moving aimlessly, but that seemed to make it worse. What I heard was a scream that seemed to come from all of them. It was bad."

The stone she touched was black with minimal swirling going on. Not as bad as the Puritan stone, but almost. I pushed a smaller diamond towards her. This one was almost empty. It looked like a huge diamond, too big for a ring, except there were wisps of smoke moving slowly through the center.

Kimmy took a deep breath and held it while she put her finger on the stone. "Oh, this is different! Like I know these people! How can that be?"

"Where's a hammer?" I asked.

Kimmy went to a cupboard where Pete pointed out the tools we have. She came back with a hammer and a handkerchief. "Should we be doing this in here?" She asked. "You said it is like a tornado when they get out."

"Right. Outside!" Pete insisted.

We went to the parking lot beside the bus. Kimmy put the stone in the handkerchief and placed it on the ground. "Here goes," she said, drawing in a lung full of air. She brought the hammer down hard on the lump.

I heard the diamond crack! I felt the air expand out as if a compressed air cylinder broke. There was no hate or anger so there was no tornado. Just a feeling of warmth and love in my heart. I watched the smoke coalesce into forms. The first came towards me.

"Gramma! It's you!" I felt overwhelmed. I knew she couldn't have been to the Gate, but, in my heart, I hadn't considered the thought that she might be trapped by Andrew Rat or his grandfather. I burst into tears.

"Susie! Sweet Susie don't cry!" She came and put her arms around me. "What happened to put you in this state? Are you all right? Are you the Gatekeeper now?"

"How did you know?!"

She pointed to the tiny key around my neck. "That and your light. You are as bright as Gabriel Snow!"

"Gabriel Snow?"

"Your grandfather, dear. The old Gatekeeper! He was a good man."

"But... but.... Kimmy can you see this?"

"I see it. But Sue, look at the others."

I looked at Kim, who was kneeling on the ground looking up, big eyed, at the small collection of ghosts. Looking at them, I almost joined Kimmy on the ground. My knees felt weak. I was looking at a group of people who where the nearest and dearest to Kimberly and me over our whole lives. Her parents, my mother, a favorite teacher. Some people I didn't recognize, but Kimmy seemed to.

The people were moving around aimlessly the way they did in the diamond as wisps of smoke. They seemed to be unaware that their circumstances had changed.

"Gramma, what's wrong with them?"

"Oh, after a while, you sort of go to sleep in that place. How did you free us? Did you use magic?"

"No. Kimmy used a hammer. How do we wake them up? They can go to the Gate now."

"The Gate," my Grandmother said with satisfaction. "I had almost given up hope. The Gate might wake them. I can't imagine anything else working."

I approached several of them calling their names. Nothing. So I reached out and sent one woman that I did not know into the Gate. The light was bright and beautiful. It shone down on all of us and for the first time, I heard the beautiful ringing of bells. The ghosts right in front of me came out of the trance that held them. They turned and stared at me.

"Hello, I am the Gatekeeper," I said. "I have freed you from captivity and will send you to the Gate so you can cross over into the light."

"Susie?" My mother said in confusion. "My little Susie, is that you?"

"Yes Mom. I'm here."

"Why are you doing this? Did my mother force you into a non-life like this? This isn't living!"

"Force? Nobody forced me anywhere! What is wrong with being the Gatekeeper?" I could feel familiar arguments rising between us. Her resentment toward her mother never ended. "Mom, do you want to go into the light? It *is* time."

"Into the light? Yes, of course I do."

Before she could say: "but...", I reached out to her and sent her to the Gate. "Goodbye Mom."

The other ghosts, quietly watching us, came closer. Kimberly stood beside me, ready to talk to them if they wanted to. None did until her mother stood in front of her.

"Kimmy, sweetie, I don't know why you are in Susie's body. You two shared everything, but this...? But you *are* beautiful! You look happy. That's all a mother wants for her child. I love you always."

"I love you too, Mom," Kim said, happy tears running down her cheeks. "I didn't get to say goodbye to you! It wasn't fair!"

"Of course it wasn't. That person who trapped us, caused the accident. He must be stopped. He is pure evil. Be very careful my sweet girl."

"I will, Mom."

"Goodbye sweetheart."

"Goodbye Mom."

I took the cue and sent her to the Gate. I could have predicted that it would be beautiful. She had been very kind to me growing up. "Okay, Gramma, that's all of them. Do you want to cross over too?"

"Actually, I don't," my grandmother said to me, stepping back. "I didn't get a chance to explore the world before or after I died. I want to see gardens."

"Gardens?" I remembered the plants she always had in her home and yard. They grew so well for her! "But, don't you want to help catch the guy who trapped you?"

"Oh no, my dear. I have complete confidence in you. You are much stronger than you realize. Just remember, don't look into the diamond that he is holding. Once you look, he has you. And he is very good at getting you to look. I know! He got me!"

"All right. But Gramma...."

"You can call if you must. I will come back to see you once in a while. Maybe when it's not so crowded." With that, poof, she disappeared.

"Oh boy," Kimmy went into the bus and sat in her favourite chair. "That was so... emotional. I don't even know how to feel right now."

"Personally, I'm angry," Pete said. "The number of people trapped in those stones, unable to rest, unable to move on... no closure! It's just wrong!"

"I agree," Derek said, beside Pete. "We have to stop him."

"All right," I said, appreciating their renewed resolve. "We just have to figure out how. So far, it has been cat and mouse. We need to trap him. It's a given that he will show up whenever there is a disaster. He could even be creating the disasters. But, *we* can't create a disaster to lure him in. People would be hurt."

"So we have to predict faster than him," Kimmy agreed with me. "Yikes! Who are *they*!?"

I looked back and saw a group of ghosts poking their heads into the bus through the walls and windows. "Doesn't the salt work anymore?" I asked Kim.

"The hose got caught on a sharp thing coming into the parking lot. It was ruined. Obviously, I need to replace it."

"And in the meantime, I do my Gatekeeping job," I said.

I went out to the parking lot, accompanied by Derek. The ghosts who were hanging on to the bus, followed us, but they looked like they wanted to talk.

"It has been a long time, waiting for you," one woman said pleasantly.

"Yes it has," I agreed. "I am so sorry that happened. I do hope that something like that does not ever happen again. But I'm here now. You can finally cross over to the light."

"Not yet," she said, holding up a finger. I suspect she had been a teacher in life. "We made a… life? No… activities for ourselves while we waited. We joined groups or formed new groups and toured the world. And we have conventions."

"We?"

"We who are dead and waiting."

"Why are you telling us this?" Derek asked.

"Because you want to catch the Rat man," she said, as if teaching a slow learner. "Everyone on this level knows about your battle now. Many of us want to help."

"All right," I said, smiling. "So you have conventions, which everyone knows about?"

"Not every one. Each group has its own way to invite newcomers and share information."

"Derek, why didn't you know about this?" I asked.

"Because he is a loner," the woman answered before he could. "The loners do not want companionship. They do not talk to others unless it is necessary." She didn't look or sound judgmental, she was just stating a fact.

"I think Derek is joining a group now," I smiled.

"You never stop growing and maturing," the woman nodded. "It's all good."

Derek looked a little embarrassed. "Okay, so what do you have in mind?"

"You want to trap that Rat person. There is going to be a convention in the Grand Canyon. There could be a lot of us out there if we put the word out."

"All right," I said nodding. "But if he is stronger than me and defeats me, you are in danger!"

"We're willing to risk it, to have you doing your job," the woman shrugged.

"When you put the word out to go there, also tell people not to look at or *in* the stones he carries," Derek suggested. "That's how he traps them."

"Thank you. We will. We will be there at sunset tomorrow."

"I'll see you then," I agreed.

The whole crowd of ghosts disappeared, not wanting to go to the Gate quite yet. We went back in to tell Kimmy the development.

"Sunset? Why sunset?"

"Because sunset in the Grand Canyon is spectacular," Derek answered. "They must be thinking that win or lose, this will be the last sight they have before they cross over or are trapped. They want it beautiful."

"That makes sense," Kimmy agreed. "But what will you do to fight him?"

"I will be in Quantum Time. I will move faster, think faster, be faster and I will catch him. But, Kimmy, in the meantime, Petroni has orders to hurt you. We need to protect you."

Kimmy agreed! Usually she would shrug off her own dangers, but she had our baby to think of and she would not risk it. She went to the head of Security at the movie studio and got help. They already had her in an apartment on the lot. Living quarters were there for various important people's needs. Usually, stars who were avoiding cameras, but the security people were prepared for anything. They focussed their own cameras and patrols around her apartment. Then, we had nothing to do but wait. Wait for ghosts to want to cross over again; wait till the end of the next day; wait for the quiet to pass.

CHAPTER 23

It was early in the afternoon when the shadows started to creep across the base of the magnificent canyon. Derek came with me and Pete stayed with Kimmy to keep her safe.

We joined the gathering crowd of ghosts, hoping to blend in and go unnoticed for a while, but I had to stand in the sunlight for my own light not to show. After a while, the ghosts started to sing to drown out my music.

There was an eerie calm waiting for Andrew Rat to show himself. I kept looking into the eyes of the people around me and was reassured by their smiles and nods of encouragement. We felt the tension build.

It really did not take as long as it felt. A loud crack of thunder and flash of lightning heralded Andrew Rat's entrance on the scene. He chose to stand on a pile of rocks that put him above everyone who stood on the canyon floor. Those along the walls of the canyon had a clear view of him even though the canyon was a mile across.

"Hello people!" Andrew Rat called out pleasantly. "What a beautiful day to meet like this. It's almost as if we planned it this way, isn't it?"

The crowd cheered! He acted like *he* had called the meeting and gave them the good weather for it!

"As much as we can appreciate the great beauty of this place, aren't you wishing for more? Don't you think it is time to rest?"

A large number of the people responded with a cheer!

"You have waited too long! You had to watch everyone you love live their lives and go on without you! As if you were never there! To *them* you are forgotten." He put a sad look on his face. "The time has come for you to rest. You don't deserve the neglect you have received from your God and his minions! You don't deserve the indifference you get from your religion! They lied to you! They said: "go to the light!" But where is this light? It was a lie! I'm telling you now that I can send you to a place where you can sleep. You don't have to watch the living go on without you. You can be at peace with the world."

The crowd cheered! The sound bounced off the canyon walls growing stronger as it went.

"This is so wrong," I said softly to those around me. "It is time."

"All you have to do is look into this gemstone. Admire its brilliance. You will go where you can rest forever."

"You lie!" I called to him.

"Well well well," he said, as if he had something bad in his mouth. "Little Susie LaMarre. I do not tell lies."

"You said they could rest. In your stones, there is no rest, only aimless wandering, constantly bumping into each other. A feeling like sardines in a can where the claustrophobia can overwhelm you and yet you cannot get out! So you scream and scream but the only ones who can hear you are just as trapped as you. Don't listen to him!"

"Who are you?" Some of the nearby ghosts asked.

"I am the Gatekeeper! I can send you to the Gate where you can cross over into the light."

"What Gate?" Andrew Rat cried out. "In sixty-five years, there has been no sign of a Gate!"

"Because *you're Grandfather* destroyed the last Gatekeeper! *My* Grandfather! Did you really believe that no one else would be able to do his job?"

All I heard was murmurs from the crowd. The tone could have been for or against me; I wasn't sure.

"Destroy someone as powerful as the so-called Gatekeeper? How could I possibly do that?"

I saw his muscles twitch. He was going to do something. I grabbed Derek's hand and went into Quantum Time. Amazingly, Andrew Rat still moved quickly. I barely had time to sidestep the thrust of energy he sent at me. Unfortunately, the ghosts behind me were not so lucky. They were slammed into the canyon wall like rag dolls. I moved to an area above the crowd so he could leave them out of the argument.

"You keep hurting the innocents," I said, moving toward him.

"*I* do not hurt them," he snarled, losing his look of composure. "*You* hurt them. *You* move out of the way instead of protecting them!"

It was a silly argument, but I could see a few battered people agreeing with him.

"Andrew Rat, it is time for you to stop trapping people in your stones! They need to complete their path in *this* life so they can move on to the next."

"There is no next!" He yelled, pointing his hand at me again.

This time, lightening shot from his palm and hit me in the left shoulder. It also hit Derek in the chest. The force ripped our grip apart. Derek ended up on the ground surrounded by the ghosts who were trying to help us. I saw what Andrew Rat was about to do, nano-seconds before he did it. Even I couldn't move fast enough to prevent it.

With a movement of his hand, he scooped up a crowd of at least twenty ghosts and threw them directly at me! I got out of their way, but I couldn't help them when they crashed into the canyon wall. Normally solid objects wouldn't hurt a ghost. I don't know how he did it, but these people were seriously injured.

The rest of the ghosts occupying the canyon that night moved back, out of the way, in a hurry. I thought they would fly away completely, but quite a few of them stayed, maybe to help, maybe just curious.

Andrew Rat started to throw rocks at me as I moved closer. Derek deftly deflected them so they fell harmlessly to the rugged ground.

"We can't keep doing this forever," Derek said. "We are weakening."

"Don't worry," I muttered. "I just have to touch him."

"Susie!" I heard the scream from within. Glancing at Derek, I could tell he didn't hear it. It came from Kimmy.

"Keep deflecting," I said. "I'll be right back. He mustn't know I'm gone." I stayed in Quantum Time and went to Kimmy.

"What is it? Are you all right?"

"I'm okay! But look!"

We were standing in the parking lot where we had parked the bus. It took me a few seconds to realize that it wasn't there anymore. Instead, there was a large hole in the ground which was rapidly filling with water.

"What?" I couldn't take the scene in quickly enough. "Kimmy! Tell me!"

"Petroni's goons came and blew up the bus." she said calmly, but quickly. "I was safely out of it, but they're not very bright. They overdid the explosive!" She was getting frustrated at my look of confusion. "They blew up the chest of gems too! There are bits of diamond dust everywhere!" She grinned at my expression as her words sank in. "Go get him Susie, now, while you can."

Still in Quantum Time, I popped back by Derek. "Are you all right?" I asked.

"Huh? That was fast. I threw a rock at him. He seems to be weakening."

"Let's get closer," I said, pulling Derek with me.

It seemed that picking things up and throwing them were Andrew Rat's main skill. Typical for such a bully. I don't know why the rocks he threw at us could actually hit and hurt us, but they did. They hurt all of the ghosts. All I could do was dodge the big ones. I had to hold Derek's hand to keep him in Quantum Time with me, making us a bigger target, even though we were faster.

"You can't keep doing this, Andrew!" I called.

"I can and I will! I will smash you and then I will trap you and I will take your ability to change time! It will be mine forever!"

"I don't think so," I said, six feet away from him. "You are losing your strength. Can't you feel it?"

For the first time, he looked uncertain. He paused, then disappeared.

"Susie! He's here!" This time it was Pete. Derek heard it too. We went there immediately.

Andrew Rat was standing at the edge of the hole looking at the glittering ground. The shiny shards of diamond were everywhere, flashing in the sunset.

"What have you done?" He screamed at Petroni, who was on the other side of the deep hole. "You let them loose!"

"Hey, I just did what you told me to! We had a deal, remember?"

"Deal? You ruined *everything*! It will take *years* to replace those stones!"

"Stones?" Petroni frowned.

"The diamonds, you fool. My diamonds were blown up with this thing!"

"So, I don't get paid?"

"Why would I pay you when you ruined everything?"

Petroni pulled a forty five caliber automatic gun out from under his jacket and shot at Andrew Rat. Of course, the bullets went harmlessly through him, but for whatever reason, the diamonds in Andrew Rat's chest pocket were not immune to bullets, any more than they were to hammers. They broke, releasing a tornado of captured ghosts. For the first time, Andrew Rat looked frightened. His rage, however, took his judgment. He moved closer to Petroni in an instant and locked his hands around the Mob Boss's throat.

"There is no point in killing *him*," I said, moving over to stand beside Andrew Rat. Finally, I had him within arm's reach. I grabbed his arm with my left hand so he couldn't leave.

"What are you going to do about it?" The Rat snarled. "You may have released the ghosts, but I will get them back! It is just a matter of time. You can't be everywhere at once. Sooner or later, I will win."

"You have forgotten something in your greed," I said, keeping an eye on the air around us.

The parking lot was filling with the ghosts he had trapped in the diamonds. They all looked angry, ready to tear him apart. I recognized the group of Puritans from the first diamond. They were pushing to get closer to Andrew Rat.

"Yeah? What's that?"

"I am the Gatekeeper. It is long past time for *you* to go to the Gate." I reached out with my right hand and touched him. I felt an electric shock go painfully up my arm.

"No!" He screamed. "Your power is not strong enough! *I will not go!*"

We were locked in a battle of wills. The electric pain pulsed through my whole being, but I would not let go. I could tell that he was in pain also. From the look of it, I suspected that he felt something worse, but he was not strong enough to break free.

A loud crack of thunder announced the opening of the Gate. It was done. He could no longer resist. I let go of his arm in relief.

He was waiting for it. He grabbed my arm in an icy vise-like grip, letting Petroni collapse to the ground.

"If I go, you go. Turn it off," he said through clenched teeth.

"No!" I gasped. "You are done here."

We were being pulled inexorably to the Gate. Derek grabbed my other arm and Pete grabbed his. I put us into Quantum Time to give us a chance.

"Pete, let go!" I demanded. "Stay with Kimmy!"

"But...."

"I need you to take care of her!"

He did let go and moved aside, letting others take his place. The Puritans were there holding Derek firmly.

"Thee cannot take her where thee will go," the angriest one growled.

Andrew Rat looked at him as if trying to figure out where he came from.

"These are all people that you and your grandfather have hurt," I said, trying to wriggle my arm out of his grasp. "They are really pissed off at you."

"They can join me in Hell," Andrew snarled, eyeing the Gate over his shoulder.

My whole body felt icy cold. I think Derek was feeling it. It might have been spreading down the line. All I was sure of, was that Derek's hand was warm and strong, holding me in place. I was the center of a tug-of-war and I felt very stretched.

"Derek, if he drags me in, let go. Save yourself," I whispered.

"Not happening," Derek said firmly. "I promised to stick with you, and stick I will do.

It will take someone much stronger than *him* to separate us."

"Oh look! Little Susie LaMarre has a lover!" Andrew Rat announced loudly, probably hoping that the Puritans would let go. He would never anticipate what they did do.

Carefully, so they could maintain the pull on my side, they had other ghosts take their places. They moved over to Andrew Rat and grabbed hold of him. The biggest man started to pull Andrew's fingers off of my arm, bending them back painfully. There was enough of them and they were determined. At the last instant before touching the Gate, I was released.

We tumbled to the ground in a pile. I missed seeing the first flash of light from the Gate when Andrew Rat touched it. I was sure it had to be dark. As the Puritans who were still holding him passed through, it was like being on the red carpet where hundreds of camera flashes are going off all the time. Some were bright and pure, others, not so much. In a few seconds, it was done. Andrew Rat had gone to the Gate.

A calm settled over the parking lot. The ghosts had nothing to say and the living seemed to sense that something big had happened, but they didn't know what. The ghosts that helped save me, untangled themselves from the pile until it was just Derek and me sitting on the ground.

"Susie, are you all right?" Kimmy said quietly, coming over to us.

"A little stretched, maybe, but I'm all right."

I must have looked a little bewildered and lost. I certainly felt it. After all this hunt and chase, he was gone. Now what?

"All right then," Kimmy said, keeping my attention. "You will need to use Quantum Time to send all of the ghosts who that Rat had trapped in the diamonds to the Gate. When you are done, come to the apartment. You need to talk this out. Okay?"

"Okay." I had a job to do and I was good at it. It didn't matter how long it would take, I could do it. I stood up and walked into the midst of the ghosts quietly waiting for me. "All right folks, I am the Gatekeeper. I will send you to the Gate so you can go into the light."

"Excuse me miss," an elderly gentleman I recognized immediately said, coming forward.

"Mr. Einstein!" I gasped. "Sir! Yes! What can I do for you?"

He smiled a slow, sad smile, looking so very tired. "Well, you just sent a group of people together to the Gate. Why not us? If we hold hands, we should be able to go together."

"You want to share the experience?"

"We are already in groups that were trapped together for many years. Going the rest of the way together would mean something to us. And it would speed up the process. I am tired. I want to go now."

There was a murmur of agreement from the crowd. So, I made sure that each group was ready before I reached out and sent them to the Gate. In spite of their cooperation, it took quite a long time. Andrew Rat had a lot of stones in his collection.

I watched the ghosts who were so eager to pass through the Gate, they did not want to talk. Some, I recognized as famous people. Others, I knew must be, even if I did not know them. There was gratitude mixed into their sense of urgency to go to the Gate. And it was quiet.

Going to the Gate and crossing over is sometimes like a festival. It is a joyous experience for all but the really bad people. These people, good and bad, were too tired to show their joy. Andrew Rat had stolen their energy. The Gate responded by passing them through quickly, silently, as if to respect their mood. I was relieved when we were done.

"Come Sue," Derek said, at my elbow. "You need a rest."

We joined Kimmy and Pete in the small apartment where the security people had put her. She looked good. Relieved.

"Susie, are you all right?" she asked.

"Yes," I sighed. "I'm just tired. I can't believe it's over."

"It's not over, dear," a familiar voice said from behind me.

"Gramma! You came back!" I walked over to her and put my arms around her. She seemed so much smaller than I remembered, that I had to take a step back and look again. "What is it?"

"There will be *more* like that. There will always be those who use people and those who help them. You are on the right side. I am so proud of you! But, now it is my time to cross over."

"But Gramma! I need you! What do I do if...."

"You follow your heart, my Susie. If you truly need me, you can come to me and then come back."

"I can come back?"

"Of course! The Gatekeeper can go to both sides of the Gate. You will learn with time. Now, please, let me go."

Reluctantly, I reached out to her and sent her to the Gate. The light was beautiful, as was the look on her face.

"Susie...," Derek said. His voice was hesitant, the look on his face concerned. "Are you all right?"

"What? Why? We won. Isn't that all right?"

He reached up and caressed my face, wiping tears away. "Susie... your tears..."

"What about them?" I leaned back and looked at his fingers. Not believing my eyes, I wiped the rest of my tears away and looked carefully at my hands. There were several perfect opal spheres rolling together in my palms. Each was the size of a small marble. The colourful fire from them was more brilliant than any I had ever seen before.

"What is this?" I asked, setting them on the table. I didn't think I had cried that much.

"Opals!" Kimmy gasped. "How is this possible? They are exquisite!"

"What is going on?" I felt very confused.

"Perhaps this is another aspect of the powers of the Gatekeeper," Pete suggested. "When the Gatekeeper cries, she sheds beautiful jewels."

"That's just weird," I snorted. "Powers of the Gatekeeper! Really!"

"Susie, you need rest," Kimmy said, ignoring the joking around by the guys. "Go somewhere quiet and rest. Things will look better in the morning."

CHAPTER 24

Kimmy was always right. In the morning, I did feel better. The world seemed brighter, people seemed more at peace with themselves, the ghosts were more orderly. Life was good.

Good until another Being came to talk to me . I was alone, sitting in the topmost branches of a giant redwood tree in California, enjoying the sunrise, when the light from the sun separated into two. I recognized that the shape was like that of the first Being, but thinner, more angular. I waited for it to speak.

"You have done well, Gatekeeper," it said softly.

"Perhaps," I agreed, "but how am I going to keep up with all the vast numbers of people? I have not caught up with the number of ghosts in North America yet, let alone the rest of the world! How do I do it? I need help."

"You are right," the Being said, to my surprise. "The population keeps growing! What one person could do before now needs several people. You must find and train others to do the work with you."

"Find and train!? How do I do that? Where do I look?"

"Through your tears," the Being said softly.

"The opals…" I murmured.

"Exactly. If a spirit can *hold* a tear, it can learn to do the job. It must touch the tear *to* another spirit to open the Gate. It will be as if you were there."

"But, who can touch them?" I asked.

That Being, just like the other, chose to leave things unanswered. I don't think I will ever like that. It laughed gently as it faded away. I felt annoyed when it left without giving me more information. I went back to Kimmy at the movie studio.

*

"*More* Gatekeepers?" Kimmy squawked. "And you have to train them? Like, being an Apprentice Gatekeeper? Wow."

"How do you find such an apprentice?" Derek asked.

"It's about the tears," I said, looking him in the eye. "The opals. If a spirit can hold a tear, then he can touch a ghost with it and send the ghost to the Gate."

"Hold… *I* held your tears."

"I know. We *do* have choices though. We *must* be able to choose."

"Did you? Was this your choice?"

I thought back over the past year since Pete's car hit me and realized that I was led every inch of the way to the job of Gatekeeper and I had had no choice at all.

"No, I guess not," I said, shaking my head. "But maybe it will be different for the apprentices."

"Wait! Before you two get all bent about it, let's do some figuring," Kimmy said firmly. "How many opals are there, and who can touch them?"

She had placed them in a small dish on the table of the apartment at the film studio. She tipped them onto a scarf so they wouldn't roll away. She reached out with her hand to spread them out.

"Hey! I can touch them!" She said surprised. "Well, my baby and I will not do *that* job!"

"Maybe it is because you are in Susie's body," Pete suggested.

"I am? Oh yeah, I forgot!" Kimmy said blushing.

Pete reached out to pick up one of the pearl sized opals. His fingers passed right through them. "Strange," he murmured, looking at his fingertips. "My fingers feel wet, as if by tears."

Derek reached out and picked one of the opals up to confirm that he could indeed touch them.

"You *could* be one of my apprentices," I said, feeling like I was going to lose my best friend. "Or you can help me find enough others so we can work together...."

"Susie, Derek, don't panic!" Kimmy said, reading the look on our faces. "Even if Derek did do the job, he will always be no more than a thought away. But he is probably the most sensitive person here. He knows when bad things are happening *way* before the rest of us. I would bet that *he* can *find* the apprentices. Sue, you have been so busy, you don't notice much else, do you?"

"You're right, I don't," I sighed. "That's why I rely on Derek. If the old Gatekeeper had had someone watching out for him, maybe he would have survived."

"So you work together to find your apprentices. Who do you look for?"

"Someone who is not a religious fanatic," I said. "They should speak other languages so they can talk to the ghosts..."

"I think we should find newly dead ghosts," Derek said. "They would be more open-minded toward the future."

"Does age matter?" Pete asked.

"I don't see why it should," Derek said. "When you die, you become the age you were when you were happiest in your life. Some don't change at all, but most appear to stay around thirty or so. Why?"

"I wander around hospitals when Kimmy is busy," Pete admitted. "I don't like the idea of someone not knowing they are dead like I did. The shock was kind of brutal."

"Oh Pete!" Kimmy cried, tears coming readily to her eyes.

"It's all right, sweetie," Pete assured her. "I just try to help when I can. Most of the time, there are family members waiting for them, when they die, but sometimes they die alone."

"Do you have someone in mind?" I asked, thinking Pete was going somewhere with this.

"Actually, yes. There is a lady who is an artist. She has stubbornly refused medical care, claiming to be ready to die, but every time she should have died, she didn't. She had Polio; she was exposed to tuberculosis; her appendix ruptured at age sixty four; she had a few heart attacks; breast cancer that went to her lungs *and* bladder cancer. Her body is shutting down now, but she doesn't seem to realize it. Her youngest daughter is with her, but I haven't seen anyone in the ghost level waiting for her. I just think I could help."

This was a challenge I had not faced before. Up until then, the ghosts had come to me. I did not have the time to wait with each person until they died.

But, if Pete thought it was important, I was willing. He took Derek and me to a very small hospital room. A frail old woman lay on the bed using all of her strength just to breathe. Her daughter sat by the bed reading to her.

"How long has this gone on?" I asked Pete.

"Two days now. The older sister is on her way, but she has a long drive. Everyone is telling the woman to hang on until the sister arrives. This lady is so strong, she's doing it!"

"Driving? Why not fly?" Derek asked.

"I don't know. Money probably. Maybe she doesn't understand that her mother is dying."

"And this one?" Derek asked.

"She understands. She has had to stand between her mother and the medical staff to make sure her mother's wishes are carried out. They want to try to heal her, but her mother has refused many times. This daughter is as adamant as her mother was."

"That must be hard," I said.

"I suspect it is the hardest thing she has ever had to do in her life," Pete said. "Watching her mother in so much pain, struggling so hard to breathe, is tough. She doesn't see the need for her mother to hang on any longer."

"What do you want us to do, Pete?" I asked, knowing he was going to stay and keep the vigil with the daughter.

"Drop in every so often," Pete smiled. "Come if I call. I just feel that this old lady is special and she deserves the best we can do for her."

"All right, Pete," I agreed. "We will be back."

We left the room and found ourselves surrounded by the many ghosts that had died in that hospital. I took them to a quiet spot and sent each of them to the Gate. Derek was right. It didn't seem to matter what age the people died at, the only ones that appeared old were the ones that appeared to have had a very hard life. It seemed sad to me that a crippled up old man stayed that way because that was the happiest time of his life. Even then, however, once they were on the way to the Gate, they all became more childlike, often giggling their way to the Gate.

It seems, I still had a lot to learn.

We went back to Pete several times that day and through the night. The hospital had a sitter on hand through the night so the woman couldn't pull the tubes out of her arms, but they discontinued the watch in the morning after she became unconscious most of the time. Clearly, they thought she would die soon. Her daughter stayed, talking to her, reading to her and just being with her.

"How's it going, Pete?" Derek asked when we arrived.

"I guess this is the way it is supposed to happen, but it sure seems to drag out a lot," Pete fretted. "The older sister will arrive today. They will have their time for goodbyes, then she should be ours."

"Is that what you are after?" I laughed and put my hand comfortingly on the daughter's shoulder. Oddly, I think she felt my presence. She smiled and looked towards me.

"I've seen her art!" Pete said defensively. "She is special!"

"Then you may be right," I smiled. "She just might like to work with us. Call when the sister arrives."

We got the call that afternoon. I popped in just behind the sister.

"Hi Mom, I'm here! We're here for you Mom, just the way you wanted. But Becky is coming Mom. Hang on till Becky gets here okay? It would mean so much to her."

"What?" the younger sister whispered. "Oh no. Let her go."

I could see how upset the younger sister was and wished I could help, but Pete did not want me to interfere. I stayed for a while watching the bustle that arrived with the older sister and her friends. They came and went while the youngest stayed, calmly letting her mother know that she wasn't alone.

"Pete, has she made any effort to leave the body?" I asked.

"No. She seems very confused. Her whole focus seems to be on breathing. When they move her, she winces and opens her eyes. She is still very much in the body."

Pete stayed. I carried on, going from place to place do do the Gatekeeping while Derek kept Kimmy informed on what was happening.

Later that night, I popped in to see nurses bustling around the bed. The old woman's breathing was extremely laboured. There was so much fluid building up in her throat, she sounded like she was drowning.

"The doctor will let us suction some of that out," the nurse was saying. "It will help for a while."

"Help how?" the younger sister asked.

"She will breathe easier," the nurse said.

"You hear that Mom?" the older sister said. "You will breathe easier so you can hang on until Becky gets here. She is flying in tomorrow. You are doing great, Mom."

"Oh dear," I said. "Do families always drag things out like that?"

"Sometimes," Pete nodded. "The nurses have talked with the younger sister and they will give the mother enough sedative that she won't remember this process."

"Too bad they can't give it to the family." I sighed. "Call me if it changes."

I returned to the room later the next day. The nurses were turning the old woman so she wouldn't drown in her fluids too quickly. She opened her eyes in pain and called out: "Lynne!"

The younger daughter rushed to her side. "I'm here Mom. I'm staying. I love you."

"I have to tell you..." the old woman gasped, but was unable to go on.

"Mom, you have told me everything you ever wanted to say. We have talked for years and I know what you want. You don't need to worry. It will be okay."

The woman relaxed a bit and the daughter went on.

"Mom, I think you are a little bit confused, so I'm telling you now. Your body is shutting down and you are going to die. But you are not afraid to die. You have *never* been afraid to die. We aren't afraid either.

This is it. So, If you happen to see a white light out there.... go for it. It is all right."

The older sister looked a little blank at that speech, but she did add a comment that her mother should wait until Becky arrived.

"Do you suppose that will make a difference?" Pete asked.

"Telling her she is dying?" I asked. "Yes, I would imagine so. It takes the confusion away. I hope that she heard it."

When I returned to the room that night, the Granddaughter and one of the Grandsons had arrived. They were sitting on either side of the bed holding the old woman's hands. The two sisters were dozing in uncomfortable chairs.

The younger sister woke with a start and told the others to wake her sister. The mother was breathing slowly, pausing between breaths. Each pause was longer, each breath shallower until, finally, there was no more.

I had expected to see the spirit leave the body sooner than it did. This woman was tough. She hung onto life through so much hardship, she wasn't just going to go easily. As the air left her lungs, she floated an inch above her body. She reached out with both arms and hugged her Granddaughter, seemingly knowing that this was going to be hardest on her. Then she looked around the room and saw me.

"Where's Gregory?" she asked. "He was supposed to meet me, wasn't he?"

"I'm here instead," I said. "I am the Gatekeeper. I can send you to the Gate so you can go into the light and be with your family, if that is what you wish. Or, if you are up to a challenge, perhaps I can train you to work with me."

"Work with you how?" She sounded interested. It was amazing! As her curiosity was peaked, she started to look younger. Her snow white hair darkened and grew down around her shoulders. She floated higher and approached me, careful not to touch any of the family members standing around her body.

"First," I said, holding an opal out on my palm, "can you touch this?"

She reached out and picked the small stone up easily. "It is an opal!" she smiled. "I used to work with opals. One of my favourite stones." She carefully placed the stone back on my palm.

"The fact that you can hold it means that you are able to work with me," I said, encouraging her. "It is your choice. Do you want to leave here?"

She turned and looked at her family, still quietly standing around her body. "I guess it's time," she said. "I can't help them now."

"I have a question," Pete said, getting her attention. "Why did you let this drag out for so long? We have been here for you for days now. You were obviously in a lot of pain. Why wait?"

"They told me to... at least, Doreen, my eldest did. I wasn't quite sure what was happening. She said: you are doing good, Mom. Hang on. So I did. Then Lynne *told* me exactly what was happening and that cleared up my confusion, but Doreen still wanted me to wait for Becky. That girl is special. I will do anything for her."

"Even with all that pain?" Pete asked.

"Pain is transitory," she shrugged. "Love is the important thing. My girls know I love them."

"What should I call you?" I asked.

"Mia," the woman smiled. "It is the name I always wanted."

"Then Mia it is. Pete, why don't you take Mia and show her what you can and cannot do. Give her a chance to make an honest choice."

I left the small stuffy room and soared up into the clouds, followed closely by Derek. I could feel the wind and the water and the tiny bit of heat from the sun that was just peeking over the horizon. I spun in place, trying to shake off the feeling of unnecessary suffering.

"Derek, I don't get it," I whispered.

"I know. I don't either. I think there is such a deep fear of death that people will suffer all kinds of horror to avoid it."

"But she claimed to be ready to die!"

"It's just words, Sue. Fear of the unknown is monumental. I don't think that fear goes away until a person is actually, finally dead. I know of another lady with similar health problems who took three months to do what Mia did in five days."

"Maybe, some day, Mia can explain it to me."

"Now, *that* sounds like a *wonderful* idea. It might help both of you."

Derek followed me as I soared above the earth. I was looking for a sign, something that could tell me where to look next. What direction my work would take me. Signs like that are notoriously hard to see, even when they slap you in the face. I certainly wasn't being slapped, but I did feel a small nudge.

"Derek, do you see that?" I asked, pointing north.

"Um. I see lightning over there," he said, staring carefully, "But those aren't storm clouds. We should investigate, but be ready for the locket, all right?"

"Always," I grinned. I did enjoy a good mystery. I hoped we would find something interesting, but not dangerous.

CHAPTER 25

What I saw *looked* like a ball of lightning. A really *big* ball of lightning. The center was as bright as the sun. The outskirts radiated with jagged blasts of electricity projecting out for great distances.

There is an area in the central part of North America where the land is flat. There are no hills or valleys to break up the landscape. The rivers that cross the plain barely have trenches to contain them. I would imagine that even a small flood would cover many acres of land.

Hovering over that flatness, the strange ball of electricity shot streams of lightning in all directions. Some of them shot down to the ground which worried me. People could get hurt.

As we neared the thing, I could see under it. A small town was either the source or the target of the strange phenomenon. I knew I would have to go there.

Derek moved first, always being chivalrous and took one large lightning bolt in the chest. It passed through him as if he wasn't there. That was reassuring. We went down to the ground and walked along the street. Not one person was outdoors, but I could see a lot of them peering out of their windows, watching. What *they* saw was darkness, like in a black and white film with so many flashes from the lightning that it looked like a strobe light. It can be very difficult to see under a strobe light.

"Derek, can you see where they are hitting the ground?" I asked.

"No... Yes! That one!" He pointed to a fence post that was charred and split down the middle. "Most of them fade away before they touch anything. The actual damage is minimal. The people are smart enough to stay indoors."

"So far. Let's go and listen to what they think is happening," I suggested, pointing to a café that had a lot of people in the window.

We went through the door above the people standing around. I still had a thing about going through people. I was afraid I would inadvertently send them to the Gate. I knew I had to have the *intention* to do that, but still, I was always careful.

"Sue, check it out!" Derek said, pointing to the back of the room.

There was a group of ghosts sitting around the only large table in the place. They held hands, closing a circle. Their eyes were shut and they were chanting in an old language that I didn't recognize. A pillar of light formed with a thread coming from each of them. The pillar went through the ceiling to the lightning ball above us.

"Excuse me!" I said loudly, above their chant. "Hey guys! What are you doing?"

One of the people, an old wizened up woman, opened her eyes and stopped the chant. The rest stopped and stared at me. The hostility was palpable.

"Who are you?" the old woman croaked in a thick accent.

"I am the Gatekeeper," I said. "I have passed through here before, why didn't you come to me?"

"Gatekeeper?" She spat! At me! I've never encountered *that* before!

"So, you don't *want* to go to the Gate to continue your life experience on the other side?"

"Other side? We know about the other side! You cannot trick us. We have been tricked before and we will not fall for it again."

"Sue!" Derek said quietly, "these people are Romani!"

"Romani? So?"

"Gypsies!"

"Oh! Well then, I suppose you do have reason not to trust," I said to the woman. "The persecution of your people is widely documented. Totally unfair, but why are you *here*? What are you doing?"

The woman looked at me as if I was stupid, asking the obvious. One of the others, a scrawny old man, said something curt and she reluctantly started to talk.

"We burn our dead and take care of them... the ashes. Everyone knows that when we die, we stay close to our bodies... or ashes... so we can keep on living. We have stayed in family groups like that since forever. That's who we are!"

"All right," I encouraged her.

"Then we came to this land." Her disgust was palpable. "Our mother's mothers, back to the beginning brought us to this place! As if this was a place to be safe!" They did not look like they had felt safe.

"Then what happened?" I urged.

"They lost us!" the woman exclaimed. "They kept us through more wars than we can count, but here... the police invaded our homes and forced our descendants to give us to them for 'proper burial'! As if we were savages or something!"

"Where did they put you?"

"In a graveyard outside this town. Then the good citizens of this fair community ran our children out of town as if they were thieves and cheats! Now, it has been so long, the children can't find us any more!"

"That's terrible! But what are you doing now? What is this ball of electricity?

"Retribution," the old woman said coldly. "This town will end in the same way that our family did. It will become lost and forgotten, buried under miles of earth."

"Miles of earth? How can you do that?"

"The lightning will create a cavern into which the town will sink, leaving them in the airless dark, to think about their sins."

"When did all this happen?" Derek asked quietly.

"Just after the North part and the South part of this land fought over slaves. Hmph. At least they had others besides the People to be their slaves. But then, they turned back to us."

"That war ended in eighteen sixty five!" Derek said. "It is now the twenty first century! The people who wronged you are long dead and gone. So are their children and their children's children! Their descendants probably don't even live here any more.

"Maybe so," the old woman snarled, "but we are stuck here, so here is where we do our retribution."

"And then what?" I asked.

"Then we will have a quiet place to grow herbs and sing songs and live happily together."

"That place already exists," I told her firmly. "It is just beyond the Gate. I am sure that your ancestors *and* descendants are already there, waiting for you."

"We do not go anywhere without our bodies! That is our connection to life!"

"This is not a life," I shook my head. I noticed that the group still had their hands clasped in their circle, probably to give each other strength. I moved quickly. "I cannot allow you to hurt innocent people based on an unprovable belief of the afterlife. But, I'm sorry to do it like this." I reached out and touched the woman on the arm.

The others tried to let go and get away as the Gate opened. It was bright and beautiful, filled with colour, which made me believe that they were good people in their lives. But, even though they became younger and more vibrant as they floated to the Gate, they all resisted the pull.

"What a strange group of people," I muttered to Derek after the Gate closed.

"From their history, they had reason," Derek said, pointing to another smaller group of ghosts gathered near the door of the café.

"Hello," I said, walking toward them. "I am the Gatekeeper. I can help you cross to the other side."

"Is that the same place *they* went?" a small elderly black woman asked nervously.

"No," I assured her. "The Gate decides where you go according to your life and beliefs. You will go to your own family. There is nothing to be afraid of."

It took almost no time at all to send the small group to the Gate.

"Just as soon as you think you understand it all, you find another mystery," I said, enjoying the sunlight on the street in front of the café. "Who would think ghosts would hold such a grudge?"

"Ghosts are just people without a body," Derek shrugged. "That's why you need apprentices. So *you* can deal with situations like this as they arise while they do the regular work. Let's see if we can find more apprentices."

We went back to Kimmy and Pete to see how they were doing. Kimmy had a definite bulge in her tummy and she really did glow! It was good to see her happy.

After the prolonged dying process that Mia went through, Pete showed her how to move around and go places. She left him to go on her own adventure, probably to check in on her family. But Pete didn't want to spend time in hospitals waiting for people to die any more. It just wasn't a smooth and easy process. He preferred to stay with Kimberley.

So, we all watched the ghosts that came to us. A few were curious, but not really interested in crossing over. I was getting better at figuring out where the Gate would send people. The ones that were too afraid of going to a bad place were not welcome to stay as far as I was concerned. I would use Quantum Time to touch them anyway. But there were a few who seemed more interested in staying just because they were having fun. They were the ones we approached.

We had nine opals. Kimmy took them to a jeweler and had them mounted on rings so they wouldn't be dropped or lost easily. The rings were made from pure silver, which Kimmy believed would do the best job.

It turned out that she was right. Starting with Mia, we found nine people who wanted to do the job and were able to wear the opal rings.

My days became more scheduled than I ever was in life. In the early morning, I went to a new area of the country where I had not been before. I sent all to the Gate when they came to my music. That was the peaceful part of my day. Usually Derek was with me, but, just to watch and enjoy the peace with me.

In the afternoon, we took the apprentices, in groups of three, to areas where there were lots of ghosts to be crossed over. We did not limit ourselves in what location we went to. We crossed Vietnam and China, knowing the death toll had been horrendous over the last sixty to seventy years. The teams learned to work together, protecting each other and bonding into very strong groups.

One aspect that I did not expect was that it didn't matter what language the ghosts spoke, we understood them and they understood us. That was one worry I was glad to shed.

In the evening, I let everyone go to their favourite spots to enjoy the world. I found it interesting that the teams were spending their time off together, as closely bonded as when they worked.

We kept that schedule for about a month until all nine apprentices came to me requesting that I let them go to work themselves. Each group chose an area of the world to work in, promising to check in with me at the end of each day. It was wonderful! I doubt if the Gate had ever been so busy in all of history.

I continued working in North and South America. Of course, when something strange came up, I was called in to check it out. In Europe, we found four more incidents of lightning balls, created by gypsies. It made me wonder if there weren't towns already buried underground from past centuries. If there were, *I* couldn't help them anymore.

For the most part, I stopped worrying.

Kimmy was growing that child in her and, basically, she was happy. The movie producer assigned an assistant to her and made sure she saw the doctor as necessary. We visited her as much as we could, but I knew she felt the absence of arms to hold her when she slept at night.

I had a little more time to pay attention to the people around me. When Mia started getting depressed, I was the first to notice. She still worked as hard as ever, but she didn't smile as much and she stopped singing. She loved to sing. I went to where her team was working in France and I took her away to a remote island in the Mediterranean Sea.

"What's wrong, Mia?" I asked.

"Wrong? What could be wrong? I can go anywhere, see anything, do whatever I want..." she sighed and a tear ran down her cheek.

"So what is it?"

"Where you ever married?" She asked. When I shook my head, she went on. "I was married to

Gregory from age eighteen until he died when I was fifty-eight. Then, I still felt married to him for the last twenty-two years. We had our problems, but he was still the one who helped me make decisions in my life. I expected to see him when I died. I was looking forward to it. I feel empty without him."

"But, he has probably gone to the Gate!" I said. "Do you want to go to the Gate and stop working here?"

"No! I want to work at this! This is the most fun I've ever had in my life!"

"Then what?"

"Can't we call through the Gate so he can hear us? There does seem to be time just before it closes."

"Then what? We reach in and pull him back to us?"

"Yes! Something like that! Can we do that?"

"I don't know. My Gramma said that there were many things I could do that others could not. She said that the Gatekeeper can pass through the Gate both ways. But I've never done it."

"So, you are afraid," Mia nodded. "Well, I'm your apprentice. I will try."

"What? No! You don't know where you could end up, unable to come back!"

"It couldn't be much worse than my life was. It is worth the risk."

"No, we will do this with caution," I insisted. "You can call him to the Gate from this side. When you hear his voice and know he is there, call me. I'm not sure that you can pass through both ways. I don't want to lose you!"

Mia looked much happier at that. She continued to work hard, but at the end of every session they had with the Gate, she would call into it, speaking clearly that she was looking for her husband Gregory.

CHAPTER 26

To my surprise, it only took three days! I was finishing clearing out a hospital somewhere in the northwest part of the United States with Derek's help when I heard her call. We both went to her where she sat, on a ledge, halfway up the Rock of Gibraltar.

"Oh Sue! I heard him! He is waiting for me! What do I do now?"

"I guess I have to go through and get him," I said.

"You're not going alone." Derek stated firmly. "We go together, or not at all."

"Me too!" Mia insisted. "I don't know what it's like over there, but from what I heard, voices and such, it is crowded. You wouldn't recognize him!"

I saw the determination on both their faces and shrugged. "All right, but we must hold hands. Keep the physical connection *at all times*. If you let go, I may not be able to find you. Got that?"

"Yes," they both agreed.

I took each of their hands, Derek on the right and Mia on the left and thought the Gate open. It was so beautiful! There was a brightness that shifted and swirled, white on white, as we neared. I had avoided being this close to the Gate in the past for fear that I would not get back home. Now, I boldly pulled us right into the center of the maelstrom.

The special effects guys for movies and television are good. Their imaginations take you into other universes in a gut-lurching slide. This was more light and less slide. We passed through a spiral opening into a colourful light show with the center being a blindingly bright White. The spiral closed behind us before another opened in front. There, we moved into an area of pure White Light.

Mia was right. There were hundreds... thousands of people milling around in the white space. The lighting was indirect. I couldn't see the source. I wasn't sure I saw walls, the mass of people extended so far. There must have been a floor and ceiling. The people were walking around all on the same level. If they could fly, they may not have felt so crowded.

I focussed on the people. They all wore white tunics and leggings. They appeared generally under thirty. A few were older children. There were various sized family groups of people who looked alike and talked happily amongst themselves. A very few loners ignored the rest of the crowd, but I thought it was the loners I could probably get answers from.

A group nearest to us had faces that I recognized. They were the last people I had sent to the Gate. I began to realize that the famous White Light and sense of Peace came from *this* reception area. But why were there still so many here?

We drifted above the crowd trying to see something to indicate what was supposed to happen next.

"There he is!" Mia cheered. "Greg! I'm here!"

She pointed to a short, kind of scrawny man, who had been talking with a group of people who in any time frame would have been termed Geeks. I held her hand tightly as she pulled us to him and gave him a warm hug.

"I have missed you," she smiled.

"I have been waiting for you," he responded. "I was there, at the hospital when she (he pointed at me!) touched me and I was here!" They both looked at me accusingly.

"That must have been the group I sent while we waited for you to die," I said. "Some of them had been waiting for the Gate for many years. It was time!"

"If you had died when you were supposed to, it wouldn't have been an issue," Derek said, rising to my defence.

"What does he mean?" Greg asked.

"Well, I wasn't thinking straight," Mia said. "The girls both wanted to be there. I remember wanting that. Then Becky... but I wasn't sure what was happening until Lynne told me. Time seemed to drag there. I don't remember how long it took."

"Five days," Derek and I chorused.

"And it looked painful and exhausting," I added.

"Hmm. I'm glad I don't remember that part," Mia said thoughtfully. "Anyway, I'm here now to see you before I go back to work!"

"Work? What work?" Greg asked.

"I am an apprentice Gatekeeper," Mia said proudly. "My team works in Europe and the Middle East. There are too many war deaths these days, but we are handling them."

"Wow, that's a special job!" Greg said, impressed. "How did you get that?"

"I'm not sure," Mia said. "They came to me."

"What's going on *here*?" Derek asked, interrupting what would end up being a long discussion.

"This is a Holding Area," Greg said. "Everyone who is good goes through the Gate and comes here. There is a door over there." He pointed to a far corner of the space. "It seems to take a long time to pass through the door. So we are bottlenecked here."

"What about the Bad Ones?" Mia asked, looking around nervously.

"I've been looking for them too," I said quietly. "I don't see any that I sent. They must have a different holding area. Let's check this out."

Mia took Greg's hand and we flew over the heads of the people. As we approached the spot Greg had indicated, I could sense a feeling of anticipation. The people were eager to move on. Finally, I found a person who was sitting at a desk with a very long list in front of him.

"Excuse me," I said.

"Hmm? Wait your turn, lady," the man said rudely. You can see me according to your number."

"Number?"

"Right. *Next*, number one hundred million, seven hundred sixty five thousand, two hundred eighty four!"

A young boy approached the desk holding a crumpled piece of paper.

"How many times do I have to tell you people not to damage the numbers!" the man complained. He smoothed out the paper, confirming the number. He pulled a thin file out of a drawer and looked through it. "All right, young man, it says here that your good deeds outweigh your bad, but while you have been here, you have had a problem with indifference."

"So?" the boy shrugged.

"So you need to learn that indifference gets you nowhere. So, I will be indifferent and you can go get a new number and wait a while longer. Then you may not be quite so bored by the proceedings." The man closed the file and pointed in the direction we had come from.

The boy rolled his eyes and sauntered away. I was ready to feel sorry for him until I saw him meet with a group of young people who high-fived him and clapped him on the back. Interesting.

"Greg, what number are you?" Mia asked.

"One hundred and six million, five hundred three thousand, four hundred and six," Greg said despairingly.

"There are six million people in here?" Derek asked stunned.

We flew up into the air, not finding a ceiling to stop us. The masses of people just went on and on. There did not seem to be any walls in the place, just a floor and white light.

"This doesn't make sense," I said, pulling us back to the man at the desk.

"One hundred million, seven hundred sixty five thousand, two hundred and eighty five," he called loudly.

"Me! That's me!" a woman who had maintained looking like she was sixty, was cheering and waving her number as if she had won the lottery. She pushed her way to the desk and presented her number to the man with a flourish.

"Oh yes," he muttered, opening a very fat file from his drawer. "Your life was difficult, but you did good in spite of it. You will go to level Alpha. Enjoy yourself." He took her hand and pressed a rubber stamp on her arm. A very colourful and ornate Greek letter alpha was left glowing on her wrist. Then she disappeared, poof, just like that!

"Excuse me," I tried again.

"Look lady, take a number! One hundred million, seven hundred sixty five thousand, two hundred and eighty six!"

"I am not here to be stamped by you," I said, getting annoyed. "I am the Gatekeeper and I would like to know what's going on here!"

"The Gatekeeper?" For the first time, he looked right at me. To me, he looked like a typical mousy little bureaucrat with more power than brains. I knew looks could be deceiving.

I saw him push a button on the desk and instantly we were surrounded by a group of them. They were all dressed in white suits with Name buttons that all said 'Next' on them.

"Next?" I asked. "It seems to take a long time for people to go to whatever is next around here."

"Well, that's *your* fault, lady! What do you think you are doing? There have been so many coming through the Gate, we can't handle them! You have no business doing that!" This Next Man was tall and black and really scary.

I quietly and quickly rearranged us so that we were still holding hands, but I was on the end with my right hand free.

"Don't you yell at me!" I said, staying calm. "I have not sent *this* number of people here! Clearly, you have to have been back logged for hundreds of years!"

"So? We get it done in our own time frame. We don't need interference from a do-gooder like you!"

"How do you know I'm a do-gooder?" I asked suspiciously.

"We have a file on you, same as everyone who ever lived."

"Is there a file on you?" I asked, stepping closer to the argumentative man.

"No! We are not from there!" He seemed horrified by the very thought.

"Then how can you understand people and how they live their lives?"

The people around us were getting interested in our talk, but they kept their distance. In general, they seemed to be afraid of these 'Next' men.

"It's not our job to understand. All we do is send them where the file tells us."

"Then why aren't you doing it?" I asked, watching the hoards of people mingling in the area.

"Look lady, they all wanted to go into the White Light. This is it! If it is crowded, it is because *you* keep sending too many our way."

"*That is my job!* I was told to get the back log cleared up. Do you have *any* idea how crowded it got there in the sixty five years when there was no Gatekeeper?"

"I think they're getting an idea," Derek said. "But if they have never been to earth, why would they care or know?"

"We *have told* them," Greg sniffed. "*They* have somewhere else to go to when they leave here. Most of the people here just want to be somewhere else doing something productive or fun. *This* is boring!"

"So where's *your* boss?" I asked the big black one who seemed to be in charge of them all. I stepped closer and he backed up. He gestured to his colleagues and they moved to surround us in a tighter circle.

"Oh dear!" Mia gasped. "This isn't good."

"Don't worry Mia," I said. "They are just bullies. There really is only one way to deal with bullies."

"What's that?" Mia asked nervously.

"Bully them back. When we are at home, I send people to the Gate by touching them. I wonder what would happen if I touched someone on *this* side of the Gate?"

The whole group of Next Men took several steps back, giving us some breathing room.

"*You* can't threaten *us!*" the spokesman snarled. "You have no *right!*"

"Yes, I understand," I nodded. "You have the power to make people stay here for an eternity, no matter how they spent their lives. I don't know everything, but I'm pretty sure there is more to the afterlife than hanging around here for millennium! You are overstepping your bounds."

"Well, if *you* would stop sending so many, *we* could handle them!"

"There has been only one of me! How many are you?"

"We are numbered the same! There is *ten* of you and *ten* of us!"

"Well then, I guess *you* will have to *speed up!*"

That made him mad. Really mad. He did not look even remotely angelic. I needed the intervention of a Being, but they only seemed to arrive after the excitement was settled. This was more excitement than I wanted.

"I don't think we are doing any good here," I said to Derek and Mia, not taking my eyes off of the Next Men. "Greg, do you want to come with us or stay here?"

"It sounds like you are having way more fun," he said. "I would like to go with you."

"Wait a minute, *you* can't take anyone *back*! The only way to leave this place is through *us*! *He stays!*"

"I don't think so," I said, thinking the Gate open.

I didn't want to risk any violence from these guys, so I put us into Quantum Time and pulled my small group through the Gate. We ended up exactly where we started from, half way up the Rock of Gibralter.

When the Gate closed, it looked different than usual. There was a darkness around the edges that I had never seen before. I thought that the difference was because we had gone through the Gate in the other direction, so I put it out of my mind.

CHAPTER 27

I called a meeting of my teams. We needed to talk. Mia had explained to all of them what we found on the other side of the Gate and we were all disturbed.

"You need to talk to your Being!" Mia insisted. Again.

"I know I do, Mia, but the Beings only seem to show up *after* I have solved the problem, to tell me I did a good job! Believe me, when this all began, I called for them a lot! They don't hear me!"

"But isn't the other side of the Gate their jurisdiction?"

"I don't know. The only thing I know for sure right now is that every good person we send through the Gate, ends up in that White Light. Greg, you were there for a few months. What was it like?"

"Months? Was that all it was? It felt like forever! At first, it was calm and peaceful, just like they say, but after a while, when nothing else happened, I started getting curious. I don't know how long it was before they gave me a number and a quick explanation. I didn't understand their laugh when they said it would take some time to be processed! Then, it got boring. Everyone is on their best behaviour for fear of being sent to the *other* waiting area. *I* never saw anything like that happen and I never talked to anyone who had, but the threat was real just the same!

"So you go there, and wait," Rob, one of my younger apprentices stated.

"That's right," Greg nodded. "Most would not complain. The feeling of calm and peace is like a drug there. Even if you are impatient, you can't get too worked up about it. The only ones that could, were the kids."

"Kids!" Rob squawked. "With the adults?"

"Kids from ages eight or nine and up," Greg amended. "The kids play. They have fun without inhibitions. Since they have no toys, they play with the people. Hide and seek is always on the go, but some of the games seem complicated. And the kids can fly! *They* don't believe in rules any more. Not physics or math *or* the demands from the guys in white suits. Their main game is to stay *there*. All of them. Not that their numbers come up that much."

"Why do they want to stay?" Mia asked.

"Because they have bonded and want to stay together. No way the Next Men will let people have what they want. *That's* not what *they* want."

"What *do* they want?" Mia asked.

"To be in control without doing too much work." Greg shrugged.

"But wouldn't controlling so many people be more work than just letting them move on?" Rob asked.

"I would have thought so," Greg agreed. "But when the numbers coming in rose so noticeably, they got really upset. The only yelling in the White Light is being done by the Next Men."

"So what do we do?" Mia asked. "Stop sending spirits to the Gate?"

"No," I said firmly. "For whatever reason, that is exactly what *they* want. We should send as many as possible. If they can't handle it, maybe a Being will make them do *their* job. At least it is a place of Peace. I'm sure, for a lot of the people, it is still better than here."

*

We made plans, deciding on a schedule that would double our work load. I told the teams that if they came across a really large group to call me. Up until then, I had not mentioned the Quantum Time to the apprentices. Now, I only told them that I *could* do it, not how. With a plan in place, Derek and I went to report to Pete and Kimmy.

"Sue, are you all right?" Pete asked.

"I'm all right. We all are." I told them about our excursion through the Gate, describing in detail my impression of the place. I wanted Kimmy's opinion, even though I knew she would feel the same way I did.

After I said my piece, Derek added his viewpoint. He had felt a different vibe from the Next Men. As far as he could tell, they had no intention of changing the way they did things. They would resist with all their might rather than acquiesce.

"Oh dear," Kimmy said, quietly. "Here we thought the backlog was on our side of the Gate! The Beings have to know what is going on! Why don't they do something there?"

"Obviously, because they can't," Pete said firmly.

"Can't?" we chorused in surprise.

"If they could, they would, so they can't," Pete nodded excitedly. "But something *must* be done, so they are bringing *you* into it!"

"*Me*?" I squawked. "What can *I* do? My work *here* is enough! What can I possibly do *there*?"

"I guess that's what we have to figure out," Kimmy sighed. "We have come so far in this, we have to see it through to the end."

"End!" Shock went through my entire being. "What do you mean the end?"

"I don't know! That's just it. You are going to have to do something where we can't help you! I'm scared!"

"Scared?"

"For you. For me, if you don't succeed and I never see you again! You know..."

"Yes. But, Gramma said I could cross back and forth through the Gate and we did it, so I'm pretty sure I can come back. I don't want to go back there right now, though. I really don't."

"All right," Kimmy relaxed a bit.

"Kimberley, when is your due date?" I asked, changing the subject. Her belly seemed to be growing very rapidly. I think I lost track of time.

"Yesterday," she groaned. "*I'm* ready. I guess the babe isn't. It will be soon."

I looked closely at her and her child. There wasn't much for me to see. The baby's soul either wasn't there yet or it was small enough to hide from me. I had to admit that I had not thought about the souls of the babies who were about to be born at an ever increasing rate across the world. I wanted to know more.

"Oh dear," Kimmy said, sitting up straight.

"What is it?" Pete asked anxiously.

"Um... it's a contraction. I've had a few over the last couple of days."

"Contraction! Call the doctor! Or a taxi! We've got to get you to the hospital!" Pete was jumping in his excitement.

"Relax," Kimmy said. "My mother told me that she was in labor for days before I was born. They sent her home three times before they agreed that it was time. I don't need *that* aggravation!"

"Kimmy," I said, getting her attention. "*My* mother was in labor for *one hour* before I popped out. If you are thinking genetics, let's get you to the hospital."

"Oh! I forgot! Let's go!" She moved quite quickly under the circumstances. One of her assistants for the movie drove her to the hospital. The young woman was more excited than we were.

*

We met up with Kim again in the delivery room.

"All right, Miss Foton, don't you have a coach to help you through this? Do you need a nurse?"

"I have coaches," Kimmy said, between contractions. "I'm fine." She grinned at Pete and me standing on either side of her. Derek stayed behind the doctor, letting us know what was happening.

The nurse spoke to the doctor quietly and he nodded, looking concerned.

"Your partner died a few months ago, did he not?"

"Yes, but he's here anyway," Kimmy gasped. She grabbed the arms of the birthing bed and squeezed tight.

"The baby is crowning!" the doctor interrupted her. "Just a couple of pushes and that will do it!"

"Sue!" Kimmy whispered, focussing on my face. "Find out who it is… was… whatever. Now, before it is too late."

I understood her and immediately went into Quantum Time, freezing everything in mid-contraction. We had discussed the possibilities of reincarnation and the baby being occupied by an older spirit. Up to that point, I had not met any spirits around her other than us. I turned slowly around, looking for some kind of sign. Even so, I did not expect what did happen.

A white light shimmered in the far corner of the small room. I saw a shape separate from the light, moving toward the bed.

"Gramma!" I said, recognizing her. "What are you doing here?"

"I am going to live another life!" she said cheerfully. "This will be fun!"

"But why? I don't understand!"

"I know sweetie. It's because of the situation in the White Light. There are only two ways to leave, you know. It is extremely boring there. Everyone wants to leave, but they can't."

"Two ways? How?"

"Either your number comes up or you reincarnate into a new life. After a while, most decide to come back and try again. You, my dear, must help resolve the situation there. Then, maybe we can create *new* souls for the babies. Until then, I get to be born again. And it is *time!*"

"But Gramma!"

"I will forget everything I know. I have to start fresh and make a new life. I am going into the best family in the universe. I will always love you Susie."

At that, she moved past the doctor and shrunk into the tiny size of the baby. I let the speed of time progress back to normal. Standing there, a silly grin on my face to reassure Kimberley, I whispered, "Gramma."

Kim's gasp of surprise coincided with the end of the last push. The baby came out wet and slippery, caught deftly by the doctor.

"It's a girl!" he cheered, cleaning the tiny child up quickly. The infant took in a breath of air without crying. When the doctor placed the baby on Kimmy's stomach to help the placenta to pass, Kimmy and the baby stared eagerly at each other. Kimmy's joy was profound.

The doctor cut the umbilical cord and the nurse took the baby to be checked over. Kimmy looked around at us, happier than I have ever seen her in her whole life.

"Have you chosen a name for her?" the doctor asked while he cleaned her up.

"Sarah Marie Foton," Kimmy said smiling at me.

"That is a lovely name," the doctor said, covering her up. He went to the sink and washed his hands. "That went very well. You have a beautiful daughter. Now you both need a rest. The nurses will take you to your room and bring Sarah to you."

"Thank you Doctor," Kimmy said, looking anything but tired.

"We had better go," I said firmly.

"Go, Why? "Kimmy whispered.

"Because if they hear you talking to us, they may lock you up and take Sarah away. You have no living people here to fight for you. So, even if Pete stays, you can't talk to him!"

"Understood," they both said. I knew I couldn't expect him to leave, but when she was tired, Kimmy could blurt out any silly thing.

Derek and I left as the nurses bustled in with a gurney.

"Sue, what happened when you were in Quantum Time?" Derek asked.

"Weren't you in it too?" I asked, surprised.

"No. You made a really tight bubble. The only way I could have been included was if you held my hand."

"Oh. Sorry. I met the spirit going into the child."

"Someone nice, I hope."

"Absolutely. It was Gramma."

"Your Grandmother? Sarah Kathleen LaMarre?"

"Right... But Gramma told me that *I* would have to fix the problem in the light. *I* am the only one who can."

"Did she say how?"

"No. But the work we are doing these days is probably going to create a crisis. If we can keep the Next Men off balance, maybe they will reveal what they want."

"We already know that they want to stop *you*."

"I need more information."

I was still wearing the lovely outfit we had created to make it look like I was exercising in the park. The gauzy, multicoloured scarves fell from my waist and shoulders, looking like an aura around me. I grabbed one of the scarves and tied the end around Derek's wrist.

"I don't know if this will be enough, but I don't want to lose you. If, somehow, they break our hold, hopefully this will keep us together."

"Because we're going back there."

"Right." I loved that I didn't have to explain everything to him. He just knew what I was thinking.

I grasped his right hand firmly in my left and thought the Gate open. I got an overwhelming sense of urgency. If we didn't hurry, we would not make it. We hurried.

The other side was no longer a peaceful, calm place to be. Even when it was at its most crowded, there was calm peacefulness. Now it was chaotic. People milling around, demanding that they be allowed to move on.

There was no sign of the Next Men.

"Hey! Here's someone who must know something!" a burly man shouted, coming right up to me.

"Me? Why would *I* know anything?"

"You are dressed differently and so is he!" The man pointed at Derek.

I hadn't thought about it before. Derek was wearing the same clothes he had on when I first met him. Blue jeans, white t-shirt, jean jacket and sturdy boots. That did stick out in a place where everyone wore white tunics and leggings.

"We came to find out what the problem is here," I said. "We want to help."

"I recognize her!" a smaller man said from behind the big man. "She is the Gatekeeper! She sent us here!"

"Why would you do that?" an aggressive woman to my right shrieked. "This place is terrible! There are bullies that push us around and punish us by keeping us here longer and longer. *My God* promised me *heaven*, not *this*!"

"I know," I said. "That's why I'm here. To see if there isn't some way to fix this."

While we talked, I could see, off to my left, the Gate opening and closing so fast it was like a strobe light. The pure beauty of it was lost in its speed. The jostling of the crowd around me came from all the newcomers passing through the Gate. My teams were hard at work.

"Well then, fix it!" another woman yelled.

I looked around at all the irate people yelling at me as if the whole thing was *my* fault!

"I suspect that this is a problem that can be solved if we all work together." I said calmly.

"Work together? It is supposed to be working right already! Why should *we* have to do anything?" That big man was getting annoying.

"Look, it really doesn't matter what it is *supposed* to be. It only matters what it *is*! If we talk to the Next Men as a unified front, they may be convinced to do their jobs!"

"You have a problem with how we do our jobs?"

I spun around, recognizing the voice of one of the Next Men trying to sound tough.

"You do not exactly have the serenity traditionally associated with the White Light," I said. "Why not?"

"Because *you* and your *minions* keep sending too many here!"

"I do not choose where they go, the Gate does," I countered. "Why don't *you* send them *on*?"

"We do our job the way it has always been done. The balance has always worked."

"But, you must work *faster*!" I said in frustration. "Don't you realize the population has increased over the last few decades?"

"We have to take care of that too," the guy said smugly. "That is *part* of our job! These souls can go back any time. They have the chance of greater understanding, living more lives."

"Who is your boss?" I asked quietly.

"You don't want to know," the man said, looking around uneasily.

"Since I can't reason with *you*, I do want to know. Who is your Boss?"

"Look, Gatekeeper, trust me on this, you don't want to know. *Our* Boss is not what you would call reasonable."

"Are you saying that I am *un*reasonable?" a soft contralto voice spoke around us.

The Next Men who had confronted me stepped into a straight line, standing at attention, but keeping their eyes firmly closed.

"No Ma'am," the spokesman said briskly.

"Uh huh." There was laughter in her voice. "Gatekeeper!" her soft voice became hard and sharp. "Why have you come here?"

I felt like a child standing in front of the principal. Derek's hand in mine was the only thing that gave me the strength to go on.

"These people should not be kept here waiting forever to go to their afterlife. It is a long, frustrating, boring existence."

"Perhaps they get what they deserve."

"No! They are good people. All of them! The Gate would not have sent them here otherwise. But look around! It is *not* a peaceful place any more because your Next Men are not doing *their* job!"

"They are doing what they have been told to do. I am satisfied with *their* reports. If, at some time, one comes to me to say we must change, then I will consider it. Until then, stay on your own side of the Gate!"

She caused the Gate to open right in front of me. One of the Next Men reached out to push me through, but I grabbed his outstretched hand and pulled him with me. I heard the woman's voice shriek just before the Gate closed.

"What did you do? Send me back!" the man screamed. "Send me back, send me back...."

We were in one of my favourite spots. The top branches of a giant redwood tree. He seemed to be terrified, but not from the height.

"Noisy, isn't he?" I asked Derek.

"I wonder how we shut him up?" Derek mused, looking sideways at the man.

I reached over and lightly slapped the man's face to get his attention. He shut up and stared wide eyed at me.

"That's better," I said. "Now, what do I call you? Do you have a name?"

He silently pointed to the badge on his lapel.

"Next? How do you know which one is being spoken to if you are all called Next?" Derek asked. The man looked at him as if he was speaking gibberish.

"All right, Next. I am Sue and this is Derek. Derek helps me do my job, which is Gatekeeper. Now, I want you to tell me about *your* job."

"My job? I just send people to the next place." He shrugged as if it was obvious.

"The next place. But it seems that most people are *not* being sent on. They are stuck in the White Light. Why?"

"Well, the Morrigan says it is necessary in order to supply the demand for all the new births in the world. Do you have any idea how many babies are born *every day*?"

"So you fill the need with unhappy, dissatisfied people who feel they have been lied to and gypped throughout their lives."

"Umm…. Well, that's not quite how we see it. We keep a desk in the far corner and when they want to go back, we send them there! It works!" He actually smiled in satisfaction.

"How many times does a person have to do that?"

"Some have gone through us hundreds of times. Some are patient and wait for their number."

"What happens when their number comes up?" Derek asked.

"They go to the place that their religion has described as heaven. There are quite a few heavens out there."

"But it takes so long!" Derek shook his head.

"Time never meant anything to anyone until *you* showed up! Now you are sending vast amounts of people in and they are noticing their surroundings! It's all *your* fault!"

"Hmm. Other people's incompetence is *my* fault. I'll have to remember that."

"It is not incompetence! This system has worked forever. We have no reason to change!"

"*People* have changed. People strongly feel that they should have a *say* in what happens to them. They do not like being told what to believe, where to go and what to say. I guess I have to teach you about people."

CHAPTER 28

Next was an unwilling participant in his education. We took him to places where people congregated like churches, schools, malls. Whenever something important came within his line of sight, he closed his eyes. He wouldn't even look at a man and woman being affectionate to each other.

In desperation, I decided to put him into a body for a while.

Pete had been doing research on coma patients. For many of them, the soul had already left the body, leaving a shell that was still too healthy to die. Some were on life-support and the body would never be able to function on its own. There were a few, however, that the body was functioning as if asleep. Pete kept me up to date on these bodies in case I had need of one.

Derek and I took Next to the same hospital where Kimmy had had her baby. We waited in the hallway so Next could see what it was like in hospitals. He just ignored all the spirits that came to me the same way he ignored them in the White Light. The ghosts that were going to a darker place really bothered Next. He peeked through fingers at them as if they were bugs in a jar. He refused to interact with any of them, so, I took him into a room and roughly put him into a sleeping form.

The heart rate increased, the breathing deepened and the eyes opened. Nurses, who had been watching the monitors ran into the room before Next had a chance to scream.

"Katie! Welcome back to us!" the nurse exclaimed. "There, there, don't try to talk. You have had a long sleep! Do you remember anything that happened to you?"

The woman in the bed looked wildly around the room, probably trying to see me or Derek. Unfortunately for her, she couldn't see or hear us any more.

"What?" she gasped. "Who? Where?"

"Stay calm," the nurse urged. "All your questions will be answered. The doctor has been called. Everything will be all right."

The woman sank back in the bed, staring around at all the electronic devices around her. She kept running her finger tips over everything within reach; her face, the covers, the tube coming out of her arm.

We knew the sensation of touch was new to her, but the staff would not.

It did not take long before a doctor came into the room.

"Hello, my dear," the doctor said cheerfully. He was an angular man. His head was long with angular planes and his body was long and thin. Even his hands were thin and bony. "I'm Doctor Sharp. I'm going to check you out and make sure everything is working right."

She did not fight the doctor or nurses as they checked her reflexes and muscle tone. She looked pretty flexible from our point of view, but she still looked like she was on the verge of a scream.

"All right, my dear. Do you remember your name?"

An irritated look came across her face as she said, "Next."

"Next? What next?" the doctor said, confused. "No, my dear, your name is Katie Konroy. We have some pictures and things brought by your family to help you remember."

"Family?"

"Yes, my dear, you have a family. At least you *had* a family. Unfortunately, they were in an accident while you were in the coma. As far as we have found out, they are all gone."

"No wonder Pete was keeping tabs on her," I muttered. "She's perfect."

Katie turned her head to look in my direction. She must have heard me! I moved to another spot, but she kept staring at the corner.

"What is it?" the doctor asked.

"I heard something. The Gatekeeper," she said, turning back to him. "What happens now?"

"We will run some tests to make sure you are healthy. You will need Physiotherapy to strengthen your muscles. You will have an Occupational Therapist and Social Worker to help you re-establish yourself in the world. You can relax for now, we won't send you out without the help you need.

"All right. Goodbye," she said, laying back on the bed. Her tone was of dismissal, which obviously shocked the doctor. I saw him give her a puzzled look before he left the room, closing the door behind him.

"Where are you?" she said, looking all around the room. "Gatekeeper, what have you done to me and why?"

"I have made you human," I said from the end of the bed. Her head whipped around to stare at the space I occupied.

"Why?"

"*Your* job deals with humans, but *you* know *nothing* about them! You need a lesson in humanity before you can deal fairly with them."

"You can't do this to me! Don't you know who I am? I can…"

"No you can't," I interrupted. "You had better remember where *you* are and who *I* am! I am the Gatekeeper and we are on *my* side of the Gate. You are going to be dealing with a lot of very nice people who want to help. If you treat them badly, or if you become a bad person, the Gate will not send you home. You will go to a much darker place."

"You wouldn't!" she gasped.

"I keep telling you, it is the Gate that chooses. All I do is send people there for the Gate to decide. You had better live this life accordingly." I grabbed Derek's hand and we left.

"I wonder…," Derek said, sitting in his comfortable spot in the treetop.

"What?"

"Do the people who go to the darker places get a chance to do it again? Do they have Next Men that send them back?"

"And give them a chance to do it right? When you look at humanity and how young some people become monsters, I would think it is a definite possibility... Am I going to have to go *there* too?"

"No... well... I wouldn't think so... hmm. Maybe."

"Great." The thought made me feel sick to my stomach. "If I do, you are not coming with me."

"What? No way!" He sat up sharply and fell off of his branch. It took a second before he was back in place, ready to argue. "I have been with you for almost every step of this thing you are on!"

"Thing?"

"Adventure, journey, job, whatever. I have helped you as much as it is possible to help. I don't want anything in return, except..."

"Except?"

"Except to be there with you. To share your fate. Susie, I love you. Life without you is nothing."

"Life?!"

"You know what I mean! We are more alive now than either of us were in our whole lifetimes!"

"That's just it! I don't want to lose you! I can go through the Gate and come back. What if I lose my grip on you? I don't want to keep doing this without you!"

I felt like we were at an impasse, but Derek looked stubborn.

"Then I will hold on harder. If you go without me, I will get Mia to send me there. I will hitch a ride on a serial killer or something, but I *will* go."

"Damn," I said, trying to think about what had to be done. "Well, we may as well get it over with. Who's working the Middle East these days?"

"Mia and her team. Let's go."

*

"Are you saying there is more chances of bad people here than anywhere else?" Mia asked, looking shocked.

"No. I'm saying there are more suicide bombers and killers here right now. There is a war here. War attracts bad people."

"All right, you have a point. We were on our way to one of them when you called. I hate it when they target the babies."

We arrived at a place that had once been a storefront. The dust had not yet settled and there was a lot of crying and yelling going on. Those who had died in the explosion were standing together looking confused. One other stood a short way apart from the others, looking excited. His anticipation showed me, more than anything else, that he was responsible for the bomb and he expected a reward for having done it.

"You!" I said, walking up to him. "*Look* at what you have done!"

"Yes, I did. Allah will praise me!"

"Maybe he will, but *I* won't," I had Derek tied to me again as well as a firm grasp on his hand. I reached out to the man and touched his shoulder, but I hung on to him too.

When the Gate opened, it was not as dark as I had seen for serial killers, but it was nonetheless dark. We moved quickly to it and tumbled through into a place without light.

At least that's what my eyes told me. Derek and I stood together trying to see something around us.

"Hey! Let go!" the killer demanded, twisting in my grip. "Where is this? Where are the virgins and slaves? I can't see!"

I let him go and waited for a while. Slowly, the space revealed itself to me with the light showing in the red part of the spectrum. I had dabbled in photography in my University days and this place looked like a standard dark room with something else added.

As my eyes adjusted more, I saw people milling around in the same way as those in the White Light. We started walking, looking for a difference.

"Look there," Derek said, pointing to a brighter area. "That looks like flames."

Sure enough, the way the light flickered on the people, there appeared to be flames, but as we approached, all we saw was the shadows on the people.

The people were different. They *all*, each and every one of them, looked terrified. Their movements seemed to be an effort to hide behind others. Since they had no idea who they were hiding from, they were all exposed in all directions anyway.

We did not have to wait very long before another light source opened above us. This one was in the ultraviolet range. People caught in this light glowed strangely, particularly their eyeballs. A group of dark men materialized around us, separating Derek and me from the crowd.

"What do you want here, Gatekeeper?" one of them asked.

"I want to know what happens here and where people go next. I gather that this is a waiting area?"

"Indeed. They must wait here until they have examined their lives. Once they see how it truly was, they can go to the next level."

"Is there a backlog?" I asked, looking at the huge number of people milling around.

"Not really. Some just take a very long time to realize where they went wrong."

"Where do they go from here?"

"There are choices. Some choose to be punished. Some prefer oblivion where their soul is scattered to the winds never to exist again. And some want to go back, to be reborn so they can try to do it right the next time."

"But, that sounds fair and reasonable!" I exclaimed.

"Why would we not be fair and reasonable?"

"Because the guys in the White Light are not!" I snorted.

"Ah. Theirs is the more difficult task," the man nodded wisely.

"More difficult? How can that be?"

"The people they see have a self satisfied attitude. They will not look to see room for improvement. And really, even a Saint can be a miserable person sometimes! A space full of people who think they are all Saints? No thank you! *We* wouldn't enjoy that. But why are you going through the Gate? Are you not busy enough on your own side?"

"I am *more* than busy enough! But there is a backlog that is disturbing the balance of the system."

The group, there were six of them, closed their eyes and thought for a second. "Ah yes," the spokesman said. "It is like a traffic jam and everyone is frustrated. When they go back to live again, they will take that frustration with them."

"So what do I do?" I muttered, not really expecting an answer.

"You *are doing* the right thing. Teach them to respect and appreciate humanity. Maybe then, they will use some kindness in their methods."

The bomber that we had come through the Gate with seemed to realize that he was not going to have the fate he had been promised. He squeezed past the dark men with the intent of hurting me. Derek stepped between and got the blow that was aimed at me. He collapsed in my arms, stunned.

"You had best go back," the closest dark man said, easily holding the bomber back. "We cannot open the Gate for you, only you can do that. Good luck in your mission."

I thought the Gate open right beside us so I could take Derek home. Oddly, it seemed to take much longer going in that direction from that place. I took Derek straight to Pete and Kimmy and laid him down on the couch in her apartment. She had just arrived home with the baby that morning.

"Derek! Sue, what happened?" Pete asked, rushing over to us.

"Derek was hit! He stepped in between. It was supposed to be me!" I found myself crying for the first time in a very long time. I buried my face in Derek's chest and sobbed. "I can't keep doing this; hurting my friends and making a bad situation worse. If he doesn't get better, it will be my fault!"

"If you remember, I insisted on going with you."

I felt his words rumble through his chest to my very tired senses. His arms wrapped around me, holding me as tight as I held him.

"I am all right," he said. "I just didn't expect that guy to be able to actually hurt us. I am too used to being a ghost, invulnerable to the actions of others... We need a vacation."

"Vacation? *Now?*" I blubbered.

"Yes, Sue. Derek's right!" Kimmy urged. "You are exhausted. I don't know where you just went, but you look like you did after you crammed for two weeks for first year University Chemistry. And remember you fell asleep in the exam and had to drop the course anyway? Don't let that stuff happen again! Get some rest!"

"When and where?" I asked, feeling befuddled.

"I have an idea," Derek said. "Pete, Kimmy, if you have to reach us, call me. Otherwise, don't look for us for two weeks. All right?"

Their agreement was suspiciously quick, but I was too tired to think about it. Derek took my hand and pulled me up, through the building, into the sky, above the clouds and into space. We kept going until we were nearing the moon. He landed us beside a few enormous rocks that had shadows extending a huge distance away from the sun.

After I shed my body, one of the things I loved most was to fly. If I had to travel, I pretended I had wings and flew. I could teleport instantaneously to a place, usually the locket. But I preferred to do that only in emergency situations. Flying was more fun. When I stopped to talk with people or just to rest, gravity did actually take hold and bring me to the ground. Not always gently.

I discovered, with Derek, that the Moon's gravity affected us the same way as with anything solid. We jumped into the air and somersaulted our way back to the ground. The landings were much softer. Even though we did not disturb the deep layer of sand and dust, it felt gentler to land on than rock.

Derek took me to a spot where, if I looked in one direction, I saw the Earth lit up and glowing from the sun in the daytime and city lights at night. Then, he turned me around and I saw the vastness of space crowded with stars. I can remember, as a child, looking at the night sky and seeing stars and great empty areas of blackness where only my imagination could put something into the emptiness. The view from the Moon showed those spaces filled with more and more stars as if they were fighting to be acknowledged. There were no empty spots at all.

On the Moon, resting in Derek's loving arms, I slept. I felt no fear or worry for a while and finally allowed myself to rest. It was wonderful.

By the time we returned to Kimmy and Pete, I was ready to deal with the situation at hand. The first task was the education of the Next Man, Katie Konroy.

When we returned to the hospital, it was to find the staff shaking their heads and Katie looking stormy.

"No, no, no, no, no, no!" she repeated over and over, sitting on the floor in the corner of her room.

There was a distinctive odour in the room that told me she had not yet learned to use the bathroom facilities.

"Fine! You can sit in it for a while!" the nurse on hand stormed out of the room, slamming the door behind her.

"What is going on?" I asked.

"Gatekeeper? Is that you? Take me back! Please! This is horrible. How can anybody live this way?" She burst into tears.

"Live like what?" I asked, rubbing my nose.

"This body keeps doing things to me! There is no warning! No reason! I don't understand."

"So, they didn't show you the toilet?"

"Toilet? That white thing in there? They showed me, but no one said what to do with it! What is it for? What do they want from me?"

"All right," I said, sitting down in front of her. "You now have a body. Your body must function properly to keep you healthy. It takes energy to live, so you have to feed your body."

"Food. Some of that is good."

"A lot of it is good. Hospital food is not the best, but it is nutritious. But your body can only use a part of the food. It filters out the unusable stuff and dumps it out."

"That?" she asked, pointing to a pile on the bed.

"That's right. That and the liquids. You can tell when your body wants it to leave by pressure in your abdomen."

"Abdomen? Pressure?"

"Any kind of discomfort. Then, you sit on the toilet and let it go out there."

"But, I can't feel it! Or, I feel too much. This body is nothing *but* discomfort!"

"Tell the nurses. They will have a much better attitude if they understand that you don't know when it's coming. You will not get out of here if you cannot control this. It is not considered socially acceptable to just let loose wherever you are! As well, there is another thing that women's bodies do in particular. It has to do with the ability to have babies."

I explained the whole process to her, then saw a puzzled look cross her face. Immediately after, a fresh puddle formed around her.

"That!" I said, moving back. "Your look showed you felt something!"

"I felt it here," she said, pressing her hand to her lower abdomen. "But what do I do?"

I sighed. "When you feel that particular feeling, *before* you relax the muscles, go to the toilet, pull the clothing out of the way and let the stuff fall into the toilet. Clean that area of your body with toilet paper, put your clothes back in place, flush the toilet and wash your hands. Don't forget to wash your hands, you don't want to spread germs."

"Gatekeeper, why did you do this to me? I have never had these 'feelings' or 'sensations' before! I don't know what to do!"

"You will learn. If you do not learn, they will move you from here and put you in a mental hospital where you will be locked up for the rest of this body's life. And I will have to go get another Next Man to teach about humanity."

"Another?! No! You can't do that! I will learn. I promise I will learn!"

"Will *your* experience be enough for all of you to understand?" I wondered.

"Yes. We join our minds. We can feel anything that happens to any one of us. If you hit one, we all hurt and have a bruise, sort of. It is enough to punish me!"

"You know, most humans don't think of life as punishment."

"I am *not* human! I don't belong here! I don't understand the rules!"

"Of course you're human!" the nurse said from behind me. She was pushing a mop and bucket to clean the room. "You're just a little confused, that's all. It's not your fault if you don't remember anything. Amnesia happens in many different ways. We assumed that since you remembered the language, you would remember the basics, like how to go to the bathroom. It is unusual, but it is not your fault. Your language ability is enough to show us that you are smart, therefore, you can learn the rest. No problem!"

The nurse worked while she talked. She stripped the bed and washed the mattress. When she was done, she helped Katie up and took her into the washroom to clean her up. Katie was subdued and watchful.

"I'm going for now," I said to Katie. "If you are smart, you won't let them know you hear voices. That puts you in the mental hospital too. I will be back to check on your progress."

"No! Gatekeeper! Don't leave me here!" she cried.

I waited to see what the nurse would do. She had obviously heard the calls to the Gatekeeper before.

"Now, now, dear, this isn't that bad. You will feel much better when you are clean and smell better. It is a fact that moods are affected by aroma."

As soon as she had Katie in the washroom, cleaning staff came in to the room to remove the soiled sheets and clothing and wash the floor. They sprayed air freshener as they left.

Satisfied with that situation, I went back to check on Kimmy and baby Sarah.

The baby was sleeping quietly, but Kimmy was going through her closet like a whirlwind.

"Kimmy! What are you doing? What is it?"

"Oh Sue, I'm so glad you're here! None of these things look good enough any more! I thought I would be back in shape, but I'm not! I still bulge!"

"But you just had a baby! Of course you bulge! What difference does it make?"

"I have to go to the premiere of the movie tonight!"

I stopped, stunned. The movie had been the backdrop of our lives for so long, I forgot it would be finished. "Tonight?"

"Tonight." Kimmy agreed, sitting on the bed.

I looked through the mess of clothes, glad that Kimmy had kept all of the things I had before I shed my body. The colourful sheer things I had made to put over my exercise clothes were all still there. I pointed to a simple black dress and one of the covers. It was a loose and filmy vest that extended beyond the hem of the dress. When Kimmy had it on, all the bulges in her tummy area were not noticeable. The eye was caught by the bright, iridescent colours of the vest.

"Susie, what would I do without you?" Kimmy sighed. "This will do. Will you guys come with me? Please?"

This was the culmination of a great deal of work on Kimmy's part. We were very proud to accompany her to this fancy deal. It was a new experience for me too.

The studio sent a limousine to pick Kimmy up. They had offered an escort, but she refused, wanting to be able to talk with us without explanation.

The front of the theater was roped off and a red carpet was laid out across the sidewalk. People with cameras lined the path. We stepped out of the limo and walked slowly to the entrance. Kimmy was carefully trying to look alone while Pete was trying to be the perfect escort. He kept saying things in her ear that made her laugh.

I had not seen her look so happy in quite a while. Her blond curls were bouncing the way they had in high school. I had to remind myself that they used to be my curls and they were never that curly.

We were ushered into the theater as the next limo drove up. Inside, there were a few reporters from various entertainment television shows, set up to interview the celebrities. One beautiful young woman, dressed *way* more expensively than Kimmy, managed to corner Kimmy in the lights.

"Ms. Foton, how do you feel about tonight?"

"Tonight is very glamourous and exciting," Kimmy said. "It is certainly a first for me!"

"Your dress is lovely! Who made it for you?"

"Oh, I'm afraid it's not one of the big names. It came from a designer who does not want publicity. Unusual, don't you think?"

"Then, how will he or she get more business?" the reporter asked, genuinely surprised.

"She does fine with word of mouth. Isn't that Katie Holmes with her daughter to see the movie?"

"Where?" the reporter spun around and Kimmy moved away.

"Well, at least I'm presentable, I guess," Kimmy muttered.

"You will become a mystery woman," I laughed. "And you will be more so when they find out how good the movie is."

We went in and sat in a sectioned off box, reserved for the writer and her guests. The world saw Kimmy sit proudly alone, looking regal and happy. At one point, just before the lights dimmed, some people pushed into the box, wanting to take some seats, but Kimmy told them that she needed the chairs and they were not invited. It was a long time later that we found out he was a famous actor with his children who wanted better seats and thought he could wow his way anywhere.

The movie started and all was quiet. I watched the strange circumstances of the past two years of my life revealed in great detail. The girl who played the part of Gatekeeper looked to be around eleven or twelve. The friendship between the two girls was unbreakable... familiar. I put my hand in Kimmy's and squeezed. She looked at me, tears in her eyes.

Our bond was something she had totally managed to portray. I was very proud of her.

At the end of the movie, the crowd went wild. There were spotlights aimed at the places where the director, writer and actors sat. Kimmy had to stand and acknowledge the enthusiastic applause from the crowd. I would say, all around, it was a successful night.

The next morning, Kimmy's assistant arrived with the reviews, but instead of staying, she made up an excuse to leave quickly. Confused, Kimmy looked at what was being said.

"The talented Kimberly Foton talks to herself!" "Kimberly Foton losing her grip on reality?" "Writer spends too much time alone! Talks to herself throughout the film!"

"What?! What can I do about this?" she gasped. "I didn't know I was being so obvious! Now what am I going to do? They think I'm crazy!"

"It's all right Kimmy. At worst, you are eccentric!" I assured her. "When they want the interview, and they *will*, you just laugh at them and their silly ideas. Then explain that you *do* talk to yourself. When you are trying to make dialogue sound right, you say it out loud. Inspiration may strike you any time or any where, so you carry a small recorder with you. You are a writer, you can do anything you want as long as you write a good story."

"Okay. I can do that. I don't want Sarah to grow up thinking her mother is crazy."

"Why would she think that?" Pete asked. "You are not crazy! Now *my* mother, *she* was crazy! But that's another story."

"Will you tell me that story some time?" Kimmy asked, smiling at him.

I was reassured. Pete did it. Kimmy's sense of humour would keep her safe.

Derek had been quiet since we had seen the movie. When we went to our tree to relax, I managed to get him to talk and tell me what was wrong.

"These movies..." he said. "How do they know? How do they take the pictures? Cameras can't see us, can they? What else can they see?"

"They did it accurately because we described it to Kimmy and she wrote it down. There are people out there, who, using computers, can show anything that can be imagined. The only people who *know* that it is *right* are the ghosts. Us. It will be interesting to see if any ghosts watch it and realize that."

"If they do, they will think the Gatekeeper is a child. They may want to walk right over you."

"Then it's a good thing I'm not!" I laughed.

A light shimmered in front of us for a few seconds before Mia and Greg appeared.

"Excuse me, I hope I'm not disturbing you," Mia said. "I know it's not our meeting time, but you need to know."

"Mia, this is just a relaxing and thinking place. Coming here is no problem! What's wrong?"

"It's Greg! Or, at least, what he did, is doing..."

"All right, Greg, what did you do?"

"Well, there's not much to do when Mia is working. I like to talk to people, mostly young people..."

"That sounds good. What's the problem?"

"Everywhere we go, he stops the young ones from going to the Gate!"

I looked at Greg in surprise. He looked like someone, caught with his hand in the cookie jar. Caught, but not sorry.

"Why?" I asked.

"Because the kids on the other side are having such a boring time of it. I thought they would enjoy helping *you* more."

"Helping me? Helping me how?"

"Digging up information, following people, whatever you need. You know... like the Baker Street Boys in Sherlock Holmes. The kids are eager to contribute!"

"Ages?"

"Twelve to sixteen. Older than that, they think they are too cool for us. Their loss."

"So, if I need someone watched twenty four hours a day, they will do it?"

"Sure! They would break it up into shifts. They would enjoy themselves. Who do you want watched?"

"The Next Man. He is in a woman's body right now. The kids will just know her as Katie. She needs to stay alive and learn about humanity. The Next Men don't seem to value what people go through in their lives to end up in that White Light. Somehow, we have to teach her. Let's go meet your young people..."

"What a sad bunch of kids," Derek said, looking at the group in front of us. "None of them died in a hospital!"

"Mia has been working in a war zone." I said, eyeing the children.

Derek was right. They all looked like they had lived off the streets and died in a bombing. Their clothes were dirty and ragged. Blood oozed from cuts, small and large. But their eyes were all bright and intelligent. They were starting to have fun, possibly for the first time in their lives.

I explained to them, the job of watching the Next Man. Some of the younger ones would get bored pretty quickly, so I needed to keep them doing other tasks as well. They were all independent, apparently taking orders only from Greg. He was grinning when he told me that they called themselves *'Greg's Ghastly Ghosts'*. I was just glad to have more people watching the Next Man.

Our lives returned to a workable, scheduled timetable that got a lot of work done without much stress. For a while, we were all happy.

Except Rose.

Rose was an apprentice that Mia had found and introduced to me. She had only just died in the past year and when Mia encouraged her to go to the Gate, she refused. She was going to stay and wait for the 'Love of her Life' to join her first. Mia asked me to put her to work as an apprentice, hoping to keep her too busy to obsess over a living person. When that didn't work, Mia came to me.

"What exactly is the problem?" I asked. "When he dies, he will get younger and be with her then," I said, watching Rose fidget in a treetop a safe distance away so she couldn't hear what we were saying.

"He is suicidal," Mia said. "But their religion says that suicides go to Hell. He has no one. No family or friends to help him. No one would even know if he was there or not."

"That is sad. In her place, I would just be tempted to take him out of his body."

"But *we* can't do that!" Mia sighed. "I think she tried, but it didn't work. Only *you* have that power."

"Then she would leave a perfectly good body to die!" Derek said, getting upset. "What a waste!"

"How old is he?" I asked.

Mia waved to Rose, signalling her to join us. "How old is he?" she repeated.

"Twenty eight," Rose said.

I looked at Derek. He was thinking the same thing I was. We both grinned.

"Take us to him," I demanded.

Within seconds, we were in a small apartment in a big city. A man was lying back on a sofa, not sleeping, but not really awake. The beer bottles around him explained some of his condition. The small amount of marijuana explained the rest. His condition suited my purposes exactly.

"Name?" I asked.

"Stephen," Rose provided.

"Stephen, can you hear me?" I called. I hadn't tried talking to the living other than Kimmy in quite a while, but I *needed* him to hear me. So far, most of my *needs* had been met. All I could do was try. "Stephen! Wake up!"

"Huh? Whazzup? Who?" He opened his eyes, but saw nothing more than a few shadows in the corners of the room.

"Stephen, listen to me!"

"Arright," he slurred. "Lissening."

"Why are you living like this?"

"What?"

"Are you trying to drink yourself to death?"

"If it cd ony wrk. Get away frm them. See Rosie. Need Rosie."

"Why do you need Rose?"

"She does the bsness. Makes evrythng make sense. She's gone. Doesn't make sense any more. I blew it. I won't make it on my own. Need my Rose."

Rose was standing behind him, tears running down her cheeks. She put a hand on his cheek. He tilted his head and put his hand over hers.

"What do you think?" I asked Derek.

"He is half way here already. The way he is going, he won't last long. He will walk in front of a car or train or something. What a waste."

"All right. Call Pete," I said, grinning. "Rose, I will do this for you for a couple of reasons. I hate to see someone do this in order to die. It is a waste of a life. But we do need a healthy body so Pete can take care of Kimmy. Stephen will agree that having a ghost around that loves you is not as good as warm loving arms. Do you understand?"

"Yes, Gatekeeper. You will take Stephen out of his body and put Pete in. Stephen will be with me forever!"

"Or for as long as you get along," I smiled. "Forever is a very long time."

Pete popped into the room in front of us looking curious.

"Pete, are you ready for a new body?" I asked.

"Am I ever!" he cheered. "Who? This guy?" He looked carefully at Stephen, still sprawled on the couch. "Is he healthy?"

"Yes, he is!" Rose said. "He has just been drinking a lot since I died."

"And of course, we can't wait till he sobers up," Pete sighed. "All right." He turned to me. "I probably won't be able to see or hear you at first. I will need Kimmy's help to get me home. I will try to find a way to let you know what I need."

"What if we assign Greg's Ghastly Ghosts to be with you?" Mia suggested. "They like helping."

The decision seemed to have been made. I looked around at the group and all I saw was eagerness, except for Stephen, of course. He had fallen asleep. I reached out with my left hand and took Pete's hand and put him into the form lying on the couch. Stephen was pushed out as if punched in the stomach. I remembered *that* sensation. It was not one *I* wanted to repeat.

Stephen sat on the floor behind the couch looking dazed. He was no longer drugged, but he was definitely confused.

"Who?" he asked, looking at us. Rose moved into his view and he lit up. "Rose! Oh my Rosie, I have missed you! What is this? What happened? Am I dead?"

"Well....," Rose said, taking his hand. "You are with *me* now. Always. That's what you wanted, isn't it?"

"Yes! I guess... but... did I kill myself? I can't have done that. What happened?"

"You were well on the way to killing yourself," I stepped closer to him. "You made it clear to the people around you that all you wanted was to be with Rose. Now, you are with her."

"But..." He looked down at his body, seeing it still breathing. "I'm breathing! So, I'm not dead?"

"You have been taken out of your body before you made it uninhabitable and someone else has been put in there for now." I was getting the feeling that perhaps I had made too hasty a decision. "You wanted to be dead."

"But, I can't commit suicide! I won't be with Rose! I have to wait."

"You did not commit suicide," I explained patiently. "Your behaviour indicated that you might have, but not yet. But you didn't and you *are* with Rose. The wait is over."

"Stephen, come with me," Rose said, pulling him away from the couch. "Let me show you the wonders of this world."

He followed her, a little reluctantly from my point of view. I hoped Rose could show him the joys of this existence.

We turned our attention to Pete.

"Pete, can you hear me?" I called.

He stirred, opened his eyes and looked around the room.

"I think I heard something in my dream," he slurred. "It's going to take time to get this shit out of my system. Maybe we should have waited till he sobered up. G'night everyone." He rolled into a more comfortable position and went back to sleep.

"I'll get the Ghastly Ghosts to watch over him," Mia said.

"Let's tell Kimmy," Derek suggested.

I agreed, but I had a feeling that we might have a problem coming up.

Kimmy was excited. She had wanted Pete in a body for a long time. She missed his warmth and smiles.

"How old is he? What does he look like? How tall is he? Tell me everything!"

"Umm," I was stumped. "He was lying down! His hair is sort of darkish. There wasn't much light. Oh dear! I'm sorry Kimmy, I didn't think about that! He is twenty eight! Pete needs to sober up the body and clean up. You must arrange transportation to get him here. But Kim..."

"What? What's wrong?"

"Stephen's reaction was a bit odd. For someone who was working so hard to die, he didn't seem to be too happy to be here. Even seeing Rose didn't make him happy."

"He was in shock," Derek said. "Give him time. He will realize this is what he wanted."

"I don't know," I said. "I hope we weren't too hasty. We have to get back to work Kimmy. I'll see you later. Mia will get the information we need when he wakes up."

"All right!" Kimmy cheered. I heard her singing to Sarah as we left.

Two days later, we found out that bringing Pete home would be harder than we thought. I stopped paying attention to Country and State borders right after I shed my body. Friendly relations between Canada and the United States always meant easy border crossing. Kimmy and I had gone South on work visas. She was able to renew hers easily since she was rich and successful. I hadn't even noticed that Stephen lived in Montreal, Quebec.

Pete went through all of Stephen's papers and found a birth certificate, two credit cards and a provincial photo identification. He found a letter telling him that his driver's license was revoked for a period of five years due to drunken driving, which occurred right after Rose died. Apparently, he crashed his car into another car and injured a passenger. He was lucky. If he had killed someone, he would be in jail.

The more Pete looked, the worse his situation seemed to be. He had no passport; he was being watched by the police; he had no money or job to tie him down, but a letter from a probation officer indicated that he was not allowed to leave. The hardest part for him was that he could not see or hear any of *us*. Kimmy phoned him, but distance made the whole situation worse.

"Oh, Derek, what have I done?"

"It's not that bad, Sue. Kimmy can come here. She's still Canadian."

"I know, but it is taking time! And Stephen doesn't seem to be happy! I really don't understand *that*!"

"When he calms down and realizes that he can be with Rose forever, he *will* cheer up."

"I hope so. Kimmy asked me to go get a description of Pete for her. Do you want to come?"

"Not this time. I want to check on Rose and Stephen. She has been unable to work since we did this."

Seconds later, we both popped into Stephen's small apartment. Pete was cleaning up. The walls and floors had been washed and he was dusting the bookshelves. Stephen was pacing on the other side of the room glaring at Rose and Pete and trying to kick the furniture as he passed. Rose was sitting miserably on the couch watching Stephen's every move."

"Why are you here?" I asked firmly.

Stephen whirled on me, pointing his finger at me. "*You* did this! You had no *right*! You stole my life and gave it to *him*!"

"I took your body. You were not making very good use of it. The only thing you kept saying was that you wanted to be with Rose."

"I was drunk! You can't believe a drunk!"

"You were drunk continually since she died! You were killing the body. I can't stand waste."

"But it was *my* body to do with as *I* chose!"

"Is *that* what your religion says? I don't believe you. You were miserable alive and now you are miserable here. Perhaps you should go through the Gate and give us some peace and quiet." It was just a threat. I was watching Rose to see her reaction and was surprised to see relief on her face.

"Stephen, I'm sorry," she said. "I really thought you wanted to be with me. Otherwise, I would have left you alone. I love you. I always have."

"You died!" he raged. "You left *me* with the consequences of what we did! I would have gotten over *you*. I had a life ahead of me! I could have dealt with *them* too!"

"You had jail ahead of you," Derek said. "Is this how you treated Rose in life? You are not good enough for her. *My* only regret here, is that in taking you out of your body, she was subjected to more abuse from you!"

"Why you..." Stephen charged Derek, intending to hurt him. I knew Derek could handle his own, but I wasn't sure I would get a better opportunity. As he rushed past me, I reached out with my right hand and sent him to the Gate.

The Gate was dark. Not the worst I had seen, but it told us that Stephen had done some really bad things in his life. Rose stared at it in horror.

"I didn't understand," she said quietly. "Sometimes, you don't know it is abuse until it stops."

"I think mental abuse is the worst of all," I agreed. "Why were you with him?"

"He made me believe he needed me. I worked two jobs to support us. I had everything worked out too! I had Uncle Bill's will and everything! We wouldn't have to struggle again. The loan sharks would be taken care of even. Now, that's all ruined!"

"Uncle Bill?" Derek asked, wondering where another person came into it.

"He's my uncle. Or, at least, he's my grandmother's brother-in-law. My aunt and I had it all worked out. I was to get everything!"

"That would be a pretty distant relative. Didn't he have anyone closer?"

"Oh yes," she shrugged. "But we convinced him to sign a will anyway. It is iron clad! We even made sure he didn't remarry when he wanted to."

Derek and I exchanged troubled looks.

"And did you collect on your Uncle's estate?" he asked.

"No! He is still alive at ninety five! I have been waiting for him to die for years! And now Stephen can't get it either! All that wealth will go to his sister's children! As if *they* needed it!"

"But they are more closely related to him," Derek said. "They are entitled."

"That's why we had the will written so well. I worked on that for five years! It was like having a savings account." She really looked stormy.

"How did you die?" Derek asked.

"A street accident. I was pushed in front of a bus. It happened so fast, I couldn't believe it for a while."

"Did you have insurance?"

"Yes. A policy that my parents started when I was young."

"Did he collect?"

"He didn't know about it. Otherwise, he would have. He was named beneficiary. I never found the right time to tell him. He hated talking about the future."

"So there is money available?" I asked.

"About one hundred thousand dollars," Rose agreed. "Those papers are in an envelope under the file holder in the desk."

"Who would look there?" Derek asked.

"Not Stephen. He was messy. It gave me time to think."

"Did *he* push you in front of the bus?" Derek asked.

The thought had not occurred to Rose. She sat, quietly thinking about the events that led up to her death. The look on her face changed from surprise to puzzled to anger. Then the tears rolled down her cheeks.

"Yes. He did," she sobbed. "Stupid, stupid, stupid. And I didn't even see it! How could I have missed that? He was getting so desperate for money!"

"You were in love?" I guessed.

"What about the police?" Derek asked, watching Pete take books off the shelves to get the dust off of them.

"I know they came around here several times after I died. They must have suspected something."

"I hope they can't prove anything," I said, fear clenching my stomach. "We have to tell Pete."

"How?" Rose asked.

"I tell Kimmy and she phones here and tells him," I said. I remembered that I was supposed to be checking out what he looked like now, so I went over and had a good look.

He was tall. Almost the exact height that Pete was originally. His eyes were the kind of grey that looked like they would change with the background. His hair was a light brown. If he got to Los Angeles, it would probably turn blond in the sun. His features were sharp. Thin angles and planes made him look angry even when he wasn't. His skin was blotchy in response to the drugs and alcohol he had consumed. And he was thin. So thin, I was sure I could count ribs if he took his shirt off.

Kimmy could fatten him up. She was a really good cook. All my best memories of food were things she had made.

But I had a sinking feeling that we had not yet found all of the problems facing us.

"Rose, I don't think we can let you continue your job," Derek said, moving in front of her.

"What? Why?"

"Because you were going to steal everything from your Uncle Bill. Tricking an old man into signing a will like that may be legal, but it is just wrong. You had no right to his money when there are closer relatives."

"No! You don't understand!" She stomped her foot at him in frustration.

Derek snatched the pearl ring from the long chain where Rose kept it tied around her neck. He moved fast and I moved faster. I sent her to the Gate where, if I understand the levels of darkness, she would spend a great deal of time with Stephen.

CHAPTER 29

Greg had six of his young ghosts staying with Pete. Some of them were just learning how to do things in the world where they found themselves, so they spent their time learning in Pete's apartment. Once they learned to move things, they could communicate with him. At Kimmy's suggestion, Pete bought a Ouija Board. Thus, they could tell him things he needed to know.

Two weeks after I sent Stephen to the Gate, I got a panic call from the kids. I rushed there to find Pete huddled in his bathtub and his apartment riddled with bullet holes.

"What on earth?"

"They were gangstahs!" one of the kids said to me. He was a young boy, dark hair and dark eyes, who looked like he had grown up in a slum. He was very excited.

"Gangsters? What did they do?"

"They came hammering on the door. I saw the guns, so I told Pete not to open it!"

"You did? How?"

He pointed to the Ouija Board that had fallen to the floor in front of the couch. "Pete stayed quiet, but those guys yelled that they knew he was there and they wanted their money! They couldn't break down the door. Now I see why he has so many locks!"

"I wondered about that too," I agreed. "So they just started shooting?"

"Yes! Pete lay in the tub and it's a good thing he did! Look at the holes! They're everywhere!"

"Then what?" I asked while I walked through the room. It truly was amazing that Pete survived. His quick thinking to get into the tub was the only reason he was alive.

"They heard sirens and left."

"Thank you. Joseph, isn't it?"

The boy nodded, grateful that I remembered his name.

"Those are the same sirens we hear now?"

He nodded again. By reflex, I had gone into Quantum Time to assess the situation. I took us back to regular time and watched.

Two burly police officers came heavily up the stairs and banged on the door. The door swung inward and fell onto the floor.

"Oh oh," the first grunted, stepping over the barricade and walking on the debris from the walls and ceiling. He looked into the bathroom and saw Pete huddled in the tub.

"He's alive!" the officer said in French.

"How did he manage that?" the second officer responded.

"He's in the tub! Get up, you!"

When Pete didn't respond, the officer poked him with his night stick and demanded again that he get up in French.

Pete got out of the tub, brushing glass and plaster bits off of himself and looked around at his apartment.

"Oh boy," he said. "Someone must be really mad at me. What a mess!"

The Police officers both pretended that they didn't understand him. Each grabbed one of Pete's arms and helped/pushed him into the middle of the living room where the coffee table used to be.

"Who did this?" the first asked, in French.

"I'm sorry, I don't speak French," Pete said, noticing a trickle of blood flowing down his arm and dripping off of his fingertips.

Again the police ignored him.

"If you keep talking in French, I won't understand you," Pete repeated. "Why don't you speak English?"

The second officer spit into a dusty pile of rubble and snorted. "English."

"Yes, English," Pete sighed. "Don't make the rumours about Quebec a reality. I know you speak English. It's part of your job requirements."

"And we know you speak French, Monsieur Stephen Dupois," the first officer said, finally in English. "Vinnie le Merde put out a contract on you. Why?"

"I don't know," Pete said, looking frightened. "Can't we let him think he succeeded?"

"So we protect *you*?" the officer snorted.

"Umm... yeah. So I get to live a little longer," Pete nodded.

"Only if you help us convict him," the officer said, squeezing Pete's injured arm.

"I would be happy to, but I don't know anything." He winced at the pain in his arm.

"You dealt drugs for him for six years! You know enough!"

"Six years!?" I could see shock on Pete's face. "What else did I do?"

"Smuggling drugs, trafficking, suspected murder..."

"Murder? Oh no."

"Oh yes. The only reason we haven't nabbed you before this, is because we can't find the motive. Maybe now we will find it."

"Motive?" Pete asked, confused. "Who?"

"Your girlfriend, Rose. Come on, we have said too much. You are coming with us."

"Can I see a doctor?" Pete asked. "I don't want my blood getting all over everything." He deliberately let a drop fall on the quieter officer's shoe.

"Merde! What did you do that for?"

"Because I am injured," Pete said, pulling his arm out of the man's grip. He rolled up his sleeve to reveal a deep gash along his biceps. "This needs stitching."

"All right, come along. Forensics will be here soon."

They took him out, still grabbing his arm. I waited with Joseph.

"How good are you at moving things?" I asked.

"Pretty good," he said, going over to the one lamp left standing and with great effort, he pushed it over.

"Not bad! Derek! We need you," I called. He arrived on the instant.

"What's up?" he asked. Then he noticed the state of the room. "What happened?"

"More trouble," I said.

"Gangstahs!" Joseph was enjoying the term. "They shot up the place!"

"Where's Pete?"

"The police are taking him in," I told him. "But there is that insurance policy in the bottom of one of the drawers in the desk that Rose mentioned. If the police find it, they will consider it motive to kill her. We have to stop them."

"All right. Joseph, can you get a couple more of the kids to stay with Pete, while we deal with this?" Derek said to the boy. "If they start to hurt him, yell loudly. We will come."

Joseph nodded seriously.

"And Joseph," I added. "If you have the opportunity to move papers or things to let Pete know you are there, go ahead. He is probably feeling all alone right now."

Joseph grinned widely and popped out of our space.

"Okay. First the insurance," Derek said, opening drawers on the desk. There were files all lined up neatly in the drawer, but when we looked in them, we found things like dress patterns, a bill of sale for the television and stereo equipment which were purchased together and a whole bunch of puzzle magazines, organized by date.

"This must belong to Rose," Derek said, pushing everything aside. "She likes puzzles. Ah! Here it is! A one million dollar policy? That's a bit steep for someone her age, isn't it?"

"She said it was one hundred thousand. She must have been salesmanned. Some of them are so good, they talk you into almost anything. I had a salesman ask me one time if making an extra fifty dollar a month payment would take food off the table! In fact, at that time, it would, but who wants to admit *that*?"

"Did you buy what he was selling?"

"No. That question was his undoing. I told him that if that was his best argument, he had better rethink his strategy. But Rose is so young! Salesmen could get her way too easily."

"Yes, but that extra zero on the policy is huge. How could she not know? Did she lie to us?" Derek was troubled by the difference from what Rose told us. "What do we do with this?"

I looked around the room again. There was a small fireplace at the end wall that looked boarded up. Book shelves were inserted into the fire box. "Clear that out and burn it," I suggested. "Why would they close off a fireplace?"

"It gets cold in the winter. Downdrafts would make this place intolerable."

We pulled the books and shelves away. Inside, we found insulation batting shoved up the chimney and above that, a balloon. As soon as the stuff was out, we burned the dangerous papers. Then, to hide what we had done, we tore up some books and burned them too.

"I hate the whole idea of burning books," I said, through gritted teeth.

"They are just story books," Derek said, reading a cover. "Romance! They must have been Rose's books."

"I know, but who's to say what books are important or not. The only reason I can do it at all, is because I know that millions of these have been printed."

We heard some banging on the stairs outside the apartment, so we stopped to watch. Two, not so burly, police officers entered the apartment, putting on latex gloves. They already had boot covers and face masks in place.

"What do they think they'll find in here?" Derek asked, surprised at their behaviour.

"It's not so much what they find. They try not to bring anything more into the scene. It is hard enough trying to figure out what happened.

"Somebody lit a fire!" the first man said, stepping over the shelving. I looked carefully at his nameplate. Doug Hastings. "This was *after* they took him away!"

"How can you tell?" the other, Gerry Osser, asked.

"The rubble from the shooting is under these shelves. René said they hadn't touched anything, they just left."

"The guys below, in the street, evacuated the building. Who could have come in here?"

"We'll find out. The desk was tampered with too. I wonder…" He looked from the desk to the fireplace and seemed to piece things together. "Papers! Maybe we can see what was burned."

I looked more closely at the fire. It had burned down to embers without absolutely destroying everything there. They mustn't see that insurance form! I went closer and blew on the embers until they flamed up again. I kept blowing until the bottom papers, the ones we needed destroyed, fell apart into tiny bits of ash.

"Merde! What did that?" Doug demanded in French. "The fire was going out!"

"Must have been a breeze," Gerry said, looking into the bathroom. "This guy was smart, getting into the tub like that."

"Yeah, but look at the spray of bullets," Doug said, moving away from the fire. "Whoever did this, knows the apartment. They shot from the door, the fire escape and the light pole over there on the street."

"That's serious," Gerry said, measuring the depth of some of the bullets in the wall. "There's only one guy with the confidence and the fire power to do this."

"Yes, but we'll have a hard time proving it."

"I know. What's with the books?"

"Books?"

"Whoever started this fire was destroying evidence. Books were burned. What was in these books?" He fished out one of the spines from the fire. The title was: 'True Love, Lost and Found.' "There may be a coded message in here!"

"Codes? That's Emile's specialty. We'd better take all of these with us." He pulled the ashes out of the fireplace, making sure the embers were out. The various pieces of paper that survived went into plastic bags.

I didn't care since I knew the important paper was destroyed. They could play their detective game all they wanted.

"I think we are safe to leave," I said to Derek. "Unless you want to freak them out."

Derek grinned at me and pushed a bag that Doug had placed on the desk. It landed on the floor, startling both men.

"Hey, careful with that!" Doug exclaimed.

"What? It wasn't me! I can't even reach that spot! What happened?"

"It must have been too close to the edge," Doug said, putting the bag into the evidence box that hey brought in.

When he turned away, Derek lifted the bag out of the box and placed it on top of the desk. Doug turned back to get another bag and noticed the book's remains out of place again. He looked over at Gerry, realizing that his partner couldn't possibly have moved it.

"Something strange is going on here," he said in a low voice.

"What?" Gerry asked, looking at him.

Derek took the opportunity to pick up another book that we had not burned, from the floor. He floated the book through the air and placed it on the desk beside the burned remains in the bag.

"Doug...!" Gerry exclaimed, sounding frightened. "What...?"

"Someone is trying to tell us something," Doug said, nervously. "These books are the key. This one: 'The Phantom Lover' must have the code as well. We'd better take all the books."

"I think we're done," Derek said. "We'd better find out what they're doing to Pete."

We located Pete in a small, curtained off area, in the emergency room of a nearby hospital. The police officers were standing on the other side of the curtain looking nervous. Joseph was giggling.

"What did you do?" I asked the boy.

"I just knocked over a bed pan," he said, trying to look innocent. I waited and he continued. "It was full of... ummm... liquid."

"Why did you do that?"

"The bully cop," he pointed to the one named René. "Wouldn't let the doctor work. He coughed all over Pete! That could infect. I know! My brother got that."

"So you dumped the bed pan...."

"All over his pants and shoes." Joseph grinned.

"So, he backed away. Good. Well done, Joseph."

I stepped through the curtain to see a female doctor swabbing iodine all around and over the cut.

"It is a clean cut along the muscle. It goes deep here, but it should heal without permanent damage."

"Thank you Doctor, I think it was a piece of glass," Pete said.

"You think? Don't you know what cut you?"

"No. Some goons came and shot up my apartment. There was glass and plaster flying everywhere."

"And this is all you got? I'm amazed!"

I hid in the bathtub," Pete sighed. "I am the victim here, but the police are taking *me* in."

"For your protection?" she suggested.

"I don't think so. That thumb print next to the cut is the cop's. They think I am a bad guy."

"And are you?" She looked curiously at Pete.

"No. I may have done things I'm not proud of, but that is over."

"Good for you. I hope it works for you." The doctor cut the thread of the last stitch and wound a bandage around Pete's arm. She put it in a sling and then opened the curtains. "Excuse me, you are blocking the pathway." She pushed past the police officers and went on to her next patient.

"All right, you," the one called René snarled. "Let's go." He reached out to grab Pete's arm, but Pete twisted away enough to deflect it.

"Don't touch me!" he said with some volume. "I'm coming with you! You don't need to hurt me!"

"We'll see. Come on."

Pete followed the other officer with René behind him. If he hesitated, René pushed him with his night stick. Derek and I were behind Rene and Joseph followed us.

"What do we do now?" I asked Derek.

"Maybe we should break him out of here. These guys are too rough."

"Yes, but to go where? We need a plan."

We followed the trio, sitting with Pete in the back of the police car. Joseph stayed, determined to do the job he was assigned. At the police station, we were taken to a small room with a table, two chairs and a two way mirror.

René pointed to the chair facing the mirror for Pete to sit in. He locked one side of his handcuffs on a table leg and the other on Pete's good wrist. He moved to sit in the opposite chair. Derek shoved that chair into the table before René could sit.

"How'd you do that?" he snarled at Pete.

"Do what?" Pete asked. He looked tired and groggy, possibly from the drugs they gave him in the hospital. Some of it, though, may have been an act. Slowly and calmly, he winked. The police man did not even notice.

"All right," I said. "He wants us to freak them out. Maybe even break him out."

Joseph and Derek both grinned like the kid Joseph was. They enjoyed freaking out the living!

"Look you!" René yelled, making Pete jump. "You are in a lot of trouble here!"

Derek picked the chair up and threw it at the wall. Pete ignored it. René couldn't stop looking at it.

"I'm in trouble because someone turned my apartment into Swiss cheese in an effort to kill me," Pete said calmly. "Are you at least going to *pretend* that you are looking for the other guys?"

"We're looking. Don't worry about that! You can't have a private war in *my* city and get away with it!"

"Private war?" Pete was incredulous. "In case you hadn't noticed, *I don't own any weapons!*"

"Then why did they want you dead?"

"I don't know!" Pete was really tired. I had never heard him slur his words like he was. I was starting to think they had drugged him. Truth serum or something, maybe? "Look, I've only been in this body for two weeks and I tell you, they are the strangest two weeks of my existence!"

Derek picked up the chair again and shoved it into the back of René's knees, forcing him to sit opposite to Pete. We wanted Pete to shut up!

"What is this BS?" René said in French.

"There you go again," Pete mumbled. "I was born in Winnipeg! The majority of people speak *English* there. And *Ukranian!* And *German! French* is the *fourth* language in that province, so I don't know what you're swearing at me, but I do consider it rude!"

René reached for his club, obviously wanting to hit Pete. Derek grabbed the heavy weapon and pulled it out of René's hand and slammed it into the mirror. The impact was so hard, it was like an explosion. Glass flew everywhere.

There was a great deal of French spoken after that. I'm pretty sure most of it was swearing. Oddly enough, after I shed my body, I was able to understand most languages, but not the swearing or the colloquialisms. It's just as well. I don't need to be pushed around by people who would swear in my face to try to force me to send them to Heaven.

René's partner burst into the room, yelling about expenses. He went over to René, who was still sitting at the table and noticed the bits of glass stuck in René's back, neck and head. Then he went to look at Pete.

Joseph had done his job well. Pete had not one scratch on him. Specks of René's blood had splattered in his direction, but even the blood missed Pete.

René's partner snarled at René to get cleaned up while he unlocked Pete to take him to another room. We went with him while René hollared for help.

Pete was put into a smaller interrogation room with a camera set up in one corner, a table and two chairs. There was no expensive mirror to break. We weren't sure what we could do. Joseph, being a typical kid, as soon as he saw the camera, sat in front of it on the table and made faces. I went to the other side of the tripod to see what was being recorded.

It was a digital camera. For some reason, Joseph was clearly sitting on the table being juvenile. There was a ghostly image of Pete sitting in the chair. The strange part was that Pete looked more like a ghost than Joseph did! Joseph must have been practising that accomplishment. Derek and I stayed out of the camera's range.

Pete sat in the chair with his hands cuffed behind his back. Clearly, they were taking no chances with him, but by the way he moved his shoulders, it was painful. Derek touched one cuff and it opened. Pete put his hands on the table in front of him.

"What the?" the cop said from the doorway. "Stand up!" he demanded as he moved toward Pete. He grabbed Pete's arms and cuffed him again, pulling his wounded arm roughly.

Pete winced at the rough treatment. He sat down and Derek opened the other cuff so he could move his arms again.

"How did you do that?" the cop demanded. This time he grabbed the cuffs, one end of which was still attached to Pete, and looked at them. Shaking his head, he hooked the loose end around a table leg. Derek touched the cuff around Pete's wrist and it popped open. Pete rubbed his wrists, but said nothing.

Another cop came in the room. "Good day, Mr. Dupois. I am Detective Benjamin Dover." He reached over to shake Pete's hand, but when he realized that Pete's handcuffs were not attached to him, he straightened up in surprise. "What happened to the cuffs?" he asked, backing up.

"They won't stay done up," the other cop said from the safety of the doorway. "I don't know how he does it. Every time I put the cuffs on, he gets them off as soon as I turn my back. Whatever he does, he's fast."

"So, Mr. Dupois, what do you have to say for yourself?"

"Hmm? Me? I don't know. I feel like I've been drugged. Did you drug me?" Pete massaged his wrists and grumbled at the cops in general.

"We do not drug the people we interrogate," Detective Dover snorted.

"Interrogate all you want," Pete said, his eyes drooping. "I need sleep. Wake me in the morning." He put his head on his injured arm on the table and fell asleep.

"No!" Detective Dover squawked, but Pete was sound asleep. "Damn!" he muttered and moved behind Pete to the camera in the corner. The rest of us moved out of the way to avoid the unpleasant sensation of him walking through us. He fiddled with the camera for a few seconds then took it off it's stand, swearing.

"What's wrong?" the other cop asked, looking surprised.

"There's something or someone in here with us," Detective Dover whispered.

"What?"

"Look! The handcuffs!"

I peered over their shoulders to see what they were talking about. The detective had rewound the image to where the other cop cuffed Pete to the table. A blurring of the image occurred at the right of the screen. It moved across the table and touched the handcuff, making it pop open.

"What was that?" the cop asked.

"I don't know," the detective whispered.

"Can we capture it?"

The detective looked at the cop, clearly thinking the man had lost his mind. "I'm not sure we can maintain the capture of *this* guy. Whatever *that* is, it doesn't want him held."

"You think it can unlock doors?"

"Why not? Locks are just mechanisms. If it can open one, then why not all?"

"But, what is it?"

"I don't know. A ghost, maybe?"

"You believe in ghosts?" The cop was mocking his superior.

Joseph, who had been behaving very well through all this, decided to get involved. He pushed the empty chair to the far corner of the room. Both cops stopped and stared at the chair.

Derek had a wicked gleam in his eye. He leaned over the camera that the detective was still holding and pushed the rewind button. The images flashed to the point where they brought Pete into the room and turned on the camera. Derek pushed play so the cops could see Joseph sitting happily on the table making faces into the camera.

"Who's that?" the detective asked sharply.

"Beat's me. The camera must be broken. Double exposed or something, but digital cameras can't do that kind of thing! Can they?"

"Not that I know of. Who's the kid? Ever see him around here before?"

"Nope. Look at our guy behind him!"

"What is it?"

"I don't know. He's all fuzzy. What are we gonna do?" The cop's voice had a definite whine.

"Watch him. Get another camera. I'd say move him to a cell with a bed, but that might be our undoing."

"Why?"

"He's asleep now. Waking him up to put him behind bars could cause more of this ghostly stuff. Let's keep him contained here."

"More ghostly stuff!" Joseph laughed and moved the chair a few inches again.

The two men moved out of the room, locking the door behind them.

"What should we do next?" Derek asked.

"You and I should go out there and look everywhere for any files or folders with Stephen Dupois' name on it. Check the computers too. Pete could do that faster, but I can find my way around most systems. Joseph, try not to wake Pete up, but if anyone comes in, lift the chair and scare them into leaving. You are doing great!"

"All right!" The child grinned at my understated compliment. He clearly was doing a job that was the most fun he had ever had in his life.

We went into the main area of the police station. It was bustling with activity, crowded around many desks. There were windows above filing cabinets along one wall, like an old time schoolroom. Derek headed off to look through the files. I went to a desk that was currently unoccupied and turned on the computer monitor.

The system opened to a search engine. I typed Stephen Dupois into it to see if it could be that easy. The file came up right away showing a mug shot and description and a long list of offenses. Each conviction would have a separate file somewhere and each suspicion of doing something would have another file.

I printed the locations and backed out of this file. I then directed the computer to delete the file. When the usual question of 'do you really want to do this?' came up, a chime sounded. One of the women officers turned to see what was happening as I hit yes.

"What's going on here?" she asked. "Who's erasing this file? Dover, is this you?"

"Me?" Detective Dover came over to the desk to stare at the screen. "Stephen Dupois? No! Make it stop!"

"It's all right," the woman said, starting to tap the keys. "I can recover it."

I got a little annoyed with that, so I made the monitor short circuit and spread sparks around the desk.

"Shit! What was that?" the woman screeched.

I went behind the desk to the cables and followed them through the floor to the main computer system for the police station in the basement. It looked like I had stepped back in time to the beginning of computers where one system took a whole room to house. This, of course, was not just one system. I wasn't sure where backup was stored or any other redundancy that would be incorporated. In my hurry, I felt that it was necessary to shut the whole thing down permanently!

I created heat. Stopping all ventilation fans, I heated the room. One after another, the computer boxes slowed and stopped, some putting out sparks, others dripping plastic from inside their casings.

"What are you doing?" Derek asked curiously from behind me.

"I'm shutting this down. I will need to find the backup place and wipe it too, but this is a start."

"You've found it," Derek said, reading the print on the side of one of the computer boxes. "They trusted this space so thoroughly, they kept it all in one room! Just different computers!"

"How about the paper files?" I asked.

"I found one really large file sitting on Dover's desk."

"Good. They're heading down here now. Maybe we can get what we need and get Pete out of here." We followed the cables back up to the squad room. A large number of the officers had charged down the stairs to find out what had happened to the computers. I went to the printer and took the pages I needed and Derek took the file from Detective Dover's desk. We went to the interrogation room to wake Pete up.

"What? What's wrong?" Pete said, looking up.

I grabbed a pen and wrote on the back of one of the printed sheets a message for Pete. "We want you out of here. Just quietly leave. Take these papers with you."

Derek unlocked the door and we calmly walked out of the station. Pete carried the papers and Joseph moved chairs out of our path. It was a very smooth escape.

"Now, where do I go?" Pete asked.

I grabbed the paper and pen again. "Taxi. Airport. Home. Winnipeg. Stay in my house until Kim gets there. You know Winnipeg better than anywhere else. All right?"

"Best idea I've heard in a long time," Pete agreed. "It wasn't supposed to go like this."

I wrote one last note. "Joseph will stay with you. We will be close. Don't worry." It had been so long since I had tried to write anything, I found the exercise exhausting on my hands. Weird.

Derek and I took the files to a nearby garbage can and read everything. There were three places that might have records on Stephen. He really had been a small time crook who thought he could beat the mob. The most dangerous information out there about him was in the hands of the mob. Derek lit the papers on fire and waited until they were totally consumed before he left the area. We went to the Vital Statistics department and did damage to their computers and some files hidden deep in the basement. We found Stephen's juvenile records at the court house along with his adult record. We just took those files away rather than burning everything. Other people needed their files intact. I did, however, consider computers to be fair game. I may not be able to purge everything out there about Stephen Dupois, but I made a good effort. After all, he *was* dead. He couldn't hurt anyone ever again.

We joined Pete at the airport. Joseph was standing beside him, looking like he would hurt anyone who crossed their path.

"What's wrong, Joseph?" I asked.

"Money!" Joseph snorted. "We had to pay with a credit card, but Pete can't do the signature very well. He faked it by saying he had carpal tunnel and it messed up his writing, but if he hadn't had his ID on him, we'd be back with the police again. I'm not *that* sure we are safe."

"It's a good thing Kimmy put a lot of money on that card," I said. "It has a plus balance and they really don't look at signatures that close. When's the flight?"

"In three hours," Joseph said. "But this is a strange place to fill time."

"Really? Why?" He was laughing and it made me curious.

"The ghosts that are here are trying to travel as if they were alive! They try to buy tickets and everything! They get on the planes to go wherever! They even want empty seats!"

"Well, *this* can't be their homes," Derek said, looking around. "Some of them know you are here, Sue." He pointed to a group that was coming our way.

I signalled to them to follow me to the roof. It didn't take long to send them to the Gate. The only one who wanted to talk to me was the last, a young woman who kept looking over her shoulder as she approached me.

"What's wrong?" I asked. "Is someone trying to hurt you?"

"Me? No!" she blurted quickly. "There is a girl... sort of... she won't come out. She said she would scratch my eyes out if I gave her away, but really, it's not healthy!"

"Okay, where is she?" I asked.

"Usually, she is in the corner, under the sandwich machine on the third floor. She seldom comes out."

"All right. Thank you. I will take care of her. Do you want to go to the Gate now?"

She nodded eagerly, so I reached out and touched her with my right hand. The Gate was a beautiful bright rainbow for her, which was very reassuring. I turned back to the problem she left with me. Somehow, I had the feeling that this ghost-in-hiding was what Joseph had really laughed about. I went searching.

To get into a space under a big machine you have to reduce your size a lot. Not as much as going into a locket, but still, a lot. I compressed myself enough to be able to walk between the machine and the wall. I could not see much beyond accumulated dirt until I turned the corner at the back of the machine. A young girl was crouched in the space hissing at me and threatening to claw me with her hands.

"Hello," I said. "Who are you? What is your problem?"

"Who are you?" she hissed, backing up.

"I'm sorry," I said. "I am the Gatekeeper. I can send you to the Gate so you can move on."

"Move on? Move on! It doesn't work that way! You don't move on anywhere!"

"Why? What happened?"

She stared at me for a minute. I made myself comfortable, sitting on a motor that was connected to a fan.

"You've heard of reincarnation?"

"Of course," I answered.

"Well, people talk about things. Stupid things. They say stuff like, come back as something else. Something like a pampered pet! Wouldn't it be nice to be a kitty cat. What a life of luxury it would be...."

"So, what happened? Were you once in the White Light?"

"Yes," she said miserably. "I was there for *so* long! I was stupid. You know, those Next Men? Have you heard of them? They won't talk to anyone. They ignore everyone who tries to talk to them and they punish people!"

"Punish how?" I felt a sinking sensation in my stomach. What were they doing now?

"I know... like, I *know* I made a pest of myself. That's what you do! At least, that's what *I* always did. You know, the squeaky wheel gets the grease. I thought... I thought if I bothered them enough, they would send me somewhere else, but it didn't work that way. They surrounded me and *yelled* at me! They *yelled* in my face saying they would send me back to be a pussy cat or something! So, I said... I said that would be better than staying there forever and then... poof! I was being born! But, I wasn't a pampered cat! Oh no! *That* would be easy! No, *my* mother was the number one barn cat for a farmer who raised cows! My brothers and sisters died over the first year from cold and sickness! The snow was so deep, I would tunnel through it, but I was the only one who knew anything! I still had my memories and knowledge from being human! I knew things that helped me survive. I stayed close to my mother and when I could, I attached myself to a human... one of the farmer's children.... That was worse." She closed her eyes and a tear ran down her cheek.

"Why?" I asked to get her talking again.

"I was the best cat I could be! I was clean. I cooperated when she dragged me around and dressed me like a doll. I *never* scratched her. I gave her all the love I could, but one day one of the Tom cats came into the house with fleas and they got on me! That was the worst thing I had come across! Ever! In both my lives! I tried to avoid the damned things by avoiding carpets and upholstery. I thought it would work, but the people thought I was crazy! It got so bad, the *people* got bit by the fleas. Then the baths started. They bathed me every day for I don't know how long. You know what they say about cats and water? It's true! Cats hate water! The panic was beyond my control! I bit my girl! Her dad was so upset, he threw me sopping wet into the snow and wouldn't let me back in. I searched for my mother, but she was gone.... None of the other cats would let me into the barn, so I went to sleep on the porch of the house. I froze to death. Now... now, I still feel like a cat and the whole world scares me so much... I don't know what to do."

"I can send you through the Gate," I offered.

"No! They would do something else to me! They made an example of me and if I show up feeling like this, everyone who is stuck waiting in the White Light will fear them more! That's just what *they* want!"

"It's been a while. Couldn't you just go there and quietly rest and recoup?"

"Look at me! My instincts are far more those of a cat! I would stick out! I know that I have to learn how to be a person again. I just don't know how!"

"All right," I nodded. "I want to help you. There is a group of young people who are having a lot of fun by helping me. Would you like to join them?"

"Young people? Dead young people?"

"Yes. Ghosts, spirits, whatever. They watch over people and follow them and help solve mysteries. Tell *them* your story. I think they would like to help you."

"How?" She was very nervous when I waved for Joseph to join us.

"We can teach you how to be human again," he said, coming up behind me. Before she could shrink farther back into the wall, Joseph moved closer and took her hand to shake it. "Hi. I'm Joseph. What's your name?"

"Snowball," she said in a timid voice.

"All right, Snowball. Stick with me. We'll have fun! And you can teach us some cool stuff."

"I can? What?"

"How to be a cat!" he grinned. "Nobody can hurt you now. We won't let them."

I knew he was wrong, but she responded to him. We left the confined space just in time to hear the boarding announcement for Pete's plane.

"There are cops coming," Derek said to me. "I'll stop the ones on the main floor and you get the ones that come up here."

I heard the sounds of crashing garbage cans almost immediately. I looked around and saw several security people reaching for their cell phones. I went into Quantum Time and dashed to each person, making their phones melt on the inside. While I was doing that, I thought there had to be a better way to shut them down. Maybe Pete could figure it out when we got him home.

The guards didn't know who they were supposed to stop, but they did realize that they were supposed to stop someone. There were two planes boarding at the gates in our vicinity. One of them was going direct to New York, the other to Vancouver with stops along the way. The guards assumed the problem was with terrorists, so they converged on the gate to the plane going to New York. Pete had no difficulty walking past them and boarding the flight that would take him to Winnipeg. The plane was in the air before the cops had convinced airport security that the threat was already in the air heading west and they had no way of knowing where he was getting off.

"That should do it," Derek said, popping in beside me. "Once he is home at your place, things should calm down. Kimmy will get there in a couple of days."

"Joseph and Snowball?"

"He took her to meet the rest of the group. That was a good idea, putting her with the kids."

"I feel like I have had too many bad ideas lately. Things were easier when I started this job."

"Sue, it's not as bad as you think. I'm going to check on Pete. You rest. It will be all right. I'm sure of it."

CHAPTER 30

I went home to my little house in Winnipeg. I guess I was feeling a little homesick. I definitely felt like things had gone wildly beyond my control. I needed to think. Pete would arrive within a few hours. Kimmy had found an earlier flight and would arrive a short time later. I had a really strong feeling that their meeting like this would complicate our lives even more.

The house looked vacant. The grass had not been cut; the mail was scattered on the front porch; someone had written a crude message in soap on the front window, probably at Halloween and the timer to turn the lights on and off seemed to be broken.

I went to the door and tried to walk through it the way I had walked through doors for months now. It felt like I walked straight into a wall! Putting my hand out, I pushed against the barrier and found it solid. Curious, I walked right around the building, looking for a gap. I had not rum into anything like this before! What was happening? As I stepped back onto the porch, I remembered. Salt! The salt barrier had been there for a long time. Years! I still had a body when I left my home! All I had to do was open the door.

I had become quiet adept at moving objects. I just needed the key to unlock the door and then I could turn the knob, push the door open and walk in.

So, the key. The hidden, spare key that I put in a spot that no burglar would find, was somewhere in a flower bed. I remember putting it in a fake stone and burying it at the base of some bright yellow flowers. That was no help. It was winter in Winnipeg! The flowers were dormant. There were stems still sticking through the snow along with the overgrown grass and weeds. There was nothing sticking up to indicate what colour the various flowers might have been and I sure couldn't remember now!

I kept walking around the house, hoping an idea would come to me. I was tired. I could go to my favourite tree to bask in the warmth of the sun, but I felt drawn to this place, where it had all started.

Of course, in my world, some things will never change. After being in the one place for a couple of hours, my music drew the ghosts from the city. They came to me like driftwood on the tide, not swift and decisive, but softly, unwillingly. Some were trying to resist the pull to come to me. This was another problem that was new and I had to figure out why.

"What's wrong?" I said to an ancient woman who supported herself with a walker to get to me. You look like you want to run away!"

"I do!" Her voice was as shaky as the hand she brought up to shade her eyes from my light. "I don't want to go there!"

"Where?" I asked.

"To the afterlife! I'm drawn by your music, but I want none of it. Don't send me there!"

"I'm the Gatekeeper!" I said, wanting to clarify my role. "I send people to the Gate. The Gate decides where they go after that. You can't avoid your destiny forever. If you have led a good life, you will go to the Light. Everything will get better for you after that."

"You still believe that?" she croaked. She was losing her voice. "I was there before! Twice! It's not Heaven! There is no Bliss! It is simply a waiting room that the only way out is to come back here to live another life."

All of the other ghosts around us were backing up, staying out of my reach.

"I'm working on that," I said, frustrated. "But when you go to the Gate, you get younger again! It is easier to cope with the Next Men when you are young and healthy. You don't want to stay like this forever, do you?"

"Forever? This is forever?" a younger woman who had probably died in a car accident, shreiked at me. I couldn't blame her. Most of the left side of her body had been burned to an unrecognizable mass.

"No! I send you to the Gate and you become whole again. The Gate *knows* where you should go!"

"Maybe," the old woman croaked, "but it does not send us there. It sends us to a limbo that drains your soul into nothingness. Fix *that* and I will go."

Fix that. It was a command put on my shoulders by everyone who was left waiting in the White Light. I could imagine the Beings of Light pushing these ghosts to demand the reparation. But, how?

"I want to fix that," I said. "I have been working on it. I have one of the Next Men living in a woman's body, trying to learn what it is like to be human. It will take time, but if they get the idea, maybe they will respond better."

"You're dreaming," the old lady snorted. "Those Next Men have no compassion and understanding. Their Boss is cold and callous. It will take a lot more than making one of them human for a while to get them to change."

"Then, what do you suggest?" I was wilting under her scorn.

"Take them *all* out of there! Including The Morrigan! She has less sympathy than them. Then the people can do it *themselves*!"

"There has been only ten of them pushing around millions of people! If the people could do it themselves, they could have easily overwhelmed them and done it! There has to be something else involved."

"The people are pussies!" the woman croaked. "They won't rock the boat for fear that they will lose their place in line! They were good all their lives and don't have it in them to be bad now!"

I burst out laughing. I couldn't help it. "So the Next Men have the perfect crowd to deal with! No one will start a revolution!"

"Right!"

"Then, why don't you?" I asked, looking directly into her angry eyes.

She mumbled something and looked away.

"What was that?" I asked, stepping closer.

"I said, I'm afraid!" she muttered, just audibly.

"Afraid? Of what?"

"Of *not* going back there! All right? I had more to deal with this past lifetime. I had hard choices to make. I don't *know* that I will end up back there." She looked like she had something bitter in her mouth.

The crowd around us stirred uncomfortably at that thought.

"So, now that you have the strength of character to lead a revolution, you think that *that* very attribute will send you to another place?"

"Umm... Maybe."

"Then we need a plan," I said. "I cannot do it all alone either. Are you willing to work *with me* to make it better?"

"Yes!" The old woman actually looked eager instead of bitter and angry.

"How about the rest of you?" I asked the crowd.

The majority of them nodded in agreement. Some stepping forward eagerly. The burned girl was among them.

"All right," I said. "I need to think. Tell the people that you come into contact with to be patient. We will probably have only one chance at this, so it has to be good."

They backed off, talking amongst themselves.

"What is happening?" Derek said from behind me. "I've been looking for you!"

I told him the situation, including my inability to find the key to the house. I felt ready to cry in frustration.

"Well, then, it's a good thing I found you, isn't it?" he said, putting his strong arms around me. "Did I ever tell you about my days prospecting in the Yukon?" He went on when I shook my head. "I was there with a partner. He was my best friend from boyhood. We were going to get rich together. But, accidents happen and I died. He was going to pack up and leave! At the time, I thought that would make my death pointless, so I found some gold and put it in his way. That's why I learned quickly how to move things. I got good at finding metal under the ground and bringing it up to the surface for him. When he finally moved, he became a very wealthy man."

"Then what happened to him?" I asked into his shoulder.

"He bought a piece of land and became a rancher. Did the family thing. When he died, he barely recognized me. He went to the Gate without a word to me. I was forgotten over time."

"Oh, I'm so sorry! That must have hurt."

"For a while. But the Gate was pretty dark when he got there, so I guess he was not the same man I grew up with. But now, I can find any metal underground that I want to. Let's find that key."

He went around the house once. Stopped at the flower bed along the south wall and picked up the fake stone. We had to combine our strength to push the door open, the power of the salt was so strong, but eventually I managed to go into my little house and relax.

"All right, what's wrong?" Derek asked, relaxing on the couch.

I sat in the old chair I got from my grandmother and shook my head.

"I have made mistakes. I rushed in, on the word of someone I didn't really know and interfered in people's lives! I have drifted from the job of Gatekeeper to something else and I don't know what that is! Those Next Men have been pushing people around for centuries and until *I* came along, they got away with it! Nobody complained!"

"So, you want people to stop complaining?"

"Yes! No! I don't know! How could they keep this going for so long without a revolution?"

"Because the people who are there are not the kind to rock the boat. As far as *they* are concerned, they are on the track to Heaven. They have been 'Good' all their lives and they expect the reward now."

"But... If they are the really good ones and the Dark place has the really bad ones, where are the rest?"

"The rest?"

"The folks who lead decent lives, but have faults. Maybe they gamble, or sleep around, or like drugs, or swear a lot. You know, the ordinary, normal people in this world."

"Oh... Them..."

"Them. Us. Or at least me. I am not particularly good *or* bad. I do my best, but really, I could never hold a candle to Gramma. She was special."

Derek laughed! "One of your most endearing features is that you don't realize how special *you* are."

I shook my head at him and rolled my eyes. "Right. But really, where *do* they go?"

"I guess we have to follow *them*," Derek grinned at me. "I would guess the Gate would be in the midpoint between light and dark."

"Right. But I don't know *that* until it happens."

"So, we need to be ready at all times. Can we do that?"

"Of course," I agreed, thinking about all the people I sent to the Gate and it was just beautiful, but not the brilliant White Light that we couldn't look at.

"But we can't go yet," Derek interrupted my thought.

"Why?"

"First we need to be sure that Kimmy and Pete are all right here. We promised to tell them when we were going to do something crazy."

"This isn't crazy!"

"Think like Kimmy!"

"Oh, all right. Hare brained idea that takes us away from her." I sank back into my chair, thinking about Kimmy. "She is going to have to accept the fact that some day I will have to go and not come back."

"Why?" Derek sounded a little uneasy.

"I think we will eventually go to a place where we can't come back, whether it is by choice or not."

"We might *choose* to go away?" He sounded skeptical.

"They always say death is the doorway to the next great adventure. We may want to go on that adventure. Who knows?"

"As long as we do it together, I'm game," Derek said, relaxing again.

"I don't think it would be as much fun alone. We make a good team."

"That we do," he grinned. "For now, we can wait here for Kimmy and Pete. They are supposed to be here this afternoon."

The wait was quiet and peaceful. The ghosts waiting outside kept the newcomers informed, so I did not feel the usual sense of anticipation that I picked up regularly from the ghosts just before I sent them to the Gate. I put my head back and slept for a while, curled up in my Grandmother's comfy old chair.

"Sue! Suzie, are you here?"

Kimmy's voice woke me up. "I'm here Kimmy!" I said, yawning. "How did you know?"

"The door was open. It was either you or a burglar. But how did you get it open?"

"With a great deal of pushing. I couldn't have done it without Derek."

"Of course not," she said, smiling to herself. "Well, I'm home. Pete will be here soon. We thought that meeting in an airport would be too strange, so I came straight here with Sarah to get organized." She brought the car seat in from the front porch.

The baby woke up with the movement and stretched luxuriously. She looked around the room, stopping to stare right at me.

"She can see me!" I said quietly. "Hello Sarah! Do you know who I am?"

The baby smiled a sweet toothless grin and waved her chubby arms at me. I reached out to touch her hand, giving her a finger to grab. To my utter amazement, she grabbed my finger and held on tightly. "Derek, do you see this?"

"I see it. It is rare. She knows you!"

Kimmy, who had not been paying attention, come over to the carrier to unhook the baby and lift her out. Sarah did not let go of my finger or take her eyes off of me.

"What'cha looking at sweetie? Hmm? Do you see something? That's nice, but now we have to change that soggy old diaper, don't we? Let's get you cleaned up before Daddy comes." She pulled Sarah away, making her lose her grasp on my finger. When she turned, putting herself between me and the baby, Sarah's chubby face crinkled up. She took in a deep breath, ready to cry, but I stepped around Kimmy and caught Sarah's attention on her other side. Instead of crying, she squealed and tried to talk to me. Kimmy seemed oblivious to the fact that it was me that Sarah was talking to. She changed Sarah's diaper and put clean clothes on her, talking baby talk the whole time.

"Here's a taxi," Derek said from the doorway. "It's Pete!... Stephen... Pete!"

"Oh good!" Kimmy responded. She put Sarah back in the baby seat and went to the door. I could see that she was nervous of meeting Pete for the first time in this body.

He ran up the steps and entered the house eagerly, but stopped in his tracks, just as nervous as Kimmy was.

"Pete?" Kimmy asked timidly.

"Yes, Kim, it's me."

That was enough. Kim ran into his arms and held him close, wanting to talk about everything, all at once, but not sure where to start.

"Okay Kimmy. Before you get lost in each other, I have to tell you something. Derek and I are going somewhere else."

"Somewhere else? No!" Kimmy gasped, turning my way. "What do you mean? Where?"

I told her about the conversation and decision Derek and I had made. She repeated everything for Pete, so they both understood what we were going to do. I expected more resistance from them, but they were really more concerned about each other than us. My timing was perfect.

CHAPTER 31

We went back out into my little yard to talk with the people there.

"What do you want us to do?" the ancient woman croaked, standing at the front of a crowd of people.

"I need to go to a different place than the White Light," I said. "There are many places that the Gate sends people. I have only been to the extremes. I hope the answer lies somewhere in the middle."

"How do you get there?" she asked.

"I have to send people to the Gate. When it is the middle amount of brightness, I have to go with them. Maybe *then* I will know what's really happening."

"Which one of us will go there?" she asked.

"That's just it!" I said. "*I* don't decide. The *Gate* decides where people go. I just send them to the Gate. I told you this before."

There was an unusual silence in the group of souls. The old woman straightened her back, letting go of her walker and squared her shoulders. "Then tell me the truth," she said clearly. "Is The Gate, God?"

"God?" I asked, surprised. "No. Not to my knowledge."

"You don't seem to have much knowledge," she said firmly. "We need to know. If the decisions are being made by The Gate, in *my* religion, that would make The Gate, God."

"Oh!" I looked over at Derek, who looked uncomfortable. He would be no help in this. "Well, as far as I understand it, The Gate is a non-physical event that responds to the energy of the person sent to it. Since The Gate is made up of energy, it is very sensitive to energy. It can detect the slightest difference between people and sends them to different places accordingly. The majority goes to the one bright place or the other, but there is still a vast number that goes somewhere less definite. I am hoping that I will learn something there."

"Then, where is God?" the woman demanded.

"I don't know!"

"How can you not know?"

"Because I have not *met* God! I don't have the answers. I am doing my best, but I suspect I am a very low level bureaucrat in this realm. Nobody tells me anything. I have to learn as I go. So, now I have to go to the middle place! That's all I know! When I know more, I will do better!"

"All right," the old woman sighed, stepping forward.

"Just remember," I said, looking her in the eyes. "If you go back to the White Light, I am working on that situation. Please stay calm and try to be ready for me. Okay?"

"All right," the woman nodded and actually smiled at me.

I grabbed Derek's hand with my left hand and reached for hers with my right. We had a good connection and it would have worked, but I saw the bright White Light showing through The Gate, so I let go of her hand and waved goodbye to her. She shrugged and waved as she approached the Gate.

"What was that? What happened?" It was the young woman who had been burned so badly. Her damaged tissue glistened in the light from the closing Gate.

"She's back in the White Light," I smiled. "She'll be all right. How about you? Can we try to come with you?"

"All right," she said nervously, holding out her hand.

Still holding Derek's hand, I reached out to the girl. Her wounds withered away as soon as our hands connected. She was young and pretty and looked really relieved as she looked toward the Gate opening before us.

"This is it!" Derek cheered. "Right in the middle!"

I squeezed her hand as we floated toward the Gate. It was bright, but the light was more colourful than the White Light. There were tinges of blue and yellow and red radiating in tendrils from the light.

We moved to the Gate rapidly and were engulfed by the colours. I discovered a sensation of joy in my heart. It was as if we were going to a party and the excitement was building. After a short while, a matter of seconds, really, we emerged into a wide open space filled with people who were having a good time.

"Jenn?" a voice called from nearby. "Jennifer! It's really you! I've been waiting for you!"

"John? But... when? How long...? Where are we?" She pulled her hand away from me to go to him.

He caressed her face where the burn had been worst.

"I guess she's in the right place," Derek said quietly. "Look at this place!"

"It's amazing! Everyone is doing something and it looks like they are enjoying it! Look over there!" I pointed at an area beyond a group of brightly dressed people. There was some kind of hut with a grass roof. We walked closer and saw the counter and stools along one wall. There were tables and chairs off to the side, some with people sitting at them, colourful drinks in front of them. An older, black man stood behind the counter, wiping it off. "That guy must be on a different level from the others." I pulled Derek behind me as I marched straight up to the man.

"Excuse me," I said, getting his attention.

"Yes, what can I get you," he responded cheerfully.

"Some answers. What is this place? Who is in charge? What happens here?"

"Didn't your family meet you?" he asked, surprised. "Families are usually there when the Gate opens. *They* answer questions."

"Do they? How do they know to be there?"

"I don't know exactly. The Gate rings a bell and deposits the person in the middle of their family. The Gate knows."

"Okay, that sort of makes sense. I hitched a ride with a girl, so we went to her family."

"Hitched a ride? How can you do that? Who are you?" He was really upset at that idea.

"I am the Gatekeeper. I need to know what happens on this side of the Gate."

"Why?" He looked upset. He started wiping the counter again with his cloth. His movements were jerky and random, as if he wasn't watching what he was doing.

"Because the process is not going smoothly and I need to know why. Is there someone in charge around here?"

"There are the Guardians. You should talk to a Guardian."

"Okay. How do I get to see a Guardian?"

"You just have to be patient, Gatekeeper, and we come to you." The voice was soft and gentle.

I turned around to see a short, ethereal woman standing behind us. She smiled and gestured for us to sit at a nearby table.

"What is the problem, Gatekeeper?" she asked pleasantly. "How can I help?"

"The problem seems to be in the White Light," I said. "The Next men are not letting people go farther, wherever farther is. The back log is horrendous and everyone is unhappy. The ghosts have become afraid to go to the Gate!"

"That *is* a problem. What do you need?"

"Information. What is *this* place called?"

"*Samsara* by some. It is the place of disambiguation. Some also call it the Universe."

"The Universe?"

"The beginning, the middle, the end. All at once. This is the pool of consciousness that the philosophers talk about."

"Pool? Everyone looks to be individual!" I said, looking around.

"True, but their thoughts and experiences merge with others in their families. They can then understand the experiences they went through in life so they can make better choices in their next life."

"Reincarnation."

"Exactly. The Gate will keep family groups together. When you were alive, didn't you hear people talk about feeling that they had met before or always knew another person?"

"Um, sometimes. So, they met them here? Did I have family here?"

"For most people, I would say yes, but you, my dear, are kind of unique. This was your first life...."

"First life?" my hand clenched Derek's tightly. He held mine solidly like a rock. "What does that mean?"

"You were created to do this job. Technically, right now, you are not dead or alive. Derek has been through here many times, but he decided on the last time through that he had to stay and learn in the ghostly plane. He won't remember that he was waiting for you, but he was chosen to be your companion long ago."

"Chosen by whom?" I asked, looking Derek in the eyes. He looked just as amazed as I was.

"There was a group of us," she smiled. "Your Grandfather was one of them. He knew there was going to be an upheaval in the Universe, so he prepared the way for his successor. The delay was unexpected."

"How could he know? That was the future. *I* don't know the future."

"You aren't ready for that yet. You have to be able to deal with the present first."

"In the present, ghosts won't go to the Gate! The word has spread around the world that it is not enough in the White Light. Everyone is afraid to go there! I don't understand why the Gate sends them there when they could come here!"

"The Gate knows the belief system that people grow up with. It cannot send someone to a place that they don't believe exists. Even your Grandmother believes that the White Light is it. She was your primary teacher in these things. It was her love for your Grandfather that made her educate you in all religions, in spite of her personal belief."

I thought back to the many discussions that Kimmy, Gramma and I had, sitting around the kitchen table. I remember Gramma looking pained when we talked about reincarnation. "And yet, she volunteered to reincarnate into Kimmy's daughter, Sarah."

"Your influence and the stress of the people in the White Light are the things that let *that* happen." The Guardian grinned a mischievous little smile.

"The Next Men seem to think they are in the *only* good place and they can do whatever they want. They started thinking like that in the Middle Ages when bubonic plague wiped out so much of the population. Europe was mainly Christian by then, so the White Light became over loaded. The belief that the White Light is the only good place is predominant in Christianity. Instead of just doing their job, The Next Men slowed down. The Morrigan enjoyed the adoration of the humans and the power she had over them. She is not bad. She just can't see any reason to change things. When the Next Men see the need, she will too."

"It sounds like they want to punish people for believing in that place!" Derek said, speaking for the first time. He sounded aghast.

"Yes! That's it!" the Guardian said. "They do not understand people."

"But, *you* seem to," I said, leaving the question open.

"To become a Guardian, you have to have lived many times. Once you have learned a lot, you can become a Guardian to help others learn, or...."

"Or?" I wanted more. I *needed* more.

"I'm sure you have heard of Nirvana. Heaven. Whatever. When we are ready, we are promoted."

"By whom? God? People keep asking me about God and I don't have an answer..."

"Okay. God is as good an answer as any. There are many questions that you don't get the answer to until you are there, and you can't take it back to tell others. There are reasons for this."

"Reasons! Why?" Derek asked.

"Every religion has a philosophy of God and truth. There are similarities in all of them, but there are differences too. It is less destructive in the world to leave it as a question."

"There have been so many wars in the name of God!" Derek said, looking stricken. "To let that happen....You call that *less* destructive!!?"

"The poor soldiers at the bottom may believe that is the reason they are fighting, but wars are always about power and money, Derek. Even when Hitler went insane, his Generals kept letting him lead, on the belief that he would get *them* more power and more money. Everything fought since *then* has been about oil money and space."

"There should be a special place in Hell for those people who cause such death," Derek grumbled.

"There is," the Guardian stated. "Don't worry, Derek. Things are working the way they should everywhere except in the White Light."

"So, how do we fix that?" I moaned. "I feel responsible! I'm sending people to a place that they don't deserve!"

"My first instinct would be to say that you don't know what they deserve, but that would be petty. You have a pretty good understanding of people for someone so new. So, all I can advise is that you educate the Next men. *They* will educate the Morrigan."

"I hijacked one and put him in a woman's body," I blurted out quickly.

"I heard something about that," she smiled. Her eyes really lit up when she smiled. "I can picture the difficulties."

"Right," I nodded. "I don't think I can keep her there for the whole lifetime. It will take too long."

"Let her out of the body once she is comfortable in it. Then, use your Key and take her places. Show her the good, bad and ugly of the world. Then, trust that you have done it right."

"Trust."

"You are doing a good job, Gatekeeper. Now you need the self-confidence to keep going." She smiled again and then disappeared.

"I've been in the ghost world for a while now, but I still find that popping in and out disconcerting," I sighed. "I guess we go home again."

"All right," Derek said, "but Sue, aren't you a little relieved?"

"With?" I asked, watching a large group of people in colourful clothes and looking very much alike, walking past, chatting excitedly.

"The White Light is not the only place that good people go to!"

"Yes," I agreed, standing and pulling Derek with me. I thought the Gate open and we stepped through.

We stepped right back into the front yard of my little house in Winnipeg.

"What is it?" Derek asked, realizing that I had not responded as happily as he did.

"There are still more questions than answers!" I was feeling frustrated. "She was reassuring me, without telling me anything!"

"Like what?" Derek was confused. I had to remember that he was apparently in on the plan to make me Gatekeeper.

"Like the *Beings* who have come to me to tell me that I was needed. Who are they?"

"I forgot about them," Derek admitted. "Sue, no matter what she said, I have no memories of a previous life, let alone a time between lives."

"So, it could be a whole lot of lies that she told me?"

"I don't know!"

"Okay," I said, taking in a deep breath. "What did we learn?"

"There is another place for good people to go to where their family is ready to care for and support them until they come back and do it again."

"There is?" A ghostly old man stood nearby, listening to our talk. "Where?"

"They call it Samsara," I said, just noticing the gathering crowd in the yard. "It looked like a fun place to be. The Gate takes you to the people you know. There are beaches and sunshine and music."

"Samsara," he repeated. "All right. I want to go there."

"You have to know that it is the Gate that decides where you go," I said, trying to slow down the eager crowd.

"Don't forget what she said, though," Derek said in my ear. "If they believe in a place, they can go there. It might work."

The crowd, at that point was almost chanting, "Samsara, Samsara, Samsara."

"All right, then. We can try it. I cannot promise anything, but I'm willing to try."

The ghosts lined up politely, eager to go somewhere else. Each of them was whispering 'Samsara' as I touched them with my right hand. The Gate opened with the light being the same as it was when it took us to Samsara.

Derek looked pleased.

I still felt troubled, but at least we had learned something new.

CHAPTER 32

"What has happened to Katie?" Pete asked when we finally went in the house, several hours later.

"Katie?" Kimmy asked.

"Katie Konroy, the Next Man," Pete clarified.

"Oh! Right! How is she doing?"

I shook my head at them. After I told them about Samsara, they shrugged it off as a place they may have to go to at some future date, but not now. I wasn't sure Kimmy would include Samsara in her Gatekeeper stories. They were more focussed on each other than anything I had to say. The Next Man, being here and now, was more important.

"I am going to check on her now," I said. "Derek is checking on the apprentices. I may be away for a few days or more. You two look after each other and Sarah. If you need me, call."

It really was funny. They were so into each other, they barely noticed my departure. I was pretty sure that I did not have to worry about them any more.

We found Katie in a hospice located in a scenic valley on the outskirts of the town where we originally found her. I saw Joseph lounging in the chandelier over the dining room table.

"Joseph, what's going on?" I asked.

"Oh, Gatekeeper! Finally! It's been happening so fast!"

"What is? What's wrong with her?" I looked down at the people sitting around the table. Katie looked shrivelled up, like a raisin.

"I think the body is allergic to the Next Man," Joseph said with confidence. "She was trying to learn, like you told her to, but everything she eats, she throws up. Whatever stays down, comes out the other end. They've run tests, but don't know why. The doctors say 'will to live' as if they know what they are talking about."

"They don't?"

"No," he snorted. "She's been talking to me. She made up her mind to try to learn like you said. The body can't hold her. She is upset by that because she wants to learn about life!"

"You've been talking? How?" I knew she couldn't see or hear him.

"You've heard of a Ouija board? She talks, I respond."

"But, the arrow thing moves from vibrations made by the people who touch it."

"*She* doesn't touch it," Joseph said, looking me in the eyes. "*I* do."

"Oh! Well, all right. She can hear me. Maybe I can talk with her."

"Be careful, Gatekeeper. Some of these folks think she's wacko because of the Ouija board. Talking to herself..."

"All right." I waited until after the meal. A nurse helped her to her room so she could lie down for a nap. When she was alone, I went and sat next to her.

"Katie, how are you?" I asked.

"Gatekeeper! Is that you?" she asked, sitting up. "Is it time? Have you come for me?"

"Yes, it's me," I said. "What happened? You were supposed to be here, learning, for a long time! What did you do?"

"I didn't *do anything*! I thought about what you said. I decided that learning about this life made sense, but, no matter what I do, I can't keep food in me. When it started, they accused me of doing things, like sticking my finger down my throat! Yuck! Then they searched my stuff for some drug that would make me sick. Why would I want that? Sick is not fun! They don't know where I came from! Now, they just know that I'm not doing it on purpose, but they don't know why it's happening. So, I won't get to see this world now that I really want to. We wasted both our times."

"I wouldn't say that," I consoled her. "Your attitude has changed. That's pretty big."

She groaned and doubled up in pain, falling to the floor. Beads of sweat popped out on her face as she fought the spasms of pain that wracked her body.

Joseph showed up beside her. Pushing a pillow off the bed, he made her more comfortable between the spasms.

"Thank you, Joseph," she said, quietly.

"How do you know that was Joseph's doing?" I asked, surprised.

"He and his friends are with me all the time," she said. "On *your* orders. Thank you. It helps. I'd never experienced *alone* before."

"Alone? If he was here...."

"At first, I didn't know it. He found the Ouija board at a flea market that my social worker took me to. She wanted to find stuff for me to move into an apartment. Then I got sick...." Another spasm of pain tore through her body. I could see the individual bumps from the bones in her spine through the t-shirt she wore. She couldn't go on like this.

"When I knew the kids were there, I wasn't so scared. Weird, isn't it?"

"But *you know* what happens when people die. Why would you be scared?"

"Not everyone goes to the White Light. What if I got sent to the wrong place? You were so mad, you might do that."

"I might, if it was up to me," I agreed. "But *I* have no control over where the Gate sends people. I told you that."

"Oh? Good." She drew in a deep breath, held it for a second and let it go. She did not breathe in again.

In a few seconds, a rather dishevelled Next Man stood before me, looking hopeful.

"May I go home now, please?" he asked politely.

"You were here for only a few months," I said. "There is more for you to learn." I took his hand with my left hand and urged Joseph to take his other hand. I went into Quantum Time to see the world.

We travelled around the world watching life unfold like a movie. I showed him the joy of childbirth along with the pain; the celebrations of children and their achievements; the fear of loss. Loss of people and things; the terror of disasters; the rage of inequity. We continued until I was sure that he understood the beauty of the human condition.

By the time we were done and back in normal time, he had a lot to think about.

"I don't understand," he said. "Why didn't you just show me all this in the beginning? Why put me in Katie?"

"I wanted to. You would not listen," I said. "You were too busy being angry. You could not see what was in front of you."

"Okay," he said, nodding. "So there is a lot more to people than whatever they are, at the last minute of their lives."

"Right! The things they suffer through and accomplish are a part of what makes them special! It cannot be shrugged away as if it doesn't matter!"

He turned to me and looked me in the eyes. "I understand. I will share this with the others. Things *will* change. Thank you. Goodbye. Goodbye Joseph."

The thank you was *way* more than I expected. I reached out with my right hand and sent him to the Gate. The light was a very bright white. He was going home.

Joseph went to tell his team about Katie and I went to my favourite treetop, waiting for Derek.

CHAPTER 33

There is a cave in the United States, in Virginia's Shenandoah Valley, called the Luray Caverns. A man, Mr. Leland Sprinkle, discovered that when he tapped the stalactites, a musical tone would sound. Over a three year period, he built the machinery to tune and hook up the stalactites to an organ. It is like being inside a pipe organ! You are totally surrounded by the sound.

I love going there late at night when the lights are out and no one is near. I have never claimed to be a musician. I won't play in front of others, but the joy of playing even a simple tune in a place like that is indescribable.

I went there to think. I closed my eyes, immersed in the beauty of the sounds. Gradually, a bright light came towards me. I put my hand up to shade my eyes, but it didn't help, so I opened my eyes to look.

A Being of light was floating in front of me.

"Hello," I said pleasantly.

"Greetings Gatekeeper. You have done well." The voice was different from either of the previous Beings. I wondered how many of them were watching the world.

"It has been difficult trying to figure out what I was supposed to do," I said. "A little hint or suggestion would have helped."

"But then your understanding would be lacking. There are things you must learn for yourself."

"All right," I said. After all, I can't argue with a Being of light! That is exactly what I did to the Next Man. "What am I supposed to do now?"

"You have managed to put everyone back to work. Spirits are going where they are meant to go. The backlog is diminishing the way it should. We are pleased."

"Good. So why do I feel like you are going to say 'but'?"

"But..." the Being laughed. The music of it's laugh resonated around the cave. It was beautiful to hear. "But indeed. There is an imbalance between the world of the living and the world of the dead."

"An imbalance? Meaning?"

"There is too much communication back and forth."

"Communication? Every psychic in the world claims to talk with ghosts. I can't shut all of them up!" I had a bad feeling in my guts.

"Their level of communication is fleeting and unsure. Very few can maintain an opening beyond five minutes. They are no threat."

I felt tears welling in my eyes. "What do you want?"

"Now that Pete has a body, you must stop talking to him and Kimberley. They have their lives to live and you cannot be there."

"Well, could I use a Ouija board the way Joseph did with the Next Man?"

"Ingenious, but no. They must believe the contact is severed so they can raise Sarah the way she needs."

"Sarah!? So this is a time limit thing?"

"Sarah will be a leader in her future. But only if she is allowed to develop without the influence of the spirit world."

"But Kimmy and I...."

"When Kimberley's time is up, you will be together again. Then you both can move on."

"Move on? What about Gatekeeping?"

"You will find the next Gatekeeper before you leave."

I know the Being was touched by the stricken look on my face. The pain in my heart. Kimmy and I had been best friends since childhood. Without her, I would feel lost.

"You are not alone, Gatekeeper. You have a good man in Derek and lots of support in your apprentices. You are all a family."

"What will happen if I stay with Kimmy?"

"Over time, the living will find out about you. These things get out. They will want to move to the Spirit world before their time. Suicides will increase dramatically. Death will become more desirable than life! Nothing will ever be the same."

"You can't know that! We could be quieter. I could avoid seeing Sarah! There must be a way!"

I couldn't say anything more. The Being shook it's head sadly. I closed my eyes, letting the tears flow down my cheeks. The bright light from the Being faded and I was alone. The music of the cave no longer felt beautiful. I left to go find Derek.

I took him with me as I went to talk with Kimmy and Pete.

"Stop all communication?" she gasped. "Everything? Forever? As if you...."

"Died..." I agreed. "But, at least, now we get to say goodbye. You can live your life knowing that I love you. I always have. They may stop us from talking, but they cannot destroy our connection. My heart and your heart will always be on the same path, no matter what."

"That's true," she said through her tears. "I don't care what they say, Sarah will always know who you are."

"Teach her to have an open heart and to enjoy every minute of life," I said. "Then, when you are all worn out and this body can't go on, we will see each other again."

"Will we? Promise?"

"I promise. I will be waiting for you. You and Pete and Derek and I have more things to do together. The Being said we will be together again. It's just a matter of time."

"Time. In spite of everything that's happened, it seems so far away."

"Kimmy, you have to live for both of us. Enjoy every minute of *your* life and write about it so *I* can feel like I was there with you. I might be allowed to watch, but that's it."

"But *you* are the level head in our team. Don't they know that?"

"They know. I have to go now. Don't forget me...."

She chuckled through her tears. "As if."

"Goodbye for now."

"Bye...."

Kimmy's sobs were too hard for me to listen to. I went with Derek to sit quietly on top of the Great Pyramid at Giza. My mood affected the weather around me. It was the first time in recorded history to have snow on the Giza plain.

CHAPTER 34

I was vibrating, I was so excited. After all that time! After all the long hours; days; weeks; years; finally I would see her again.

"Sue, calm down!" Derek, looking the same as he always had, laughed at my excitement. "What's going on?"

"Another Being! After all this time, another Being came to me!"

"Why?"

"It said enough time has passed. The time has come that we will all be together again!"

"Together? Kimmy and Pete?" Derek asked, looking stricken.

"Yes! Isn't it exciting!"

"But, that means they will die!"

"Well... oh..." I had forgotten that part. Isn't it silly that there I am, the Gatekeeper, and I forgot that to see my dear Kimmy, she would have to die? That was the deal that the Beings made me agree to and I kept my end even if it did hurt.

"What is going to happen?" Derek asked.

"It didn't say. It just said that I am to pass the key over to my successor and get her started. Then, we will not go to the Gate. We are to meet the Being at the place where it began! Where did it begin? What is it talking about?"

"Wouldn't that be your little house in Winnipeg?"

"Winnipeg! Right! But Kimmy sold that, didn't she?"

"No. She gave it to Sarah to use. Sarah made some additions to make it bigger, but not too much. It still looks the same on the outside."

"Wait a minute, how do you know all that?"

"The Being restricted our contact and you're watching of them. So I have been watching."

"You didn't tell me! Why?"

"Because every time you thought about them, you cried."

"So you kept me too busy to think." I had to appreciate his effort. "All right, what has happened? How long has it been?"

"Long enough for Sarah to grow up and have a child."

I exclaimed in surprise, but he raised a finger to tell me more. "Her child, Suzette, is a University student right now."

"Suzette?" I was torn between the honour of having her named after me and hating the name.

"She doesn't like it either," Derek said, reading my expression. "They call her Sue."

"So they will be okay when they lose Kimmy and Pete?"

"They know about you. It is family tradition and history now. I guess it depends on how it happens. What else did the Being say? When is it supposed to happen?"

"I don't know! We'd better go find out! Who wears the locket now?"

"Sarah does. Kimmy gave it to her on her eighteenth birthday."

"You have gone to birthdays?"

"Just Kimmy and Sarah's!" Derek looked sheepish, as if I would be mad that he kept an eye on them.

"What did you give them?"

"Kimmy... usually flowers. Sarah... Toys, then jewelry."

We were moving quickly, taking ourselves to Winnipeg to see if we could find Kimmy and Pete before they were killed. Once there, we would have to search for them.

*

It was spring. The rivers were high. We saw people hard at work piling sandbags along the river bank, trying to protect the houses. It was not new, but every few years, conditions arose to make the water overflow everything. After all this time, you would think that people would build safer, but no, south of the city there were islands, surrounded by dikes of sandbags, in a sea of water. More homes were swamped, the rise of the flood moving faster than the dikes.

Moving in the general direction of the Red river, I saw some of the old familiar structures that had been there when I was growing up. They looked a little weatherbeaten and worn out, especially in the flood.

I neared the Provencher Bridge with it silly restaurant in the middle of it and the towering sculpture above it. At least, I always thought it was sculpture. The cables were frayed at the top. I did not know they were load bearing, but apparently they must have been. The first cable broke and fell onto the bridge causing the cars to swerve to miss it. The cars hit each other instead. The road bed going onto the bridge was being washed away in the flood. The people in the cars didn't seem to realize they should stay off the bridge.

Another cable snapped and the bridge shuddered, causing the whole thing to sway to the north. Some of the cars tried to keep moving, to get out of danger. Some succeeded. Several people abandoned their cars and ran off the bridge. One person in a large, black SUV decided to push his way off the bridge. There was only one car in his way, so he pushed it forward into the guard rail in order to go past. I could hear the people in the car scream just as another cable let go. The guard rail collapsed, the deck of the bridge dropped and both the car and the SUV plunged into the freezing water.

I recognized the scream.

Derek and I rushed down into the river to see what we could do. Pete was driving. Kimmy was beside him and the young woman, presumably Sarah, was in the back. Derek helped her with her seatbelt and provided an air bubble along the roof. She hung on for quite a while, but it took the rescue team a long time to get there.

Kimmy and Pete stayed with their bodies until they were brought ashore. They sat on the stretchers looking confused and watching the efforts being made to resuscitate Sarah. We all breathed a sigh of relief when she coughed and sputtered back to life.

I went and stood in front of Kimberly. She looked at me in surprise.

"Sue? Susie, is it really you?"

"Yes Kim, it really is me."

"You haven't changed a bit! You're still wearing the exercise thing we made! You look exactly the same!"

"Yes, but *you* don't! You aged!" I could see all the aging signs in her wrinkled, sagging skin, and graying hair.

"Hey, I *earned* these wrinkles! I do not begrudge *any* of them. But it will be nice to let them go." She stood up, leaving her body on the stretcher and came to me to give me a hug. We both cried. It had been too long. Kim stepped back, looking around. "Pete?" She asked. We both turned to see Derek and Pete slapping each other on the back. Pete was back to looking as he did right after he hit me with his car. The image of Stephen was long gone. Kimmy would have adjustments to make. She walked over to him and nestled into his arms as if she had always been there. I guess she always had.

We all went over to Sarah to see how she was.

"Mom? Is that you?" She asked, staring right at me. She could see me! She could see all of us!

"I'm sorry ma'am," the medic said to her, "the other passengers have been taken to the hospital. Just lay back, we will take you there too."

She was smart enough to stop talking, but she didn't take her eyes off of us, so we went with her to the hospital. They put her into a room in emergency so that they could tell her that both her parents had not survived the accident. She wouldn't take her eyes off of us in the meantime, so they seemed to think she was in shock.

"Tell them you need to be alone for a few minutes," I suggested.

"I need to be alone for a few minutes, please," Sarah said, finally looking at the doctor.

He nodded and left, closing the door behind him.

"You can see me!" I grinned.

"Yes, but what's going on, Mom? You *sound* different."

"Mom? Oh Mom! Well, actually, I'm Sue. That's Kimberly," I said, pointing to Kimmy, who was standing at the foot of the bed grinning. "And that's Pete beside her and Derek here."

"You mean the stories are *true*?" Sarah gasped. "It really *happened*?"

"The stories that I told *you*. Not the books so much, but what I told *you* was the truth. I thought you had a right to know."

"So you switched *bodies*?"

"It was necessary at the time," I said, wondering why our altered looks was the important thing to her. "I had to keep working the Gatekeeping job."

"... it is really true?"

"Not only that, but it is time for me to turn the job over to a successor."

"Successor? Who?"

She knew. I know she knew. I could see it in the way she straightened her back and squared her shoulders. "You," I said.

From the foot of the bed, Kimmy gasped.

"The Beings have said it is time." I reached up to the back of my neck and unclasped the chain that held the Quantum Key. There had never been a clasp on that chain before. Even Kimmy moved closer to see it. I reached out and put the chain around Sarah's neck. Kimmy and I both saw the clasp disappear.

"That's strange," Kimmy said, quietly. "Sarah, this is not my first choice for your future, but I learned a long time ago that we are not always in control of our choices. Sometimes we just have to go along with it. I suggest that you get Kirsten to help you. A best friend is important."

"A best friend is everything," I agreed. "Even if you don't see them for a long time. The bond will always be there." I took Kimmy's hand and grinned at her.

"So what happens now?" Kimmy asked. "Do we all go to the Gate?"

"No," I said, taking Derek's hand and nodding for Pete to take Kimmy's other hand. "The Being has other plans for *us*."

"Wait! You can't just leave me like this!" Sarah cried out. "I don't know what to do!"

"You know more than I did," I laughed. "It will be fine. The apprentices will come to you and will teach you. Perhaps someday in the future we will be together again."

I took us first to the yard of my little house. The yard was smaller now that an extra room had been built onto the house, but it was still nice. It felt like home.

Within seconds of arriving, the Being showed itself to all of us. "You have done well Gatekeeper," It said softly. I could feel the others react to the musical beauty of the voice.

"Thank you," I said. "What happens now?"

"You have all earned the right to bypass traditional destination. You are going to meet the Fates."

"Fates?" I asked. The term rang a bell in my memory. "You mean the Weird Sisters?"

I could hear the laugh even though it felt like petals falling on my skin. "I don't think I would mention that term to them," the Being laughed. "As times grow and change, we must grow and change with them. The challenge of the Fates has increased and become more complicated. You are to help them. You *will* be together forever."

That was the only explanation. The Being took Derek's hand and led us through a wrinkle in space, beyond which there is no description.

I left this story for Sarah. She can handle the truth now. We will miss her, but I think we will all be reunited someday. In the meantime, a strange new land was coming into view ahead of us.

The End